For Shawn, as always

Praise for
Tall, Dark & Dead

"What's not to adore about a heroine who frets equally about the Vatican and ripped pantyhose, an herbalist who dresses like one of the Jets in *West Side Story*, and a fascinating 'other world' most of us could never imagine, much less write about? Tate Hallaway has a wonderful gift, Garnet is a gem of a heroine, and *Tall, Dark & Dead* is enthralling from the first page. I hope this is the first of many more books from Tate Hallaway."　　　—MaryJanice Davidson,
　　New York Times bestselling author of *Undead and Undermined*

"Curl up on the couch and settle in—*Tall, Dark & Dead* is a great way to pass an evening."　　　—Lynsay Sands,
　　New York Times bestselling author of *The Reluctant Vampire*

"Tate Hallaway kept me on the edge of my seat with *Tall, Dark & Dead*. Every time I thought I knew where the story was going, she threw something new into the mix. A thoroughly enjoyable read!"　　　—Julie Kenner,
　　USA Today bestselling author of *Aphrodite's Kiss*

"Hallaway's entertaining debut paranormal romance will appeal to readers of Charlaine Harris's Sookie Stackhouse series."　　　—*Booklist*

"A funny and captivating paranormal story . . . Look out fans of the paranormal, there's a new supernatural heroine in town sure to become an instant favorite."
　　　—*Romance Reviews Today*

"I love how Garnet handled everything that came her way with grit, humor, and attitude as she kicked some serious butt! . . . Hallaway keeps you glued to the pages."
　　　—*Romance Junkies*

BERKLEY PUBLISHING GROUP
Published by The Penguin Group
Penguin Group (USA) Inc.

375 Hudson Street, New York, New York 10014, USA

Penguin Group (Canada), 90 Eglinton Avenue East, Suite 700, Toronto, Ontario M4P 2Y3, Canada
(a division of Pearson Penguin Canada Inc.) • Penguin Books Ltd., 80 Strand, London WC2R 0RL,
England • Penguin Group (Ireland), 25 St. Stephen's Green, Dublin 2, Ireland (a division of
Penguin Books Ltd.) • Penguin Group (Australia), 250 Camberwell Road, Camberwell, Victoria 3124,
Australia (a division of Pearson Australia Group Pty. Ltd.) • Penguin Books India Pvt. Ltd., 11 Community
Centre, Panchsheel Park, New Delhi—110 017, India • Penguin Group (NZ), 67 Apollo
Drive, Rosedale, North Shore 0632, New Zealand (a division of Pearson New Zealand Ltd.) • Penguin
Books (South Africa) (Pty.) Ltd., 24 Sturdee Avenue, Rosebank, Johannesburg 2196, South Africa

Tall, Dark & Dead

TATE HALLAWAY

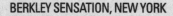

BERKLEY SENSATION, NEW YORK

Penguin   Canada
(a divisic   2R 0RL,
England   Penguin
Books Ltd   , Australia
(a divisi   mmunity
Centre   Drive,
Rosedale   in Books
(Sou   frica

Penguin Books Ltd., Registered Offices: 80 Strand, London WC2R 0RL, England

This is a work of fiction. Names, characters, places, and incidents either are the product of the author's imagination or are used fictitiously, and any resemblance to actual persons, living or dead, business establishments, events, or locales is entirely coincidental. The publisher does not have any control over and does not assume any responsibility for author or third-party websites or their content.

TALL, DARK & DEAD

A Berkley Sensation Book / published by arrangement with the author

PUBLISHING HISTORY
Berkley trade paperback edition / May 2006
Berkley Sensation mass-market edition / April 2012

Copyright © 2006 by Lyda Morehouse.
Cover design by Monica Benalcazar. Cover art by Margarete Gockel.
Interior text design by Kristin del Rosario.

ISBN: 978-0-425-24700-6

BERKLEY SENSATION®
Berkley Sensation Books are published by The Berkley Publishing Group,
a division of Penguin Group (USA) Inc.,
375 Hudson Street, New York, New York 10014.
BERKLEY SENSATION® is a registered trademark of Penguin Group (USA) Inc.
The "B" design is a trademark of Penguin Group (USA) Inc.

PRINTED IN THE UNITED STATES OF AMERICA

10 9 8 7 6 5 4 3 2 1

ALWAYS LEARNING   PEARSON

Acknowledgments

This book would not exist but for the vision of John Morgan and the tender loving care of Anne Sowards. I also have to thank my agent, Martha Millard, for all of her hard work and continued enthusiasm.

The support of my friends and family was also invaluable. A big, huge, hearty thanks to Miss Ember for Meadow Spring and "you know what," and to my other midnight-hour readers: Shawn Rounds, Naomi Kritzer, Sean Michael Murphy (to whom special credit regarding Hebrew translation goes), and Kelly McCullough.

If only I hadn't been late.

When I opened the door, I'd expected some halfhearted admonishments from my coven for being tardy once again, a joke or two about "Garnet-time."

I hadn't expected all that blood.

Black spatters blotted the walls and floor, obscuring the white pentacle painted on the dining room floor. A dozen bodies lay in the center, curled into fetal positions as though trying to protect something. Eyes, usually full of amusement, glazed over, staring and empty.

All of the coven—my friends, all the family I had—were dead. Among the bodies walked the Vatican assassins who'd done it, calmly sprinkling holy water on battered faces, and, of all things, administering last rites.

They hadn't seen me yet. By the time they looked up, it was too late. I had summoned into me the Goddess Lilith, a terrible vengeance, and they saw their fate in the changing color of my eyes.

Lilith's eyes . . .

First House

❧

What's the best way to keep Vatican Witch hunters off your scent? Dress to kill.

After clasping the last silver skull buckle on my knee-high, black leather, ass-whupping boots, I straightened my velvet miniskirt. The mini tended to ride up my thighs thanks to the sparkly spiderweb hose. I glanced out the bathroom door toward my closet, contemplating a change into a leather skirt. But I might be pushing the dress code already with my scandalous hemline, and as store manager I really needed to provide a good example for my coworkers. Or, as I liked to refer to them, my minions.

To finish off the look, I applied a layer of Egyptian kohl around my eyes. Regarding the result in the mirror, I smiled: total Goth chick. No one would take me seriously as a Witch dressed like this. A Vatican agent would take one look at the large, silver-plated ankh bouncing off the too-tight décolletage of my fanged Hello Kitty shirt and think: *Poseur.*

Exactly what I wanted.

Yeah, I'd be all right, as long as no one looked in my eyes long enough to see *Her* lurking inside. Trouble was, my eyes tended to attract attention. I've had customers gasp when they looked into my eyes. Not a lot of people have purple eyes. Just me and Liz Taylor. And I think mine are prettier. But, really, I think I garner the stunned reaction because, on some instinctual level, people recognize Her, the Goddess inside me.

I've tried covering the color with tinted contacts—blue, brown, even black—but the Goddess always shines through. She wants me to have purple eyes, so purple eyes I have.

I checked my wallet for cash. My driver's license still said boring Minnesota-Norwegian blue; the picture showed a woman with shoulder-length blond hair, not a dyed-black pixie cut. The only thing accurate was my name: Garnet Lacey.

I needed to get to the DMV one of these days. I'd never tested for a Wisconsin license, even though I think I was legally required to do that within thirty days of moving. I'd left Minneapolis almost eight months ago now. The license was a last tie, and though it was a trivial one, my subconscious seemed reluctant to break it.

Just that quick glance at my old self brought back the nightmare night I found my coven dead. I could feel the Goddess stirring, roused by memories. Bile rose in the back of my throat. The hand holding my driver's license trembled with rage and grief. A dark curtain began to descend in front of my eyes as I felt Her rising.

It always started with a cramp shuddering across my abdomen. Then came the rush. Heat, like fire, pulsed upward from between my legs. My thighs quivered. With each heartbeat the heat rose, higher, higher, spreading along my stomach, up my rib cage. My body shook with pleasure.

It felt so good, but I had to stop Her. If She brought me

to the crescendo, I would no longer be in control. And what I would destroy, because destroy She always did, I wouldn't know until I came to in time to pick up the pieces or bury the bodies.

My fingertips tingled with unreleased power. In the mirror, I saw Her. My eyes had changed once again. My pupils darkened to the bloodred of the poisonous fruit of the nightshade.

She was coming.

Pitching myself forward, I slammed down hard on my knees. The pain brought me back into focus.

I smacked my head against the sink as hard as I could stand and whispered, "There is nothing here for you. There is nothing here for you." She had to know it was true. The Vatican agents were gone. They were just a memory. The only thing to kill in the house were some potted herbs and my cat. This would *not* satisfy Lilith. Not by half.

Perhaps She understood me, or maybe She sensed that the danger was long gone and that her need would not be satiated. She left. I felt the heat extinguish like someone had thrown cold water on a roaring flame.

My body ached. Not unpleasantly, but definitely . . . unsatisfactorily. My legs felt rubbery, and my heart pounded in my eardrums.

I knelt there on the bathroom floor, eyes closed, and concentrated on getting my breathing back to normal. I counted to six, breathed in. Counted again, and breathed out. I did this for several breaths until I could no longer feel a banging in my chest with every heartbeat.

When I opened my eyes, the driver's license was a melted blob in my hand. Blue flames danced for a moment in the center of my palm, then died. I scraped off the remains of the plastic card on the rim of the wastepaper basket.

There was a little blister in the center of my palm where the license had been. Taking a final deep breath, I lay my head on the cool porcelain rim of the claw-foot tub. She was so near the surface these days, it frightened me. Thankfully, I had no roommates to witness my strange behavior . . . or for Her to—no, that didn't bear thinking about. I lived alone not by choice but by necessity.

Uncurling my now numb legs, I noticed I'd managed to rip the knee of my black lace panty hose. Damn. They cost me twenty bucks. Ah, well, the torn look added to the whole Goth ensemble.

As I got up to fetch my clear nail polish from the medicine cabinet to stop the run before it got any worse, Barney made her usual dramatic entrance. The door flew open as she put her weight against it, and then she casually paraded in to sniff disdainfully at her water bowl. Barney was a gray, striped fluff ball of a Maine coon. She blinked her yellow cat eyes at me and then sneezed. Barney was allergic to magic.

Or at least she pretended to be.

Rubbing her nose with her paw, she gave another dramatic yet somehow dainty sneeze. She was telling me she didn't approve.

"As if I had any choice, Ms. Puss," I said to her while scratching behind her ears.

A slow blink told me she was skeptical, and then, as if bored of the whole conversation, she hopped up onto the toilet lid and began fiercely cleaning herself.

Barney was my familiar.

Most people *thought* they understood what their cats said with all their little movements, but I really did know. Before, when I used my magic more freely, Barney had a voice. I heard her talking in my head. Yeah, the line between magic and insanity was pretty thin. I knew that. That's part of why I quit. I was a Witch no more. I'd gone cold turkey. Never touched the stuff. Nope. No exceptions.

I'd had to. The Goddess fed on magic. The more I used it, the closer to the surface She came. What bothered me now was that I hadn't cast a spell in six months. I'd been feeling pretty good about myself. Yet there She was at the slightest provocation.

A petite yet noticeable sneeze broke my reverie.

"Yeah, okay. Look, I'm trying to quit. Everything," I said as I finished daubing at the torn edge of my hose. Although I still kept up with astrology. That couldn't count as real magic, surely. Returning the bottle to its spot in the cabinet, I added, "It's not that easy. I'd like to see you try."

Barney yawned, her pink tongue curling in an almost complete circle inside her wide-open mouth.

"So you say," I told her, giving her another fond scratch, "but you wouldn't last a week."

She snorted. Leaping off the toilet seat, she padded delicately out the door. I knew where she was headed: the kitchen. I fed her, then dutifully wolfed down a bowl of flax flakes while Barney watched over me. I gulped down coffee, nearly scalding my tongue. Pouring the remains of the pot of coffee into a thermos, I tucked it into my backpack. I double-checked the contents of my bag: Kleenex, black lipstick, bottled water, bike lock, and the latest issue of *Mountain Astrologer* to read at my lunch break.

I felt along the rim of the canvas until I found the hidden compartment. After opening it up, I methodically recounted the two thousand dollars in cash I kept there. It wasn't nearly enough if I had to run again, but it was a better start than I'd had before. I replaced the money.

Barney mewed. I mussed the fur on the top of her head. "I'd come back for you; I promise."

She rippled her back and stalked off to her sunny spot among the herbs I had growing in the tower room adjacent to the kitchen. I put my bowl in the sink with the other dirty dishes I promised myself I'd clean soon.

Before closing the compartment, I carefully removed Jasmine's prayer necklace. Jasmine and I had gone to college together. I'd talked her into joining the coven, even though she'd always said she enjoyed the craft part of "the Craft" more than the magic. The prayer necklace was proof. It was a piece of art. Jasmine had twisted the silver wire herself and strung mother-of-pearl and amethyst beads in groups of three. I held the pieces in my hand.

"The circle is open, but unbroken," I whispered. We'd ended each ritual that way. Except this time it wasn't true. When the Vatican agents attacked Jasmine, a jump ring had snapped, and the circle was *broken*.

Reverently, I tucked the necklace back into the compartment. There was one other item I kept hidden, but I refused to look at it: a blood-covered crucifix. I'd torn it from the body of a Vatican agent. Or rather, the Goddess had.

With a tremor that clenched my gut, I checked my watch. I was running late for work. I couldn't allow myself to be late. Not ever again.

I live on the upper floor of a creaky Victorian. Locking the door behind me, I headed down the stairs. The stairwell and a narrow hallway were the only common areas in the house. This place had seen its share of students, since it was less than a mile from campus, and nowhere did it show more than in these spaces. Relentless grunge and wear had given the wood a dark patina. The stair runner, which might have been red at some point in its life, had faded to a dull brown. A big crack ran down the center of the glass of the window at the landing. Original plaster clung tenaciously to hundred-year-old laths.

Despite mistreatment, it was still a grand old house. A chandelier with tulip shades hung on a brass chain fastened to a tin medallion. The banister, though dinged and nicked, still had all of its spindles and had been built at a slight curve, which gave it a sweeping effect. Dusty wainscoting lined the walls.

I grabbed my mountain bike from its spot in the hall and headed out. It was late May, and the days were finally starting to be consistently warm. Spring-green buds tipped the branches of the trees. From under piles of leaves and mulch, fiddleheads and columbine struggled toward the light. Though the air held a nip, the sun glittered across the lake. Seagulls soared lazily overhead.

I pushed myself hard, pumping my legs the whole way. I was covered in a light sweat by the time I hit State Street.

State Street was Madison's main tourist destination. The white marble State Capitol building anchored the "top" of the pedestrian mall; the University of Wisconsin-Madison's campus occupied the "bottom." The several intervening blocks held hat boutiques, novelty shops, Nepali restaurants, sports bars, artisan clothiers, the world's only toilet paper museum, and Mercury Crossing, where I worked. After locking my bike in the back alley, I checked my watch. Damn. Despite my best efforts, I was five minutes late. An irrational shiver of fear fluttered in my stomach as I opened the door.

My shoulders relaxed the second I smelled the incense. It was sweet with a touch of spice and smelled like every magic shop from here to Poughkeepsie.

Crystal wind chimes decorated with tourmaline, amethyst, and other semiprecious stones hung from the ceiling. I made my way past crowded aisles crammed with books and tarot cards to the checkout counter in the center of the shop, which was surrounded by display cases full of wands, jade Buddhas, necklaces, gazing globes, and Goddess jewelry of every kind.

I loved this place. It felt like home to me.

Probably, if I wanted to avoid magic, I should work at

the deli two blocks down. One thing they always told people in recovery from drugs and alcohol was to stay away from old companions, old places, and old things.

I told myself working here was all part of my "cover." No self-respecting true Witch would come within a mile of this New Age, Warlock-wannabe haven. Well, okay, we would, but we'd come in really early or over our lunch breaks. There just aren't enough places like this for Witches to be too picky.

But we sold black, hooded cloaks for crying out loud! Not only that, one of our big sellers was the dashboard glow-in-the-dark parking space goddess to protect the owner from meter maids. We had computer gargoyles. We carried the entire line of How to be a Teenage Witch books.

Then there was the other full-time employee, William, or was it Wolfsbane this week? William/Wolfsbane had intense hazel eyes and the typical gaunt, gawky, college freshman build. His hair matched his eyes, which is to say it was light brown with amber and green highlights. This week his interest appeared to be Irish magic. He had Celtic knotwork everywhere: earring, bracelet, necklace, and even his T-shirt showed two dragons intertwined. I swore that boy blew his entire salary here at the shop, since he had a new interest and a new wardrobe every two weeks.

William was what the Belief.net quizzes would determine to be "a sincere seeker." A Libra with a Pisces Rising, he jumped from one cause to another with both feet. Indecisive yet polite to a fault, I had to make sure he wasn't in charge when the salespeople came through because he couldn't say no to anyone, much less make a firm decision.

"Hey, guy," I said cautiously, afraid he might have changed his name again.

William looked up from the book his nose had been pressed into and gave me a worried look. "Are you okay?"

"I overslept." It was easier to lie than to say I had to fight down a Goddess who wanted to kill them, kill them all.

"It happens," William said, not noticing my shift in mood or choosing to ignore it. "Anyway, it was spooky. Is there some kind of lateness planet transiting your getting-to-work-on-time house?" he teased with a fond smile, but his eyes held a touch of seriousness. William counted on me for astrological tidbits. "Are the planets doing something weird or what? Today feels all retrograde to me."

That's when it hit me. I hadn't progressed my natal chart to see what would happen today. I'd gotten in the habit of doing it every morning during breakfast. I had all the books I needed in the kitchen shelved next to my cookbooks and recipe cards. "Well," I said, "judging by my morning, I'd guess Mars went retrograde."

I stowed my bag behind the counter and grabbed my handy yearly ephemeris. After finding the month, I scanned the columns for today's date. Mars was direct, it appeared, but not much else. Jupiter, Neptune, and Pluto were all retrograde. *Retrograde* in astronomical terms means that a planet appears to be moving backwards in the sky from the vantage point of the earth. It had something to do with orbital velocities. I didn't really know all the science. What I did know was that astrologically, it was bad news: screwed-up, blocked energy.

Usually, I didn't put much stock in outer planets. Anything past Jupiter moved too slowly to really affect daily life. When a bunch of planets ganged up like that, well . . . seemed pretty ominous to me.

"Well?" William asked. He crouched beside me, peering intently at the rows of numbers. "What does it say?"

"I'm not really sure," I admitted, standing back up. William followed my motion like a nervous shadow. "Neptune retrograde in a natal chart is all about self-deception and mysterious circumstances. Pluto means secrets and other people's money. So," I added with a laugh, "we could lose out on an inheritance and not even know it."

William chuckled, but I could tell I'd worried him. He adjusted the counter display of polished gemstones. "Anything else?"

"Yeah," I said. I moved out from behind the counter to unlock the door. "Jupiter's moving backwards, too. In a birth chart, I'd say you'd be a fundamentalist in your religious outlook. What it means about today, I haven't a clue. Maybe we can look it up in one of the books." I gestured in the direction of the astrology section.

When I got to the door, I jumped. To my surprise, there were two people waiting for us to open. I let them in with a smile. Inwardly, I groaned. Looked like it was going to be a busy day.

And it was. William and I spent the rest of the day rushed off our feet. We never did have the time to find out what it meant that Jupiter had gone retrograde.

I don't know what it is about spring. Maybe the same natural force that draws plants from the ground brings out the New Age tendencies in Midwestern housewives. I must have sold a zillion leather-bound diaries and witchcraft starter kits today.

To be fair, it was a new season, a new semester. Everyone was in the mood for starting fresh. Though I really should have been closing up, I found myself scanning the Burpee catalogue that came in the mail, wondering if we should try selling some of the more exotic herb seedlings.

William's girlfriend had picked him up as the shift ended. There was something about her that made me wary. I couldn't put my finger on it, but . . . well, I was probably being silly. William always provoked my latent maternal instincts. He seemed in need of protection. Plus, I'd been working here for several months and she'd never once come in and introduced herself. She always just waited for him in the car. I found that odd.

The tills were cashed out and the lights dimmed. In fact, I'd have sworn I'd locked the door until I heard the telltale jangle of bells.

"I need mandrake, a whole root," a masculine voice called out from the doorway. "Harvested by new moon. Best if from a crossroads."

I laughed. "Why not just ask for it grown under a gallows?"

"My God, yes. Do you have it?"

"No." I was being sarcastic, anyway. I was about to explain to this dimwit that there hadn't been a public hanging in America for several decades now, when I found myself struck dumb. Glancing up from my catalog, I gazed into the most gorgeous brown eyes I'd ever seen.

I mean, they were really beautiful. Besides being almost perfectly almond-shaped, his eyes had those long, thick lashes usually reserved for very young boys.

Eyes aren't usually the first things I notice on a man. Though I hate to admit it, normally, what I check out is "the ratio." That is to say, shoulder to waist. I like that triangular shape of broad to narrow.

This man had it. In fact, I'd say his body spelled out a perfect T, for tall, tough, and tasty.

And trouble.

Despite a slight, cultured British accent, he dressed like a hoodlum. He wore a leather jacket, broken-in blue jeans, and a white T-shirt just tight enough that it hinted at a hardworking body underneath. His long, black hair was pulled back into a loose ponytail at the nape of his neck. And, just to drive me absolutely wild, a touch of stubble dotted a chiseled jaw. I hate that. Pretty men make me stupid. Suddenly, all I could think about was stroking my finger along his high cheekbones down to the hollow of his throat.

I pulled myself away from that image only to get lost in those damn eyes again. They were the color of polished oak in sunlight. In fact, they had that kind of captivating, enchanting, inner glow that I'd come to associate with the dead, or rather, undead.

"Well, can you get it?" he asked insistently.

"What?" I asked, still staring stupidly.

"The mandrake."

"Uhm, probably," I said.

I leaned a little over the counter, trying to smell him. I caught a whiff of motorcycle exhaust and leather. I couldn't detect the scent of human sweat, which unnerved me a bit. So I let my eyes unfocus and scanned for an aura. Just as I suspected: none. Not even that faint purple glimmer you get from a well-made zombie. He was definitely a dead man walking.

Wow.

Well, today just got a lot more interesting.

"Could you check?" he asked.

"On what?" I asked, thinking about his aura, or rather, lack thereof.

"On the mandrake." He backed up a step, as if he thought *my* behavior strange.

I wanted to point out that *he* was the dead guy standing around in my store, but I didn't. "Uhm," I stalled as I tried to collect my thoughts. "There is this place that does hand-harvesting by moon phases. New Moon Wimmin's Herb Collective or something like that. I think I have them bookmarked on the computer. They might grow mandrake in their greenhouse. I mean, I assume you want the real deal, not American mandrake." American mandrake was sometimes called mayapple. I had some of that under my pine tree. It was pretty common throughout Canada and the East Coast, though I'd cultivated it purposely.

"I need *Atropa mandragora*." He spoke the Latin perfectly and without even the tiniest hesitation. When he was alive, this man had either been a serious herbalist or a Church scholar.

"Yeah, I figured," I said as I searched the Collective's Web site. "Looks like they have mandrake root harvested by new moon. I can order you one or however many you want, but if you need it in a hurry, it looks like it's going to cost you."

He didn't even ask how much, he just pulled out his wallet. The fold was crammed with bills of every denomination. I was relieved to see cash. I really didn't want to take credit card information from a dead guy. Just my luck, he'd have been murdered, and I'd become a suspect. No cop in the world would believe me if I said, "Oh, yeah, he came in two days after he died and just gave me his account information. Honest."

"How soon can they get it here?"

I filled out the online form, pressed Enter, and waited for the mailing information options to appear on the screen. "Looks like they can promise two to three business days."

"Fuck me," he swore. While I was thinking, *Yes, I'd like to*, he said, "I really needed it today."

"We have mandrake powder," I offered. When he shook his head, I pointed to the herbal section of the bookshelf. "You could see if there's a substitution." Though probably not for something involving mandrake. That was kind of a specialty herb, and, frankly, a bit out of most tree-hugging Witches' leagues.

He gave a sad little laugh like he thought I was the biggest idiot on the planet.

"Should I order this?" I asked, pointing to the screen. "It's going to be a hundred and fifty bucks."

He rubbed his chin as he considered his options. His gestures all seemed pretty normal for a dead guy. He was either so recently dead that it hadn't sunk in yet, or he'd been dead so long he'd gotten used to it.

My next thought would normally have been: vampire. Problem was, the sun was still high in the sky. On Mondays, we were only open until six. I gave a meaningful glance at the light shining though the windows, "Aren't you up a little early?"

"Sorry?"

"Uhm, I'll need a name and address for the order form. You know, and a number where I can reach you when it comes in." He seemed so genuinely startled by my question that I decided to change tactics.

Maybe this guy didn't know he was dead.

He gave me another slightly nervous look. Then he pulled a business card out of the inside pocket of his jacket. The buckles jangled. I loved that sound. He laid the business card on the glass counter. I got a glance at his fingernails. Short and trimmed, not broken or bleeding—but there *was* something dark, like dirt, encrusted under a few nails. I'd have wondered if he recently clawed his way out of a grave, but with the funerary regulations of concrete and steel vaults, few people could do that anymore.

Unless someone had hurriedly buried him in a shallow grave.

"Order it," he said finally. "I don't think I have any other choice."

The name on the card said Sebastian Von Traum, herbalist. On the back was a local address, e-mail, Web site, and phone numbers. I keyed all the information in. Though I could have had them send it directly to his home address, I did a bad thing. I wanted to see him again, so I entered the store's address instead. Feeling a tiny bit guilty, I said, "I'll call you the instant it comes in."

As I pressed the Order button, Sebastian let out a tiny, sad sigh that almost broke my heart. Those beautiful eyes held the look of a man who knew his time on earth was limited. I felt like the cad who'd signed his death warrant by telling him I couldn't get the root today.

"Look," I said. "I'll give them a call tomorrow and explain the situation. Maybe we can arrange something so you can get it sooner."

Of course, I had no idea what I'd say to them. "Hey, could you rush it because this very sweet reanimated corpse really, really needs mandrake, or I think he might suffer Final Death?" sounded a little strange, even if it might be true.

"That's brilliant. Thanks." Sebastian flashed one of those gorgeous smiles that usually only belongs to movie stars. I found myself grinning back foolishly, even while I scanned for fangs. His canines were long, but the smile was gone so quickly I couldn't decide if they were sharper than average.

I hated to say it, but I had to. "I can't promise anything. What are you going to do if we can't get it?"

He shrugged. "I guess I'll have to look into those substitutions."

The tone in his voice made it clear he didn't believe anything else would work. I wanted desperately to see that smile again, so I said, "Well, if I can't get you the root, I could see if I could score you a hand of glory. Those are always good in reanimation spells." Personally, I found the whole concept of the hand of glory creepy as sin. They were wax-dipped severed hands—*real* hands, like, that were once on living people—usually from a murderer, the fingers of which the practitioner would light like a candle. "Ooh! Or maybe some graveyard dust. I think I have a vial of that under the counter."

"No thank you. I have all that already, though I prefer grave mold myself," Sebastian said.

It took me a moment to realize he was joking. The broad smile tipped me off.

"Oh, yeah," I said lamely, smiling back. "Handy." I instantly thought of the hand of glory after saying that. "Oh, ick! No pun intended."

He laughed. Sebastian had one of those hearty, open laughs that puts a person instantly at ease. A strange quality for a dead guy, but even so, I found myself laughing along. I mean, if the guy were a vampire I could chalk his charming manner up to glamour—their unearthly attractiveness. My experience with vampires was that when they laughed it was usually *not* a good thing. Sort of like when a hit man chuckles.

No, this was a nice laugh, a damn-you're-so-cute-why-the-hell-haven't-you-asked-me-out-for-coffee-yet? laugh. Too bad he was dead. It was ruining the romance for me.

"Why do you think I need the mandrake for a reanimation spell?" he asked.

I was tempted to point out the obvious, but instead I asked, "Isn't it called the funeral herb?"

"It is," Sebastian said with a hint of surprise in his tone, like he hadn't expected even such basic knowledge from me. "Though it's also a laxative."

I smiled. "Are you telling me you're desperate for gallows-grown mandrake because you're constipated?"

"No," he said, with that infectious chuckle. "I wouldn't say that."

"It's also a narcotic," I pointed out. "Maybe you're some kind of mandrake junkie."

"Maybe I am," he said with a wouldn't-you-like-to-know smile.

And, indeed, I did. There were several other things I wanted to know, too, like what it would feel like to untie that luxurious looking hair and run it through my fingers.

Vampires tended to have long hair. After all, once cut, it didn't grow back. The hair follicles being dead and all that made it difficult to be a slave to fashion. Sometimes you could tell how old a vamp was by the style of their hair. I kind of felt sorry for those guys who died in 1789 or whenever and had shaved heads because they wore wigs most of the time. Though the bald tough-guy look was coming back, it was often hard for a former fop to pull off.

Sebastian didn't look like he'd been a fop. Oh, no, not with *that* body.

I wondered when Sebastian had died. I really, really wanted to ask, but it seemed so rude, particularly since he clearly didn't want to talk about it. Between my sun obsession and the reanimation bit, I'd given him several opportunities to come out, as it were. I sighed. Too bad he didn't seem as into me as I was him.

I picked up his card and put it beside the register. Letting my eyes feast on his masculine beauty one last time, I was about to open my mouth to regretfully kick him out of the store so I could close up when he read my mind.

"You look hungry," he said. "Can I buy you a pastry or some coffee next door?"

Finally.

"Sure."

We went out the side door, which connected directly to Holy Grounds, the coffee shop adjacent to Mercury Crossing. I waved at my best friend Izzy, who was serving behind the bar, but she was too busy with a customer to see me.

Sebastian chose a table near the window. Though the sun had begun to set, a bright shaft of light shone precisely on his seat. I had to bite my lip to hold back a gasp of fear as he sat in it. Despite the evidence to the contrary, I still figured him for a vampire.

I checked his aura again. Yep, still dead.

"Too bright for you?" he asked, apparently mistaking my squint.

"No, I guess it's all right," I said, watching for tendrils of smoke snaking up from the top of his head. Nothing, except the usual swirl of dust motes dancing through the air. I sat across from him, scanning his face. His skin had none of the waxen, gray slack of a zombie. In fact, if anything, he looked a bit tanned.

Weird.

Of course, he derailed my investigation completely by taking off his jacket. The muscles on his arms couldn't be called anything other than sculpted. When he was alive he'd worked out, or he'd worked hard, but no matter which it was, it'd produced magnificent results. "What did you do?" I asked. "I mean, I don't imagine you made your living as an herbalist."

"I'm a mechanic these days. I work down at Jensen's Service Station near Vilas."

A day job. Present tense. This poor man *doesn't* know he's dead. "Wow."

He shrugged. The slight, unconcerned lift of his shoulders was such a normal-guy, mundane gesture, it seemed wrong to me. The dead should be stiff, or at least stately. "It's a job. I like working on the classic cars. These new ones with their computers annoy me."

"What? Why?"

"Cars should run on fire, water, and air. It's alchemical. Magic. Computers interfere with the elemental nature of engines, as far as I'm concerned."

"Huh," was all I could think to say; I was totally in love with the man at that moment.

"So, what can I get you?" he asked, standing up.

Now he was offering to pay? A mystical car mechanic *and* a gentleman . . . he could have me on this table right now, even with the whole dead thing. "I like the honey latte," I said. "And if they have a croissant or something like that?"

"Right. Coming up."

Because the coffeehouse and the magic shop had once been jointly owned, they had a similar flavor. The Holy Grounds had gone for New Age couture. Lush oil paintings of Gods and Goddesses hung on exposed brick walls. Each table had a candle nestled in a glass holder that was surrounded by five vaguely feminine iron figures connected in a circle. Across from me, in the space by the front door, hung a large poster of the chart I'd cast for the business using the date it opened. Brightly colored construction paper stars hung from thin strings in front of the window, and moon-shaped lights snaked around the bookshelf in the back near the comfortable couches and overstuffed chairs. A group of Renaissance Festival types dressed in peasant shirts and woolen cloaks sat there, softly drumming on borhans and dumbeks.

I watched as Izzy leaned in very close to take Sebastian's order. Izzy, née Isadora Penn, was undeniably beautiful. Her skin was several shades darker than the mocha lattes she served, but it was just as creamy and smooth. She kept her tight curls clipped close to her head, and her profile always reminded me of that famous bust of Nefertiti. If Sebastian were like every other red-blooded man I knew, it would be difficult for him not to notice her.

Yet somehow, though she flirted outrageously throughout the entire transaction, he seemed uninterested. In fact, when he paid, he pointed to where I was sitting. Izzy's eyes searched the room jealously but brightened when she saw me. She gave me a wave, and, when Sebastian wasn't looking, a big thumbs-up. I returned Izzy's smile.

As Sebastian walked past a long, narrow mirror hanging above the booths, I found myself relieved to see his reflection. Then I chided myself. Of course he had one. *Every*thing does. I never understood how the storybook vampires could make their clothes disappear as well. I mean, shouldn't you still see whatever they were wearing?

I returned my attention to watching Sebastian make his way back to our table. I grinned; even his walk was sexy. Some men stomp across a room, but Sebastian had such grace he seemed to glide.

Gliding. That was like floating, and floating wasn't sexy at all; it was creepy.

I peered at Sebastian's feet. They touched the ground. His gait had none of that odd tiptoe-glide of a ghost-possessed corpse. Of course, neither was he Chinese, and it was those ghosts who possessed people by sliding underneath the soles of their victim's feet.

Plus, he cast a shadow. Not to mention the fact that a regular ghost would have trouble carrying my latte and the saucer with my croissant on it. Sebastian didn't. In fact, he slid my food so deftly in front of me that I had to ask, "Were you a waiter once?"

"Oh, more than once," he said. "I worked my way across several continents waiting tables. It's a good job to have done because there's almost always work."

"True enough," I agreed. I'd done a stint waitressing while in college.

"Can I ask a small favor?" He looked vaguely sheepish, and I was wondering if he was going to bum some money from me to cover the food and drinks.

"Sure," I said suspiciously.

"Would you tell me your name?"

"Garnet Lacey," I said, then instantly regretted it. My stomach twisted in that way it does right after you've given the cute stranger you just met at the bar your *real* home phone number. Oh, yes, dead guy, here, have my true name. Why don't I just hand over some fingernails and a lock of hair, too, so you can have complete control over me?

I should have given him my ritual name. Because of the constant threat of Vatican spies infiltrating the coven, it was standard protocol to have an assumed name, one that was used primarily among other Witches. My coven had been strict about it, secrecy had been drilled into me, and here I was exchanging private information with a dead guy I'd only just met. *Super, Garnet.*

"Well, Garnet." He smiled that harmless smile I wanted to trust but couldn't quite. "It's nice to be officially introduced. My name is Sebastian Von Traum."

Well, at least he appeared to have returned the favor. If this guy didn't know magic, he certainly knew the right questions to ask and how to phrase the responses. After all, he didn't just say: "I'm Sebastian" or "I'm called Sebastian," he said, "My name is." It was an offer of trust. Or a happy accident. The glow in those brown eyes made me doubt it was the latter.

"Sebastian is kind of an old-fashioned name," I said, trying to be sly about sussing out his age. After all, at this point in the conversation it seemed a little gauche to ask him how long he'd been dead.

"It is," he agreed, glancing out the window at a drunken gaggle of college frat boys in full barhopping mode. "I'm named after the saint, no less."

"I'm not big on Christian saints," I said. "Which one was he?"

"Praetorian guardsman, pierced by arrows, though apparently that wasn't what killed him in the end."

"You've lost me."

Sebastian smiled. At that moment in the conversation— i.e., me having declared my stupidity—I normally would have taken such an expression as condescending. Instead, Sebastian's grin seemed self-deprecating, almost shy.

"I do that," he said. Again, on other men, I'd have assumed arrogance, but there was something about the way he said the words that cast them in a softer, kinder tone. "He lived through the arrows. He got beaten to death with a stick. Anyway, do you know what I find truly bizarre?

Here's this poor guy who gets shot with a zillion arrows, and do you know what he becomes? The patron saint of archers. Doesn't that seem wrong to you?"

"It does," I admitted with a laugh.

Sebastian took a sip of his drink. He'd bought something dark that came in a big yellow coffee mug. From here, it smelled like a dark roast of some kind. Most dead things I'd run across so far could drink if they wanted to, even zombies—at first, anyway. So, it didn't surprise me to find him able to do it. I just wondered at his choice.

"You have the strangest expression on your face right now," he said to me.

"You're drinking regular coffee," I said.

"So I am," he said. "Though this is organic, shade-grown, fair-trade, and bicycle-delivered."

Of all the things to spend your money on, I thought. Here this guy is dead and he doesn't even spring for a fancy latte or a shot of anything. What a waste of precious digestive juices. I mean, I believed in the power of a normal cup of joe, but when you were going out for coffee, a person should go for broke. And, if you're dead . . . well, you should really whoop it up.

"Does it offend you?" he asked cautiously.

"No. It's just . . . don't you want something more special?"

"Why?"

"To mark the occasion." He raised his eyebrows in a way that reminded me that he wasn't privy to my inner thoughts, and I probably sounded like a complete idiot. "I mean, you can make that stuff at home."

"Ah, but at home I can't spend three dollars for the privilege."

"Exactly my point," I said with a smile.

"You're a very odd woman, but you have the loveliest smile," he said. "It attracted me instantly. It's rather enchanting, actually."

Like your eyes, I almost said. Instead, I pulled myself away from those amber depths and stared at the napkin I'd been folding into a tiny triangle. "So, uh, Von Traum . . . What kind of name is that?"

"Austrian," he said a bit perfunctorily, as though he'd been asked about it a number of times.

I felt bad not acknowledging his earlier compliment, but I didn't know what to do about his/our attraction. The fact remained that he was dead. As a doornail. And dating doornails was no fun. Trust me, I tried being with a dead guy once, and it was miserable. I found that whole cold skin thing a big turnoff in the bedroom. You can only do so many things in a hot bath or shower, and even then the heat didn't . . . well, penetrate, if you know what I mean.

I banished that thought with a sip of my latte. The honey and milk tasted sweet on my tongue, and the hint of espresso gave the drink a perfect kick. Izzy sure knew her stuff. I looked up to see her smiling at me from behind the counter.

Meanwhile, Sebastian's attention had wandered to the street again. Two women walked by, loaded down with shopping bags. One of them wore a dress with the price tag still hanging from the sleeve. I cleared my throat to draw him away from the two laughing women. "I'd have thought you were English from your accent."

"I was educated in Britain," he replied distractedly. I got the sense he'd been asked both these questions a lot.

Since I was asking all the traditional getting-to-know-you questions, I might as well go right down the list. "How long have you lived in Madison?"

He sighed. "Since my dreams of becoming a rock star died."

"Seriously?"

"No, my best singing is done in the shower," he said with a smile.

My imagination suddenly flashed to an image of Sebastian naked and wet. I could almost feel my hands sliding easily over slick shoulders and down the flat planes of that broad chest to—

"I moved here from Phoenix a couple of months ago."

I blinked, banishing my fantasy with a quick shake of the head. "Uhm, so," I said, wishing we could talk more about what Sebastian did while wet. "What were you doing there?"

"I was a tour guide at the botanical garden." Before I could ask him more about that, he turned the conversation back to me. "What about you? Have you always lived in Madison?"

I shook my head. "No, I'm a world traveler, like yourself. I must have come three, four, five hundred miles in my entire lifetime. I was born in Finlayson." He gave me the blank look I often got when I mentioned my hometown. "Minnesota. A speck on the map, really. I left there for college as soon as I could."

"So, you're at UW?"

"No, I'm done. I got my degree in Minneapolis."

He gave me a skeptical look, as though he didn't think I was old enough to be a college graduate. I was, in point of fact, nearly thirty. It was the clothes; I always got carded when I went Goth.

"If you don't mind me saying so," Sebastian said. "Garnet is an unusual name, as well."

This was the question *I* got asked all the time. I was the only Garnet anywhere I went, and thus I'd had to endure a lot of playground teasing in my formative years. Though I loved the uniqueness of my name, I'd developed a love/hate relationship with it. Frankly, I always thought Garnet Lacey sounded a bit like a stripper.

I had a pat little story I always told to try to explain the origin of my name. "What can I say? Even though it was the late seventies, my parents hadn't given up on flower power. They'd moved to a farm to live off the land—they're raising organic chickens today. Anyway, they always used to joke that they were so into being 'back to the earth' they named their only child after a rock."

He laughed. A lot of people laughed when they heard the story of my name, but he seemed to share my amusement at my crazy, organic folks. "You're not serious."

"Not entirely. Garnet is also my birthstone."

"January," he said without hesitation. "So, does that make you a Capricorn or an Aquarius?"

"Come on," I laughed. "Look at me. Do I seem like a Capricorn to you?"

His gaze seemed to take in the pixie hair, ankh, and miniskirt in one measuring glance. "So, you're saying you're not somber and reserved?"

"Something like that."

"I'm a Capricorn," he said with a slight crinkle of a smile.

Oops. Before I could apologize for implying I wouldn't want to be a Capricorn, Izzy interrupted us with Sebastian's tuna sandwich. After she handed it over with a professional, "Here you are, sir," she waited until he wasn't looking and made the telephone sign to me with her fingers to her ear to let me know she wanted all the dirt later.

"I know Capricorns get a bad rep as being the boring, responsible sign, but you're more than that," I said.

He gave me a look over the rim of his coffee mug that seemed to say, "You bet I am."

What I'd meant was that a person's sun sign was only one small aspect of their natal chart. Among a myriad of things there was the ascendant, the Moon sign, hard and soft aspects, and houses to consider. "What time were you born?"

"If you're asking my ascendant, it's Sagittarius." I supposed I should be surprised he knew, but I wasn't. I mean, he had walked into my shop looking for mandrake.

As he ate, I thought about his sun/ascendant combination. A person's sun sign represents core personality traits, but the ascendant, or rising sign, is one's mask to the outside world—how you present yourself. My first thought was: philosophical scientist. No wonder he was a mystical car mechanic. It might also explain the various jobs. His Sagittarian soul was seeking new learning experiences, while the Capricorn sun insisted he master all his chosen trades. *Hmmm,* I thought, *attractive.*

Ugh. What was I doing? I was sizing up my compatibility with someone who was dead. I squinted at his aura one more time: still nothing.

Watching him dig into his food, I decided he was certainly hungry enough to be a ghost. Vampires tended not to eat. Zombies couldn't.

I picked at my croissant and tried to think if there was any other kind of reanimation I knew about. I squinted at his lack of aura again. If he'd been serious about the rock star thing, I'd have asked Sebastian if he'd sold his immortal soul to Satan for a record contract or something. But, I didn't believe in Satan.

If it was about the lack of a soul, Sebastian certainly had the muscles to be a golem. The most famous one had been made to protect the Jews of Prague from attack. If that were the case, he'd have the Hebrew word for life written on his forehead. I chewed another piece of pastry. I supposed that part of the legend could be some kind of metaphor. Or maybe if he frowned just right, it'd appear in wrinkles. It would help if I read Hebrew, of course. Still, Kabalistic rabbis would probably spawn an Orthodox golem, so I just had to figure out a way to ask him if he was Jewish. I could wait until we had sex and look, but circumcision was so common these days that it really wouldn't be proof of anything.

"We could go out to a proper dinner, you know, if you're still hungry," I suggested, giving a meaningful glance at his empty plate. "There's this great deli down the street if you need to keep kosher."

He arched his eyebrow as he wiped his mouth with a paper napkin. "The only religious dietary restriction I'd even consider is the Pope's requirement that I eat fish on Fridays during Lent. But that's only because they have the best fish frys down at Syl's."

"You're Catholic?"

"Sort of," he said with a wry smile. "I was. Well, technically, I still am. I was excommunicated."

"Really? Wow. What did you have to do to warrant that?"

"Dabble in the dark arts," he said with a smile that showed off his canines. Were they a little too sharp after all? "Catholics frown on Witchcraft."

I should know. The Vatican Witch hunters destroyed my previous life. His comment made me curious about whether or not he was familiar with the assassins. Not everyone was. And those in the know tended to be very circumspect about talking about the Vatican and real magic in public. Of course, I'd already given Sebastian my true name, which was a big no-no among the hunted.

Yet somehow I wasn't quite ready to talk about the Witch hunters. Probably because talking about killer priests out loud made me sound like a stark raving lunatic with a conspiracy theory complex. I still wanted to make a good impression on Sebastian, so I changed the subject somewhat. "What kind of magic do you practice?"

I was expecting him to mention Alexandrian or Seax-Wiccan, or Feri, but instead he said, "Alchemy."

It was an odd answer, but it wouldn't account for the lack of an aura.

Damn. I was running out of ideas. "Can I see your palm?"

"Are you Romany?" He offered his hand, palm up, without question.

"I may have a little Romany blood," I said, taking his hand in mine. "Family lore has it that Mother's grandmother was."

I peered intently at his palm, though I'd asked for it with an ulterior motive. His flesh was warm. What I now knew was grease had worked its way under his fingernails, but he had no cuts, bruises, or scrapes anywhere on his hands. Which implied his flesh might be immutable or regenerative, since he worked with sharp and heavy car parts all day.

I ran my fingers along his wrist. There was no pulse.

"What do you see?" Sebastian asked.

I looked up into those gorgeous brown eyes with their unearthly light, which seemed only to have gotten brighter now that the sun had slipped below the horizon. He seemed genuinely interested in the fortune I might read, so I took a more serious look at his palm. I wasn't an expert palm reader by any stretch, but I understood that the curved crease nearest the thumb was called the lifeline. His was broken in the middle where it split into two lines. I pointed to it.

"Well, if you weren't sitting here with me, I'd say you died young," I told him.

My hand cradled his, so I could feel his muscles clench, though to my eyes he barely twitched. He knew he was dead, and now he knew I knew it.

"What else?" he asked, not bothering to respond to my implication.

I was almost out of tricks. Then I remembered one other thing my grandmother had showed me. I turned his hand to the side and looked at the skin underneath his pointer finger. There were no creases. "You will have no children."

For some reason that pissed him off. He jerked his hand away. "Do you really believe in this stuff?" he asked, though from the way his jaw worked I thought it was pretty clear that he did.

I shrugged and sipped my latte. "I don't know. People have been reading palms and stars for millennia."

"Ignorant people," he all but spat.

"Newton was an—" I started, but before I could go through my list of famous, intelligent people who believed in any number of "superstitions," Sebastian interrupted me.

"Isaac Newton was an asshole. And mad as a hatter. He used to poke sticks in his eyes to test his optics theories."

I crossed my arms in front of my chest. "You sound like you've had dinner with him."

Sebastian's lips twitched. "I have a master's in history of science. I take this stuff personally."

A dead, English-educated auto mechanic/tour guide with a history of science degree who did herbalism on the side . . . If all of it was true, Sebastian was sounding more and more like a man who'd been kicking around for a few centuries and had a lot of time to pick up skills and interests.

Sebastian frowned out the window at the deepening twilight. The electric light caught the amber highlights in his eyes. I wanted to ask him about his strange reaction to my comment about children, but I didn't know what to say or how to phrase it. I sensed it was a subject I needed to tread carefully around. Sebastian certainly seemed deeply troubled, and I doubted his mood was a result of talking about Isaac Newton.

I reached across the table to caress the back of his hand where it wrapped around his coffee mug. At my touch, our eyes met. Oh, and what a look. It was one of those zing-we've-got-chemistry, smoldering, penetrating, I-can-almost-see-a-hint-of-your-soul meaningful glances.

My breath quickened. Sebastian leaned closer—maybe to say something, maybe to kiss me. I stretched across the table, and a tingle of anticipation shot through me. He looked like he'd be a fantastic kisser, and I was dying to find out for sure.

I found myself watching his mouth, reveling in the thin line of his lips . . . the sharp glint of his canines. The what? Before I could take a closer look, Sebastian turned away. "Sorry," he muttered into his hand. "I have a transmission to rebuild tomorrow. Call me when the mandrake comes in, okay?"

"Uh." Watching him stand up and shrug into his leather jacket, I was too stunned to say anything else. "But . . ."

His hand squeezed my shoulder as he headed for the door. The warmth of his palm lingered momentarily along the curve of my neck. "I had a great time. Really," he said. "I hope to see you again, Lilith."

"Yeah," I said to the jangle of bells on the door as he walked out of my life. I replayed the last part of our conversation in my head, noting the various places I'd screwed up . . . or did I? I was on my fifth go-round when I nearly choked on my latte.

"He called me Lilith," I said out loud, my heart pounding in my chest. *"Lilith."*

I shouldn't have done it, but I had to know. I shut my eyes for a moment, visualizing a doorway. In my mind's eye, it was steel with a combination lock, like a safe or a bank's vault. I imagined the tumbler spinning, all the while letting my breathing slow as my senses searched for the elements: earth, air, fire, water, spirit. The door swung open, and I felt the old power settle around my shoulders like a warm shawl.

Searching for a trace of residual magic, I reached for the rim of Sebastian's abandoned coffee mug. My fingers jumped back after the lightest brush. The cup glowed red-hot with his presence. In fact, when I looked around the room with my magical eyes, I could see trails of everywhere he'd been, like wisps of black smoke.

I was so stupid. It was so obvious. He wasn't dead; he was highly magical. Perhaps Sebastian was a necromancer or a dark Witch of some high degree. He'd have to be one wicked-powerful magician in order to recognize Her.

Vampires often saw Her. They didn't always call Her by name, but they somehow seemed to sense that power riding me. It was probably why none of them had ever tried to kill me, even when I recognized them for what they were. Vampires lived in secret. They didn't like it when people pointed to them and said, "Hey, bloodsucker, what's up?" Not that I'd ever done that, but, well, sometimes my mouth started up before I found the off switch. Witness my exchange with Sebastian. I could stand to learn some subtlety.

Izzy plunked down in the chair Sebastian had occupied and grinned into my face. "So, who was the hottie? And why didn't you go home with him?"

I hadn't put away my magic, so I could see the remaining wisps of Sebastian's energy scatter from Izzy's bright blue aura like snakes recoiling from a sudden light. I shook my head and took a deep breath. It was always more difficult to close down the magic than to free it. "Give me a second," I told Izzy.

Izzy was used to my weirdness. Though she anxiously fiddled with Sebastian's mug, she didn't interrupt as I gathered myself together and mentally relocked the door. When I opened my eyes again, the world had returned to normal. Mostly. I could still see a glimmer of Sebastian here and there, like the afterimage of a Fourth of July sparkler.

"So . . ." Izzy prompted, "where'd you dig him up?"

I laughed. Izzy always surprised me, even though I'd done her natal chart and knew full well she was a latent psychic. "Sebastian came into the shop looking for some mandrake root."

"Ooooh." Izzy feigned horror. "Satan's root, that makes him some kind of evil magician, right?"

"Right," I said a little too seriously.

Izzy and her damned intuition picked up on it right

away. "Okay, what's going on, girl? Normally, you'd be all giddy after hanging out with a handsome, grown-up man instead of one of those pimply college boys who want to initiate themselves at your altar. Something's wrong. Seriously wrong."

I rubbed my eyes. They always felt tingly after I used the magical sight. "Yeah, I don't know, I guess it doesn't really matter." So Sebastian was a powerful, potentially evil necromancer. That really didn't have anything to do with me. Well, other than the fact that I should probably put aside my desire to date him. I also felt slightly less inclined to help him obtain his mandrake. Whatever he planned to reanimate probably wasn't a good thing.

"Look at you, you're all googly-eyed. You've totally fallen for this guy."

Once again, Izzy was probably right. "That's such a bad idea."

"Why?"

"I don't know much about him," I said lamely. Actually, I knew quite a bit, but all of it was confusing, frustrating, or sexy. I was actually kind of surprised that Izzy didn't seem to know Sebastian. She loved to dish, and thanks to a Libra Sun and a Gemini Rising, she could usually charm any information out of anyone. "So, you've never seen him before? Never heard anything about a Sebastian Von Traum?"

"Honey, I'd remember a man like that."

"I know him. I sold him his house."

We both turned to stare at a woman who sat at the table behind us. She nodded. "Sebastian, right?"

My first impression was: this woman is completely forgettable. She had a soccer-mom bob of some undistinguished brownish color, a matching skirt and blouse. She completed the look with brown, low-heeled pumps. They weren't Birkenstock-comfortable shoes by any stretch of the imagination, but they were the kind of dress shoes worn by women who had to be on their feet all day. Because I always looked, I noticed the small golden cross that hung around her neck. A nice Christian real estate agent, then. I wondered what she'd think if she knew she'd sold a house to a necromancer.

"I didn't mean to eavesdrop," she said. "Sebastian Von Traum is such an unusual name, I recognized it instantly."

Despite Izzy's disapproving look, I motioned the woman over to the table. "He's Austrian, I guess," I offered, curious to know what else she could tell me about Sebastian. "English-educated."

"Yes, I understand Mr. Von Traum is some kind of horticulturist at University," she said. "I sold him his property."

The way the real estate agent said "at University" pegged her as a foreigner. Nearly every Madisonian referred to it as UW. Most of the rest of America tended to add a "the" before speaking of higher education. "I thought he was a car mechanic."

She gave a little disdainful laugh. "A car mechanic? With an original Picasso? I think not."

I could almost hear the growl of murderous rage in Izzy's throat before she spoke. "What are you saying? A car mechanic can't own decent art?"

The agent raised a frosty blond eyebrow and looked to me—the other white woman at the table—for help. I gave her none. In fact, I added, "Most college professors make much less than mechanics."

"He doesn't own it anymore," the agent said. "He sold it at auction a couple of months ago."

Which was about the time Sebastian said he'd moved to Madison. At least the agent seemed to have the timing of Sebastian's relocation correct.

"I suppose mechanics can only own velvet Elvises," Izzy muttered into her coffee cup.

"Where did you say he worked?" she asked me, ignoring the hostile gaze shooting from Izzy's eyes.

"I didn't," I said, while thinking, *Wouldn't that have been on the loan application?* Surely the woman must know where he works if she knows what he owns. What, did Sebastian hock the Picasso to buy the farm? "Why do you want to know?"

Her eyes slid from mine momentarily. Then, as if deciding on the lie she wanted to hand me, she looked up suddenly and said, "Networking. I get my best referrals from former clients. I like to stop by people's workplaces. Sometimes they can introduce me to friends on the spot."

Big fat lie. Not even a good one at that.

I frowned suspiciously at her. She was getting information from us, not the other way around. But I couldn't understand it; I thought maybe she might be tracking Sebastian down for money owed or something. After all, she seemed to be trying to locate him, but if she sold him his house, she must remember the address. "What kind of property does Sebastian own?"

The agent studied her coffee cup for a noticeable moment before she spoke. "One with space for all those herbs of his."

She had no clue. *I*, however, had typed his address into my computer less than twenty minutes ago. Sebastian had a farm just outside the city in Dane County.

"No mandrake, though, I guess," Izzy said before I could kick her shin under the table. "Mandrake's a Witch's herb," she added, clearly playing the freak-out-the-mundane game, which was especially odd, considering that she was a Christian of some kind herself. Izzy must have been hopping mad about the classist remark the agent had made earlier for her latent psychic abilities not to catch my mental screams to shut it. "He was buying it over at Garnet's shop. Probably for some spell, right, Garnet?"

"I've never heard of mandrake," the agent said. "Does that grow around here?"

"It's very common," I said trying to sound casually disinterested. Though I didn't know why, I hesitated to give this woman any more information about Sebastian than we already had.

"No, it's not," Izzy countered. "You've got to special order it. A bunch of naked lesbians have to harvest it by the full moon."

Normally, that would be game over. Your average mundane would have blushed, stammered, or fled at the mention of skyclad women wielding scythes. Our real estate agent merely blinked.

A creepy-crawly feeling twisted across my stomach.

"So, he'll be back," the agent said. "Well, this was a very interesting conversation, ladies, but I should really go. Maybe I'll see you again, Garnet."

When she hefted her purse onto her shoulder, the fabric at the back of her blouse shifted so that the V-neck exposed a bit of skin under her collarbone, revealing the hint of tattooed numbers. I didn't have to see them clearly to know exactly what was inked in bloodred: 22:18. It was a reference to the biblical book of Exodus, which read: "Thou shall not suffer a Witch to live."

She was no real estate agent; she was a Vatican killer.

Second House

KEYWORDS:

Evaluation, Entanglement, Order

My fingers gripped the strap of my backpack as I watched the agent disappear into State Street's evening crowd.

"I need to go," I heard myself say over the roar in my ears. I stood but I couldn't move. I had to leave town right now. I should walk to the bus station, buy a ticket, and go. *Don't hesitate, girl*, I told myself, these are the killers who murdered your entire coven.

My feet refused to move. My head knew what I should do, but my heart wasn't willing. I felt overwhelmed by a desire to leave responsibly this time. There was so much to do. The bus station was close, but I'd promised Barney I'd go back for her. I needed to turn in my keys, call Eugene, get my shifts covered . . . and I should warn Sebastian.

A hand on mine stopped me. I hadn't realized I'd started moving. Izzy smiled up at me. "You look frazzled, honey. No need to rush off. I'll get you another latte. Sit for a second."

I blinked. In her intuitive way, Izzy was right. Running would only draw attention. I should wait for a moment and try to form a plan of action. I drew in a deep breath and rolled my shoulders, trying to relax them. "Yeah, okay."

Dutifully, I sat. When Izzy got up to fetch the drink, it took all my resolve not to grab her and beg her to stay. She must have seen the panic in my eyes, because she paused and gave me a reassuring smile. "I'll be right back."

"Good," I said, letting out the breath I hadn't even realized I was holding.

I needed a plan, but all I could think was, *Oh shit, a Vatican agent. Here.*

Through the iron candleholder, the flame cast a flickering shadow on the table that looked like women dancing in a circle.

For a moment, I saw them all alive again: Jasmine and the others. We stood with our hands clasped together. Wren's rich alto led us in song. It was a moment of perfect trust, perfect peace. Though I tried to hold on to that image, the memory of blood overwhelmed me. Still in a circle, some still holding hands, they lay sprawled on the floor. Their nakedness, which had in life always felt so safe, so powerful, made them look vulnerable and small. The black robes of the Vatican stood out in stark contrast to the pale corpses.

I used my fingers to extinguish the candle. With the shadows gone, my memory faded. Glancing toward the counter, I saw Izzy busy preparing my latte. I had to warn Sebastian. He might be engaged in a kind of black magic I disapproved of, but I couldn't sentence him to death. Not by their hands.

Even though my knees threatened to buckle, I stood up. "I left something in the store," I said to Izzy, just as I realized she was about to set the drinks at our table. Sebastian's contact information was on the card I'd left next to the register, including a phone number. In what I hoped was a more sane tone, I added, "I have to go."

Izzy made some kind of protest, but I was already pulling the keys from my pocket.

My fingers trembled as I punched in the security code to turn off the alarm. In the dark, the familiar surroundings took on a sinister cast. The aisle felt too narrow, the ceiling too crowded, too close. I put my hand on a bookshelf to steady myself, only to knock over the turquoise feng shui dragon statuette Eugene insisted on setting in the east corner of the store. It shattered into tiny porcelain shards when it hit the floor.

There went my luck.

I started to stoop to clean up the pieces but decided to take care of Sebastian first. I made my way to the checkout counter without breaking anything else. Finding Sebastian's business card, I used the telephone under the counter to call his cell. The first time I dialed, I forgot to press 9 to get an outside line. The second time, I got the numbers screwed up and connected to a bait shop.

When the overhead lights flicked on, I shrieked, dropping the receiver on the counter so hard it bounced. "Holy Mother," I swore.

"Are you okay?" It was Izzy. She poked her head in from around the side door. "I heard a crash."

"I just destroyed Eugene's luck," I said through shallow breaths. "It's okay."

"Not the dragon?" Izzy asked with a low whistle. "He's going to kill you."

"He's not the only one," I whispered. To Izzy, I said, "I'm okay, I just need to make a quick call."

There was silence as she stared thoughtfully at me. Her brow furrowed slightly, then she said, "Okay, but when you're done, come back. Finish your latte, then I'll give you a ride home."

That was a sweet offer. I found I was actually able to smile a little bit. "Thanks."

She shut the door behind her, and I carefully dialed Sebastian's cell again. I held my breath as it rang. When it picked up, I almost started to yell, "The Vatican is coming!" but then realized I'd reached his voice mail. I took a deep breath to calm myself as I waited for the beep.

"Don't come back here, Sebastian," I started, and then stopped. He wouldn't recognize my voice; we'd only just met. "I mean, that is, this is Garnet. We just had coffee. Anyway, it's too dangerous." I paused again. Did he know about the Order? He seemed like he might, but if he'd been solitary this whole time . . . How did I explain on voice mail that the Vatican had a crack team of Witch hunters without sounding like a freak? Or, should I say, *more* like a freak. "Call me, and I can explain everything," I finished lamely, and gave him my number at home. "Tonight," I insisted. "It's really important."

I pressed the option to mark the call "priority" and then hung up.

He was never going to call; I sounded like a complete idiot.

Grabbing the broom and dustpan, I went to clean up the feng shui disaster. Well, when I got home, I'd try Sebastian again. Returning the cleaning supplies to their place behind the counter, I grabbed his card and tucked it into my pocket. My fingers hovered over the phone, but I told myself I didn't need to call again right away. After all, the assassin couldn't really know where he lived, or she'd have gone directly there. She wouldn't have needed to wheedle the information from us. He probably had some time. The agent would be watching the store, watching me; so as long as I didn't lead her to him, it would be all right.

* * *

On the drive home, I borrowed Izzy's cell to try to reach Sebastian again. I called both numbers listed on his card. No answer. I tried not to let that worry me. Maybe he was the sort to turn his cell off when he was out. Or perhaps he was at some noisy bar and couldn't hear the ring. I told myself he was a big boy; he could take care of himself.

I just wanted to do whatever I could to spare anyone else a run-in with the Vatican.

Izzy filled the rest of the ride with idle chitchat. I watched Madison roll by outside my window. I liked this town. It was a perfect mixture of urban and park spaces. There was a beautiful parkway that stretched from downtown to the lakes and along neighborhoods full of grand old houses like my own. Burr and white oak branches formed canopies over the broad avenues. I was going to miss this place. I wondered where I'd settle next.

A wave of nausea passed over me at the thought of leaving everything I'd come to love. I gripped my pack with whitening knuckles. I didn't want to do it. I loved my apartment, my job, and this town. Finally, after months of being alone, I'd made good friends again . . . people I could trust. I glanced at Izzy. Could I tell her about the Vatican agents? About my past?

I was still considering when we pulled up to my duplex.

"Do you want me to come in?" She popped the trunk and came out to help me pull the bike out from where we'd stowed it.

"I'm good," I said, but I think the tremble in my voice betrayed me.

I stood on the sidewalk, my bike resting against my hip. Izzy leaned on the hood of her car. The streetlight at the end of the block lit half of Izzy's face in stark white contrasts, like a harlequin mask. She gave me a deeply skeptical frown. "I can stay here until I know you're in safely."

I could have cried at her kindness. I was going to miss

having a friend like her. "No, I'm feeling restless. I might hit the grocery store or maybe just go for a ride."

She nodded, but I could tell she disapproved. "You sure you don't need the company?"

"I'd love the company, but I don't think I'm up for it," I said honestly. "I've got some thinking to do."

"I'd love to know about what."

"When I get it sorted out, I'll tell you, promise."

"It has to do with that man, doesn't it?"

"It does."

"Hmmm," she said through pursed lips. "Men," she said. "You can always count on them for trouble."

I smiled. "Take care," I said, as she got in the car. On impulse I added, "I love you."

She paused to shoot me an I'm-worried-when-you-say-things-like-that grimace, then gave me a fond wave as she started up the car. I didn't care if she thought I was strange. I probably would never see her again after tonight, and, anyway, I did love her. Izzy had been good to me when I needed a friend.

I watched her drive away with my hands resting on the handles of the bicycle.

Clouds had rolled in, and a haze formed a halo around the moon. Though the air was warm, I shivered. I looked at the address again. I thought I knew the place. It was a long way out but doable by bike. Besides, if the Vatican agent followed Izzy and me this far, I was sure I'd spot her if I took the bike. It's very difficult to follow a bicyclist when you're in a car. I'm no speed racer, so someone creeping along at fifteen miles an hour would be easy to spot. Besides, my mountain bike said All Terrain right there on the crossbar. If I had to lose someone, I'd off-road it.

Anyway, I was restless to be going—somewhere, anywhere.

Shouldering my backpack, I glanced behind me at my

apartment. I could see Barney in the window, silhouetted by the purplish glow of the grow lights. Her eyes were on my back as I hopped on my bike and headed out.

Somewhere outside of the city limits the rain started. I was too far out to turn back; Sebastian's place was closer than home at that point. It was only a light drizzle. I could feel myself calming down with the exercise. The county highway was deserted. The smooth asphalt curved around farms and fields of newly planted corn and alfalfa. I could smell the pungent scent of manure on the warm breeze.

My shoulders relaxed. I didn't have to leave town. The Vatican agent was concentrating on Sebastian. She might not even know I was a Witch. I'd heard through the grapevine that the Vatican employed psychics who could sense the presence of magic, but she might not be one of them. Even if she were, she was on assignment to deal with Sebastian first. That would buy me time. Time to entrench. Time to make a stand.

If I ran now, it would be the beginning of a life on the run, of starting over from scratch. I'd spend the rest of my life lonely because, just as I made friends, I'd have to leave them. It was bad enough to think about doing that twice, but forever? It was too much.

I wouldn't go. Maybe I could find a way to face down the threat that would solve the problem permanently.

Lilith tightened my stomach.

Well, maybe not that kind of permanent. I'd think of some way—some *other* way.

Nighthawks darted through the air chasing mosquitoes, flashing white stripes on the underside of their wings as they passed overhead. Well, I'd think about all that later. My first order of business was to warn Sebastian.

The raindrops grew heavier as the miles wore on. I

checked the address again. Up ahead I was happy to see
what I assumed must be his farm. A graveyard occupied the
lot next to Sebastian's. It was one of those odd country
cemeteries that existed between fields, surrounded by a
chain link fence, with no church for miles. The monuments
listed on ground made uneven by time, the wooden coffins
underneath having long since disintegrated. A nearby yard
light illuminated neatly trimmed grass, though a few markers were nearly obliterated by cedar bushes and other over-
grown offerings.

I could see how this place might appeal to a necromancer.

Just as I pulled into his drive, the rain officially became a
downpour. I dragged my bike through the mud of the path-
way to his front door and hauled it and myself up onto the
open porch. A damp, rotting-wood smell permeated the
porch. When I leaned my bike against the railing, the section gave so much that I was afraid I'd come away with
wood in my hands. The porch rail mostly hid the bicycle
from the road. Not that anyone would be looking at this de-
crepit place.

A heap of curled, yellowing newspapers lay in front of a
screen door, which hung precariously by a single hinge.

The farm looked abandoned.

Fan-fucking-tastic.

Leaning up close to a dust-covered window, I peered into
the darkened interior. I thought I could make out furniture
of some kind. No lights were on anywhere. Maybe I was at
the wrong place? I checked the card again. The address was
painted clearly above the door. The numbers matched.

Gingerly propping the screen door against my shoulder,
I knocked on the door. No answer. I pounded a little harder,
then leaned up to try to look in the window of the door. To
my horror, it popped open, the latch slipping open under
the extra pressure.

There was something overly familiar about this scene,

which caused my magic radar to ping. The go-away vibes were so overwhelmingly strong that I started to suspect they weren't real at all, but a spell designed to keep people away.

Even so, I hesitated, my foot on the threshold. The rain fell in sheets, sluicing down the slanted porch roof. My mini clung heavily to my butt, growing colder with each gust of wind. Going back wasn't an option, not with the constant flashes of lightning and miles of open, flat farmland.

So, the only course was the fool's errand. If only my life were a movie, I thought, then I could just listen for the swell of operatic music and know if my decision was the wrong one.

"Hello?" I ventured, stepping over the threshold. "Sebastian? Anyone?"

I peeked around the door into the house. Blessed warmth hit my face. The interior smelled of woodsmoke and cinnamon.

"Sebastian?" I called out again, taking a bolder step inside.

Turning, I saw a man-sized shadow, and I nearly jumped out of my skin until I realized it was just a coat rack with a jacket hanging on one of the pegs. I let out a sigh of relief. Reaching out a hand, I felt leather and heard buckles knock into each other. Sebastian's coat.

Right house, at least.

A cold draft rushed along the edges of the soaked skirt. I wanted to shut the door behind me, but somehow I felt less like I was trespassing as long as it remained open. I dripped self-consciously onto the hardwood floor. "Hello?"

As my eyes adjusted to the darkness, the room in front of me began to take shape. On the far left wall was a fireplace with a simple carved-wood mantle. A couple of overstuffed chairs and a couch nestled in front of it, as though huddled close for warmth. A built-in buffet took up most of the wall opposite me. Cabinet shelves and leaded glass framed a pass-through opening that presumably led into a kitchen or dining room. I heard rattling of pots coming from the back of the house. Someone was here. "Sebastian? It's me, Garnet."

The storm shook the window.

A hiss like rain spattering asphalt seemed to tickle my ear. "Trespasser."

I turned at the words but saw no one. The feeling of being watched crept across my skin. Behind me, nothing but water pelted down, silver needles reflecting in the yard light.

As I turned my attention back to the interior of the house, my peripheral vision registered the coat rack as man-shaped again. This time, however, I could have sworn it lunged toward me, and I took a step back before I remembered what it was.

"Trespasser."

Either my overly guilty conscience just sprouted an "outside voice," or the coat rack just talked to me.

"Hello?"

The wind pushed the door shut with a slam. I jumped and yelped at the same time. At least my first impression was that it was the wind, but part of my brain said, *Breezes usually blow outside in, not the other way around.*

"Is someone there?" I heard a voice call out from upstairs.

"Sebastian! It's me, Garnet."

"Don't move!" Sebastian shouted.

"Don't move, trespasser." The second voice came from behind me. I spun around at the sound. Lightning flashed, revealing the shadow of someone holding an upraised knife. Instinctively, I called Her name.

The darkness instantly became light to my magical eyes. A gaunt man dressed in ragged overalls and galoshes stared at me with bugged-out eyes. His mouth was twisted with rage. The knife came down in a slashing motion. The hand I'd stretched out to ward off the blow felt a slight shudder as the blade clattered uselessly against Her psychic shield, which surrounded me like an obsidian bubble. The man looked around frantically. *Yes,* I thought, *you should be nervous, little ghost.*

I could feel a smile twitch across my lips as She began to rise.

"Benjamin, no!" I heard a shout from the stairs. I saw Sebastian coming down, a towel wrapped around his waist, his hair dripping with soap. At Sebastian's command, Benjamin disappeared, fading like a wisp of smoke.

My enemy was gone, but the tremors had already started cutting across my abdomen. The fire consumed me. Before I could stop Her, She was upon me.

Lilith didn't share very well. When She controlled my body, I went away. Total blackout. When I came to, I always checked three things: how much time I'd lost, how bruised I felt, and how much damage I'd done.

Through closed eyes, I could tell I lay on the couch. Pillows propped up my head, and a warm, fuzzy blanket had been wrapped around me. I smelled hot chocolate. A fire popped and hissed nearby. What I couldn't feel was the sticky sensation of blood congealing under my fingernails, or anywhere else for that matter. Some experimental twitches revealed few, if any, bruises. I did, however, appear to be missing my clothes; I was naked.

A curious turn of events.

Yet I still didn't want to open my eyes. I didn't want to see Sebastian dismembered on the floor—or worse. I didn't want to know what had happened this time. It was too horrible to imagine that I'd come all this way to warn him, only to be the death of him.

"Are you all right in there?"

My eyes popped open at the sound of Sebastian's voice.

Sebastian occupied one of the chairs next to a roaring fire. His fingers made a steeple in front of his lips as he watched me. He, I noted, had gotten dressed. Sebastian seemed to favor what I would call typical male attire: a black T-shirt advertising what I assumed to be some heavy metal rock band called Slither, jeans of the same hue, and bare feet. His hair was still damp.

I stared at him for a long time. Not only had he found a way to look even sexier than he had the first moment he walked into my store, but also I couldn't get over the fact that he seemed to have all his parts in their original order.

"I didn't kill you."

"Apparently not." I couldn't tell by the sound of his voice whether or not he was happy about the situation, but a smile kept twitching at his lips.

I started to sit up, but the feeling of the blanket sliding over bare skin stopped me. Pulling the covers tighter around me, I asked, "Uh, where are my clothes?"

"In the dryer," he said. "Well, not the velvet skirt or the lace hose, those are hanging on the shower rod upstairs."

Practical. The man knew how to take care of a woman's delicates. Trying to stifle the beginning of an ear-to-ear blush, I asked, "You undressed me? Why didn't Lilith kill you?"

Behind his fingers, he flashed me a wolfish grin. "Only a fool would take something from Lilith she didn't give freely."

I tried to picture the scene: Lilith, Queen of Evil, Mother of Demons, politely asking Sebastian to wash my clothes for me—but for Goddess' sake don't ruin the velvet! I shook my head at the image. Lilith didn't joke around. At least, she never had before.

"Uh," I said, my imagination failing me. "So what exactly happened?"

"I am extraordinarily fortunate She recognized me as kin."

Slowly, and careful to keep my modesty, I sat up. Sebastian

hadn't moved, except to speak. Lilith was mother of all things that went bump in the night, and Sebastian had just implied that She had spared his life because She understood him to be one of Hers. He was admitting to being a monster.

"Kin?" I repeated, giving him an opportunity to change his story if he wanted.

"Blood, if you prefer."

"Blood," I said again skeptically.

He inclined his head slightly in confirmation. His eyes studied me, as if trying to ascertain whether or not I understood the full implication. Oh, I got it, all right. He was telling me he was a vampire, but the problem was, I wasn't buying it.

"Really?" I pressed.

He raised an eyebrow and broke from his posture to reach for a second mug of cocoa on the edge the table between us. Our eyes met before he settled back, and I had a flash of déjà vu, as a spark of passion arched between us. I felt keenly aware of the fact that he had seen me naked, and I still had no clothes on.

Sebastian held my gaze as he said, "You sound as if you don't believe me."

I started to shrug but realized the motion would undo the careful arrangement of blanket. "Creatures of the night usually, well, hang out at night, Sebastian."

My astute observation was rewarded by a hearty laugh. After he got himself under control, he said, "You've obviously never read *Dracula*."

Ouch. Okay, so I wasn't up on my vampire literature. "And?"

"And daylight isn't a problem for the most famous 'creature of the night,' as you put it."

"I hate to be the one to point this out, Sebastian, but Dracula wasn't real."

This time he almost snorted his cocoa. I guess my timing

was improving. "There was a historical Dracula. Vlad Tepes. He was an Austrian, no less. You know the Transylvanian Alps are in territory that was once part of the Austro-Hungarian empire."

I arched my eyebrow. "Now you're Dracula?"

"I'm not saying that. I've just always enjoyed the irony." He shook his head, and I suddenly realized his hair was loose. Long, straight locks settled mid-chest. There was something about the way it hung that made him look other-timely. That is to say, it would be easy to imagine hair like that accompanying a Renaissance-era tunic or whatever they called them back then. Weirdly, the style of his hair gave his claim of being a vampire some credence. He'd still come off as crazy, however, if he tried to tell me he was Vlad the Impaler.

"Exactly what *are* you saying?" I asked.

"The sun is not my enemy." He took a sip of his cocoa and stretched his feet toward the logs in the fireplace.

Neither, apparently, was fire. A lot of vampires studiously avoided open flames. They tended toward paranoia, as if their bodies made better kindling than those of the living.

Still, his comment begged the question: Who or what *was* his enemy?

Before I could ask, Sebastian let out a sigh. "Well, it hasn't been for a millennium."

A millennium? As in a thousand years? I gave Sebastian a more serious looking over. Could he really be that old? Weirdly, that made him even sexier. Longevity in a vampire implied a strong survival instinct, a wolf-eat-wolf, heavy-on-the-testosterone kind of lifestyle, which, embarrassingly, appealed to me.

Anyway, that was beside the point. All vampires shriveled in the sun like plastic in a campfire. "How come you're so special?"

"What do you mean?"

I gave him the are-you-seriously-this-dense look.

He responded with the yeah-I-am-what-of-it glare.

"The vampires I've met are sun-averse, Sebastian."

"You've met others?"

Okay, I dated one, once. It was an extreme lapse of judgment, and if I were to get introspective about it, probably a major self-destructive phase in my life. Parrish was a good lover, though, and, as it turned out, someone I could count on in a pinch. More importantly, he gave me all sorts of knowledge about vampires and, I'm happy to say, not all of it was carnal.

After the big breakup with Parrish, I seemed to spot vampires everywhere. And they noticed me. Once I was aware of them, they seemed to home in on me. So, I had my share of run-ins. If I was honest about it, I could only claim about a half-dozen sightings, one or two extended conversations, and the one intimate relationship. Still, I considered myself pretty well-informed about the vampire community. Most people didn't even know they existed.

"Yeah. A few."

Sebastian looked as if he were about to ask more when the sound of glass breaking came from the kitchen. Then a pot crashed to the floor, followed by several others.

Each noise made me jump. I clutched the blanket tighter, and shouted, "Shouldn't you go see what's going on?"

"My poltergeist is throwing a tantrum," he said nonchalantly.

"Benjamin." The name came back to me, as did the image of him fading at Sebastian's command. "He's a ghost."

"Technically, as I said, poltergeist. He's slightly more material than your average ghost. Hence, the throwing part of throwing a tantrum. Anyway, he came with the house," Sebastian said with an uninterested shrug, as though discussing the weather. "He upped the property value for me, frankly."

The mention of real estate reminded me why I'd made my sojourn. "The Vatican is after you, Sebastian."

Silverware rained on the floor. A wooden thud, like the sound of someone tossing aside a cabinet drawer, echoed from the kitchen. Sebastian stood up angrily. "All right, that's enough," he said, striding past me to the kitchen door. "Outside, Benjamin. Now."

One last petulant crash, and then I heard the sound of a door opening and slamming shut.

"Sorry about that. He's always like this around the full moon. I guess, you know, it happened on a full moon," Sebastian said.

It? Did I want to know? The guy was a ghost now, a fairly murderous one, I might add, so things hadn't ended well. I decided to let that ride for now.

Before returning to his chair, he crouched beside the fire and stirred the embers with a poker. "What were you saying?"

"The Order," I repeated. "They're after you." When he'd opened the chain screen in front of the fire, heat poured into the room. My skin was still damp enough that the warmth felt divine. I itched to relocate closer to the flames, but the blanket restricted me. "Don't you have a T-shirt or something you could loan me?"

He glanced over his shoulder, his gaze lingering on my face for a long moment. "Sure. I'll go get something." He stood up as if to go, but hesitated. "What Order?"

"The hunters," I explained. "The Order of Eustace."

"Eustace?" he chuckled. "Am I supposed to be afraid of an organization with a name like Eustace?"

My fists clenched. "They could be named the pansy-ass froufrou club for all I care. They're killers, Sebastian. Stone cold."

"So am I." Sebastian's tone carried no arrogance or boasting, merely a statement of fact. His gaze held mine steadily for a moment longer, then shifted uneasily to the floor.

"I'll get those clothes for you," he said.

I nodded mutely. The rain had softened to a hushed, steady rhythm on the roof. The house was quiet except for the creak of floorboards as Sebastian made his way up the stairs. It wasn't as if his admission should come as such a shock. I knew vampires killed people. I mean, they were predators. It was their nature.

I learned from Parrish that vampires could, and most often did, survive on the small amount of blood that they took from consensual partners. The majority of vampires in Parrish's circle courted a certain kind of groupie who enjoyed the thrill of the bite, which, I had to admit, had no small appeal. I let Parrish bite me once, out of curiosity, I suppose, or that before-mentioned self-destructiveness, and I instantly understood why Parrish never lacked for volunteers in that regard. The pain was addictive. My attraction to it must have scared me on some level, or I wasn't nearly as suicidal as I feared, because somehow I managed to studiously avoid the role of ghoul with Parrish. We were lovers; he got his nourishment elsewhere.

I guess that's how I'd fooled myself.

Parrish had been pretty up-front about the fact that he'd made his living as a "gentleman of the highway," as he called it, and had a tendency toward murder even before the Change. Somehow he'd made his lifestyle—past and present—all seem so charming, so . . . harmless. I supposed it behooved him not to remind me that vampires regularly murdered people. That sort of thing was probably a turnoff for a potential partner.

Sebastian had certainly changed the mood with his comment. I wasn't precisely disgusted by him, but I certainly felt . . . sobered. I think what disturbed me the most was the comparison. When I thought about the Order, it was personal. Those bastards had taken the lives of my friends.

Was there someone out there who hated Sebastian for the life—or lives—he'd taken the way I despised the Order?

Of course, I was a fine one to talk. Lilith had killed through me. I was a murderer, too. Though I preferred to think of it as vengeance. If I thought of it at all.

The squeak of the stairs alerted me to Sebastian's return. He handed me a white T-shirt and navy sweatpants with UW's logo on the hip. "I thought you might find these comfortable." He gathered up the cocoa mugs, avoiding my gaze. "I'll freshen these up, shall I, while you change?"

He was already through the kitchen door before I could acknowledge his kindness. I quickly pulled on the clothes. The shirt fell way past my hips, and I had to roll up the legs of the sweats before I could even see my feet, but he was right. The plush fabric of the pants felt really comfortable against my skin, although the softness made me hyperaware of the fact that my underwear was in Sebastian's dryer.

I thought about calling him back into the room to let him know I was decently dressed, but the sounds of broom and dustpan came from the kitchen. I took the opportunity to snoop.

Despite claiming to be sun-loving, Sebastian had not turned on any lamps. The fire cast the majority of the light, accented by a couple of tall tapers on the built-in glass-fronted cabinet. Though clearly designed to display china, Sebastian had filled the shelves with books—tomes, really. The books Sebastian had looked nothing like any reading material I'd ever owned in my life. For one thing, none of them were published by the major New Age publishing house, Llewellyn Press, and anyway, these things were leather-bound and serious-looking. Most of them were not in English, or if they were, they were in some dialect so ancient it wasn't recognizable to me as such.

The books seemed very vampire, almost stereotypical fashion-by-Vlad. What surprised me were some of the curios among the books: a toy '65 Mustang with working doors and trunk, a jeweled frog with a compartment that held a rose quartz rosary, and—most curious of all—a framed photo of Sebastian with guy friends dressed in climbing gear on some mountainside.

I looked at the photo for a long time. The sky was crystal-blue behind the men. Sebastian looked . . . tanned. Actually, it was a really good picture of him; it showed off his muscles, but that was just a distraction from how strange the whole thing was. A vampire who mountain climbed? With buddies? In the sun?

I was still staring at the photo when Sebastian came back into the room. I suppose I should have replaced the picture guiltily, but I just couldn't get over it. "You mountain climb?"

He smiled fondly with the memory. "Oh, yeah, I got into it for a while there. That was taken in Alaska." He came up beside me and pointed to one of his friends in the picture. "This is Smitty. He's a crazy Australian. You'd like him, I think. He has a bit of a wicked side. This is Ron—"

My expression must have halted his reminiscence.

"What?" he asked; it was that incredulous yet I-could-be-guilty-if-I-knew-for-sure-what-you-were-thinking-of what.

"You mountain climb?"

"Rock climb, really," he said, his eyes lingering on the photo in my hands. "Not anymore, though. Too dangerous."

I nodded. I was thinking that the danger of being exposed as a vampire had to increase exponentially when you were alone in the wilderness with a bunch of living men. The logistics of his expedition made me ask, "How much blood do you have to consume in order to go out in the daylight?"

Sebastian let out an embarrassed laugh. "That's a bit of an indelicate question, isn't it? See how I've diplomatically avoided asking you how you came to be part killer Goddess?"

I started to deny it, but stopped. I kept forgetting that

Sebastian knew about Lilith—had seen her—and lived. "Tact has never been my strong suit," I admitted.

"I've noticed." He smiled, handing me a refilled cup of cocoa. "Luckily, I find it dead charming."

In order to take the cup, I had to replace the photo on the shelf. All the shuffling made for a good excuse not to show Sebastian how pleased I was to hear his compliment.

Sebastian must have noticed how flustered I was, because he changed the subject. "Tell me more about these Vatican agents of yours."

"Not mine," I said abruptly, though I'd known full well what he'd meant.

He raised his hands as though in surrender. "Sorry."

I shook my head. "No, I didn't mean to snap. I just have a history with the Order."

"So I've gathered."

Sebastian took my place on the couch, so I snuggled into one of the overstuffed chairs close to the fire.

After taking a sip of chocolate, I asked, "What do you want to know?"

"Why do you think they're after me, for one?"

I recounted the tale of the real estate agent for Sebastian. "It was pretty obvious."

He nodded. "It's strange that they care more that I'm a Witch than a vampire. You'd think that being one of the walking dead would be a bigger sin."

"It's biblical, I guess," I said with a shrug. "Vampires aren't mentioned in the Bible; Witches are."

"The whole suffer the Witch to live thing?" he asked.

I nodded.

"Well, that's just bad biblical scholarship. A much more accurate translation of the Hebrew would be something more like, 'Thou shalt not support a Witch in her livelihood.' Or, 'Don't give the fortune-teller your dime.'"

I'd also heard that originally the word had been "poisoner"

and had gotten changed over time. Anyway, it hardly mattered. "Be sure to explain that to the assassins when they come," I said with a grimace. "I'm certain they'd love to engage you in a little semantic debate before they gut you."

"They? I thought you said there was only one."

I shrugged. "Where there's one, there's bound to be more."

Sebastian took a contemplative sip of his cocoa, then asked, "Why Eustace? The Vatican had a fairly efficient group of Witch hunters in the Order of the Inquisition."

I shrugged. "Eustace *is* the Inquisition, as far as I can tell. Officially, of course, it's a different story, but when the Inquisition fell out of favor, the new order carried on its business covertly. I think the Inquisition was embarrassed because it never uncovered real magic. The Order of Eustace has."

Sebastian nodded. "So what's their plan?" Sebastian asked, setting his cocoa cup down on the table between us. I watched the firelight play across the ripple of his muscles with a smile. "The Order, I mean. Total destruction of Witches? Containment? Control?"

I sipped my cocoa and thought about for it for a moment. It wasn't like the Order had a published mission statement anywhere, but the Witchcraft community talked and speculated and spun conspiracy theories. "There's a lot of debate about that," I said. "The general consensus is destruction, but to what degree, no one seems to know."

Sebastian sat forward in his chair. As the conversation intensified, so did his body language. "I thought you said they were being literal with the 'Thou shall not suffer a Witch to live.' That seems pretty straightforward, doesn't it? Not a lot of room for shades of gray."

"Well, yeah, that's what I'd think, too, except the Vatican employs Witches."

"Really?"

"That's the rumor," I said with a shrug. "Fight magic with magic, I guess."

"So," he said with a wicked smile that showed off the points of his canines warming his tone. "Instead of excommunicating me, they should have recruited me."

The thought of Sebastian fighting for the other side sent a shiver though my body. He radiated magical power, even dead. "Goddess forbid," I said.

He laughed. "I'm not that scary," he said.

"Yeah, loads of people stare down Lilith and live," I said, sarcasm oozing in my tone. "Please."

Sebastian caught my gaze and held it. The fire reflected the amber starburst that encircled his pupils. Intense. Intense and deeply, deeply sexy.

We fell silent for a moment, both lost in thought. My thoughts mostly fell under the category of the things I wanted to do with Sebastian naked, with nothing between us but the heat of those eyes. I broke away first. "Do you think the Vatican knows you're a vampire, Sebastian? With all this rock-climbing and having a day job, they might have come to the same conclusion I did."

"Oh? And what was that?"

"Well, at first I thought you were some other kind of animated corpse."

He laughed. "Nice."

I gave him a hard glance. "You *are* an animated corpse, Sebastian."

"*Re*animated, technically, but, well, I was hoping to make a better first impression." His smile was warm and flirtatious. "What tipped you off?"

"You have no aura," I explained, smiling back. Damn that infectious grin of his. "I figured you had to be dead, but then I decided maybe you were just such a powerful magician that you'd learned to cloak it."

"To what end? Why would I not want to seem alive?"

I blushed. I didn't want to say what I'd been thinking, but he stared at me with such a curious expression that I finally relented. "I thought you were a necromancer. I thought you were trying to pass as dead. You know, to be cool."

Sebastian gave me a look that told me exactly how wrong I was about that idea. "Who the hell thinks it's cool to be dead?"

If I'd been wearing my ankh, I would have pointed to it. Instead, I twirled a piece of my dyed black hair with my bloodred fingernails. "There's a certain type."

And then he actually said, "Egad."

I hid my smile behind my cocoa mug. "More importantly, how do you think you came to the Vatican's attention?"

"It's odd. I've always been very low profile." He watched the flames dance on the logs. "It's how I survive."

"As a vampire," I offered. "What about as a Witch? Joined any covens lately?"

"Dabble, remember? I'm no Witch," he said, with, I noted, a slight tone of contempt. "I'm an alchemist."

"Same difference," I said just to tease him. "Anyway, what self-respecting 'scientist' needs mandrake harvested by full moon? You're a spell worker, Sebastian Von Traum, admit it."

He opened his mouth to protest but then stopped when he saw my smile. "I suppose I am, at that."

"Tell me the truth," I said, pointing my finger at him with faux seriousness, "Mine isn't the first shop you went to for your mandrake, was it?"

"Hmmm, I suppose I shouldn't have gone to all those co-ops and health food stores if I wanted to be secret about it, eh?"

We grinned at each other, but neither of us could really work up to a full-fledged laugh. The situation was just too damned serious. I chewed on my fingernail, listening to the rain tapping against the window.

Sebastian's eyes roamed over my body thoughtfully, as though trying to understand something without having to ask. Finally, he said, "You never mentioned. What kind of Witch are you?"

Oh, the loaded question. This was that moment of vetting I always hated, when Witches tossed around lineage and degrees and dropped names copiously. Luckily, I had an answer that satisfied most people. "I've been kicking around the magical community for a decade or so. I was a third-degree Gardnerian when I got frustrated with hierarchies and all the politics of a structured order. The last coven I was in was Eclectic, which suited my temperament better. Now . . . now I'm solitary."

It was hard to say *solitary*. The word itself felt foreign and thick on my tongue. I loved being part of group magic, and I missed it so much I almost felt a physical pain in my chest. I tried not to let my hurt show, but Sebastian reached across the table and took my hand. I squeezed it, enjoying the comfort in his strength.

"I'm sorry," he said.

"Yeah, me, too." Impulsively, I moved to the couch.

I nuzzled under his arm. He smelled good, musk-manly and something spicy, like cinnamon. It felt good to be held. His fingers stroked my hair.

Oops. Suddenly I was all turned on. His presence, his smell, the rock-hard smoothness of his muscles had me thinking about kissing and grunting and sweating. Problem? He was being all brotherly comforting, and it would be wildly inappropriate to grab a handful of his silky black hair and plunge lips-first into a bruiser of a kiss.

What to do now? How could I transform this moment of sympathy into hot, sweaty sex? I pushed myself closer under his arm, wiggled a bit, then felt foolish for even thinking about jumping Sebastian under these circumstances. I took in a deep breath and tried to be satisfied with the moment.

Nope. Too hot and bothered.

I straightened out of his embrace. "It's late, isn't it," I said glancing around the room for a clock. "I should probably call a taxi if I'm going to get home at a decent hour."

"I'm afraid all the decent hours have already passed," Sebastian said. "It's quarter of midnight. Anyway, the guest room is already made up. You can stay here tonight."

I liked the sound of his proposition minus the guest bedroom part. Ah, well, I supposed he was being gentlemanly about it all and not presuming.

"Yeah," I said, trying to hide my disappointment. "That would be fine."

The room Sebastian showed me smelled of dust and lavender. Lace valances, white curtains, calico comforter, and doilies all seemed perfectly preserved from someone else's life. Somehow, I couldn't picture Sebastian collecting a wooden darning egg and displaying it so artfully next to a brass-bottomed kerosene lamp.

"Whose room was this?" I asked.

"Vivian," he said, glancing at the window as if looking for something.

When he didn't volunteer any more information, I prompted, "Vivian?"

"The former lady of the house," he said. Then, almost as an afterthought, he added, "But it's perfectly safe now."

Safe? That sounded very bad. I got the sense that I didn't want to know the answer, but I asked anyway. "She died in this room, didn't she?"

He nodded. "Kept the house off the market for years. Apparently, the whole murder-suicide thing was very spectacular."

"I'll bet," I said. "So, which one was Benjamin? The murder or the suicide?"

"Suicide."

I should have figured. "And you kept the room the same?"

"Not me. Benjamin." Picking up an embroidered sachet of potpourri from the end table beside the bed, he tossed it on the bed. "That'll drive him spare."

"Let me see . . ." I said, working this story out in my head, "Every time you try to change this room, Benjamin fixes it?"

"The good thing is that his obsession makes him an excellent housekeeper. Sometimes I can get him to clean other parts of house by putting her things around."

"This is supposed to make me feel better?" I looked at the bed with its deceptively homey pile of throw pillows. "No way. I'm sleeping on the couch."

Sebastian tried to insist that Benjamin wouldn't try to ax-murder me in my sleep, but I was able to convince him that there was no chance of me closing my eyes for one minute if I stayed in Vivian's room. After helping Sebastian gather some pillows and blankets from the hall linen closet, I made myself a comfortable nest on the couch downstairs.

The rain continued to fall softly on the window. "Are you sure you'd prefer to sleep here?" Sebastian asked for the seventh time since I had backed hastily out of Vivian's room. "It's only that Benjamin will probably rattle around all night, and . . . well, I'd prefer to have you closer."

Closer? I liked the sound of that, but I wasn't sure how he meant it. "Oh?"

I could have sworn I saw the hint of a blush color his cheek. "Yes, well, in case of . . . emergency."

Were we talking hormonal emergency or something else? I assumed he meant if the Order somehow followed me here or if the ghost tried to kill me. "Do you honestly think Benjamin is that dangerous? Maybe I shouldn't stay here at all tonight."

"Oh, no. It's safe. Really," he said quickly. Sebastian put another log on the fire, replaced the screen, and stood up.

"Benjamin can't come inside unless I allow it. He can stay outside tonight."

I glanced at the rain-spattered windows and thought about an angry ghost shuffling around outside. "Aw," I said. I felt weirdly guilty for putting an evil spirit out in the cold. "This is *his* house. I mean—"

Sebastian put up a finger up to shush me. "This is *my* house. And you are *my* guest for the evening. Benjamin doesn't mind the cold. Weather doesn't bother him. Besides, if he doesn't like it here, there are places he can go."

Like Hell? I wondered, but I didn't really want to start a discussion about the transmigration of souls with a dead guy, so I fluffed my pillow and said, "Okay."

"Well, good night, then," Sebastian said.

"Good night," I said, waiting for him to head upstairs before settling down.

Instead, he stood there, staring at me. I knew that look. He wanted me. But he'd decided to play the gentleman, and now he was stuck in the role. I suppose I should have said something inviting, but I couldn't think of anything other than "Hey, so, you wanna . . . ?" And while that might be effective, it could also completely turn Sebastian off.

Besides, part of me really wanted *him* to be the one to make the first move.

"Right, then," he said finally. "I'm off."

"Yeah," I said, adjusting the blankets, wondering if I could stroke them seductively enough for him to get the idea that it would be more than okay to stay.

"Eh," he said, and marched determinedly up the stairs.

With a defeated sigh, I pulled the covers over my head and tried to sleep.

It's never easy to sleep in a strange place. Add to that a restless ghost and some serious sexual frustration, and it was nearly impossible. I spent a lot of the night listening to the mantel clock ticking softly, wondering if I should creep upstairs and quietly slip into Sebastian's bed. If nothing else, being snuggled up to him would be warmer. More importantly, I'd be spared the image of Benjamin's pale face pressed against the glass window and the occasional rattle as he tried the doorknob. The wind sounded very frustrated as it moaned through the gables.

Man, this house was freaky. I hoped Sebastian got it cheap.

Which made me think of the Vatican agent who claimed to be his real estate agent. I didn't think I'd impressed upon Sebastian the seriousness of his situation. He seemed pretty blasé about having a Witch hunter after him. Of course, the man had a murderous ghost for a roommate.

As though on cue, Benjamin rapped his knuckles on the window again, making me twitch. I'd be a nervous wreck if I lived here. It made me wonder if Sebastian had many lovers stay over. I mean, how did you explain the ghost roomie to a mundane? Or did they usually have some kind of signal system on the nights Sebastian wanted to bring someone back to his place? Benjamin didn't seem very tolerant of women in general. I had no idea what happened with Vivian, but it didn't seem good that she'd died in bed.

Benjamin tried the doorknob again, and I put the pillow over my head. Maybe sleeping in the dead woman's room was better than this.

Honestly, I'd rather be sleeping with Sebastian.

I wished I'd been more forward. It's not like I'd never been the aggressor in a relationship before, but, other than my previous vampire, I tended to bag the weaker members of the herd. The sick, slow ones. Okay, it wasn't that bad, but Mercury Crossing wasn't exactly happy hunting grounds for alpha males. The kinds of guys who came to my shop fell under the classification of safe, even for Madison, which I'd discovered produced more than its fair share of SNAGs, otherwise known as "sensitive New Age guys." In fact, the majority of the men I dated were more than safe, they were feminists; they respected my Goddessness. Which was all well and good, but I'd gotten out of the habit of dealing with a man like Sebastian.

I'd forgotten how complicated things could get. Especially since Sebastian sincerely intrigued me. I wanted to know more about him. How was it he came to have power over Benjamin? Why could he walk around in the sun? Was he really a thousand years old? Was he ever married? Who was he before? How did he die?

My interest gave him power over me. If I wasn't so fascinated, I would be able to think more clearly. I'd be able to control the direction of the relationship better. As it was, I watched the flickering shadows of the firelight elongate the cracks on his ceiling, trying not to be bothered by the insistent tapping on the window.

Above me, I heard the floorboards creak. Sebastian was awake. Would he come down? Should I pretend to be asleep? Act more frightened of Benjamin than I was? I seriously considered playing the helpless female and cowering in the corner—maybe even whimpering—but I couldn't do it. I didn't want Sebastian to lose respect for me. Not even if it meant getting into his bed.

How I got into his bed that first time really mattered to me.

Man, I was in deep. Or I needed to get some serious sleep. Probably both.

I heard the toilet flush, and more creaking boards. Damn. Sebastian hadn't been thinking about me at all, just getting up for a midnight piss.

After ruminating on that depressing thought for a moment, I fell asleep.

* * *

I woke up to the smell of frying bacon. I absolutely adored that smell. It was such a fucking shame I was a vegetarian.

Sebastian looked even more gorgeous in the morning. When I let myself into his kitchen, I found him busily chopping up red peppers, his back to me. And what a beautiful, broad back it was. I could inspect every inch of his muscled frame because he had no shirt. The only thing he wore was a pair of light cotton pajama bottoms covered with cartoon pictures of cherry-red Volkswagen Bugs. The radio was on and tuned to a country station. Sebastian hummed along to Johnny Cash as he washed mushrooms in the sink.

Man, but he was cute. I had this crazy desire to tickle him. I snuck closer as quietly as I could; Johnny helped cover the sounds of my bare feet on the linoleum. I was within striking range when he turned to toss the veggies into a frying pan, and the sun highlighted a nasty scar that ran from his shoulder blade to his butt. I must have made some noise, because he turned to face me. We were inches apart. Which is how I came to be staring at the second, even uglier scar near his sternum.

"Holy Mother, Sebastian," I said, touching the rough skin just under his heart, "at some point you were, like, Swiss cheese."

Absently, his fingers rested lightly on mine, as though protecting the wound. "Alas, 'twas the killing blow."

I looked up, startled. "You were killed?"

He gave me a you-silly grin and put a finger on my chin as though to chide me. "That would be the part before my *re*animation."

"Well, yeah, I mean, I knew you *died*. It's just that, I guess I thought, you know, another vampire was involved."

"No." His jaw muscle twitched, as though this were some kind of bone of contention for him.

"Not at all?"

"Not at all." He turned away from me, back to the frying pan. Pulling a spatula from a drawer under the counter, he stirred the vegetables. The pleasant odor of onion and peppers filled the air.

Clearly there was something about this I wasn't getting—something important, something that bothered Sebastian. Frowning at his back for a moment, I tried to puzzle it out. I didn't know that much about the Awakening or whatever vampires called the moment they woke up dead, but I knew Parrish's story. He'd been out on some English highway robbing a coach when one of his intended victims tried to make a meal out of him. Parrish said he'd have died except that, in a moment of fear-inspired chutzpah, he bit her back. She'd been impressed and took him under her wing.

Truth was, vampires were relatively rare. I had no idea if Parrish's story was typical or not. He made me believe it was, but then, he had that whole charm/glamour thing going on generally. Hell, he'd made me believe he was a nice guy for a while, too, and that had turned out to be a lie.

So no vampire had been involved in Sebastian's reanimation. How did that work? I supposed there had to be a first, but even if Sebastian was as old as he claimed to be, he didn't give off übermaster vibes.

But then, what did I really know about it? Although he had sort of implied he was Dracula earlier. . . .

Ugh. I needed coffee if I was going to think this hard. So I gave up. Slipping my hands onto Sebastian's shoulders, I leaned around him to look at the sauté.

"Smells good," I offered, by way of an apology for whatever had so clearly distressed him. "I hope your eggs are organic," I teased, giving him a playful poke in the ribs.

He laughed. "Free range, nest laid. Only the best for you, darling."

And without even thinking about it, he leaned down to

kiss me. I think it was meant to be a friendly sort of playful peck on the cheek, but I turned into it with my mouth open, ready with a witty retort. Which I think had been going to be the stunningly clever "Yeah, right," but instead it came out a smooshed "Yum."

His arms slipped over my shoulders, and I let my hands do what they'd ached to do since the moment I saw his naked skin. My fingertips discovered strong muscles and a few more scars and that oh-so-slender waist and a firm, tight—

Then he broke the kiss.

"Oh, *now* what?" I said, digging my fingernails into the cotton of his pajama bottoms, just to let him know I wasn't letting go without a fight.

His eyes registered a bit of surprise, then a wolfish smile spread across his face. "I just thought I'd better turn off the stove."

Even I had to admit that was probably a good idea. "Okay," I allowed, "but hurry back."

Reaching around me, he clicked the gas off. I pressed myself closer and raked my fingernails over his ribs, just to make the job harder. "Knock it off," he said half-seriously. "You're going to get us killed."

Of course an admonishment like that just encouraged my misbehavior. I kissed his chest and ran my hands down the length of his back, slowly. I let my fingers caress the shape of him, taking in muscle and bone like a blind woman exploring a statue. My hands paused when I reached the drawstrings of his pajama bottoms, and I looked into his eyes. Sebastian stared back intently. Sunlight reflected an amber starburst that encircled his pupils. *Witch's eyes,* I thought. Then, *No, a wolf's.*

His body had gone preternaturally still, as though he'd held his breath in anticipation and simply forgotten to start again. I started to ask him what was wrong when I saw them. His fangs had descended.

Well. At least I knew he was in the mood.

Stretching up on my tiptoes, I kissed him again. I let my tongue slide across the sharp tips of his fangs, purposefully cutting myself just a little. Blood mingled in our mouths.

That got him moving again.

Sebastian's arms encircled my waist, suddenly, crushingly. With his superhuman strength, he lifted me up, closer to him. I loved the power and strength of his arms as they enveloped me. The fingers that reached under my shirt were rough and calloused from hard work.

I threw my arms around his neck and my legs around his waist and started nibbling at his ear. He smelled like breakfast; the scent of onions and peppers clung to his hair. He tasted of salt. Despite myself, my stomach growled.

He let out a little predatory chuckle and murmured into my shoulder: "That's supposed to be my line."

I shivered but returned my attention to his earlobe. I was distracted again when he started walking. When he used my back to push open the kitchen door, I stopped my ministrations entirely. "Where are you taking me?"

"You have your choice, my darling," he said. I noticed that, although he carried me in a very awkward position, he didn't strain at all. His breath wasn't even short. "The couch or the bedroom."

"Which one's closer?"

"I like the way you think," he said with that dark, vaguely evil chuckle.

I found myself reconsidering the wisdom of getting naked and vulnerable with someone who, under different circumstances, considered me food. "Uhm," I started.

Then all the air rushed out my lungs as he tossed me onto the couch. I caught my breath in a little gasp. I braced myself for what I thought would come next. I assumed he'd throw himself on top of me and the ripping off of clothes would commence.

Instead, Sebastian stared. He stood at the foot of the couch, looming really, hungrily taking in the sight of me struggling to catch my breath and regain my composure. Sebastian cut quite an imposing figure. I'm not sure I'd registered just how big he really was. Somehow, without his shirt, he managed to appear taller and broader. Maybe he looked so strong because white-hot sun pooled in the hollow of his collarbone. Blazing strips lay along the line of his taut stomach muscles and continued down the sharp angle of his hip. Meanwhile, he smiled at me, showing fangs.

The whole look in his eyes was very predatory . . . very metahuman . . . very masterful. All I wanted to do was blush and squirm under his intense scrutiny, like some helpless harem slave, but the part of me that had merged with Lilith would not allow it.

I pulled my shirt off. Slowly. Teasingly. As if to say, *You want something to look at, boy? Here I am.*

The cold air and his gaze sweeping across my skin teased my nipples into stiff peaks. While Sebastian continued to stand there, I stroked my thumbs across the tips, giving myself a hot spike of pleasure between my legs.

His eyes registered a hint of surprise, but the expression on his face seemed to me to be one of cool amusement, as if my exhibition were some kind of pleasant distraction. It didn't help matters that, standing as he was, Sebastian looked down his aquiline nose at me, dark black hair framing strong, aristocratic features.

I ran my hands along the swell of my breasts, down along the soft curves of stomach and hips. Hooking my thumbs in the elastic of my sweatpants, I lowered them just enough to expose a little more skin.

Sebastian grabbed the cuffs of the pants and gave them a good yank. I stopped what I was doing long enough to help wriggle my legs free. Now I was naked, and he still had on his pajamas. A situation that would soon need correcting, in my opinion, but at least he'd become an active partner once more. Sebastian caught my ankle and bent to kiss my foot tenderly. His lips tickled the skin of my sole and, involuntarily, my foot jerked. He held it firmly, and purposefully, deliberately spread my legs.

I felt a little like a doll being moved into place, so I attempted to show my disapproval by giving Sebastian a playful nudge with my free foot. Before my toe even touched his stomach, he caught my ankle. Meanwhile, he'd begun to work his way up my inner thigh with his tongue. Each kiss caressed my skin lovingly. His breath tickled warmly and sent a shiver of pleasure up the length of my leg.

His progress was maddeningly slow. I twisted and squirmed just like I swore I wouldn't do earlier. I was, in fact, this close to begging him to speed things along, and I had to bite my lip to keep from uttering any words I might regret later like, *Oh, master, please.*

Attempting to sit up, I made a grab with the intention of dragging his head up to the part of me that was burning for his attention. Expertly, he lifted my legs into the air, over his shoulders, so my back flopped hard against the rough upholstery of the couch. I would have felt defeated except that his mouth found its way exactly to where I most needed it. His long hair tickled the inside of my thighs as his tongue and teeth slid hard against me.

The section of my mind that was able to form coherent thoughts kept worrying about those extra-pointy canines being so close to my tenderest parts. The sharp tip of tooth shot an intense wave of pain/pleasure deep into my core.

"Oh, Sebastian, no." I'd meant to say something a bit more comprehensible like, *Actually, what you're doing is great; just don't draw blood, okay?* but apparently that kind of complex sentence structure was beyond my current abilities.

Unfortunately, he took me literally. He stopped what he was doing entirely. I tried not to sob, but a whimper escaped my throat anyway. His golden eyes watched me over the mound of my belly as if to ask, *no, what?*

I didn't want to say, because I wasn't entirely sure what I wanted at this point; I just wanted him closer, a lot closer. So my hands clutched his hair, and I pulled him closer for a kiss. As he crawled upward, I could feel his body slide on top of mine, strong, solid, and very, very hard. That made me smile. Dead guys could be tricky in that department. Parrish had always been able to perform, but he hadn't been dead nearly as long as Sebastian.

What I wasn't expecting was the heat. The warmth from Sebastian's body enveloped me, and the spot where my flesh met his pajama bottoms fairly burned.

Great Goddess, he still had his pants on.

My hands moved to quickly remove the obstacle, but the feel of hipbone and smooth, firm buttock distracted me. As my hands moved, so did my own hips, arching up to grind against him. At that he let out a frustrated growl. With a jerk, I undid the string on his pajamas.

"Is there something you want?" I teased him.

His answer involved pulling down his pants and reaching down to guide himself into me.

Despite evidence to the contrary, I still braced myself for the shock of the cold, dead flesh. When his heat filled me, I gasped in surprise. I kissed him full on the mouth, lest he misinterpret my noises.

We began rocking together, slow at first. Sebastian grew more urgent with each thrust, and I responded in kind. I clutched at him, pulling him deeper into me. I wanted more, harder, faster. The smile he flashed me at that moment, especially with the fangs showing, made me feel at his mercy. The pounding tempo he set didn't help matters.

My back pressed deeper and deeper into the couch with each thrust. He held himself on his arms, over me, grinning wickedly.

Who dares?

My fingernails dug deep into the flesh of his back, but Sebastian barely flinched. I bucked wildly beneath him, but I was completely pinned.

Not for long.

And then suddenly we were on the floor wedged between the couch and the coffee table. He was on his back, and I straddled him. Somehow, our bodies were still entwined. A nasty set of scratch marks marred his cheek. Oh, and I held his wrists.

"I take it you want to be on top." He flashed a weak smile to try to cover the obvious pain in his voice.

Lilith.

I let his hands go by way of apology and sat up so that I knelt over him. Moving slowly, I worked at rekindling the passion. It didn't take long for Sebastian to figure out the advantages of this position. His hands covered my breasts, pulling and teasing at already taut nipples. In no time, we had the rhythm back.

I lost myself in the motion of our bodies. I could feel myself getting closer, then, without warning, he pulled me down into a tight embrace. His teeth sank into my shoulder. It was a deep, hard, full-mouthed bite.

Blood wasn't the only thing that came out in a rush.

The pleasure didn't stop there. Sebastian kept moving inside me, while he sucked and licked at my shoulder. His need added desperation to each thrust, driving harder and harder. When Sebastian was finally satisfied, I'd been there done that a half-dozen times. He released me, and I rolled limp and panting onto the floor.

"You suck," I mumbled into the short nap of the Persian rug. My shoulder throbbed painfully where it lay under the weight of my body. I briefly worried about bloodstains on what was clearly an expensive weave, and then I giggled at my sudden fastidiousness.

Sebastian pulled one of the blankets from the couch and wrapped it around me tenderly. Then he got up and left. I heard the door to the kitchen swing open and shut. Just like that.

I'd have felt wounded at being thus discarded if I had any energy to feel anything other than just plain wounded. I might even have gone after him and told him a thing or two about how to treat lovers if any part of my body were still under my command. As it was, I felt about as sturdy as Jell-O.

"You really, really suck," I told the rug, my brain incapable of coming up with anything more vehement to say about Sebastian's insensitivity.

However, I had to retract my sentiment when he returned with breakfast. He helped me sit up and all but held the glass of orange juice for me to drink.

"It helps with the blood loss," he said matter-of-factly.

I leaned my back against the couch. The plate, still hot from the microwave, rested in my lap. The heat felt good. So good, in fact, I wanted to just curl up in a fetal position around the warmth of it. That was when I realized how cold I was. "How much did you take?"

"Too much, probably," he said, embarrassed. My blood flushed his cheeks a bright red.

"I look good on you," I told him, tracing the blush with a clumsy fingertip.

His gaze dropped to the plate. He picked up the bacon as though to offer it to me. "You should eat something. Or take a nap."

"Meat is murder," I said teasingly, pushing away the bacon. Then I started giggling again a bit hysterically. I mean, it just seemed so pathetic. I wouldn't eat something already dead, and yet he didn't hesitate to have me for breakfast.

Sebastian failed to find the humor. Or he was sincerely worried about my sanity, I couldn't tell which. Very carefully he replaced the bacon on the plate and offered me more juice once I stopped laughing. He put his arms around me as I drank the rest of the glass and then, without meaning to, I fell asleep with my head against his shoulder.

I dreamt of Lilith.

At first, I was just running . . . from something, someone close, too close, just behind. I had to keep moving. A moonlit jungle surrounded me. Primate screams echoed though a canopy of trees. Thick, sharp leaves cut at my face, pulled at my body. A tangle of mud and vegetation sucked the soles of my feet, making it difficult to keep up my pace.

Water dripped from broad palm leaves. The hum of insects filled my ears. Sweat clung to my skin. I felt like I was suffocating in the heat and darkness.

I came upon a clearing with an apple tree . . . or was it pomegranate . . . growing in the center. Lilith reclined in a hollow of the tree, which had gnarled and warped over time into a seat, a throne. Above her head, ripe fruit and white blossoms hung.

She was naked. Long, serpentine twists of white-gold hair partially hid shriveled, dry breasts. Her hips were narrow and slender, almost boyish, yet her pose exuded sexuality and seduction. "You were careless," *she admonished me, her voice a hiss.* "Perhaps I should not have spared him."

Sebastian.

No, *I wanted to say,* you did the right thing; he's a good guy, *but my mouth felt full of cotton, and I found I could only shake my head mutely.*

"He takes liberties with us," *she said, twirling a tight ringlet of hair in her fingers. An owl screeched overhead.* "We will take something from him in return."

"No," *I started,* "I don't want to play this game. You're not—"

But she was already fading into the mist of dreamworld. Beating wings brushed at my ears as the sun of the waking world stabbed at my eyes.

"You're not the boss of me," I continued for my own satisfaction. "So not."

The sun continued to shine cruelly through the dusty window in a broad, blinding sheet. I pulled the covers over my head and groaned. My shoulder twinged. He *did* take liberties with us. What time was it? Noon? I had the sinking feeling I was supposed to be at work several hours ago. I started to sit up to look for a phone, when the world spun around, and I fell back to the couch, feeling faint.

Where was that bastard, anyway?

If he'd abandoned me again, there'd at least better be a note and some hot coffee, or there'd be hell to pay.

When I found the energy to sit up again, I found half of what I needed tucked under the orange juice glass. It took me a moment to translate Sebastian's almost feminine, curling cursive, to read: "My dearest Garnet, very sorry, but transmission couldn't wait. Will be back at noon. Coffeepot is on. While I await our reunion, I remain, your humble, loving servant, Sebastian."

Okay, so I wouldn't kill him right away, if only because I found the "your servant" part charming.

I drained the dregs of the OJ, even though it was tepid and clung fuzzily to the back of my throat. Stumbling into the kitchen, not even bothering to try to find my clothes, I helped myself to as much of the pot of coffee as I could drink. Though my stomach lurched at the sight of soggy, wilted remains of the peppers, I ate all of the egg concoction Sebastian had started earlier. On top of that, I added two cartons of yogurt and a bowl and a half of frosted-something-crunchy with milk.

Then I had another cup of coffee.

Somehow the caffeine and the calories did nothing to improve my mood. Usually, this was my favorite part of a relationship: the first morning after. This was the time I tended to gather up sentimental memories: the quaintness of the red-and-white-checked tablecloth, the glow of the sun on the polished oak of the cabinets, the god-awful crooning of Toby Keith on the radio . . . and the complete lack of a lover sitting across from me. That last part made me especially grouchy.

And now there was no more coffee.

I put my head down on the table, remembering the other reason I never let Parrish bite me. Not only did the mark sting like a sonuvabitch, it wiped me out. I felt like I got the ugliest hangover from a party I wasn't even invited to.

Meanwhile, Sebastian ended up with so much energy, he hadn't stayed around and waited for me to wake up. He was off merrily rebuilding the whatcha-ma-dingee.

At work, no less. Somehow I could forgive him more if he'd gone off to putter in his garden. No, he took off for town, for a job.

I started to build up a good angry burn, which might have fueled a trip all the way upstairs to the shower, when the back door opened.

A very pretty boy stopped dead in his tracks when he saw me sitting naked in the kitchen. His features were delicate, almost Asian, and he had long, silken black hair that, though it was cut short above his ears, artfully fell in front of his eyes. Something about him looked familiar—the cut of his jaw and the slope of his nose?—but whatever it was, he reminded me of Sebastian, actually.

He wore a deep purple silk shirt and black fitted jeans. The shoes he wore made him look European, since they were black and polished. He was slender to the point of being reedy and awkward. I guessed him to be about seventeen.

I watched his expression as I tried to hide my nudity under the table. His gaze was measured, distant, jaded—like somehow he'd already seen his share of naked women sitting at kitchen tables. He appeared to have no concern for my discomfort but took me all in, pausing with some interest to linger on the bruise/bite on my shoulder. That made him smile. I couldn't say it was a friendly smile. There was something about the cruel turn of his lips that made him look downright mean.

"I see you've met my father," he said. "Is he around?"

Third House

KEYWORDS:

Visitors, Delinquency, Improvisation

"I'm sorry," the pretty young man continued, though he sounded anything but. "I should have called first, but I'm sure you know how Papa is with phones."

He let himself all the way inside the kitchen. Leaning a hip against the doorframe, he crossed his arms in front of his slight chest. There was something about the man that reminded me of a cat. Perhaps it was the deep golden color of his irises or the way sunlight occasionally appeared to refract a green glow, mirrorlike, from the center of his pupils. Maybe it was just the languid threat of his posture.

"Do you think you could give him a message for me? That is," he paused to chuckle slightly, "*if* you plan to see him again."

Oh, what a piece of work.

"He's at the garage," I said, trying to affect a casual tone while hiding my chest under the kitchen tabletop. "Go tell him yourself."

I tried not to make my words sound too much like *go fuck*

yourself, but I could see by the sharp rise of his eyebrows that
Sonny Boy got my meaning.

Other than that slight acknowledgment, however, he
gave me no indication he was fazed by the situation, my
nakedness, or my anger. He continued to lean there, relaxed,
while I blushed furiously. "Ah," he said, feigning concern.
"The lies begin so soon."

"What are you talking about?"

"I was just at the garage twenty minutes ago. None of
the guys had seen him all morning. When did you two . . .
ah, part ways?"

"You mean he wasn't there? He wasn't at Jensen's?" Suddenly I remembered how focused the Vatican agent had
been on finding out more about Sebastian's day job.

"That's usually what—"

"Shut up," I snapped, standing up, my nakedness ceasing
to matter. "We have to find him. Now."

I told Sonny Boy to cool his heels while I rounded up
some clothes. I'd thought about going to look for the washer
and dryer, but there was something about a vampire's basement I just didn't want to explore. Even in daylight.

So instead I checked on my mini upstairs, finding it
hanging neatly over the shower curtain rod along with my
panty hose. Dampness, however, still clung to both.

I headed to Sebastian's bedroom with the intention of
borrowing another pair of sweatpants and possibly a shirt.
Besides Vivian's room, there were two closed doors. The first
one I tried was locked. Who locks a room in their own house?
Very Bluebeard/Dorian Gray, I thought. The other opened to
what I assumed must be his bedroom. I crept over the threshold, feeling like a trespasser in his sanctum sanctorum.

No, I thought, that would be the door with the lock.

I'd had the fantasy of the four-poster bed with the gauzy

canopy, but Sebastian had more utilitarian tastes. The bed was king-sized and unmade. Though the sheets appeared to be plain white cotton, Sebastian had a soft-looking maroon comforter and tons of pillows. A dressing table with a triptych mirror rested against a wall. Several large windows had been thrown open to the morning breeze, and curtains fluttered in the manure-scented air. Ah, farm life.

No coffin, at least. Maybe that was in the locked room. Part of me wanted to check under the bed for it or for sacks of Austrian dirt, but the clock was ticking. Sebastian could be fighting for his life right now.

Finding his closet, I rummaged quickly through his things. Grabbing the first T-shirt I found—a campaign shirt for Jimmy Carter—I pulled it over my head. Then I borrowed a pair of dark green sweatpants out of the bottom dresser drawer Sebastian had conveniently left open. I'd noticed several interesting things in my quick perusal of his room: the man had an opera coat and a jewelry chest. I smiled; there was a little bit of the literary vampire in him, after all.

I came downstairs to find Sebastian's son perched on the arm of the couch. He'd taken the opportunity to dispose of our dirty linens. I tried not to think about hot, naked Sebastian flesh, but a blush rose to my cheeks as I stalked past Sonny Boy to retrieve my boots from where they'd sat near the fire all night.

"That's certainly a look," he said, checking out my butt.

I still had no underwear. "Oh, shut up."

"Ah, your witty repartee stings me," he said.

Plunking down on the couch, I pulled on my boots. I wiggled my toe experimentally; the interior was only a little squishy with residual moisture. It would have to do.

Sebastian's son shook his head slightly, as though in disbelief. "Tell me again why I'm following the orders of Daddy's newest little chew toy?"

I swallowed my anger with some difficulty but managed to explain through clenched teeth, "Someone is trying to kill your Sire, you insensitive jerk."

"Sire?" His mouth curled up in a mocking smile. Throwing an arm casually over the back of the couch, he leaned in closer to where I sat struggling with the damp buckles of my boots. "Girlfriend," he drawled. "Perhaps it has escaped your notice, but my *father* can take care of himself. He's not exactly easy to kill."

"What would you know about it?"

"Dhampyrs traditionally hunt vampires."

I tried to hide my confusion by frowning at a particularly stubborn strap.

"You have no idea what that is, do you?" He put a hand to his chest, feigning concern. "He did . . . that is, you at least know what my father is, don't you?"

He ended his sentence with that irritatingly smug chuckle again.

"Of course I know what he is," I snapped. *I just don't know what you are.* I thought I had. When he'd said Sebastian was his father, I assumed he meant through blood, as in his Maker or Master or Sire or whatever vampires were calling the one that transformed them these days. Thanks to Sebastian I'd gotten used to the idea of vampires who walk around in the daylight.

So, Sonny Boy was not a vampire? Was he saying he was a dhampyr? And what the hell was that? I began to suspect it might have something to do with being a vampire's biological son, but that still didn't give me a clue.

I gave Sonny Boy the mystical once-over. His aura was a strange muted green-gold, like his eyes, extending several inches from his body. Squinting harder, I saw flashes of silver. A very active aura usually meant magic. Since he implied he was a dhampyr, I guessed that probably accounted for it. The fact that he had an aura at all meant that, despite his attitude, he had a living, beating heart somewhere in there. Hard to believe.

I wondered if Sebastian's son was older than he looked. He'd have to be if Sebastian was the age he claimed. Vampires couldn't have children after they died, could they? I'd never heard of it.

Maybe this kid was lying. Sebastian had acted all freaked out when I read in his palm that he had no children. Then again, I thought, giving Sonny Boy a sharp glance, if this jerk was my only offspring, I'd want to disavow him, too.

I looked up expectantly when the front door swung open. To my great relief, Sebastian walked in with an armload full of groceries. He smiled to see me, but when he registered the presence of Sonny Boy lounging on the arm of the couch, Sebastian's expression darkened noticeably. His jaw twitched, like he wanted to say something, but instead Sebastian refused to look at Sonny Boy. He said to me, "I brought in some supplies."

"Thank the Goddess you're all right," I said, standing up.

"Your new friend seemed to think you were in mortal danger, Papa. We were both terribly worried."

Sebastian put his bags down beside the door and hung up his coat. His back was to us as he said, "I'd really hoped my wards would keep you away from my house and my friends, Mátyás."

Now Sonny Boy had a name: Mátyás. I had to say that the thick, Slavic sound of it fit his Euro-trash look.

Mátyás ignored Sebastian's jibe. To me, he said, "My father finds it clever for people to have to be invited into a vampire's home."

"I wasn't invited," I said.

"Perhaps not explicitly, but you probably had something of his like . . . say, his business card?"

"Mátyás," Sebastian cut in sharply. "Garnet does not need a lesson in magic from you."

Maybe I did. Wards. I'd thought so, but now I knew for certain. They must have been extremely well-crafted in order to be subtle enough that I didn't catch more than a whiff of them.

"No? So you found yourself another little Witch, did you? Is she Romany, as well? Mama would be so pleased."

Sebastian flushed. I couldn't tell if it was with anger or shame. "You will not speak of your mother in that tone."

"Of course," Mátyás said, his tone dripping with false acquiescence. "As you wish."

Breakfast churned uncomfortably in my stomach. I wondered if I should sit down, but I didn't want to seem even more like a spectator of this train wreck of a father-son reunion.

"I visited Mama's grave." Mátyás turned toward the fireplace, casually inspecting his finely manicured fingernails. "She's still dead."

"I imagine she would be," Sebastian said. His tone sounded disinterested, but his eyes stayed riveted to Mátyás's back. "You should really stop disinterring her. It's costing me a fortune in reburial fees."

Was he serious? I glanced over at Mátyás, who shrugged. To me, he said, "She's still beautiful. Completely uncorrupted by time. Yet she doesn't walk."

"She's dead, Mátyás," Sebastian said softly. There was a hint of something—remorse? regret?—in his tone. "Leave her be."

"Is she, though? Dead, I mean." Mátyás directed his question to me. "I've used mediums, psychics, Ouija boards, even necromancy, and no one can find her on the other side."

Sebastian's mouth was set in a grim line. He hefted the grocery bags into his arms and started for the kitchen. At the door, he paused. Turning to Mátyás, he said, "Have you considered the possibility that she simply doesn't want to talk to *you*?"

Ouch. Score one for Dad, but that was pretty harsh. I looked at Mátyás after the door to the kitchen swung shut. Despite myself, I said, "I'm sure he didn't mean that."

"I'm sure he did." Mátyás stood up and flicked imaginary dust from his pants. Our eyes met, and for a moment he seemed to drop his guard. The look he gave me was pure sadness. His fingers reached for the spot under my tee where Sebastian's "love bite" still ached, but he stopped before actual physical contact. "Don't let that happen too often, or you'll end up like my mother."

"Trust me," I said. "I won't."

"Good." He nodded, and he seemed genuinely relieved by my answer. Then his cold smile returned. "Oh, and I hope you kids played it safe. Just because he's dead doesn't mean accidents can't happen. Look at me."

"What? Are you saying Sebastian fathered you after the Change?"

Mátyás merely smirked.

So that's what a dhampyr was. Holy shit. I mean, I'd thought dead was dead—as in, all parts, even, well, sperm. That was my impression anyway. Parrish had never suggested we needed to worry, although, of course, I'm on the Pill. Which reminded me I hadn't taken it today, and I hadn't insisted on condoms because . . . "How can that even be possible?"

"Magic, little Witch. Magic."

Our brief bonding moment had come to an abrupt end with the return of that know-it-all smile. I wondered if the Vatican agents would consider adding dhampyrs to their list. Maybe they had some kind of hotline I could call.

"How did you get to be such a jerk at such a young age?" I asked him as he headed toward the door.

"Hard work and practice, my dear."

"No, I mean it. You're seriously irritating. What did anyone ever do to you?"

Apparently, that was the question to ask, because Mátyás's constant, annoying little grin finally faded. Though
his hand had been reaching for the door, he pulled it back.
"My mother begged him—on her hands and knees—for
the dark gift, and he refused her. Instead, she wasted away
from consumption. He could have saved her life, but he
didn't."

I frowned, thinking of my own mother. How would I feel
if I knew my father had a cure but wouldn't share it?

"He wasn't even there when she finally died," Mátyás
said, turning back to the door. "She was alone. I was on my
way home when I heard the news. A stranger, a neighbor,
was the one to tell me."

Okay. That might make anyone bitter, I decided. I
couldn't meet his eyes any longer for the hurt I saw there.

"Oh, I'm not as young as I look," he said, his voice crack-
ing the way adolescent boys' often do. "Papa's little gift to
me: a century of being sixteen."

I thought of all the ages I'd want to be forever, and anything that ended *teen* would not be one of them. Especially
since Mátyás was alive, as opposed to being glamorously undead. That meant a hundred years of acne, a hundred years
of screwed-up, constantly revved-up hormones, a hundred
years of high school.

Well, probably not that last part literally, at least, but
emotionally?

Okay, I was *getting* the bitter.

"I'm sorry," I said.

"That's very kind of you," he said simply, quietly. Then
he left.

When I let myself in the kitchen, I found Sebastian
leaning over the sink, his head bowed. The sacks of groceries sat on the counter beside him.

"So," he said, his face still hidden. "He told you."

"I'm sure there's more to the story," I said charitably.

Sebastian turned to face me. We stared at each other over the kitchen table, which was still covered with the scattered detritus of my breakfast feast. "I *couldn't* give Teréza the dark gift."

"Don't you just have to bite her and have her bite back?" That's what Parrish had told me, but maybe there was more to it.

"We did that."

"Then it's not your fault she died."

"Yes, but it might be my fault that she's not completely dead."

"Oh."

Sebastian nodded. "Mátyás suspects as much. The animation in the body is gone, but some kind of life remains. To what extent her spirit is there, Mátyás and I disagree. So, you see, the gift worked, but only sort of. The result is . . . unthinkable."

Oh, but I thought about it anyway. Your spirit trapped inside a corpse forever. And then buried alive? My skin started to crawl. "You're not biting me ever again," I told him. "Oh, and you're buying the condoms. I think one Mátyás in the world is enough."

I'd meant it as a kind of joke, but the second the words left my mouth I wanted to issue a recall notice. As Sebastian stared at me darkly, his fists resting on the kitchen table, I struggled to come up with an apology that would sound sincere. Problem was, I really, truly disliked Mátyás. Okay, so he'd scored some sympathy with me, but he was still a pretty obnoxious kid.

"Uh," I started. "I mean . . . that is . . ."

Sebastian let out a long sigh, then rubbed at his eyes. "You're probably right," he said. "That boy will be the death of me."

"He certainly seems to think that's his function. I mean, as a dhampyr."

Sebastian pulled out a carton of eggs from one of the grocery bags and took it over to the refrigerator. As he put it away, he glanced at me over the top of the door. "He told you a lot."

The hard look in Sebastian's eyes made me believe that Mátyás hadn't lied when he told me what he was. Otherwise, Sebastian would have corrected my comment in some way. I really wanted to press Sebastian for more information about dhampyrs, but he was in such a foul mood and, honestly, I didn't want to seem stupid. Besides, I'd already managed to put my foot in it about Mátyás once, and I really didn't relish the idea of spending the rest of the afternoon apologizing.

"I guess," I said. "You didn't run into any Witch hunters at work, did you?"

"I didn't end up going to work," Sebastian said. He shot me a wry grin as he unpacked celery and carrots. "I decided I didn't want to be away from you that long."

"Oh." Well. That was by far the most romantic thing anyone had said to me in a long, long time. "So, the transmission-y thing could wait after all?"

He set the vegetables on the counter and dug out a package wrapped in butcher paper. I thought I'd mentioned that I didn't eat meat. Then it occurred to me that it was possible I wasn't invited for dinner, or that he might have other plans. I felt suddenly sheepish and a little slutty.

He gave me a shy glance. "I get pretty . . . er, keyed up after. I took off without really thinking things through. I have to apologize for making you seem less important to me than my job. That's no way to treat a lover."

Lover. It was such a sexy word, and so much more appealing than girlfriend/boyfriend, which always seemed high schoolish to me. Still, Sebastian was pouring on the charm pretty hard, considering we had just met the night before. "You don't owe me anything," I said with a shrug that sent a stab of pain down my arm. I kept forgetting about that damned bite.

Perhaps noticing my flinch, he said, "Maybe not, but let me pamper you anyway. Spend the day with me."

My encounter with Mátyás put a damper on some of my enthusiasm toward Sebastian. I mean, he implied that Teréza was trapped in her corpse, but he kept reburying her. I didn't know all the details, but the whole idea troubled me. Besides, earlier this morning Sebastian had been a single, sexy vampire. Part of the fun of dating vampires was that they didn't come with families. No in-laws, as it were, to meet and greet. Sebastian had a kid and a kind of dead ex-wife or whatever Mátyás's mother was to Sebastian. Things had suddenly become more complicated than I'd bargained for, and I hadn't sorted out how I felt about all of them.

"It'll give me a chance to explain myself," Sebastian added, as though reading my mind. I continued to hesitate until he said, "Anyway, I bought everything I need to fix us a proper English tea."

Who could resist that?

While I called work, Sebastian set up lawn chairs and a table in the shade of a sugar maple in his backyard. I watched him from the porch, which wrapped around the southeast corner of the house. The day had turned warm, and the air was infused with the fresh scent of loamy earth after a rainstorm.

Once William was on the phone I decided to be blunt about my reasons for not showing up at work today. Not having to lie about playing hooky seemed like it ought to be one of the perks of being the manager. "I had great sex, and I haven't quite recovered yet. I'll be in tomorrow," I said without a hint of shame.

On the other end of the phone, I heard William choke. "Oh, okay. It's been slow anyway. Have . . . uh, well, have a good time."

"I did," I said. "And I will."

"Oh," William said. "A sales rep for Llewellyn is supposed to come today. Should I take care of it?"

"No!" I shouted, remembering his inability to be cruel to people. "Give me the number, and I'll reschedule."

As William searched through the computer files for the number, I scanned Sebastian's property. The gravel road I'd come up last night extended past the house to an old-fashioned red barn, complete with grain silo. I surmised that Sebastian owned only the buildings and a couple of acres, because thin green lines of new corn stretched for miles in all directions, no doubt maintained by some local farmer.

Low lilac bushes lined a wooden fence surrounding a mowed section of grass that took up a small portion of the property near the house. Bright yellow dandelions dotted the lawn. On the other side of the fence, I could see the beginnings of Sebastian's herb garden. A twisted path of flagstone made a curious route through newly turned dirt. I had the distinct impression it was meant to be a magical symbol, but it wasn't anything I recognized. I'd ask Sebastian about it later.

William got me the number, and I was able to remember it by repeating it over and over. I quickly left a message to reschedule and prayed that the rep hadn't already left the office. Ah, well, if William overbought on anything, I could always see about making an exchange later. I hung up the phone and went to join Sebastian under the shade of the maple.

Bless him, he was just setting out a fresh pot of coffee. He'd gone all English gentleman on me. He'd set a linen-covered folding table out between the two chairs. The bone china had a delicately painted peach and yellow Art Deco geometric design on the border, and there were lace-trimmed place mats under each service. "I didn't know straight guys even owned things like this," I said, admiring the teacup before I took a sip of the coffee.

"It was once fashionable to lay out a good tea," Sebastian said. "Speaking of which, I've got some sandwiches to make. Wait here. Enjoy the view."

I sat down and let out a long, contented sigh. A pair of white butterflies danced around the unopened lilac buds. Unfortunately, just beyond them I could see the headstones of the graveyard.

Probably *not* the view Sebastian intended for me to enjoy.

Especially since it made me think about being buried alive again. At least this Teréza of his wasn't rotting in her grave. No, I thought, feeling breakfast swirl around in my guts again, I wasn't sure anything made it better.

Tearing my gaze away from the granite markers, I tried to focus on the delicate pink-and-white flowers of the bleeding hearts Sebastian had planted along the side of his house. Okay, I thought, the guy tends gardens. He's a killer who sets a gorgeous table. Maybe he had his reasons for his apparent cruelty to Teréza.

Sebastian came out with a silver platter full of honest-to-Goddess cucumber sandwiches cut into cute little triangles.

"This is amazing. They look too pretty to eat."

Sebastian nodded his head slightly and then turned the lawn chair around so that, when he sat, he faced me. "Just try the damned sandwiches," he said playfully.

I dutifully took a bite, tasting a crisp cucumber, a hint of dill and lemon, and something soft and smooth, like, "Cream cheese?"

He nodded. "Good, aren't they?"

Surprisingly, they were. And here I'd only heard disparaging remarks about British food. My eyes strayed back to the headstones, and I couldn't contain my questions any longer. "She's not buried next door, is she?"

"I doubt she's buried at all right now."

Eew? "What does that mean?"

"Mátyás habitually runs off with Teréza's body. If he's come to taunt me, he has her."

There was so much I wanted to say, but all I could think of was, "Your family is really fucked up."

Sebastian took a sip of his coffee. "Yeah, it is."

I didn't quite know how to ask the question I wanted to, so I plowed ahead. "Would destroying her body free her spirit? I mean, you have *had* the body, right? So why not just . . . you know, let her go?" I asked, wondering if I was on dangerous ground. Sebastian's eyes stared straight ahead, and his face betrayed no emotion, so I continued. "Like, well, cremate her?"

A male cardinal alighted on the wooden fence and let out a loud peep. Sebastian turned to glance at it as it darted away, a red flash against a blue sky. Our eyes met, and he said, "I have considered it. I've even, almost . . . How can I explain how difficult it is to stand over the corpse of your lover with a spade in your hand, ready to decapitate her? I loved Teréza, and she's *not* dead. Not entirely."

Sebastian paused, taking a long draught of his coffee. The leaves of the maple had not entirely filled out, so sunlight filtered through in patches. The air was cool in the shade, and the coffee cup felt good in my hands.

I could understand Sebastian's reaction, a little. My very first cat, Yeep, had died under somewhat mysterious circumstances—a seizure in the middle of the night—and I'd balked at the idea of an autopsy when my vet suggested it. Something about cutting up poor old Yeep's body, just to answer medical curiosity, hadn't sat well with my grief. Yeep had always hated going to the doctor's while he was alive, and I couldn't stand the idea of bits of him ending up in vials to be scrutinized and poked in some sterile medical lab. I just wanted him to have the rest I felt he deserved, even though I knew his spirit was long gone from the limp body I'd handed over to the vet to cremate. Looking back at it, I'd probably been overly sentimental, but that didn't change my reaction.

And, Yeep, faithful companion though he was, had not been my lover. Still, I'd been weirdly protective of a body I knew to be devoid of spirit; I was certain Yeep's soul had crossed over to the great mouse fields of the Summerland. Even with my squeamishness about Teréza's situation, I could allow Sebastian some of the eccentricities of his grief.

I helped myself to another sandwich. A chipmunk dashed across the grass with a crocus bud between its teeth. I smiled to watch its striped tail curl close to its body as it made off with breakfast. Sebastian's bite had drained me, quite literally, and I felt, despite everything, I could sink back into the cloth weave of the chair and sleep forever. "Do you think she suffers?"

"She seems at peace," Sebastian said. "If she had breath, I'd say she slept deeply."

That was something, at least. "So, you don't think she knows she's trapped?"

"She may not."

"But she might?" I asked around another bite of sandwich. "How can you bury her, if . . . well, if you think she might be at all aware of that?"

"What would you have me do?" Despite the question, Sebastian's voice didn't strain. He merely sounded tired. "She's a corpse, Garnet. Hospices usually consider their work done once people are, in point of fact, dead. It's not like I can prop her up in a chair at a dinner party. Besides, she died over a hundred years ago. I certainly would have attracted some attention by now if I hauled a corpse along with me everywhere I went. Talk about an albatross around your neck. The grave is the safest place for her. No one besides Mátyás disturbs her there."

"Wait," I said, sitting up a little straighter, "How long? How long has she been dead?"

Sebastian's shoulders hunched in a slight shrug. "Really, it's more like a hundred and fifty years."

A hundred and fifty years of being dead/not dead? "You still love her so much after all this time that you can't . . . I mean, you're willing to bury her in the ground, but you can't hand her over to a mortician to cremate her?"

"Things have gotten complicated," Sebastian admitted. "Not just emotionally. Though, truthfully, Mátyás's constant devotion to his mother doesn't help me gain any kind of distance. Also, you can't just show up at a funeral home with a body. They need a death certificate and any number of other things. Sure, I could break in and somehow perform the work myself, I suppose, but then we're back to the problem of my inability to do her bodily harm in this suspended state."

"Is the mandrake for her?" I'm not quite sure why I asked, but it suddenly occurred to me that maybe Sebastian was holding out hope for a cure for Teréza, after all.

He met my eyes for the first time since we started talking about her. "Partially, yes."

I put my hand on his arm. "You can't cure death, Sebastian."

"Actually, I can." Even in the semidarkness of the shade, I could see Sebastian's eyes glitter.

"What are you talking about?"

"Magic and science. Alchemy. I devoted my entire lifetime trying to cure death. And, at some point I stumbled across the answer. After all, I'm living proof."

I scratched the back of my neck. "What are you saying exactly? You became a vampire through alchemy?"

"I did." He flashed me a very satisfied grin. It wasn't at

all like Mátyás's snotty, smug smiles, but instead was pure boyish isn't-it-cool enthusiasm. I felt the corners of my mouth tipping and my heart melting.

"You're cute," I said.

His eyebrows raised skeptically. "I am?"

I leaned over to kiss him on the nose. "Yeah, you are."

He put an arm around my shoulders, holding us close. "I always thought cute was a bit of an insult. Shouldn't I be handsome or powerfully sexy or . . . ?"

I gave him a more serious kiss, hard and full. His tongue tasted of dill. I lingered long enough to let him know exactly how hot I thought he was. "You're definitely all that, Sebastian. But, cute, in this case, is good. Trust me."

"I guess I'll have to."

I smiled warmly at him. I could live with the whole buried/not-dead lover thing, I decided. Sebastian had a good soul, even if I couldn't see his aura. I was curious about something, though. Something that could complicate my newly sparked feelings toward him. "Are you hoping to use alchemy to revive Teréza?"

"Yes." He paused and chewed on his lip, his eyes focused on some internal argument, to which he responded, "Well, no." He looked at me and let out a sigh. "I don't really know."

I frowned, unable to follow his thoughts.

"Teréza's situation is complicated," Sebastian said. "At this point, she's been dead, or rather, undead for a long time. If I could duplicate the formula successfully, which I'm not even sure I could, how can I make her swallow it? An injection wouldn't work, either. It's not like her blood is flowing anymore. I'd have to come up with something that could be absorbed through dead skin, and again you really need blood flow for all of that to work properly. . . ."

His voice trailed off. Perhaps he realized how much like Dr. Frankenstein he sounded, or maybe he just noticed the horrified look on my face. I wanted to say, *Great Goddess, Sebastian, what are you thinking? You don't reanimate a corpse after a hundred and fifty years. Have you never read "The Monkey's Paw"?* It occurred to me his whole life, or, rather, existence after death, was one big *Pet Sematary* moment after another. Of course, it seemed reasonable to him.

"I have to re-create the elixir somehow," Sebastian said sounding nonchalant again, as though we were discussing something completely ordinary. Settling back down in his chair, he turned away from me. "I can feel the effects fading. If I can't rework my magic, I'll soon be a prisoner of the night . . . or, well, I'm not sure."

"So, the potion that made you a vampire also protects you from the sun?"

Sebastian's jaw worked for a moment, then he said, "Yes."

I waited for more, because there was something about his simple affirmation that seemed to suggest a *but* or an *and.* Instead, he stood up. Walking over to the fence, he pulled up a weed that had sprouted near the base of one of the posts. Methodically, he began moving along the perimeter, gathering up the offending plant matter.

For the moment, at least, the sun seemed to love Sebastian. The brightness that reflected from his white shirt as he stooped and dipped almost hurt my eyes. I sipped more coffee and popped another sandwich in my mouth. As I reclined deeper in the lawn chair, I felt like that old joke, "I love work—I can watch someone else do it all day."

I must have dozed, because I dreamt. In my dream, a blue jay hopped out of the maple tree to perch on the linen-covered table. It scolded me with a loud cawing, which somehow I understood as words. The jay said, *Get Sebastian's formula, Garnet. It is our demand for what he's taken from us.*

Shooing the bird with my hand, I said, "No way. Anyway, what does a Goddess need with a vampire's magic potion?"

The bird hopped deftly out of my reach and flapped back onto the table. It pecked at the sandwiches, then cocked its head to glare at me with a glittering black eye. This time I heard its reply in my mind. *The formula is more powerful than he admits. It makes life. That is a woman's power. It should belong to womankind. We want it. It is owed to us.*

"We want it, my precious," I hissed, mocking the Goddess. "You sound crazy. Forget it."

"Channeling Tolkien, are we?"

A blue pitcher of ice water sat in the spot the jay had occupied. I blinked, trying to pull myself from my dream/vision. "Uh, sorry," I said. "I'm still kind of woozy, I guess. I was kind of dreaming or something."

He looked sheepish. "Yes, well, I got caught up in the moment. It won't happen again."

A lascivious smile crept across my face; I certainly hoped it would. I remembered Mátyás's remark, and my expression sobered. "It's not dangerous if I don't bite back, right? I mean, that is, if you . . . we . . . had an accident."

He grinned lightly. "I don't think so. No one else that I've . . . uh . . . well, let's just say, there's only one Teréza."

"Mátyás made it sound like—"

"Mátyás would prefer it if I didn't have a sex life."

Made sense. I mean, I didn't always want to think about my folks getting hot and heavy, and they were married. Sebastian sounded pretty terse about it, though, which made me wonder if there was some history of Mátyás coming between his father and a lover. I started to ask him about it, but what came out of my mouth was completely different.

"So, about your formula. You wrote it down?" *What? Why had I asked him that?* Focus on Mátyás, Garnet. I opened my mouth and, "You have notes at least, right?" came out instead.

"A grimoire." He nodded. When Sebastian sat back down, I detected the sweet, grassy odor of pineapple weed on his skin. He smelled surprisingly good for someone who'd been working in the hot sun. There was no hint of sweat. "I have a ton of notes."

"What did you mean when you said alchemy made you?" I asked, trying to sound casual. Somewhere, deep inside, I felt the Goddess smile.

He poured himself a large glass of ice water before answering. He drank it in several fast gulps. "Just what I said," he replied. Then, after a moment of consideration, he continued, "No. The truth is, I'm not certain how I became a vampire."

How could he not know? "Isn't it kind of a big moment, the Awakening?"

Sebastian sputtered out a laugh. "The 'Awakening'? Where do you *get* your vocabulary?"

I blushed furiously. "What is it supposed to be called? Anyway, you said, 'dark gift.' That's pretty damn cheesy, too."

He nodded. "Good point. I also think I talked about being a prisoner of the night."

"Yeah," I said. "So there."

Taking a sandwich, he smiled to himself. "Still, 'the Awakening.' Do other vampires say that?"

"You've never talked to any?"

He shook his head. "Not many. And those few I've met have not really been the sort to hang out and swap terminology with. I find other vampires to be, well, somewhat territorial."

Well, there was that.

"Yeah, they do call it the Awakening, as a matter of fact," I said since he couldn't refute my claim, taking the last of the sandwiches out of spite. After I'd swallowed the final delicious bite, I added, "Anyway, I still don't get how you could not remember the big waking-up-dead moment."

"Oh, I remember *that*," Sebastian agreed, with a wistful look at the crumb-filled plate. "Who could forget the moment you realize you've been left for dead and buried in a mass grave? Many of us were killed the night the Turks attacked the stronghold. I wasn't the only person to claw his way out from the dirt and bodies. A lot of people had been left for dead, but I wasn't weakened. In fact, I possessed surprising strength and speed to defend the others from the wolves. Still, I would probably have thought nothing of it, if it wasn't for this," he touched the spot above his sternum where the scar lay beneath his shirt. "And, of course, the Hunger."

Despite the seriousness of his revelation, I couldn't help but tease him, "The Hunger?"

He laughed, but shook his head with the memory. "It's a startling thing, the Hunger. Even after all this time, I find it somewhat disturbing when it comes upon me. And, then, when I wasn't expecting it . . ."

A car sped down the highway. I craned to watch its approach, afraid it might be the Vatican agent. I didn't get a good look except an impression that it was silver or maybe gray. At any rate, it zipped by without slowing.

I glanced at Sebastian, who was chewing on his lip, apparently lost in thought. "So, you weren't expecting to become a vampire?"

"People were telling me I would become a vampire my whole life."

"Huh?"

"I was born on Christmas."

"Okay," I said, feeling intensely dense. "That still doesn't make any sense to me. Shouldn't that make you holy?"

Sebastian shook his head. "It's an old superstition. Where I'm from it was once considered sacrilegious to share a birthday with Our Savior. The thought was that one's parents were committing carnal sin on the same night the Blessed Virgin received the Holy Ghost."

"You're not two thousand years old," I said.

"I'm not saying it made any sense," Sebastian said. "Though it made me a wildly unpopular kid, especially since vampirism was considered contagious."

"That must have sucked."

Sebastian nodded and took a sip of his coffee. A cool breeze rustled the leaves of the maple, sending dappled light dancing across his shoulder. He shrugged. "It gave me a lot of time to read."

"Occult stuff," I reasoned. "Since you ended up an alchemist."

"Cause and effect," Sebastian smiled.

"So I guess they *were* right." The passage of the car made me anxious. I shifted in my chair, no longer feeling content to stay still. A tremor passed across my stomach. I clutched at it, as though to say, *Down, girl.*

I found myself on my feet. "I have to pee. Then I should go home."

What? Why had I said that? I mean, yeah, I had to pee, but I was really enjoying hanging out with Sebastian in the cool shade of the maple. I felt Lilith rumbling restlessly under my skin, pushing me forward. I headed back toward the house only half under my own control.

Sebastian caught my arm. "Go? I thought you took the day off work."

"I'm more worried about leaving William at the store on his own than I realized." It was a lie, and my lips said it without any go-ahead from my brain.

"Right." He sounded a little hurt, but he rallied quickly. "Well, allow me to treat you to dinner, then."

"Yeah," I said, wondering if he'd really want me back if he knew what *We* were planning. "That would be nice."

The entire pot of coffee I'd had this morning had made its way through my system. The first stop I made was, in fact, the bathroom. I didn't flush right away, however, just in case Sebastian followed me inside. I wanted him to think

I was still on the toilet while I investigated the locked room.

I put my hand on the doorknob and shut my eyes. Lilith's power rose easily in me like a bubble. With a slight magical nudge, I slid the bar back. Slowly and as noiselessly as possible, I swung the door open. Just as I suspected, the room was Sebastian's sanctum.

The smell of old books permeated the space, which was no surprise, considering the fact that hundreds, possibly thousands, of volumes crowded the floor-to-ceiling shelves. All of them were about magic in some form or other. Many more were open and piled on two long oak tables set in the shape of an *L*, which had been lifted straight from my memory of fifth-period chemistry class, complete with stainless steel sinks and racks of test tubes. It was not my image of an alchemist's lab. Instead of greenish liquid bubbling in various bits of glassware, all the test tubes were arranged by size in a rack. An unlit Bunsen burner had been stored neatly and carefully to one side of all the books.

Despite the evil laboratory look, the room was sunny. Morning light streamed in from large windows, and an open doorway led to a sun porch. A framed picture of something abstract hung on the wall. I took a closer look. A signed Cézanne.

I poked my head through the doorway into the porch. Besides the ubiquitous crammed bookshelves, a comfortable chaise lounge and a reading table were nestled into the sunniest corner. A leather-bound journal, the kind we sold at Mercury Crossing for forty bucks, lay open to a page partially filled with Sebastian's distinctive cursive. A fat, silver Montblanc pen had been tucked into the seam of the book. I doubted this was the book I was looking for, however. This looked more like a personal diary not a Witchy one, from what I could see.

Sebastian had implied that the spell had been recorded a long time ago. With a defeated sigh, I scanned the shelves.

How on earth would I find what I was looking for among all of these books?

Well, I told myself, his book of shadows would be old. If Sebastian were actually the age he claimed to be, the book would likely be hand-bound. That presumed, of course, that he hadn't recopied his original grimoire or, fuck me, just scanned it onto a CD. Great Mother, it could be any one of these.

Why was I doing this anyway? It suddenly occurred to me that my entire obsession with Sebastian's grimoire wasn't mine at all but Lilith's. I wasn't going to do this. It was bad enough I'd broken into his special room; no way would I violate his trust even more.

So resolved, I headed off to grab my clothes from the shower curtain and flush the toilet. My foot had just about crossed the threshold into the hallway when I felt the sensation of being pushed aside. It was a relatively gentle shove, and my center of gravity shifted just slightly to the left.

Except, when my body turned around and headed back into the room, somehow, I didn't. That is to say, the part of me that was me, disconnected. "I" became a camera-eye view stuck in the doorway of Sebastian's sanctum, a helpless watcher, as I strode purposely around the room, my hand trailing across the bookshelves, eyes closed. Even not being me at that moment, I knew what I was doing. I, or rather Lilith, used magic to attempt to locate Sebastian's book of shadows.

Whoa.

Nothing like *this* had ever happened before.

When Lilith took over in the past, I blacked out. This time, I was riding shotgun in my own body, watching myself from the outside.

Weird.

She/I paused at a bookshelf near the entryway into the

sun porch. I hated to admit it, but I looked very silly in Goddess mode. The slight bluish glow at my fingertips rocked, but the smudge of mascara and the freakish bedhead thing my hair had going on marred the stately look of concentration on my face. Oh and Mátyás was right; the sweatpants/ass-kicking knee-high boots combination really did nothing for me.

My assessment of my current fashion choices came to an abrupt halt when a slow smile crept across my face. Lilith had found her quarry, I was certain. I watched helplessly as I crouched down and scattered a row of books from the bottom shelf onto the floor. Reaching deep into the case, I removed a leather-bound volume.

Stop, I tried to make my mouth say, but my disembodied self stayed rooted to the spot where I'd been booted from my own flesh. Talk about taking liberties. *You get back here with my body,* I tried to shout, but I was too busy leafing through the grimoire to notice me.

Downstairs, I heard the door open.

She/I shut the book with a snap. I gave myself another thin, cold smile. If Lilith hadn't been in possession of my spine, shivers would have crawled up and down it. As it was, I felt a tightening, as though in response to that evil gaze, my spirit tried to curl itself into a small ball. *You're not supposed to be able to cast me aside so easily,* I'd have said with my mouth, if I'd had one. *You're breaking the rules.*

"You're the one who called me down, mortal. You begged me to make your body my vessel. We're just getting more . . . comfortable, is all," I whispered, standing up. I moved toward the threshold, and for a moment I thought I might leave myself floating in the doorway forever. Instead, I held out a hand, fingers open, like a net, and then I felt myself being pulled along just out of step with my body. "I have asked for little in return for all that I have done for you. If you will not willingly offer tithe, I shall take it."

She/I wrapped Sebastian's grimoire in my still damp mini and tucked it under my arm. I grabbed my spiderweb lace hose, flushed the toilet, and headed downstairs. It was weird not to have the physical sensations that corresponded with my movements. For instance, I knew that the mini would be wet where it pressed against my ribs, but instead I felt nothing. I was an impotent, disconnected observer of my own body. *Let me back in,* I demanded wordlessly. *You have the grimoire now. If Sebastian sees you, he'll know you're not me.*

She laughed. "I don't trust you to follow our plan."

Your plan.

"Very well," Lilith conceded. "My plan."

Stopping in the kitchen, She commandeered one of Sebastian's empty grocery bags. She unwrapped the grimoire, put it inside the sack, and dumped my damp clothes on top.

Then, turning, Lilith/I headed for the front door. *Aren't we even going to say good-bye to him?*

"He's a thief, Garnet. I don't share your sympathetic opinion of him. He beheld me, and despite my kindness in allowing him to live, he attempted to possess us sexually, and took our blood. *Our* blood, Garnet. The blood of a Goddess." I saw myself puff up with righteous indignation. After a moment of consideration, Lilith added, "You couldn't even take the active role during sex. I wouldn't let the first man conquer me that way, and I'll be damned if I let this thieving corpse do it."

Hey, I liked sex. And it's my body.

Lilith let that comment pass without anything other than a disparaging *whatever* lift of my eyebrows.

Anyway, aren't you, er, we the thief, taking his book and all that?

"Blood is a metaphor for life," the Goddess said with my cheery alto voice. "He dares to consume my very essence."

It's my *blood,* I insisted.

"I have been with you since the beginning, and I am that which is attained at the end of desire."

Stop quoting the "Charge of the Goddess" and stick with the program.

Lilith had no reply. Apparently, being disembodied, I was easy to ignore.

We opened the door to the sight of Sebastian shoving my bicycle into the trunk of his car. Seeing me, he waved.

"It's the least I can do," he said. "It's a long way back into town, and, well, you haven't been all that steady on your feet." The grin he gave was one of pure sheepish guilt.

Lilith barred my teeth in a snarl. Sebastian had said the wrong thing, reminding Her of the damage his bite had done to my/our body. I had to run interference, or She'd strike him down for his insolence.

Is it worth losing the grimoire? I asked simply.

"If I kill him I could have everything. Even revenge," She whispered.

Yeah, but what kind of revenge? I asked, hoping to play to a Goddess's sense of drama and ritual. *Would it really be tit for tat to rip his throat out here and now?*

A tiny tug, and I was back behind my own eyes.

Sebastian drove one of those mafia cars from the late thirties. Big, black, and shiny, it reminded me of a June bug on wheels. Wedging my mountain bike into the skinny trunk was a bit of a challenge, but Sebastian clearly had a system involving lots of brightly colored bungee cords and a rope.

The interior smelled like axle grease, but the crushed red velvet upholstery was unstained and unfaded. His car was even more fastidiously maintained than his house. There were no empty pop cans on the floorboards. When I sat down, the wide-open feel of the bench seat and the complete lack of seat belt disconcerted me. Apparently noticing my discomfort, Sebastian dug into the seat and produced a clunky-looking buckle like those popular in the seventies. It looked like an airplane seat belt, only fatter.

"The strap is somewhere in there. I had to add them to make it street legal," he said.

I found the other part in question and buckled up, feeling strangely naked without the standard shoulder strap. I held the grocery bag on my lap, self-conscious about its contents. *I should give the book back to him,* I thought.

Lilith growled.

Sebastian looked at me. "Still hungry?"

"Uh." What did I say here? No, that was just my inner Goddess letting me know I shouldn't narc on Her. I glanced guiltily at the grocery bag. "Well, actually, I . . ."

Pain shot through my stomach.

"Uhm," I managed to say, "Yeah, I guess. Or maybe I'm just digesting. Good sandwiches, by the way."

"Thanks. Say, that reminds me, do you eat fish?" he asked casually.

"What?"

"Fish. I was thinking about dinner tonight. Are you vegetarian or vegan or what?"

"I could eat fish," I said absently, watching in rapt fascination as Sebastian went through some strange rituals to start the car, part of which included pressing a button on the dashboard. The engine, when it sprang to life, surprised me by being relatively quiet. I'd expected the car to sound like a jalopy, since it was old. Of course, I should have realized Sebastian would keep all the parts in perfect working order.

"Did you buy this when it was new?" I asked. As I watched him expertly work the column-mounted stick shift, I tried to imagine Sebastian in the gangster era dressed in a zoot suit, fedora, and fangs.

"Good God, no," he said. "I didn't even know this car existed when it was new. I was in Senegal. I got this off eBay."

There were so many questions that his response produced in my brain that I opted not to ask any of them. Besides, I was busy trying to revise my image of Sebastian to include a working familiarity with eBay, while simultaneously trying to remember in which continent Senegal belonged. Africa? Asia? Cripes, my high school social studies teacher would be so disappointed in me (again).

"Anyway, like everybody else, I lost a lot of money during the crash," he continued, as we rolled out onto the county highway I'd biked the night before. "Many world markets crashed, too, not just America's."

"Huh," I said with what I hoped was interested politeness. It wasn't that I wasn't curious about Sebastian's past, but I could feel the weight of his grimoire on my thighs. Looking at the bag, I swore I could see a distinctly square shape at the bottom. What would I say if he noticed it? *Sorry about stealing your book, but my Goddess made me do it.*

"Luckily, I had expert advice from a London stockjobber in the late seventeen hundreds. Diversify, he told me, and never entirely trust paper money. He was well before his time, he was."

"So, you're rich?" I hadn't really meant to ask that, but all this talk of money and investments made me wonder. I mean, fiscal responsibility was such a foreign language to me that when people talk about IRAs, my first assumption is that they're referring to gun-toting Irish nationalists.

"When I realized I'd conquered the grave, I started thinking about long-term survival. Money is part of that."

"So, you're rich?"

He gave me a half grimace, half smile. "Yes."

"Like, I-can-live-comfortably rich, or I-have-so-many-Swiss-bank-accounts-I-have-to-hire-someone-to-keep-track-of-them-all astronomically rich?"

Sebastian frowned at the road. We whizzed past a herd of cows standing in a pasture. The smell of their manure briefly overwhelmed the air.

"That rich, huh?" I said when he didn't respond. "Why are you living in Madison, then?"

"What's wrong with Madison?"

"Nothing, it just doesn't seem like a haven for billionaires." Or vampires, for that matter.

"I like my house. I like being able to live in the country, but also be within minutes of a decent, medium-sized city. I like the smell of alfalfa, and I like the people here."

"Why work? If you've got money, why not . . ."

"Do nothing? Nothing is boring. You can only read so many books."

I almost said, *Are you sure, because you have a ton of them,* but stopped myself just in time. Sebastian didn't know I'd been inside his private, locked study.

I glanced over at Sebastian. He'd rolled his window down partway, and his hair swirled around him in the breeze. His face was pulled tightly into a frown. Though his eyes stayed darkly focused on the road in front of us, I could tell his mind was miles away. Brooding, clearly.

I had to admit that discovering Sebastian had money bothered me much more than knowing he was a vampire. Vampires I could deal with. Rich? I didn't know the first fucking thing.

"Do you have a Learjet?"

"No."

"Yacht?"

"No."

"Mansion?" I asked, then added, gleefully, "Oh! A castle?"

"No."

"A history at Yale that involves membership in Skull and Bones?"

"No."

"You're violating all my stereotypes about rich people," I said in faux exasperation.

"Good." It was the first time since admitting to having money that Sebastian smiled at me. It was a warm look that made me grin back.

"You do realize that from now on if we go Dutch, I'll totally think you're some kind of Scrooge McDuck."

Somehow the laughter that followed relieved all of the tension that had come up between us, and I forgot for the moment about the stolen book of shadows in the bag on my lap, Mátyás, and even the Vatican agents hunting us.

We talked about nothing of any real consequence on the rest of the ride home: the weather, the strangeness of living in such a groovy-political town like Madison, and the appeal of manual over automatic transmissions.

He'd released my bike from the bungee-cord death grip and leaned it against the streetlamp. "Right, well, then I'll pick you up tonight at say, eight?"

"Tonight?" I asked, clutching the grocery bag full of stolen goods to my chest.

"Dinner."

Which is what he'd want to make of me when he discovered I had his grimoire. "Uh."

Sebastian misread my hesitation. He rested his hands lightly on my shoulders, turning me toward him gently. "You're not going off me, are you?"

I shook my head. What did I say at this juncture? *Why don't we just wait and see if you're still interested in me in say, a half an hour or so when you've discovered I not only invaded your sanctum but also took your most personally valuable property? What I should do is confess,* I told myself. *Tell him now.*

Of course, that's when he chose to kiss me.

It wasn't just a friendly peck on the cheek, either; it was full-body-contact passion. My lips tingled, and I felt myself swept up into it, until the grimoire poked me in the ribs. It was smashed into the space between our bodies. My heart pounded. Did Sebastian feel the sharp edge of the book? If he did, he never broke the kiss. Despite my nervousness,

I delighted in the strength of his arms around my waist, the faint scent of cinnamon that always seemed to cling to him, and the way his hair tickled against my ear when the wind blew.

When he released me and looked anxiously into my face for a response, I was sure he could see the heat on my cheeks. "It's not you." Jesus, that sounds lame, I thought, and watching his face crumble a little, I felt the need to continue, despite a nagging sense that less was more. "I mean, I want to, but . . ." *But what, Garnet?* What was the point of breaking his heart on top of stealing his stuff? Why not just end things happily before he came to hunt me down like a dog? "But, nothing," I finished, letting out the breath I didn't realize I was holding. "That would be great, Sebastian. I'm looking forward to it. Seriously."

"I know I'm rushing things," he said. "And you'd think with the long life I've had I could be a bit more patient, but, to be truthful, the longer I exist, the more I've come to realize that there's no point in not saying what you feel when you feel it. Seize the day, and all that. It's true, you know. I want to see you. I don't really want you to leave at all, but I understand that you have a lot to digest, what with Mátyás showing up like that, and—"

I cut him off with a finger to his lips. "I'll see you tonight," I said. And, one way or another, that was probably true. "Let's make it eight thirty. I need a nap."

He smiled at that. "Good. I'll be here at eight thirty, then."

"I'm looking forward to it." With trepidation, but, hey. "Great."

He gave me another kiss, this one quicker, though still passionate enough that the grimoire poked me again.

After Sebastian carried my bike up the outside stairs, we said good-bye with a few more kisses. He was a good kisser. Part of me wanted to invite him upstairs for an afternoon of spooning on the couch. A corollary advantage to that would be to delay the whole discovery of my theft, but I was tired enough that a nap held a tiny bit of higher appeal. Besides, my apartment was a mess.

"Okay," I said, finally giving his chin a light push, "Enough now, you. You want me well-rested for this evening, don't you?"

Sebastian flashed me a wolfish grin. "I do."

"Then you'd better go," I told him, making shooing motions with my hand. "Go on."

He blew me a final kiss as he slipped out, and I felt a pang of regret as I watched the door close. We could have had a nice relationship, I thought as I trudged up the stairs. Or at least a lot of hot sex.

At the top of the stairs, I reached into the pocket of the sweatpants for the keys to my apartment and came up empty. Of course, these were Sebastian's pants, and I just realized I'd left my emergency bag at Sebastian's.

I *had* to get it back.

That bag had my emergency money in it, two thousand dollars' worth. It contained Jasmine's prayer beads, the only memento I had left of the coven. My mouth went dry at the thought of having to abandon it, but what else could I do? Sebastian would never agree to anything short of an exchange of property, and though it was not my idea to steal the grimoire in the first place, I was certain it was worth more than two thousand dollars and personal effects to Lilith.

I was wondering about the wisdom of a preemptive strike—maybe a quick taxi out to Sebastian's farm, some even quicker talking—when I heard a delicate cat sneeze from the other side of the door. What would be causing Barney's allergic reaction to magic *inside* my apartment?

Another sneeze, this time closer to the door. A paw stretched through the gap between the door and the floor.

Maybe, I considered, it was me that made Barney so miserable. Thanks to a pleasant chat with Sebastian, I'd successfully avoided thinking about the fact that Lilith now apparently rode so close to the surface that she could shove me out of the way whenever she wanted something.

"I hope it's not me, Puss," I said. I hustled downstairs to grab the spare keys from where I kept them hidden behind a loose baseboard. I'd managed to lock myself out of my apartment enough times in the past to always keep a set on site.

As I opened the door, I set the grocery bag on the floor and reached to pick Barney up. She purred contentedly in my arms, but her claws dug into the skin of my shoulder. I looked up with the intention of finding a surface to set her onto, when I saw a figure shrouded in shadow sitting in the middle of the room. I reached for the light.

"Don't," came a voice from my past. "This place is already too bright."

It was Parrish. Daniel Parrish, my long-lost vampire lover.

Fourth House

KEYWORDS:

Home, Concealment, Addiction

Parrish had managed to make my living room surpris-
ingly dark. The old Victorian had a number of windows,
and since I was on the second floor, I never bothered with
heavy curtains. The previous renters had abandoned lace
ones, and Parrish had pulled those—for good measure, I
guess, since blankets of all sizes and colors had been tacked
to the window frames. Including, I noticed with some irri-
tation, my grandmother's hand-stitched quilt.

He sat in my oversized beanbag, which he'd pulled into
the middle of the room. Compared to Sebastian, Parrish
hulked. His body dwarfed the chair, making him look a little bit ridiculous lounging as he did on the black vinyl
lump. With his auburn heavy-metal curls, poet-shirt, and
leather pants, Parrish exuded sexuality.

"You've been out all night," he observed dryly. "Should I
be jealous?"

The possessive tone in Parrish's voice should have made

me angry, but instead I found myself flushing with a frustrating combination of annoyance and excitement. Mostly, I was annoyed at myself for still finding Parrish so damned attractive. He was such an obvious bad boy, and he played the part to the hilt. I should know better than to be charmed, but . . . well, Parrish and I were very unresolved, honestly.

My coven had never liked him. The group's disapproval had caused a lot of friction in our relationship. The majority of them felt that vampires fell under the category of black magic. They managed to convince me.

Of course, I ended up saddled with Lilith less than a day after I broke up with Parrish. The coven probably wouldn't much like that development, either. It was strange to think that Lilith and Parrish had never officially met, in fact.

Parrish had never been part of my coven, so he wasn't there when I first called Lilith into me.

"How many times do I have to tell you that women don't find men who break into their apartments and lay in wait for them attractive?" I tried to sound serious, but I couldn't quite hide a fond smile.

"How about ones that help them bury bodies?"

I did phone him afterward to help me dispose of the agents' remains.

Parrish had proven himself a true friend in that regard. Dead bodies wrapped in landscaping cloth turned out to be heavier than I could lift on my own. Without Lilith, I hadn't been up to chopping the corpses to bits. Of course, that was the first thing Parrish suggested when he answered my desperate phone call, but, in the end, he agreed to do things my way. He'd said something about the killer's prerogative. Ugh. I'd forgotten that particular bit until just now.

Seeing Parrish brought back all sorts of uncomfortable thoughts. Not the least of which was a desire to curl up beside him and stroke that gorgeous mane of hair. "What do you want?"

"What I've always wanted, darling. You."

"Right," I said, trying to sound sarcastic, despite the flutter in my stomach that his flattery evoked. "What do you really want? How did you find me, anyway?"

He sat perfectly still, not moving a muscle. Meanwhile, I held my ground with my back to the partially open door. Barney, I noticed, had fled down the stairs. I could hear her plaintive mewing at the main entrance.

"It wasn't difficult. You're still using your real name. You only moved three hundred miles from Minneapolis."

I hated to hear Parrish mock me. Starting over had been one of the hardest things I'd ever done. Okay, so maybe I didn't excel as a criminal mastermind; that was never supposed to be my gig.

Besides, despite what Parrish implied, I *had* been careful. The coven was dead. All the Vatican agents were dead. The covenstead had burned to the ground. None of us had ever used our real names, not even in the privacy of the magical circle. I doubted anyone other than Parrish could connect Goth-chick Garnet Lacey with blond, blue-eyed Meadow Spring.

The memory of that night surfaced again. I could smell the fresh-baked chocolate chip cookies I'd made for the "wine and cakes" part of the ritual. The sound of the shattering plate echoed in my ears.

"Why are you here?"

"To warn you," he said.

"I've already seen the Vatican agent," I assured him.

"Vatican?" He shook his head, sending waves of curls bouncing on his shoulders. "No. Despite all your—well, *our*—careful work, one of the bodies surfaced, Garnet. A drought lowered the cemetery's lake. Murder, as you know, has no statute of limitations."

"Murder?" I bristled. "Self-defense."

"I imagine that rationale would be more convincing had

you not so expertly concealed the bodies." Parrish hadn't moved. He was so completely still that he seemed to be barely breathing. Not that he needed to take in air—well other than to talk—but Parrish, like most vampires, breathed out of reflex.

I began to wonder if, during the daylight hours, he was somehow paralyzed. I'd never seen Parrish during the sunlight hours, despite all of our time together. Like a lot of vampires, he was really secretive about where he slept. Before I could ask him more about it, he continued, "The Minneapolis papers suggested the FBI might get involved, or, possibly, it was hinted, Interpol."

"Interpol?"

"It's possible the police suspect your victims were residents of Vatican City."

"My victims?"

"You tore their throats out, Garnet, what would you have me call them?"

Not me, I wanted to say, *Lilith.* But, Parrish didn't know about Her and, anyway, he would only remind me that wasn't how a jury would see it. My fingerprints were on the bodies, my DNA in the strands of hair, no doubt, carelessly scattered throughout the crime scene.

Although, probably the bodies were mush by now, eight months later.

I comforted myself with the fact that I had never committed a crime of any sort prior to Lilith's murderous rage. I'd never even been pulled over for speeding. All the forensic evidence in the world was useless unless they had something to compare it to. There was no record of my fingerprints anywhere, and, thankfully, any DNA signature would not actually spell out my name.

"Yeah, about that night," I started.

Parrish graced me with a bedroom smile. "I usually dread conversations that start this way."

"I wasn't alone," I said, ignoring the sexual twinkle behind his eye.

"I know."

"You know?"

He smiled. "I was happy to be of service," he said. "But I don't leave behind fingerprints." He held up his hands as though to demonstrate. "No sweat. No oil. They'll never come looking for me."

"No, I don't suppose they will. So, why are you here?"

Parrish's face was obscured by the darkness, but I thought I detected the quick flash of a smirk. "I'd hate to see you come to harm, my dear Meadow Spring."

"You are such a bullshitter, Daniel Parrish." I couldn't contain the smile this time.

A stiff nod, which confirmed my supposition that being awake during daylight hours crippled Parrish. Normally, he'd have done some kind of grand sweeping gesture, like a courtly bow or some such. At any rate, it would have been graceful. Parrish was nothing if not a man of style and aplomb. "Very well," he said. "I'm thinking about relocating to Madison. Any chance I could stay with you until I get a few bob in my pocket?"

He wanted to crash here? I should have known. Parrish was always a freeloader. I wanted to tell him to scram, but I couldn't push him out into the sunlight. Despite what he implied about my character, I had no stomach for cold-blooded murder, even if the guy was already dead. Besides, he had warned me about the investigation into the death of the Vatican agents. He didn't have to do that.

"I don't know," I admitted. I mean, rooming with an ex-boyfriend seemed like more than just a bad idea; it had the potential for a real recipe for disaster. Especially considering I'd just taken up with the local vampire. There would be rivalry on all sorts of levels. Although considering how pissed Sebastian was probably going to be when he discovered

I stole his journal, having another vampire around might come in handy.

"Look, no offense, but quite truthfully, I'm going to need a much darker place sooner rather than later," he said. "I can't impose on you forever."

I frowned at Parrish's inert shadow. Another suspicious thought occurred to me. "You're running from someone, too, aren't you?"

"Let's just say an unfortunate incident caused me to consider a permanent relocation."

"You pissed someone off," I translated.

"Not precisely. Unless you consider that someone myself."

"I'm confused," I admitted.

"I'll tell you all about it come nightfall. I promise. That is, if I can stay here?"

I let out a sigh that let him know he'd won.

"Thank you," he said. Then his head flopped down against the beanbag, and Parrish went back to the sleep of the dead.

With Parrish passed out on my favorite napping spot, I had no excuse not to do the dishes. I don't really enjoy washing up, but the apartment didn't come with a dishwasher, and I've discovered that there's a certain rhythm to the work that gets me kind of Zen: scrub, rinse, stack, repeat.

Besides, the kitchen was sunny and cozy. An archway led to the tower, a small, circular room with windows on all sides. Sunlight streamed in everywhere. I'd opened them to let in the smell of the neighbor mowing his lawn. The door was closed to protect the sleeping Parrish from the harmful UV light.

I loved my kitchen. As a Witch, I'd very consciously worked at making the hearth the heart of my home. Maple cabinets stretched from floor to ceiling, and like most kitchens built in the Victorian era, mine was narrow and cramped. Instead of trying to work against that, I brought the walls in closer with a peachy-yellow paint and filled the shelves with books and various knickknacks. I displayed my grandmother's needlework in frames on the walls. The kitchen was my nest.

As I worked at a particularly tenacious glob of melted cheese stuck to the side of my favorite copper-bottomed pot, I thought about the last few days. They'd been doozies, starting with Lilith's destruction of my driver's license.

Lilith certainly had been omnipresent in the past forty-eight hours. Never since the first night we merged had She been so . . . there. We used to share this body without a lot of hassle. Honestly, most days I barely remembered She possessed me. On average, She let me live a fairly routine life. Sometimes I'd have to control her rising when I felt a particularly strong emotion, like anger or, well, even sexual desire, but I'd always won before. I'd always been able to contain Her.

I shivered, remembering the helplessness of being discorporate. How had She done that? And not one, but two dreams in which She spoke to me?

Something was seriously wrong.

I had to put a lot of elbow grease into dislodging the goop, and the bite mark on my shoulder throbbed in protest. Then there was Sebastian. Lilith didn't like him; that much was obvious. I liked him quite a bit, but he definitely came with complications: an irritating son, the corpse of a lover who was dead/not dead whom he clearly still pined after, and . . . well, and now there was the matter of the stolen book, which was not entirely my fault, but a difficulty nonetheless.

Now to top off an insanely bizarre couple of days, the only other vampire lover of my life shows up, unannounced, looking for a place to stay. Damned if Parrish's appearance didn't seem a bit too coincidental for my taste. I couldn't see how all the pieces fit together yet, but I felt a strong sense that everything was connected somehow.

Barney jumped onto the countertop and made a slow, deliberate procession across the back of the sink, delicately stepping around the faucets. Pausing at the pile of dishes blocking her way, she glared meaningfully at me, as if to say, "This obstructs me. Remove it."

"I'll put the dishes away in a minute," I lied. I had no intention of touching the pile of drip-drying dishes and utensils I'd precariously stacked in the drainer on the counter. I disliked washing, but I absolutely loathed putting things away. Why put everything back in the cabinets, if you're only going to pull them out again? Much easier to just retrieve them from the counter, I figured.

Instead, I pulled the plug. Barney and I watched the scummy soapsuds disappear down the drain. "What's your theory?" I asked her. "Why is Parrish really here?"

Her drawn-out meow sounded a bit like "Idunno."

"What about Lilith?" I asked my cat. "Why is She so powerful right now?"

Barney apparently had an answer to that, because she leapt over to the bookcase that held all my recipes and the ephemeris, which I used to cast my daily progress chart.

I spent the next several hours poring over my astrological textbooks.

First of all, I read up on Jupiter. Jupiter is called the "great benefic." It's the astrological symbol of fortune, luck, optimism, and generosity. When any planet goes retrograde, its energy is considered blocked. So the short of it was that with Jupiter retrograde, I couldn't count on getting a lucky break. Anything that could go wrong, would.

Which fit directly with my next discovery.

Lilith, the asteroid, had moved into a powerful new position in my natal chart. That is to say, the asteroid had returned to the precise location in the sky it had been on the day of my birth. Not surprisingly, Lilith was, as we say in the astrological business, well aspected in my birth chart—almost all of my major planets interacted with the asteroid in one way or the other. Thus, Lilith influenced every part of my life. With Lilith's return to the same placement, all those bonds were reenergized.

"Wow," I said when I looked up at Barney, who lay sprawled across the pile of books and papers I'd spread all over the kitchen table. "Lilith must be drawing on all this activity to boost Her power over me."

Barney cracked open one yellow eye. She extended her front paws until the flash of claw showed. Then settling back down, she rested her chin on her outstretched limbs with a huff of a sigh.

"Well, excuse me for being so slow," I muttered, rubbing her exposed belly fur.

Barney shifted onto her back so I could reach more of her tummy and began purring contentedly.

According to my computations, the asteroid would be in this position on and off for the next several days. Lilith the Goddess would be able to tap into this power during that entire time. Picking up my pencil, I chewed on the eraser.

Barney looked briefly put out that I'd stopped single-mindedly rubbing her belly, but after a little shift of her shoulder blades so she could cover more of my pile of papers with her body, she shut her eyes.

Closing the book I'd been consulting, I sat back in my chair. I tapped the pencil against my chin. So now that I knew where Lilith got the strength to take over my body, how could I stop her from doing it again whenever she liked—especially since the transit was supposed to last until next Wednesday? And then, in the way of the "wanderers," would be back again for another few hits over the next few days.

I got up ostensibly to get myself a soda from the fridge but, really, I think best on my feet. Barney, who had started to snore, didn't even twitch a whisker as I made my way across the creaky linoleum, which was good, because I knew she wouldn't approve of the answer already forming in my head.

Magic.

What else was there, really? The true question was, what kind of spell should I use? Would a general protection spell counter the celestial vibrations from the asteroid? I could certainly perform a quickie protection spell this afternoon that would cover me for a month and a day. Considering the company I was keeping and the threat of the Vatican agents, it was probably a good idea, anyway. I made plans to do one as soon as I could work my way to my bedroom and the attic door.

Barney's nose twitched in her sleep. She huffed, cracked open her eyes to give me a dirty look, stretched a paw to cover more of my books and papers, then settled back into her nap.

Grabbing a soda from the bottom shelf of the fridge, I contemplated something more serious. Maybe it was time to excise Lilith completely. I'd considered evicting Lilith before. I even made a couple attempts right after we bonded, but found that I just didn't command enough power alone. She always knew what I was up to and fought against me. I figured if I was going to succeed, I needed the full strength of a coven behind me, or at the very least another Witch who was in on the plan. Yeah, it would be handy if I hadn't pissed off Sebastian, because a Witch his caliber was probably just what the doctor ordered.

Although . . . in the last couple of hours, Lilith had taken over twice now without any fatal consequences: first when she defended against the ghost and again when she stole the book. She apparently had some kind of chat with Sebastian the first time I unleashed Her, and the second time She just used my body to steal his book.

Crap. The book. It was still in the grocery bag by the door in the living room.

My first impulse was to scurry in there while Parrish still slept and retrieve it quickly so I could hide it somewhere. Then again, it was probably smarter to leave it where it was so as not to draw attention to it.

Leaning against the windowsill, I cracked open the top of my pop and took a long swig. The sun warmed my back, and the smell of freshly cut grass drifted in through the window. I set the can down with a sigh.

I laid a hand on my stomach. Lilith thought Sebastian's grimoire held the key to life. Something she wanted only women to have.

Okay, I *was* curious.

I tiptoed over to the kitchen door and slowly swung it open. I made sure to keep the light out of the path of Parrish's inert body. He hadn't moved—not one muscle. His body draped casually, conversationally in the beanbag. Other than the fact that his head now flopped back, he looked startlingly like he'd just sat down for a friendly little chat.

I had to laugh. I mean, the guy must have known he'd be stuck in whatever position he lay down in, and so gone to the effort to artfully arrange himself for maximum sex appeal. There was something both pathetic and endearing about that.

Parrish seemed intensely passed out, but I crept across the hardwood, conscious of every creak and squeak. When I bent to pull the book out of the bag, I heard him mumble, "Nice view."

"I thought you were asleep," I said, turning around, clutching the book to my chest.

He'd lifted his head, and blinked slowly. "I am."

"Aren't you really vulnerable right now?" I asked him. "I mean, what if I decided I was still pissed off about the way we broke up, and I pulled all the curtains off?"

"You broke up with me."

"That's not the point," I said, waving off my desire to remind him of some of his more hurtful parting words. "You took a big risk coming here."

"I did," he admitted.

"Why?"

Parrish pursed his lips, which in itself, I realized, took monumental effort. "It frustrates me no end that you refuse to entertain even the slightest possibility that my motivations might have been, for once, altruistic."

I shook my head. It's not that I didn't *want* to believe Parrish might have acted selflessly; it scared me just a little. Parrish and I had once been very intense, and I didn't want that to ruin anything I might have with Sebastian— provided he ever spoke to me again. "Listen, Parrish, don't give me that. You yourself admitted that you needed a place to crash."

"Yes, but I'm still disappointed you won't even let me play the gallant."

I took in the long, lean form of his leather-clad body. Parrish represented the exact opposite of a gentleman; he was a con artist extraordinaire. He knew just how to worm his way back into my affections, and, perversely, that was part of his charm. Still, if we were going to be roommates, things had to remain platonic. "Go back to bed, Parrish."

"You wound me, lady."

"Good night, sweet prince."

I caught the flash of a genuine smile before his head hit the beanbag with a muffled thump.

* * *

Barney started sneezing the instant I shut the kitchen
door and set Sebastian's book on the table. "Oh, come on," I
said, "It's just a grimoire."

She let out a string of snorts and then shook her head vi-
olently. With a yellow-eyed glare, she hopped off the table
and stalked out of the kitchen through the archway toward
the adjacent tower room. Bounding up onto the windowsill
the farthest from the offending book, she turned her back
on me.

If anything, Barney's display made me more curious
about the contents of Sebastian's book of shadows. With
some anticipation, I opened it up and then immediately felt
like a complete idiot.

It wasn't in English.

I mean, of course not. I knew Sebastian was Austrian;
he'd told me that. Even if I could read German or Latin or
whatever, I doubted I could decipher any of this. Languages
tended to change over the course of a thousand years. I
might have a shot if it were Latin, because it was no longer
a living language, but, honestly, my Latin was limited to
the occasional botanical term and the phrase *deus ex machina,*
one of which I could use right now.

Since I had nothing better to do, I flipped randomly
through the book. I assumed Sebastian must have recopied
his notes, since the paper or vellum or whatever it was didn't
completely crumble to the touch, though it felt pretty fragile. The pages smelled a little moldy, but I was impressed
that the grimoire held together after all this time.

Returning to the start, I noticed Sebastian had written
1824 inside the cover followed by some words I couldn't
read, then 1206. Feeling pretty brilliant, I surmised that
the first was the date of the recopy, and the second the date
for the original.

I was off to a good start.

There were other Arabic numerals scattered throughout

the text, but none of them made any sense to me, not even the mathematical formula that took up several pages. I did, however, recognize some astrological symbols. I spent several minutes puzzling out something that looked vaguely like a natal chart, but gave up when I realized the houses were organized by some arcane method. Plus, it offended my modern sensibilities to be missing Uranus, Neptune, and Pluto, none of which had been discovered at the time.

I shut the book, feeling overwhelmed. Rubbing my neck, I decided what I needed more than anything was a shower and a nap, not necessarily in that order.

I crept past Parrish to my bedroom. When I thought I saw him lift his head a bit, I hurried my step and slipped into the room before he could say anything.

My door didn't have a lock, at least not a physical one. Shutting my eyes, I allowed my magic to surface. Extending my senses outward, I found the elements I kept on the shelf altar in my room for just this purpose: a polished river pebble for earth, a goose feather for air, a book of matches for fire, a silver goblet for water, and a black onyx Nile Goddess statue for spirit. A tingle of power rose from my feet like water drawn up the roots of a tree. When I felt it cascade out from the crown of my head, I put my left palm on the door. My right hand I placed on my abdomen, over my womb. Normally, a Witch would hold her hand upward for the Goddess, but mine resided within me.

"Unless I ask, none shall pass," I said. "So I will, so mote it be."

I traced a pentacle in the center of the door, then pushed a thread of power into it.

The thread appeared in my mind's eye like gold wire. I wove it in and out of the deep purple pentagram, like a stitch. When I finished, the pentagram glittered with gold. I would be safe behind the door now. No one could enter.

Since I was in magical mode, I grabbed my athame off the shelf and headed for the attic to perform my quickie protection spell. I always kept the door to the attic locked, though I left the key hanging on the knob. It was another reminder to me that I had left magic behind. I reasoned that if I had to go to the effort of opening the door each time, I'd be more conscious of why I was there.

I had a twinge of guilt when I turned the skeleton key. I'd feel pretty darn violated if I discovered someone had rifled through *my* personal space. I had a book of shadows, a grimoire. I wrote down my rituals, spell work, and kept a kind of journal of my Witchy experiences in it. It was not unlike a diary, actually, full of secrets and personal observations about my Craft. Of course, mine was in English, and Sebastian could read it, if he'd taken it.

I walked up the steep, dusty wooden stairs. Though I'd painted the walls to correspond with the directions, they were unfinished, exposed rafters. My landlord, who always started more than he could handle, had put a skylight into the south-facing ceiling, and a shaft of sunlight fell directly on my altar. Otherwise the dormers disappeared into darkness.

My altar was a round, knee-high table, which was still draped in the green cloth I'd used for Oestre, Spring Equinox. A brass chalice I'd picked up at a church basement rummage sale sat in the center. The altar looked woefully empty to me. Often a Witch's altar was a kind of collage of personal meaning. The altar I'd left behind in Minneapolis had overflowed with things I'd collected over a lifetime: images from books, statuary, tarot cards, curios, crystals, rocks pocketed in the midst of meaningful adventures, and even a favorite Valentine's card from a friend.

Though it looked sort of sad, I'd purposely left this altar

bare. I could, of course, have purchased any number of adornments from the store. That would have been a cheat. Anything I bought would have been devoid of real meaning. I didn't want to simply crowd up my altar for the sake of filling it. In a way, I used its emptiness to remind me of why I kept practicing when it might be easier to give up my Witchcraft all together. The bareness was a memorial to those I'd left behind, slain by the Order.

I stood for a moment at the threshold. My altar sat in the center of a white pentacle I'd painted on the floor. I took a deep, calming breath before setting foot inside the circle. I loved having a permanent sacred space. At my apartment in Minneapolis, I hadn't had access to the whole attic, not to mention the fact that my previous landlady was the only holdout Republican in the Seward neighborhood.

I remembered leaving that morning after. Parrish dropped me off at my apartment, and I made a mad dash through my Minneapolis apartment, trying to decide what to take with me. Barney got stuffed in her carrier with only Grandma's quilt for comfort. Into my duffel, I'd shoved my toothbrush, a bottle of vitamins, a comb, makeup bag, a pair of jeans, and as many shirts and tops as I could jam in. I had a shoe box full of photos I'd meant to organize one day, but even though I tore apart all of the closet space in the apartment, I never found it. In the end I decided losing it was for the best. If I remembered who I used to be, it would break my resolve, my heart.

As I went through the traditions of casting the circle and calling quarters, I felt the outside world slip away. I was between the worlds now, in a space that belonged to the Goddess and me. Time stopped.

From a banker's box I kept under the table, I pulled out a large white candle and some matches. I lit the candle. It was unscented and had the image of two gold rings joined together. It was obviously meant for a wedding; I'd bought it from a factory outlet. I liked the idea of using it for a ritual, though, since in many ways ritual space was in that same place—the meeting of two circles, one anchored in earth, the other not.

I rifled through my box for the other items I'd need: a flask of rainwater and a silver coin: a Mercury dime someone passed me at the store without realizing what it was. I took it thinking I'd use it for a spell someday, since it's otherwise hard to find coins made from silver.

I poured the water into the chalice. Previously, under the light of a full moon, I'd charged the water. That is, I'd poured my energy into it, consecrating it, making it magical by investing it with purpose. Pagan holy water. The Order would *love* that.

Of course, I shouldn't have been charging water at all. That was spell work. I was supposed to have given up all that. I'd just woken up one night with a craving. It was embarrassing; I was a serious magic junkie. No wonder Lilith continued to get stronger. I fed her constantly.

I shook my head to banish the thought. I concentrated on the task at hand. Into the goblet filled with water, I dropped the silver coin.

I held the cup up to the sunlight, which I imaged as the strong, loving arms of a protective, peaceful Goddess.

"O Goddess Bright, hold me tight. Watch over me now, day and night."

I held my breath, waiting for Lilith to surface. I'd been purposefully vague in my request. I didn't want to name another Goddess specifically, since I thought that might give Lilith a target for any jealous rage she might feel.

Miraculously, Lilith didn't stir. I'd been obtuse enough to escape Her notice. Although that probably also meant that the ritual failed on some level, since Lilith would likely be more ticked off to find Herself warded against.

The sun felt warm on my face. I took a drink of the

water, then set it aside to drain as a libation into my potted plants later. I fished the coin out of the chalice to keep in my pocket as a talisman. I thanked whatever Bright Goddess had touched this ritual with Her presence, which I felt as the heat of the light on my skin, and then began the unwinding of the magic. I released the quarters. Walking counterclockwise along the painted edge of the pentacle, I opened the circle.

"The circle is open, but—" I started the traditional closing words, and then choked. I hadn't been able to say the words as part of a ritual since that night. Hurriedly, I finished with, "So mote it be."

That finished, I went downstairs, locked the door behind me, crawled under the comforter, and slept.

Sebastian's grimoire figured prominently in my dreams.

Numbers and symbols danced around in my head, making a jumble whose meaning lay always just out of reach. At first, in the way of dreams, I was somehow inside the pages, standing beside the words and images. In the next moment, I was outside, looking down at the pages, when a hand touched my shoulder.

I looked around. Though I saw no one, I felt watched. The flutter of black wings against a moonlit sky skittered along my peripheral vision. When I glanced back at the book, the words had become English. Over and over, it read: "I want my fucking grimoire back, you thieving bitch."

I woke up to the sensation that someone was pounding on my door. Tense, I waited to hear the sound again. "Sebastian?" I called, albeit softly. "Parrish?"

No answer, other than a plaintive mew and a scratch.

"Come in, Barney," I said, standing up to unlatch the door. "I should get up anyway."

Barney wiggled herself inside. She sat upright on the bed

and curled her tail over her paws. Once she was certain she had my attention, Barney sneezed.

"I'm sorry, okay?" I said, picking up the ceremonial knife, the athame, from its spot on the shelf altar. I made a slashing motion at the door, effectively breaking the warding spell. Destruction was infinitely easier than construction.

I'd slept much longer than I'd intended. A glance at the alarm informed me that it was already past seven. Outside, the streetlights flickered on in response to the encroaching darkness. Twilight. Parrish would be mobile.

Changing out of Sebastian's clothes, I rooted around in my closet until I came up with something casual and sexy. After a quick trip to the shower, I slipped into a black lace-up-the-front teddy and pulled on my most faded, threadbare blue jeans. From the pocket of the sweats I removed the Mercury dime and slipped it into the watch pocket of the jeans.

Checking the look in the mirror, I decided I looked pretty good in a slutty sort of way, especially with wet hair and mascara-smudged eyes and the very faint bruise on my shoulder. Sebastian would approve, I was certain, and probably Parrish as well.

Speaking of my new roommate, I found Parrish in the kitchen, reading Sebastian's grimoire.

Oh, crap.

I felt so stupid that I'd left it out in the open like that. This was not good.

Could Parrish possibly know how important the grimoire was? I told myself there was no reason to believe he could read ancient German any better than I. Maybe if I could act casual, Parrish would never suspect anything.

How likely was that?

Parrish had made himself a cup of tea. I saw it steaming by his elbow. While I watched, he touched the rim of the cup to his lips but didn't drink—an affectation left over from a lifetime of consuming food and liquids. Parrish's eyes scanned the page slowly. I suddenly realized he *could* read it.

"Hey," I said. "You read German?"

He was so startled he nearly spilled his drink. "How long have you been spying on me?"

I laughed. He was a fine one to talk, sitting there perusing Sebastian's secrets. Of course, I had stolen them. My righteous indignation evaporated with a shrug. "Not long." I pulled up a chair to sit beside him. "So, you can read it?"

"Not really," he said. He closed the book, sending the scent of dust and mold into the air. "Seeing the book made me nostalgic. It was new when I was young."

I rolled my eyes at him. "Next you're going to say they don't make books like that anymore."

"They don't." The teacup went to his lips again, and I watched as he breathed in the orange blossom scent of Lady Gray. "Where did you get it?"

Leaning an elbow on the table, I batted my eyelashes innocently. "I stole it."

A smile twitched across his lips, as if a million snarky replies occurred to him, and he couldn't decide which one to use. "Ah," he said. "I see."

"Okay, fine," I said, as if he'd refuted my claim, which, in a way, he had. I mean, his tone fairly dripped with I-so-don't-think-you-have-it-in-you derision. "Lilith stole it."

"Lilith?"

Right. I hadn't gotten around to telling Parrish about Lilith and that night. Still, I found myself more frustrated by my apparent credibility gap. "You'd have no problem believing I can cut the throats of Vatican agents in cold blood, but you have a hard time picturing me taking someone's book?"

Parrish raised a finger as though to count off his first point. "Not cold blood. Passion." Then, he flashed me the European "two," thumb and forefinger. "This is clearly a rare book, Garnet. I can only think that the university's special collection would have such an item, and I'm trying to imagine you pulling a caper that would involve scaling walls in the middle of the night." He broke into a smile. "Though I can easily see you in a skintight catsuit. You'd make a lovely burglar."

"Thanks." I got up to pour myself my own cup of tea. Parrish had, in the parlance of his people, left the kettle on. The gas flame glowed low and blue under the blue-and-black-speckled teakettle. Steam escaped through the spout. I pulled a mug from the cast-iron tree under the cabinets. The cup was a nondescript yellow, exactly like the one Parrish had. I'd bought them from the discount bin at the big department store on the edge of town on highway whatever. My favorite mug, a blue and brown glazed, hand-thrown pottery one made for me by my friend Frank out in Oregon, had been left with so many other important things in Minneapolis.

"So," he prompted when I didn't offer anything else. "Did you use a grappling hook? Are you holding the book for ransom?"

I laughed. "It's not from the library. It's—" I stopped myself. Was he fishing? Leaning against the kitchen counter, I fiddled with the box of tea bags as I tried to gauge Parrish's expression. He'd folded his hands on top of Sebastian's grimoire, and he gazed at me with a bemused expression as though still trying to imagine me in full thief mode.

The overhead lamp radiated harsh light on Parrish's pale white skin and cast a fluorescent halo around his auburn curls. I was struck by how unhealthy he looked compared to Sebastian, which was silly, considering that they were both equally dead. You don't get any sicker than dead.

"What?" Parrish prompted. "It's what?"

Turning my back to him for a moment, I poured water into my cup. Could I trust him? I wanted to. After all, he was the guy I called when I needed to bury bodies. He was good at keeping secrets. Plus, I desperately needed to ask an expert about Sebastian's vampirism, such as it was.

Pulling a spoon from the drawer, I stirred some honey into my tea and made a decision. "Have you ever met a vampire who could walk around in the daylight?" I asked, returning to the chair I'd pulled up beside him.

He snorted a laugh. "How could I?"

"Well, *he* can walk around at night. Anyway, have you ever *heard* of one?"

He rolled his eyes. "Of course. Vampires love urban legends as much as the next fellow," Parrish said, sniffing the contents of his cup again. "Since my conception, rumors have circulated about a mad scientist and a mystical formula. It's the Holy Grail for vampires. Why? Have you found it?" He looked down at the grimoire lying underneath his hand. His face became serious. "Good God, Garnet. You're not saying this is it?"

I hadn't really intended to say anything of the kind, but Parrish was always smarter than I gave him credit for. "I don't know," I said. "Maybe."

"Is he the one who bit you?" Parrish asked.

I started to protest, but then I realized my choice in clothing had left Sebastian's love bite exposed. I hadn't really thought about covering it up because it hadn't bruised as much as I expected, plus the puncture wounds were magically nearly faded. Now I felt a blush creep up my neck. "I . . ." I had no idea what to say.

Parrish gave me a long, appraising look. "Impressive," he said finally. "The rest of us have been chasing after a ghost for centuries, and you find him in Madison, Wisconsin. You haven't even lived here that long."

"Are you jealous?"

"No," he said a little too quickly, and, moreover, the twitch of his jaw told me otherwise. Then Parrish affected a more casual air. "You know, if word of this were to get out, every vampire on the planet would be after you."

"Well, they'll have to stand in line," I grumbled into my mug, thinking of the FBI and Vatican agents. I started to take a swallow of my drink, then stopped. "Would that include you?"

We both stared down at the grimoire. One of Parrish's hands still rested casually on its tooled leather cover. "No," he said. "Because I already have it."

A disturbingly good point.

"It belongs to Sebastian, Parrish. I should give it back. He . . ." I wanted to explain that Sebastian needed it, but I hesitated. I didn't think Sebastian would want another vampire to know about his weakness.

"For someone who had no problem dispatching a half dozen Vatican agents single-handedly, you're distressingly ethical," Parrish said, his fingers tracing the gilt border.

"It's one of my charms," I said. I held out my hand. "The book, Parrish. Give it back."

"Do you know what this is worth on the open market? There are vampires who would pay millions of pounds—or euros or whatever the hell—for the chance to walk around in daylight again. I could become a very rich man." Parrish glanced at me. "Or we could."

Nice to be included. I shook my head. "It was never my idea to take it. I just want to give it back."

Parrish nodded slowly. "Then let me borrow it. I'll take it to Kinko's. We can sell the copy."

"Uh . . ." Okay, so there was nothing inherently wrong with the idea of letting Parrish walk off with the grimoire for a couple of hours, but I just didn't think that if I did, I'd ever see him or the book again, and Sebastian needed the spell in that to survive.

Parrish, for his part, looked completely unthreatened. He made no sudden move to run off with the grimoire, but neither did he remove his hand. Leaning back in his chair slightly, as though to get a better look at me, Parrish clearly waited patiently for my next move.

What would it be? My little five-foot-something self had no chance of overpowering him physically. Not unless I called on Lilith, which was kind of an endgame, especially since I got the impression from the cold calmness in Parrish's eyes that he would fight me for the grimoire. I could feel Lilith rising to the challenge, but I held Her back with the thought and the power of the recently woven spell.

"Yeah . . . okay," I said, as though finishing my earlier thought.

"You *want* me to take the grimoire?" Parrish's eyes were as wide as saucers.

Did I? Well, I sure as hell didn't want to fight him for it, not if it meant that Lilith would rise up and kill him. He said he'd bring it back. He was a thief, but he loved the idea of being an honorable one. Not more than a couple of hours ago, he begged me to consider him a gentleman. I played that card now. "You said you wanted me to believe you were a good guy; well, here's your chance to prove it." Besides, I told myself. If he didn't come back, I'd let Lilith find him. She was my ace in the hole. "I'm trusting you with this, Daniel."

No one ever called him by his first name. I never knew why, but I'd always followed what appeared to be protocol in the matter. Maybe he didn't like it, maybe he thought it was too Biblical, but he smiled warmly at me now. "I shall not fail you, lady," he said.

I might actually see him—and Sebastian's grimoire—again. "Thank you."

After Parrish left, I puttered with my herbs in the tower room. The space was no more than ten feet in diameter, and was mostly windows. The room faced south, so the plants loved it. Culinary herbs crowded together in a big clay pot in the center of the room: oregano, thyme, rosemary, basil, and cilantro. Rubbing my fingers on the rosemary leaves, I sniffed its distinctive, sharp, piney scent. In separate pots, I also cultivated a few weeds, some of which I transplanted from roadside ditches: Queen Anne's lace, chicory, cowslips, and catchfly.

Ivy and philodendron vines twined around the circular ceiling and had begun to follow the star-shaped string trellis that I'd rigged up. By next spring, it would be a completed pentacle of living plants.

Barney rubbed against my leg. I crouched down to pet her, which is how I managed to avoid the bullet that cracked through the window with a loud smack.

Fifth House

❧

KEYWORDS:

Luck, Arrogance, Creativity

The bullet punched through the plaster of the opposite wall. Barney and I stared in horror at the dust blooming from the hole in the archway.

"Was that a bullet? That was a bullet! Someone fucking shot at us," I said to Barney. A dime-sized circle of warmth near the right side of my hip reminded me of the protective talisman tucked into my pocket. Staring at the puckered spot on my window that looked like an inverted nipple with a hole in the center, I thanked the Goddess for inspiring Barney to need a cuddle just then.

Barney, for her part, hissed and scrambled out of the room.

Fighting the desire to look out the window to see where the shot came from, I flattened myself on the floor and told myself to stay there. My hammering heart wanted me to flee. Meanwhile, my brain was conflicted on the subject. Mostly, lying still seemed like a good idea, but then there was the door. I doubted Parrish had locked it, since I'd neglected to give him a key. What was to stop the shooter from coming upstairs and doing me in, execution style, while I quivered helplessly on the floor?

I compromised. Crab-crawling into the kitchen, I made my way toward the front door. I froze when I heard the sound of footsteps on the stairway. My first instinct was to hide behind the couch. The couch was one of those massive rummage-sale foldout beds that had nearly killed my friends and me dragging it up the stairs. Despite being plaid and sagging in the middle, it had enough steel in it that it might actually qualify as armor.

The second creak on the steps decided things for me. I scuttled behind the couch and cowered. When I saw Barney's furry, gray tail sticking out from under the dust ruffle, I felt I'd made a good choice.

The sounds stopped. I held my breath. Beside me, Barney's tail flicked once in irritated anticipation.

A loud rap on the door made me nearly choke on my own heart.

What kind of freakishly polite son of a bitch knocks before coming in to kill you? Had they knocked before killing my coven? Had someone let them in?

The second knock took me by surprise.

Okay, once seemed like maybe it could be part of some assassin's handbook, i.e., step one, see if the mark is stupid enough to let you in, but to knock again? What, was the killer really expecting an invitation?

Another knock.

"She stood me up," Sebastian muttered on the other side of the door. "Christ."

I started to stand up but stopped myself just in time. I had no idea if Sebastian needed to be invited in—Parrish hadn't—but this was no time to mess around with details. "Come in, Sebastian," I shouted as loudly as I could. "Stay low and lock the door behind you. They've got a gun. They're shooting at me."

"Garnet?"

"Get in here!" The last thing I wanted was for the Vatican agent to come running in while Sebastian hesitated at the door. "Now, goddamn it."

I heard the door open, close, and the click of the lock. Then came the sound of cloth rubbing against something, which I realized must have been Sebastian's coat sliding down the door as he sat himself down on the floor. "Well," he said. "This is different."

"Did you see anyone outside?" I poked my head out from behind the couch to look at him.

Sebastian sat in a half lotus with his back on my door, just as I'd expected. He'd dressed up for our date: black jeans, white shirt, black tie, and a sexy-as-hell leather trench coat. His hair was neatly tied back in a thick ponytail, which showed off the strong line of his neck.

"Like a sniper?" he asked.

"Yes, like a sniper," I said, crawling the rest of the way out. The kitchen was at the back of the house, opposite the large living room/dining room space. So, when I thought about it, it wasn't likely that Sebastian would have passed through the sniper's line of fire at all. *Well, duh, Garnet. Or he'd have been shot, too.* Still, I kept talking. My mind was still trying to process this whole thing. "Or anyone out of the ordinary."

Sebastian grimaced. "This is Madison, Garnet. There were plenty of strange people on the street."

I started to ask if he'd seen anyone suspicious-looking, but then I remembered how forgettable the real estate agent had been. Great Mother, that image was going to make me paranoid. Now everyone, even the ubiquitous tie-dyed hippie on a bicycle, could be a Vatican killer.

"Someone tried to shoot me," I said.

"So I gathered." The words sounded irritated, but the smile he flashed me was warm. "You look frazzled. Are you all right? Did anyone get hurt?"

"Not unless you count a window and a plaster wall." I crawled out from behind the couch.

"Did they scream?"

"No."

"Then it's fine," he smiled.

It was nice of him to try to make a joke, but I couldn't quite shake the feeling that danger lurked just outside. I shifted so I could rest my back against the seat of the couch, because, though I wanted to seem casual, I couldn't quite bring myself to stand up.

"Do you think it was the Order?" Sebastian asked more seriously, perhaps noticing his inability to shake my mood.

"Undoubtedly," I said.

"You don't think there's any way it could have been random? A drive-by shooting or something?"

"From the alley?"

"Oh," Sebastian said. "Well, less likely then."

Although the fact that no one had, so far, followed up to do me in, did make me wonder a bit. I mean, the "real estate" agent had led me to believe she was after Sebastian, not me. If the shooter had been anywhere nearby, they must have seen Sebastian pull up. This would be the perfect opportunity to kill us both. Maybe they were biding their time, waiting for us to let down our guard, to leave together. "You have to stay here," I said. "We can never leave."

"So, the answer is no, I take it?"

"To what?"

"To the idea that this could all be a coincidence." When my only reply was a hot, angry glare, Sebastian switched gears. "You know more about these people than I do, but do you really think they'd just shoot you from a distance? That doesn't seem very moral high ground, does it?"

"What are you talking about?"

"I don't know, but isn't killing someone at such a great distance a bit of a cheat? You'd think the Church would expect its enforcers to get in close, try to save the souls of the sinners, or at the very least look into the eyes of the accused."

"They don't give people a chance to repent, Sebastian. You're already tried and sentenced if the Order is after you."

"That's not very sporting," he said with a frown.

"Well, no shit."

I glared at him for a while, waiting for the seriousness of the situation to finally sink in. Instead, he took in the various blankets Parrish had tacked to the windows and said, "Nice place."

"Get used to it. I was serious when I said I'm never leaving."

"Well," he said. Standing up, he smoothed out his jeans. "If the Order does have a sniper outside, they can't see us in here. We could at least sit together on the couch and watch a movie or something. Maybe order a pizza. My treat."

"Why aren't you more afraid of them?"

"From what you've told me, they sound like cowards."

My anger flared again. "These cowards slaughtered my friends."

Sebastian's face softened with compassion. "Yes. And I assume your friends were mortals, not even soldiers. Did your friends even have any weapons of their own?"

"Ritual knives," I said, but Sebastian was right, the coven had been defenseless, unaware.

"And the Order carries guns."

I nodded. They did; I'd found guns, even rifles, on their bodies. They also had a whole arsenal of edged weapons from swords to stilettos.

"Cowards," he repeated, as he plunked himself down on my couch. He took in the living room in all of its cinderblock-and-board-bookshelf glory. "Where's your TV?"

"Don't have one," I said, feeling oddly sheepish about it. It was less of a political decision on my part than an economic one, but I tended to let most people think no TV

went part and parcel with my alternative lifestyle as a vegetarian Witch.

"Right. That cancels the movie option, then. Still up for
a pizza?"

"I can't eat while someone could still be out there."

Sebastian looked into my eyes for a long moment. Then,
very slowly, very seriously, he said, "Of course you can, Garnet. You're stronger than the entire Order, and you know it.
Or if you don't, you should. Lilith is a Goddess."

"She can't stop bullets."

"I watched her stop Benjamin's knife. Are you sure?"

I gave a grim laugh. "Well, not enough to bet my life on
it, no. Anyway," I added as an afterthought, "Lilith and I
don't always share the same agenda."

Sebastian leaned an elbow on the arm of the sofa in order
to shoot me a long, appraising look. With his designer
leather coat and perfectly combed hair, he made my couch
look extraordinarily ugly. "So whose idea was it to steal my
grimoire?"

The question had the air of being casual, but I felt cold-
ness behind his eyes that made me wish I hadn't been so
quick to invite him into my apartment.

Using my elbows, I leveraged myself up onto the couch to
sit beside him. I didn't want to have this fight while sitting
at Sebastian's feet. I also got the sense that it didn't much
matter what the answer to his question was. The result was
the same. He'd been betrayed, and I'd taken part in it.

"Lilith," I said, even though I wasn't sure it mattered.

A knock on the door startled both of us, as did the voice
from the other side, which proclaimed in an authoritative
male voice, "This is the police. Is everyone all right in
there? We got a call about a shot fired."

Sebastian and I looked at each other. I could tell we shared
the same concern: could it be the Vatican shooter trying to

gain entrance? Neither of us moved toward the door. I wanted to play dumb, but, unfortunately, I'd been unable to contain a squeak of surprise, so whoever it was out there knew someone was home. Anyway, we'd both been talking just before the knock came.

"Sir? Ma'am?" came the voice again. "It would be really helpful if we could talk to you for just a minute. I'd really like to know that everyone is okay in there."

At times like this I'd kill to be telepathic. What was Sebastian thinking? Did he also think the guy sounded fairly convincing as a cop? Or did he think that was part of what made this whole thing suspicious? I had no idea what to do. I was actually relieved when Sebastian got up and gestured for me to get out of the line of sight of the door. I scurried back behind the couch. Okay, it was not the most heroic of spots, but I still preferred to have steel between any ricocheting bullets and my fragile flesh and blood.

Then a thought occurred to me. If these were real cops, there'd be cop car parked out front. So I lifted the edge of Parrish's makeshift curtain to peer out. Oh, shit. No car. "Uh, Sebastian," I started.

He turned. He'd been about to put his foot in front of the door when it opened. I ducked.

I heard a strange twang, like someone releasing a high-tension wire, followed by a strangled cry and a very heavy sounding thud. My fingernails dug into the upholstery of the couch.

Oh, my God, I've just killed my boyfriend.

"That should hold him for a while," the authoritative male voice said. "Search the apartment. The source said it would be here."

Boots scuffed to do the leader's bidding. I heard a voice say, "I thought an arrow through the heart would kill a vampire. He's looking pretty pissed off."

The good news was that Sebastian was apparently still alive; the bad news seemed to be that he was staked through the heart by some method involving an arrow.

"The source told us that a stake of ash keeps the vampire transfixed, doesn't kill him."

"Ah, that's right," Sebastian said, sounding a little pleased. "You're not vampire hunters at all, are you? Aren't you a bit out of your league? Don't you usually kill unarmed tree-huggers?"

Hey, I wanted to say, *that's not fair!* But I realized Sebastian was just goading them.

When they didn't rise to it, he continued. "I hope you trust this source of yours. A longbow—very inventive, though awfully risky. What would you have done if it hadn't worked?" Sebastian hissed. He sounded as though he spoke through teeth clenched in pain. "You do know that if you want to finish me off you have to decapitate me with a single blow? Which one of you bastards thinks he has the balls to come close enough to attempt that?"

"Ignore him," leader said. "Go help the others find the journal."

Holy Mother, they were searching for the grimoire. How long would it take them to look under the couch?

Barney decided to be brave. She streaked out from under the couch with a yowl. Someone, most likely Leader Guy, cursed loudly, and then came a feline yipe followed by the quick retreat of padded paws. I imagined Barney must have scored a hit and lived to fight another day.

"Why are there always cats?" Leader Guy muttered between curses. "Why don't these people ever have goldfish familiars?"

My breathing sounded so loud in my own ears, I wondered why no one had found me yet. And, though I desperately needed to shift my weight, I didn't dare. I was afraid the creaky hardwood would betray me.

Sebastian groaned. At least, I thought it must be Sebastian, especially since the authoritative man suddenly demanded, "Where is it, Von Traum? Where's the grimoire?"

"It was stolen. Lilith has it."

"Who's Lilith?"

"A good religious man like yourself has never heard of Adam's first wife? Shame on you, Padre."

The rapid discharge of a machine gun tore through the air. I sprawled flatter, hugging hardwood, trying to slide farther under the protective shield of the couch. My ears rang, and suddenly all sound receded inside my head. Great. Now I was deaf as well as blind.

The echo of voices tried to reach my eardrums. Far, far away and underwater people were shouting. I prayed that one of them was Sebastian. I refused to even contemplate what a machine gun could do at close range to a body, and, luckily, I had no real-life previous experience to give seed to my imagination.

I told myself that shredded Sebastian meat wouldn't do the Vatican any good if they wanted information out of him. They wouldn't have cut him in half—not if they wanted him talking. No vampire could take that kind of damage lightly, not even with their supernatural regenerative abilities. So I chose to believe that Leader Guy had shot up my lathe and plaster as a demonstration, a show of power, a shot across the bow, and Sebastian remained unharmed, other than, apparently, being impaled on a longbow arrow.

If I thought otherwise, I'd cry, and this was no time for sobbing histrionics. Especially since any noise would give away my location.

I wished I could see. Or hear. At least previously I'd had some sense of the action. Now my world had shrunk to the harsh sound of my own breathing and the disgusting view of the enormous dust bunnies that populated the underside of my couch.

I might be able to visualize the action from the astral plane, but I didn't want to risk using magic. I'd heard that the Vatican employed sensitives, psychics who could sniff out spell work in progress. Of course, that would be just the kind of rumor the Vatican might plant in our community to keep someone like me from using my magic to kick their asses.

Lilith chose that moment to remind me that I was not without a weapon. A spasm jittered across my abdomen, as though to say, *Let me at 'em.* I winced from the pain, but also because at that same moment, artificial light streamed in under the couch. Fingers had lifted the ruffle and, mere inches from my own face, eyes widened in surprise at seeing me looking back. There were a couple of seconds of shallow breathing and mutual staring, then a return to darkness.

I waited, not breathing, for what seemed like an eternity. I even entertained the idea that the soldier boy who'd spotted me might have had some kind of crisis of conscience and had told his fearless leader that there was nothing to see here, move along. Then, quite suddenly, the couch was heaved up and over. I lay exposed on the floor surrounded by a perfect rectangle of dust, a set of keys, and sixty-two cents in change.

Sixth House

KEYWORDS:

Stress, Cleanliness, Weakness

I looked up to see three priests in black suits and collars with heavy weaponry, all of which was pointed at me. Including, I realized, a redheaded guy holding a bow so slender and long I had to assume it was the longbow Sebastian had talked about earlier. The redhead regarded me warily over the fletching of his arrow. I thought I recognized his gray-green eyes as those that had spotted mine under the couch.

Just as I pictured in my mind's eye, I found Sebastian pinned to the oak window frame by a huge arrow sticking out of his chest.

Something about the way he hung there, unmoving, made Sebastian seem more than just skewered. The slackness in his body reminded me of Parrish's earlier behavior. I wondered if the "transfixing" Leader Guy mentioned was a kind of magic keeping Sebastian immobilized, but he was able to flash me a weak smile when he saw me.

The machine gun *had* ripped up a space next to his feet, and there was plaster dust and wood splinters everywhere, not to mention a ragged hole in the wall.

I was so never getting my security deposit back.

Especially considering all the bloodshed about to come.

Wary of the guns trained on me, I sat upright very slowly. Leader Guy stepped forward. Or, at least, I assumed it was him from the machine gun he toted in his beefy hand. Plus he looked the part: silver hair chopped into a flattop, perpetual grimace, steely gray eyes. All he was really missing was the stub of a cigar sticking out of the corner of his mouth; otherwise he fit the whole sergeant-of-a-secret-armed-religious-force to a *T*. I was happy to notice the rake of Barney's claws across his cheek.

"Where's the book?" He growled at me, or, at least I think he did.

I put a finger in my ear and wiggled it, trying to kick-start my eardrum. My hearing was returning, but there was still a nasty roaring sound that overlaid everything.

"If you're talking, I can't hear you," I said, or, I imagine, shouted, since I could hardly make out the sound of my own words.

He brought the barrel of the machine gun level with my nose. "Listen carefully, miss. I'll ask you once again. Where is the grimoire?"

Lilith uncoiled in my guts, searing me with a whiplike sting. I clutched at my stomach, fighting not to double over. One of the other priests, a black guy with a gorgeous knot of short dreads, had the sense to take a step back and sight his weapon. I wondered if he was their sensitive. The fear I saw growing in his eyes made me fairly certain he was. It'd be such a shame to bury him; I hoped he was smart enough to run.

"Safe-deposit box," Sebastian volunteered quite suddenly. "I have the key with me."

"You've decided to talk?" Leader Guy sounded as incredulous as I felt.

"I hate seeing a damsel in distress," Sebastian said. He tried to shrug, but the arrow's spell, or whatever magic kept him pinned, made the motion more of an awkward jerk.

Lilith slithered back to watchful sleep. My stomach unclenched, and I took a deep breath. Sensitive, however, kept his eyes and his gun trained on me.

Leader dug into Sebastian's coat pockets until he came up with a set of keys. "How do I know this is the real deal?"

"You don't," Sebastian said. I had to admit I was impressed with his ability to keep cool in this situation. Unable to move, Sebastian was vulnerable. Leader Guy could deal him the Final Death pretty easily. "Let me suggest you not kill us in case it's not. You'll want to be able to harass us again if I've led you astray."

Leader Guy actually laughed. It wasn't precisely a pleasant chuckle, more like an appreciative snort. "Interesting bargaining point. You want me to believe in the possibility that the safe-deposit key is a trick so I don't just take it and finish you off."

"More or less correct," Sebastian admitted. "Question is, what's your primary agenda: to kill us, or to bring home the book?"

"What if the answer is both?"

"Then you'll have to let us go for now."

"We could take you with us as hostages," Leader Guy said. "Throw you in the back of the van until we find out if this grimoire is the one we're looking for."

"Yes, that sounds excellent." Sebastian said with a smile that didn't touch his eyes. His hand shook with the effort, but he crooked a finger at Leader Guy. "Come here and pull this arrow out. Maybe we could do a little one-on-one, hand-to-hand. Wonder which one of us would win, mortal?"

Leader Guy took a step back. "We could take your girl-friend."

Sebastian didn't even hesitate. "You're welcome to try."

Leader Guy seemed a touch unsettled by Sebastian's dark smile. He turned and graced me with the what-the-hell-does-that-mean once-over. Then he glanced at Sensitive, who shot back a very serious shake of the head, which I interpreted as *Let's not screw with her.* Apparently so did Leader Guy, who shoved Sebastian's key ring into his own pocket.

"Which bank?" Leader Guy asked.

"Wells Fargo. Downtown."

He checked his watch and frowned. I glanced at the clock on the wall. It was well after eight. The bank was closed for the day.

Leader Guy glanced at Sensitive again, who shook his head more vehemently. Sensitive never took his eyes off me.

"Well, why the hell not?" Leader Guy asked. "She'd make great collateral."

Lilith rippled across my stomach. I put a hand on my belly to hold her back.

"No, Monsignor, she would not." Sensitive had an accent of some kind. I couldn't place it but thought it might be Caribbean. "We'll all be dead."

"Let me get this straight. I can't take the vampire with me because if I remove the stake, he can kill us all. Now, I can't take the girl because she's . . . what? Some kind of ninja Witch?"

Sensitive didn't bother to reply. Or maybe he didn't know the answer.

"You can't counteract her long enough for us to tie her up or something?" Leader Guy wanted to know.

"Too powerful," Sensitive said with a wave of his hand. "Not my kind of magic."

Leader Guy looked really pissed off. I wondered if he would shoot me out of frustration.

"Magic more powerful than the Catholic Church," Sebastian mused. "That's kind of heretical thinking, now isn't it?"

"Soon the Church will be more powerful than any of you," Leader Guy said, gracing Sebastian and me with a meaningful glance. To his soldiers, he said, "We're going. For now." Turning his attention to Sebastian, he added, "If this key turns out to be a fake, we're coming back for you. Both of you."

"I have no doubt, Monsignor," Sebastian said.

To make his point, or maybe just because he was a jerk, Leader Guy removed a small handgun from somewhere under his suit and shot Sebastian right in the stomach. I saw it coming in enough time to cover my ears.

"Good," he said. Motioning to his team, they backed out, their guns flicking back and forth between Sebastian and me. That is, all except Sensitive, whose eyes never left mine until he closed the door.

"I wonder if I should have mentioned that they're looking for microfilm," Sebastian mused, after the sound of jackboots in the stairwell had faded. He tried to sound light, but I could hear the strain in his voice.

I ran over to where he was pinioned to the wall. A dark red stain spread on Sebastian's white shirt where the bullet had punctured his stomach. Blood. *My* blood. He was going to have to hunt up a transfusion as soon as I could get him unstuck from my wall. "You're going to be okay," I said, wrapping my hands around the arrow. It was thick; the shaft had a diameter about the size of a dime. I gave it a pull with all my might. It didn't budge. "Oh crap."

"The bastard had good aim," he said. "And for a bunch of Christians they know a lot about gypsy magic."

"What do you mean?" I asked, while tugging on the arrow using both hands now.

"A stake through the heart. Immobilizes vampires."

I had to admit I fell into the same camp as the Vatican

agents when it came to this sort of thing. "So, it doesn't kill you?"

"No, the killing is done by decapitation or burning. Although I understand you can do something with removing the heart, or maybe it was the liver. . . ."

"You're babbling, Sebastian. I think it's shock." I gave another heave-ho, but my hands slid uselessly over the smooth wood. "I'm going to need reinforcements."

I waited outside for my friends to arrive. I'd tried to stay with Sebastian to comfort him, but he needed blood so badly that my presence was clearly driving him crazy. His fangs dropped, and his eyes intently watched my every move like a wild cat. I felt stalked. I had to leave.

The concrete under my butt felt cold and clammy. Gnats swarmed around the porch light globe. Clouds covered the moon, and the night felt hazy. The street was dark. I tensed every time I saw the red brake lights of a car, but none stopped.

Finally, William showed up twenty minutes later with his girlfriend in tow. She introduced herself as Feather, which I first mistook for Heather, but she politely corrected me. "No, as in bird feather," she said, pointing to the dyed-black goose feather in her hair.

As we sat on the stoop outside waiting for Izzy, I couldn't see how either of them would be much help. Feather was taller than me, but thinner. Her shoulder-length blond hair had pink and blue streaks, and she wore a T-shirt that showed a cartoon cat sleeping on a pile of books which read, "So many books, so little time."

William had changed denominations again. He was in full Druid mode as far as I could tell, including a heavy wool cloak, complete with hood and carved staff. He had the most muscles of any of us, but that wasn't saying much.

All I could think was that I hoped Izzy thought to bring her tools.

Izzy pulled up to the curb with a honk and a wave. I jumped up and met her on the sidewalk. "You going to tell us what this is all about?" Izzy asked as we walked back to where William and Feather sat. "You were awfully cryptic on the phone."

"I know. I'm sorry. There's no easy way to explain this," I said, once they all found a spot on the stoop. I remained standing, anxious to get the rescue under way. "I have a very weird problem. My boyfriend is upstairs and he's . . . uh, well, there's a huge arrow sticking him to the wall, and I can't get it out. Oh, and he's been shot. He's losing a lot of blood."

My friends sat in silence, looking at me. Then they glanced at each other. Izzy spoke first. "You're serious?"

William put his fingers on his temples, rubbing them, as though he suddenly had developed a splitting headache, and who could blame him? "Why is he not dead? Or is he dead? You're not asking us to aid and abet a murder, are you?"

"He's a vampire."

I took a step up toward the door. I looked back at my friends. Feather chewed on her fingernail. William went back to rubbing his head. Izzy gave me a sad, pitying look, like she just now realized that her best friend was completely insane.

Most people, even magically initiated people, didn't believe that real vampires existed. Why would they? After all, vampires were relatively rare. I'd asked Parrish about it, and he'd said something about predators and sustainable food sources. Basically, what I got was that there weren't enough of us to feed a lot of them, and the slow, stupid vamps starved to death.

Of course, everyone had come across a fictional version of vampires at some point in their lives, but most people assumed that bloodsuckers were the stuff of folklore. Even I, who'd dated a real one, had my Hollywood assumptions.

Vampires liked things that way. They preferred people not to know the real deal was out there. They had a good reason for secrecy: it made scoring a meal a lot easier, for one.

Feather cleared her throat. "How much blood has he lost?"

Izzy glanced at Feather and then at me. Izzy's eyes were full of disbelief, but she had a look on her face that told me she'd decided our friendship was more important than the temporary insanity of this situation.

"A lot," I said. Glancing up toward the apartment, I took another step up. "He was shot in the stomach."

She nodded sagely. "He needs to eat. Can you keep him from killing me?"

"Yes," I said with more certainty than I felt.

"Okay. I'll feed him."

William had pulled his hands away from his face when Feather started talking; now he frowned deeply at her. Glasses I wasn't sure he needed glinted under the street-lights. "What are you planning on feeding him, exactly? Chicken soup?"

We all stared at her, waiting to see what she would say.

"Ah . . ." She started, giving me the help-me glance. I shot back the you're-on-your-own-for-this-one shake of the head. "Well," she continued, "I was thinking blood, actually."

William raked his fingers through his lanky brown and green locks. "Where are you going to get blood?"

Now we all stared at William; even Izzy was starting to give me the oh-please-help-him-out-even-I-get-it look. I finally couldn't take it anymore and said, "We need to get upstairs."

I turned and led the way upstairs, hoping the others would follow.

The open door to my apartment revealed the sight of

Sebastian, head bowed, hanging limply where the arrow pressed him between the windows. Black blood soaked the lower half of his shirt and pooled on the floor beneath his feet. Everyone stopped at the doorway and fell silent, but I noticed Feather's breath quickened when she saw Sebastian's fangs.

"Wow," William breathed. "There's plenty of blood *here*."

"Has anybody called the cops? The place looks chewed up by bullets," Izzy asked. "Are your neighbors deaf?"

"Just drunk," I said. In fact, my neighbors' total inability to notice weirdness had made renting this place so appealing to me. I did wonder why the cops hadn't shown yet. Maybe they were on their way. All the more reason to hurry. "Look, can we focus on the task at hand, please?"

"How are we going to get all this blood back into him?"

This time Sebastian cracked an eye open to join us in staring incredulously at William.

"I think I have a handsaw in my trunk," Izzy said, as she turned to head back outside. "That ought to help with the arrow."

I suspected Izzy beat a hasty retreat in order to catch a breath of fresh air and to chew on all this craziness. I'd noticed in the past that she often resorted to physical labor when her brain stopped functioning. I envied her. I tried not to gag at the close, coppery smell. I had an urge to open the window, but I still worried the Vatican might be prowling around with snipers.

"Hospitals have blood. I think he needs a transfusion. I'll call an ambulance." William reached into his cloak for his cell phone. I grabbed it before he could finish punching 911.

"William, he's a vampire. He can't go to the hospital."

"He's going to die, Garnet. Look at all that blood."

"He's dead," I said.

"That's pretty harsh."

"No, I mean, he was dead before the arrow hit him."

William opened his mouth for another protest, and I pushed him toward the doorway gently. "I think Izzy needs help, don't you?"

"Oh, okay," William said in his beta male acquiescent way.

When I turned back, Feather had crept up close to Sebastian. Her hands caressed the contours of his body under his trench coat, and she stood on her tiptoes to lean her lips close to his ear. I couldn't hear the words she murmured to him, but his gaze dropped to the pale outline of her neck, and his jaw twitched as though in anticipation. Her fingers touched his face, his hair, as she slowly drew his mouth to her body.

"Hey," I said. "What the fuck is this?"

Feather jumped away guiltily. "Oh. I thought you'd left. Uh, with William, I mean."

Obviously.

Sebastian shot me a dark, almost angry look. No, there was nothing *almost* about it. He was pissed.

"I thought you understood," Feather said, the cat and the books of her T-shirt smudged with Sebastian's blood where she'd pressed against him. "What I offered, that is. If you'd rather do it . . . I mean, he's yours."

I couldn't decide whether I wanted to recoil in horror at the thought of *Mine?* or to shout, *Damn straight, he's mine!* Anyway, I could tell Feather's offer was lip service; she could barely keep her eyes off Sebastian's fangs she wanted the bite so bad.

I was spared the need to respond by the arrival of Izzy, William, and the handsaw. Izzy, still needing to do, rather than think, crossed the room to Sebastian in four quick strides. "You might want to brace yourself if you can," she told him. "I'm going to try to be as steady as possible."

My eyes daring Feather to move, I rushed over to help hold the arrow and to keep Sebastian in place.

With each ripping jerk of the saw, Sebastian looked a bit paler. "Sorry," I told him.

"You never answered her question," Sebastian whispered.

I ignored him, concentrating instead on watching Izzy's quick, even strokes.

"Are you going to fight her for the privilege?"

Izzy raised her eyebrows but continued to work on the arrow. We were almost through.

"You can have her," I said through gritted teeth. This conversation was reminding me far too much of ones I used to have with Parrish. "I'm not interested in the privilege of being your food."

"I didn't think so," Sebastian agreed darkly, sliding his gaze over to where Feather watched the proceeding with a hungry look. William was talking to her about something, but she only had eyes for Sebastian.

I hated their mutual obsession, even though my brain understood that, for him, at least, right now, this was about survival. He needed the blood to regenerate. It still felt like I was complicit in my own betrayal. Queasy with shame, I insisted, "I want to watch."

Sebastian's jaw flicked, but his eyes stayed locked on Feather like a panther sighting its prey. "Fine."

The last bit of the arrow splintered, and Izzy broke the shaft deftly with a quick twist. She nodded for me to grab an arm, and the two of us pulled. Sebastian inched painfully forward. Another heave, and the arrow cleared enough of his heart that he was able to help us by stepping forward the last little bit. He stumbled, and though Izzy and I tried to support him, Sebastian ended up on his knees. Feather rushed to help so fast, I nearly fell on her.

Sebastian wasted no time. His teeth were at her throat before I could suggest to William that he might want to avert his eyes.

Blood, by the way, pulses out of a punctured jugular in hot jets.

Though Sebastian's mouth covered the wound, he couldn't swallow fast enough. The heat of Feather's blood speckled my face. Izzy screamed. She clawed at the spots where blood clung to her skin, while trying to back away from the quickly spreading viscous mass at our feet. Some part of my mind reminded me that Mr. Saunders, my tenth grade biology teacher, once told us that a person could bleed to death in something like three minutes if their jugular is slashed. However, having that information didn't help me know what to do. If I pushed Sebastian away, Feather would only bleed faster. It's not like I could put a tourniquet around her neck. I had the sinking realization that Feather was going to die, and that I couldn't do anything to save her.

William stood near my bookshelf, his hands fiddling with the miniature cast-iron statue of Kali I picked up at an estate sale the previous month. He looked sick, stricken.

I looked into his lost, dazed eyes and felt inspired. I'd called a Goddess of destruction once when I'd needed strength; I could call on one of healing to help me now. I shut my eyes and remembered. That night had been much like tonight. Vatican agents and blood. No time to really think, to really prepare. I'd just reached out in desperation for someone, anyone.

The world around me evaporated. Time slowed. I felt the coin in my pocket glow red-hot. Astrally, I reached out a hand in desperation. I repeated the words I had that Halloween night, only this time I added a modifier, "*Bright* Goddess, help me!"

Someone took my hand in Hers.

I felt something . . . a presence—the feel of armor on my shoulders, the weight of bronze, and the constant hiss of snakes, of the aegis . . . ? Then it was gone.

Instead, Lilith's voice said through my lips, "Stop, child."

Sebastian looked up, his mouth still pressed to Feather's neck. My hand, of its own volition, slid along her neck until it covered the pulsing tear mark left by Sebastian's teeth. Sebastian looked down in surprise, no doubt as uncertain as I was as to how my hand came between him and his meal. He growled deep in his throat, his eyes narrow with uncontained hatred.

I thought for a moment he would pounce on me next, but he was out the door and gone with the speed only the undead possess. William dropped the statue and sat down hard on the floor.

"Is she dead?" Izzy croaked from where she'd collapsed under the window.

Where it pressed against Feather's flesh, my hand felt tingly with pinpricks, as though it had fallen asleep. Lilith answered for me, "I shall not allow it."

Feather's eyelids fluttered, and her skin against my palm felt warmer than it had any right to be, considering how much blood she'd lost.

"Can I call an ambulance now?" William wanted to know in a small voice.

Izzy was already dialing the numbers. To us she asked, "What the hell do we tell them?"

"Nothing," Feather said, her voice surprisingly strong. I wouldn't have thought she'd have vocal cords intact after that nasty bite. "I'm fine."

"The hell you are," Izzy said, but she clicked off her cell all the same.

"I could use a little orange juice, though," she said.

I felt myself blush deeply, remembering how Sebastian had fed me orange juice just this morning. Was OJ some kind of ritual for the bloodletees?

None of us moved to get her any juice, however.

I kept my hand on her throat, though the part of me that was Lilith knew the danger of Feather bleeding to death was past.

Feather's face looked pale in the soft spotlight cast by the floor lamp, which now stood alone in that corner of the room, surrounded by dust. Previously, it had peeked over the edge of the couch, but the couch was still propped against the wall where the Vatican agents had tipped it. Parrish's makeshift curtains blocked out any natural moonlight and made the room seem uncomfortably close and dark.

Izzy's back pressed against the ruined wall, and she hugged her knees close to her chest. Freckles of blood dotted her cheek. Her eyes were riveted to the pool of sticky blackness that spread out in a circle around Feather's head and drowned the blond strands of her hair.

William sat on the floor, his hand resting limply between his outstretched legs. His head was bowed. I thought he might be hyperventilating until I heard him let out a huff of a sigh. "So," he said. "Vampires are real, huh?"

I nodded mutely. What could I say? He'd seen the evidence. Hell, the evidence was spattered all over three of us, covered parts of the plaster wall, and slowly seeped into the seams of the hardwood floor.

William's eyes stayed focused on the space between his tennis shoes. "Can he turn into mist or a wolf or a bat? It's just that a stake through the heart clearly didn't kill him."

"Crosses don't help, either," I heard Izzy mutter. "I was wearing mine."

"Yeah," William continued, opening his eyes to look at me. "So, like, what's real and what's not?"

I wasn't ready for such an existential question. Besides, I didn't know. Sebastian was a different kind of vampire from the others I'd met. For all I knew he *could* turn into a bat.

Honestly, since the moment he tore into Feather's throat, I doubted I really knew anything about him at all. The look in his eyes had been so cold, so predatory. This was not the herb gardener who listened to Johnny Cash and sautéed bell peppers for breakfast.

I didn't know this man at all.

"Vampires aren't shape-shifters, generally." It was Feather who answered. Entwining her fingers under her breasts, she continued in a psuedo-academic tone. "That's just physically not possible. Conservation of mass and all that."

"Oh. No werewolves, then?" William asked.

"No, not like you're thinking, anyway," she said with an air of authority, which amused me, since I doubted Feather gave a shit about anything beyond her addiction to the bite. Speaking of which, I removed my hand from her throat cautiously. No blood came spurting out. I wiped my hand on my jeans, leaving a smear of brown-black.

I looked down at the smudge. I had to get some cold water on that before it set.

A tear trickled down my cheek. I pushed it away with my forearm and stood up to fetch the bleach and paper towels.

"What about zombies? Are there zombies?" William was asking as I stepped over Feather to get to the kitchen. I didn't even want to hear her answer to that, so I quickly made my way to the sink and turned the faucets on full blast. I used sweetgrass-scented soap to wash my face and hands.

"Me next." I nearly jumped at the sound of Izzy's voice.

I handed her the soap and moved out of the way.

She gave me a terse grimace. "Your taste in men leaves a lot to be desired, girl."

"You're the one who gave me the big thumbs-up the other night."

"Shit," she said, looking up from the sink with a face full of suds. "That was the same guy? I didn't recognize him."

"You're not the only one," I said.

Izzy finished rinsing and vigorously rubbed her face and

neck with the hand towel. She tossed it into the sink and leaned a hip against the counter. "That sounds serious."

"He would have killed Feather."

She nodded. "Yeah," she said, her eyes averted, as though she didn't want to think about it. "I got that."

"That's not cool, Izzy," I said. "I know she offered herself, but he doesn't have to kill to get what he needs."

"He doesn't?"

"No."

"Oh," she said. "That changes things."

It did. I understood that Sebastian had been hurting, but he'd ripped into Feather like a beast, like a monster. I grappled with how to feel about that. Once again, I found myself feeling stupid. I mean, he'd told me he was a killer. This shouldn't be any kind of shock to me; I knew preying on humans was part of his nature. Even so, it was much easier to romanticize the notion of dating a vampire when you didn't have to look forward to scrubbing someone's blood off your floor.

I grabbed the mop bucket and the bleach from under the sink. Izzy found my paper towels and tucked a handful of cotton rags under her armpit. She seemed relieved to have a mission. Thus armed, we marched back into the living room.

The sight of the mess instantly disheartened me. Plaster dust and blood mingled together on the floor, no doubt turning to some kind of sanguine concrete. The hole in the wall gaped like an open wound.

"Yeah, but how does that work?" William was saying, "How can blood really sustain someone after death? It makes no sense."

William sat up a little straighter, engaged in the debate, but Feather hadn't moved from where she lay in the quickly congealing pool of blood.

"Lots of cultures believe blood is the essence of life."

I tried to decide what to clean first. I checked the clock: ten thirty. At least the Vatican probably wouldn't be back tonight.

"Sure," William conceded with a sharp nod of his head, his glasses glinting in the darkness. "But, that's, like, a metaphor. What's the science? How can drinking blood keep a person alive past death?" He stopped himself. "Oh, magic. Right. I keep forgetting it really works."

I set the bucket down next to Feather's head, careful to keep it out of her blood-soaked hair. "Are you strong enough for a shower? You could use one."

"I can help her," William offered, brightening at the opportunity to be useful.

Izzy, William, and I all aided Feather to her feet. William got his shoulders underneath her arm and surprised me by being strong enough to support her weight. I guess hauling all the boxes of inventory around the store had finally paid off for him.

Once I got the two of them situated with towels and soap and directions on how to use the showerhead, Izzy and I bent to the task of scrubbing out the gore. Even after we'd gotten rid of the obvious stains left by Sebastian and Feather, I kept finding tiny flecks of it everywhere: on the windowsill, on the wall, and even on the ceiling.

We'd opened the windows and pulled down a few of the curtains that would need washing. The distant sounds of evening traffic drifted in on a cool, refreshing breeze. Somewhere out there Sebastian hunted.

Parrish, too, for that matter; though knowing him, he'd already scored some more-than-willing-and-able masochist. Or maybe a dozen, all lined up for—what had Sebastian said?—"the privilege"?

I didn't know which of them I found more repulsive at this moment. I pulled off my bloodstained shirt and grabbed something clean from my closet.

When I came back into the room, Izzy had returned from the kitchen with the third bucket of clean water. She put a hand on her hip. "You and Feather. You're not the same, right?"

I wondered how long she'd been stewing over how to ask me that question. "No," I said. "Feather is a junkie. I usually don't let them bite me."

"Usually."

I shrugged, conscious of the exposed bruise on my shoulder. "The bite can be highly . . . pleasurable in the right circumstances."

"Uh-huh."

"Look," I said. "I don't seek it out. That's the difference." More to the point, while I might enjoy the biting, I hated the aftermath.

I stared back hard as Izzy scrutinized me for any signs that I was lying. Apparently satisfied, she said, "All right, then, but you got to stop dating boys like that."

I laughed. "Deal."

Izzy and I righted the couch, and I plunked down in the middle of it, surveying the room. Other than the ten inches of sawed-off arrow stuck in the wood of the window frame and the antiseptic smell that clung to everything, you could hardly tell that there'd been a barely averted massacre here.

Well, except for the big hole in the wall chewed by the machine gun fire. "Crap," I said, pointing to it. "What should I do about that?"

Izzy glanced around my apartment. Getting up, she walked through the dining room area to the kitchen. I thought I heard her rooting around in the tower room. Just as I was going to get up to investigate, she came back hauling a big potted plant—my dwarf Teddy Bear sunflowers to be precise. She set it in front of the hole. The flowers didn't quite cover everything, but they were tall and wide enough to distract the eye.

I nodded my approval.

A knock on the door startled me. "It's the police," a male voice said from the other side.

Oh, like I was going to fall for that one again. I ran to the window and looked out. Oh, okay. This time the car was there.

"Your neighbors called about some noise?"

His voice didn't sound like Leader Guy's at all. Even so, I was reluctant to open the door. Izzy stared at me with eyes that asked, *Shouldn't you let them in?*

I cautiously opened the door a crack. I made a mental note to invest in one of those chain locks. I'd never gotten one before because the building was supposed to be secure, but my deadbeat downstairs neighbors tended to forget to lock the front door.

On the other side was the traditional blue-and-black uniform. A nice shiny, silver badge rested over the breast pocket. An even shinier blond, blue-eyed farm boy's face squinted suspiciously at me. He totally looked like all the jocks I went to high school with in Finlayson.

The officer, whose name appeared to be Heillman, at least according the embroidery on his pocket, gave me a classic cop grimace-smile. "I'd just like to talk to you for a moment, ma'am. Your neighbors say there's been some kind of argument going on up here. Do you think I could come in?"

I almost laughed. Argument? Yeah, like a shoot-out.

"My boyfriend and I had a little fight," I said, not moving from the doorway. I thought I remembered that I didn't have to let the police in if I didn't want to. "He's gone now."

Officer Heillman craned his neck, trying to look past me into the apartment. I wondered if he smelled all the bleach. His eyes strayed over my face and my clothes. I resisted the urge to check to make sure no blood showed.

"You're all right then?" He asked, though it was more of a statement. I almost thought I detected a hint of disappointment from Officer Heillman.

"I am. Thank you for your concern."

He stared at me. I could tell he wanted to check out my apartment, maybe find those shell casings I tossed in the garbage not less than five minutes ago. Officer Heillman's jaw twitched, but he gave me a pleasant enough smile. "You take care."

"Yes, sir, I will."

When he turned to head down the stairs, I closed the door. Tomorrow I'd go shopping for industrial-sized dead bolts and security chains.

I leaned my head against the doorframe, feeling bone tired.

"What are you going to do now?" Izzy had curled herself into the beanbag chair. She raked her fingers through the tight curls at the side of her head.

I'd just formulated an answer when I heard shouting from the bathroom. William and Feather were arguing about something. Great. And the cop wasn't even out the front door by now.

"Shhh!" I hissed.

"You pay them?" I heard William shout. "Are you fuck-ing serious?"

"I'm not talking about this anymore." Feather came into the living room, her multicolored hair wet and featherless. She'd gotten dressed. She'd borrowed my favorite Hello Kitty T-shirt, but since I had her cats-and-books shirt hostage in the basement washing machine, I figured I'd get it back.

She paused to take in the clean floor and the bucket of filthy water we hadn't gotten around to emptying yet. "Yeah, so it was nice to meet you both," she said, as she continued toward the exit. "It was certainly a fun evening."

William followed close on her heels. He wore only jeans, which wasn't actually a bad look on him if you liked your boys thin and wiry. "He nearly killed her, didn't he?"

William gave us both a back-me-up-here look. "This was serious, wasn't it?"

I started to agree when Feather cut in with, "I already told you, I've been bitten much harder before. It's no big deal."

No she hadn't, and everyone in this room, including her, knew it. Izzy shifted uncomfortably in the beanbag. I probably should have been embarrassed for Feather, as well, but my eyes were glued to the two of them like I was watching a soap opera.

"Yeah," William said, clearly hurt. "What you didn't say was how many times."

"A few," she said, shrugging into her coat. "Not that it's any of your business."

"I'm your boyfriend."

"Not my keeper."

Oh, ouch. I managed to tear my eyes away from the hurt expression on William's face.

"Fine," he said. "If that's the way you want it."

"That's the way it *is*, William."

And, with a clatter of rubber soles on stairs, she left.

William let her go. His shoulders slumped, and he pinched the space between his eyes. He'd apparently left his glasses in the same place as most of his clothes.

To Izzy and me, he said, "I don't understand it. Why would she purposely put herself into situations like this, like what happened tonight? Three hours ago I didn't even know there were vampires. Now I find out my girlfriend's addicted to them? It's too much, man."

I didn't want to break it to William that Feather probably had one specific "master" she saw on a regular basis. She probably drove to Minneapolis or Chicago or Milwaukee to see the guy . . . or gal. I hadn't heard that Madison had a resident vamp. Of course, now we had two.

Izzy nodded her head. "I hear you, brother."

"She says she pays for it sometimes."

I glanced up at that. Vampires were ultra-possessive of their ghouls. They kept a kind of revolving harem, bound together in secrecy and need. At least, Parrish had. Another reason dating him had been awkward to say the least.

"Who would pay for *that*?" Izzy asked, looking at the spot on the floor where the majority of the blood had been.

"A lot of people," I said, considering it. "Tonight . . . Sebastian was unusually harsh. A little blood can sustain a vampire for quite a while. Sebastian was wounded. Normally, they don't go for the kill like that."

Nobody said anything for a while.

With a sweeping glance, William took in all of our cleaning. His gaze lingered on the stub of the arrow, as if trying to will himself to remember what had happened here. "You guys worked hard. Looks nice."

"Thanks," I said.

Izzy stood up and pulled at the hem of her blue buttondown shirt. Black stains made a Rorschach pattern on the cloth. "My turn for the shower."

"Borrow anything that catches your fancy in my closet," I offered, though I wondered if any of it would fit. Izzy was several inches taller and a few sizes thinner than me. After Izzy disappeared into the bathroom, William and I exchanged a long look. He ran his fingers through his hair, then sauntered over to sit beside me on the couch.

"So, you're dating this guy . . . this vampire?"

Was I? I had thought so, but now I had trouble envisioning a scenario where I really wanted to see Sebastian again, romantically speaking. I shook my head mutely. "I was."

"He's the guy you played hooky for though, right?" I nodded, but William barely registered my response before going on to his next thought. "Wait. That was this morning. Like, daylight. Vampires can go out in the daytime? That blows."

"Not all of them."

"Well, thank Father Odin for that."

It took me a second to parse out what he'd said. "Aren't you a Druid now?"

"Fuck," he muttered. "I meant, Oak and Ash, or something like that."

I started to stifle a laugh but then decided I needed one, even if it was at William's expense. He smiled along. "Sorry," I said, with a shake of my head. "It's been a long day."

"Yeah," he said, leaning back into the couch. "I was going to see if you guys wanted to hit an IHOP or something, but you look beat."

And I wasn't really in company mood anymore. I understood his desire to debrief, however. "Maybe Izzy would be up for it."

"Yeah," he said. With a lascivious wiggle of his eyebrows, he cocked his head in the direction of the sound of the shower and added, "You think I should go ask her?"

I smiled, but I felt suddenly, inexplicably sad. Maybe it was the brave show of camaraderie William attempted, especially considering his girlfriend had all but dumped him five minutes ago. Or perhaps it was regret—regret that I was pushing away friends who deserved better.

"Let's ask her together when she comes out," I told William. "I've changed my mind. I feel restless. I need to go out."

"Cool," William said.

I nodded. It would be good to get out of this apartment for a while. I was fairly certain the Vatican wouldn't be back tonight, at least. Despite my conviction, I just didn't want to stay here at this moment. The whole place felt violated, unsafe.

Barney came out of hiding to twine around William's feet. He reached down to scratch her on the flat space between her ears. She purred loudly and bonked her head against his hand.

Izzy emerged a few minutes later wearing my black bustier. "Honey, you have the closet of a slut," she said, making all of us laugh.

After William explained our plan and Izzy dug out something more decent to wear, I took my turn in the shower. I changed into a new pair of jeans and a sage-green shirt. I didn't have the energy to work on being pretty. Grabbing the change off my dresser, I dug through my junk drawer until I found a pen and some paper. I wrote a quick note to Parrish. I didn't want him to freak when he came in, smelled the blood, and saw the arrow and bullet holes. He might think I was dead. Or fled again. So I just wrote, "Don't worry. I'll be back."

I started to sign it "Meadow Spring." I stopped when I realized what I was doing. Then it occurred to me that using my Craft name might be enough of a hint to Parrish to keep an eye out for Vatican agents. It was worth a shot.

"Got a new roomie?" Izzy's voice startled me.

"A friend from Minneapolis is crashing on my couch." I resisted the urge to cover the note guiltily, and, instead, grabbed a piece of tape to post it on my apartment door.

"Hmmm."

She sounded suspicious, but she waited until we were all in her car before dropping the bomb. "How did your boyfriend end up stuck on the wall, Garnet? Sex games gone awry?"

I sat in the backseat. I could see Izzy watching me in the rearview.

William looked shocked. "Jesus, Izzy," he said.

She turned down McKinley Drive. Streetlamps illuminated the lakeshore. In the darkness the water appeared black, reminding me of blood.

"The Order of Eustace," I said, not caring how fantastical or crazy the whole thing sounded. After all, both of them had met a vampire for the first time tonight. Finding out about a secret Catholic Witch-hunting order wasn't going to be that big of a stretch. "They take very seriously the verse in Exodus about not suffering a Witch to live. They're after Sebastian."

I left out the part about the grimoire for now. I wanted to see how Izzy and William would react to this information first.

"They hunt vampires?" William asked, turning in his seat so he could face me. He'd put on his glasses, and he was the only one of us who hadn't had to change. "The Pope has vampire hunters?"

"Witch hunters," I corrected. "Sebastian is also a Witch." In fact, I imagined that the fact that the Order had to rely on their "source" for information on vampires was the only reason I was alive. They seemed scattershot in their approach to Sebastian, like they were operating on the fly. I think Sebastian might have been right: they were out of their league when dealing with him."

It worried me that the real estate agent hadn't been part of Leader Guy's posse. For some reason, she scared me more than the others.

"Really? A vampire can also be a Witch?" William frowned. "Being dead doesn't really jive with Wicca, does it? It's not very life affirming to suck people's blood, is it?"

I wasn't in the mood to give William a Pagan 101 class.

Izzy said nothing, just toyed with the cross she wore around her neck. I'd known she was Christian, but I suddenly wondered what denomination. She had always been so cool and open about my magic that I'd figured her for Unitarian.

"There's other kinds of magic besides Wicca," I said.

William nodded, thinking about this. "Are all vampires Witches?"

"No, William, I don't think so," I said. "Sebastian is definitely unusual. That's why the Vatican is after him." That much was certainly true, though they clearly wanted his spell. It occurred to me to wonder why the Order wanted Sebastian's grimoire so damn much. What were they planning on doing with it?

"They might not be Witches, but they must all be magical," William was saying. "Feather said that was part of their appeal."

"She's just into the pain," I said, aware that I wasn't being entirely fair.

William's face crumpled slightly. "Yeah," he said. "I suppose that's true. Explains some things, actually."

I didn't want to know any more about William's sex life, so I asked, "Are you okay? Are you going to see her again?"

William shrugged and turned back toward the front. "I don't know. No offense, Garnet, but I find all this vampire shit hard to take. I've been struggling my whole life to find true magic, and the first supernatural thing I encounter is, well, not something I want to emulate, let's just say. Jesus."

He fell silent, clearly lost in his own thoughts. Izzy chewed her lip and pretended to watch the road.

Though it was probably only about eleven thirty or so, the streets were pretty deserted. Izzy's car was a newish steel-gray Toyota. The detritus of her life lay scattered on the seat and the floorboards. Bill stubs, discarded sweaters, magazines, one blue sequined shoe, and an unopened case of soda. There was nothing dirty—no sticky empty cans or wadded-up fast-food containers—just clutter.

"Is any of the good stuff true?" William said absently. "It just seems unfair, you know? Vampires. Zombies. Killer monks. How about faeries or tree nymphs or angels? Tell me we have those, too."

You wouldn't want to meet a real angel in a dark alley, I thought but didn't say. "Sure," I lied. "There's good stuff."

"Magic works, right? Otherwise the Pope wouldn't want it suppressed."

"Right," I said, and that, at least, was true. "They're afraid of our power. Always have been."

"The Burning Times. Right," William said, referencing the era when the Inquisition burned thousands of Witches—or those just accused of Witchcraft—at the stake. "Well, I guess that's something."

Izzy, who had remained silent all this time, looked at me through the rearview again. "You haven't told us all of it. If this Order or whatever you call it is after Sebastian, they did a piss-poor job of it, especially considering they had him nailed to the wall. How did you manage to get away? Or are they just really bad at their jobs?"

I couldn't look at her when I lied. "I don't know."

Izzy wasn't buying any of it. "Why you keeping the truth from us, girl? We risked our lives to help your boyfriend out, and you won't even tell us the whole damn story."

She was right. I had put them at risk. I knew how hungry Sebastian was when I brought them to my apartment, but I didn't warn them; I didn't even really explain the danger.

"Okay," I said. "The Order left us alone because they were scared of me."

Then I told them everything.

Izzy drove aimlessly through the streets of Madison as I talked. I explained meeting Sebastian, my suspicions about the real estate agent, the grimoire, Lilith, Parrish . . . everything. They sat quietly through the whole thing, never even interrupting with questions when I mentioned I'd run into agents before, in Minneapolis. It was spooky, honestly, especially William's silence. I began to wonder if I'd finally given him too much information and his brain had simply checked out, gone: tilt.

"Uh," I said, after a moment of silence had elapsed. "So, what do you think?"

Izzy just shook her head. William had removed his glasses and was rubbing the bridge of his nose again.

"Shit, Garnet," Izzy said. "Don't you think one vampire boyfriend is enough?"

"Parrish and I are exes."

"Ri-ight." She didn't sound convinced. She pulled the Toyota into a parking spot in front of an IHOP. It was late, but they were still open, catering to the post-bar rush.

"So, there really are Goddesses?" William's voice was quiet. "Again, though, with the dark and scary. Couldn't you have channeled Fortuna or something?"

"At the time, Lilith was an appropriate choice," I said. The one thing I had not told them was the hows and whys Lilith had become attached to me. I preferred not to spell out details.

Or maybe it was more that I didn't like how crazy I'd sound if I just blurted out, *I walked in the door of the covenstead and interrupted the last rites. As the Vatican agents were getting a bead on me, I called out to the most destructive, evil Goddess I could think of. She answered. They died. I woke up later. Yeah, that's right, I don't remember a thing, but the blood was on my hands.* The last part made me sound the most insane. I could almost hear the expert witness for the prosecution explaining how people with split personalities act just like this.

How had my life become so complicated?

"You just drew the Goddess into you?" William asked. I could see the twinkle behind his eyes returning as he contemplated the nature of the Craft involved in my merging with Lilith. "And she stayed? Weren't you in a protective circle? Didn't you ground?"

"No, William, I didn't. I didn't cast a circle, or meditate, or put on a hemp robe and chant." That came out harsher than I intended because he was right. In a moment of panic, I'd thrown years of safe practice out the window. Just like tonight, I'd just reached out to whoever was closest. I suddenly remembered the comforting weight of armor on my shoulder. Had I been close to accepting another more benevolent Goddess tonight?

"Man, how lucky is that?" I looked up to see William in full pout, his arms crossed in front of his chest, chin thrust out. "I can't even meditate without falling asleep."

"Boy, you can barely tie your own shoes without help," Izzy said with a kind smile.

"Hey," he started to protest until he saw her grin. Then, he shrugged, "Yeah, you're right. I suppose if I could finally settle on a pantheon, that would help."

I smiled, but I was still trying to decide if I felt lucky. I knew what William meant. He was asking why some people had an affinity to magic and others didn't. There didn't seem to be an easy answer. I'd learned magic the way a lot of people do: I'd studied books, practiced with the coven, and attuned my senses to the hidden world. But William was right. Some people seemed to get it relatively easily; others never did.

All I could say was that when I looked, I saw—I saw those things other people missed. I'd been able to read auras since as long as I could remember, though I hadn't understood what they were at first. It had nothing to do with my upbringing as far as I could tell. Sure, my parents were open to transcendental experiences, being aging hippies and all that, but they hadn't raised me Pagan, just, perhaps, open. My Romany grandmother was the closest thing I had to a claim at a family tradition, but when I was honest about it, she had been much more interested in teaching me quilting than palm reading.

Maybe affinity to magic was random, like some kind of recessive gene that popped up in some people like violet eyes.

In the darkness and the reflection of the car window, my eyes looked gray. I also looked exhausted. The shower had added a nice fluff to my pixie cut, but maybe because I hadn't bothered with much makeup, my face seemed washed out and old. I sighed. I wasn't up for this. I didn't feel hungry. I just wanted to curl up under my comforter and cry.

Izzy and William must have been having similar thoughts. "You know," said Izzy, starting up the car. "I'm not really in the mood for a burger, are you guys?"

"I just want to go home," I admitted.

"You know what?" William said. "This works out. I mean, if everything you've said is true, Garnet. I've got to get busy. Magic is really out there. I just have to find it. I'm going to meditate for real tonight. Maybe some God will inhabit me."

"Be careful," I said softly, not even certain he heard me over the roar of the engine.

We drove in contemplative silence, me watching out the window for favorite landmarks: the Capitol dome with its gleaming white Federal columns, the carousel, the lakes and parkways. I caught a glimpse of State Street as we passed it, teeming with the post-bar crowd.

"Did you see that?" asked William. "I think that guy was a gigolo."

I craned my head to see.

"In Madison?" Izzy said, "Probably he just had bad fashion sense."

"No, I swear," William insisted. "He was totally doing that 'Pretty Woman' thing with the cars."

"It's called cruising," I suggested, though there'd been something familiar in that swagger. Did I know the guy? I hadn't really gotten a good look at him; it was more likely he just reminded me of someone. "He's probably just gay."

"He could still be a gigolo," William insisted.

We argued amiably about the viability of prostitution in Madison the rest of the ride home.

*   *   *

Despite the open windows, the tang of bleach greeted me when I walked in the apartment door. I frowned at the arrow stub in the window frame and the hole behind the potted sunflowers. I'd really hoped to come home to discover it had all been a silly dream. Fuck.

Both Izzy and William had offered me crash space, but I'd declined.

I sighed in the direction of the smashed plaster and laths. Well, the Vatican now certainly knew about my existence. An earlier version of me would have pulled out the packed suitcase from the back of my bedroom closet, packed up Barney, cut my losses, and run at this point. After what happened tonight with Sebastian and Feather and everyone, I felt a deep bond forming. If I left now, it would be at the expense of my friendships. Last time, when I fled, I had nothing more to lose. Now it was different. I stayed for myself, yes, but for everyone else, too.

I straightened a few of the pictures on the wall, dusted the counters, and did a couple of other tidying/nesting things, and then finally I felt so exhausted that I couldn't keep my eyes open. I retreated to the bedroom, threw off my clothes, and crawled into bed. Barney hopped up on the mattress and snuggled on my chest. I ran a hand along her gray ruff and paused to scratch behind an ear. She purred contentedly. "Tomorrow," I told her, "we hunt Vatican agents."

I sat bolt upright when I heard the door creak open. The Vatican. I reached for the oversized sweatshirt I kept at the foot of the bed and dragged it over my head. A weapon, I thought. I need a goddamned weapon.

Standing up quietly, I glanced at the athame on the altar. It was a cheap reproduction dagger I'd bought at the Renaissance Festival, and it was duller than shit. Though I loved the black-velvet-covered grip, the old thing could barely cut through the apple I sacrificed every year during my Halloween ritual. I had serious doubts it could damage a fully grown priest/assassin. Besides, the Order had turned the coven's daggers against them. The prospect of the same thing happening to me seemed far too likely.

So I dropped it in favor of the fist-sized sandstone rock I'd "liberated" from the Valley of Fire National Park in Nevada during my vacation there a couple of months back. It felt heavy and solid in my hands and serious enough to bash a head in.

Even so armed, I hesitated at the door before opening it. I listened carefully. For a moment I thought I'd dreamed the noise until I heard cursing coming from the living room. Either the priests had extraordinarily foul mouths, or it was Parrish tripping over the pile of books I'd purposely left in front of the door.

Leaving the rock on the altar, I grabbed Sebastian's sweatpants from where I'd tossed them over a chair earlier today and stomped into them.

"I didn't expect you back," I called as I made my way into the living room.

"Ever?" Parrish had found a change of clothes somewhere, and, amazingly, looked trashier than usual. He still favored leather pants, but he now had on, of all things, a tank top that clung to his chest like a second skin. It was very nineties, and it should have looked ridiculous on him, but it was all I could do to tear my eyes away from the muscles of his washboard stomach.

"I thought you'd sell Sebastian's grimoire off to the highest bidder and skip town," I confessed.

He acknowledged the possibility with a faint shrug that set the fabric of his shirt stretching along the hard planes of his pectorals. "I considered it."

I'd wanted to play it cool, but I couldn't help but ask, "Is it safe?"

"Yes," he said, with a glance at a pile of leather in the corner that my brain eventually parsed as saddlebags for a motorcycle. "I even brought it back."

My apartment wasn't the best place for the grimoire, especially since the Vatican would be back in the morning. Even so, part of me was relieved. I wanted it close.

Parrish's finger stroked the shaft of the sawed-off arrow. The soft, almost loving, caress he gave the wood sent goose pimples rising on my arms. "You've had some fun without me, I see."

I crossed my arms in front of my chest lest Parrish see the effect he was having on other parts of me. "I wouldn't call it fun, precisely."

"No? From your note I'd guess you had a visit from our friends from Rome. Besides, this place stinks of spilled blood." His mouth twitched up in an admiring smile. "How many did you bury this time, Garnet?"

"None," I said, unable to keep the bitterness from my voice. Parrish made it sound like a game, but the Vatican could easily have killed Sebastian, like they'd murdered my friends before. "Sorry to disappoint you."

"You never disappoint, Garnet." A seductive smile spread across his face. "I'd tell you how ravishing you look, but you wouldn't believe me."

I laughed, feeling an old familiar warmth stir deep in my breast. Parrish *had* come back. His actions showed me what I had always known: he was trustworthy. I could count on him in a pinch. When the world fell apart, Parrish would be there to help pick up the pieces.

Not like Sebastian. He'd proved to be something other than I'd expected tonight.

"Baggy sweats turn you on, do they?" I said more than a little flirtatiously.

He nodded, very seriously—far too seriously, in fact. "I've never gotten used to women in slacks. It's so . . .

revealing. Without a corset and petticoats, you might as well be bare, the way your body moves under that fabric."

I suddenly felt the absence of a bra keenly. To hide my consternation, I said, "Why are you working so hard, Parrish? You look like you've fed tonight."

Even though the room was mostly dark, other than the lamp I'd left on for him, his skin looked healthier, more natural. I suspected he'd spent his time away in the arms of some willing victim of his many charms.

He gave me the barest twitch of a smile, and his eyes studied the floor almost as though he were embarrassed. When we were dating, I will admit I never liked the fact he had sexual or at the very least near-sexual relationships with his "donors." I tried to tolerate it. I mean, he had to drink to survive. Parrish had usually blustered at my jealousy. The way he studied his boots made me think he seemed almost ashamed.

"What's wrong, Parrish?" I asked.

He sat down on the couch with his arms resting along the back, opened in a welcoming, come-hither pose. With the barely there shirt accenting his muscles and the slight spread of his legs, he looked like a *Playgirl* calendar boy.

Oh, shit. Now I knew who the gigolo we saw on State Street reminded me of: Parrish.

Could it be? Was Parrish selling himself—or his bite— on the street?

No, no way.

But then I remembered what he'd said about leaving Minneapolis. He was out of money. He had . . . what had he implied? Some embarrassing incident caused him to beat a hasty retreat?

"Nothing," he said. It was unnerving that he wouldn't meet my eyes.

I plopped myself down on the couch and settled in the crook of his arm. I wedged an arm around his back and gave

him a bear hug. His skin was cold, like the wind that blew
in over the lakes. He'd been outside, probably for a long
time. The more he'd been exposed to the elements, the
longer it took his body to warm up to room temperature. I
wanted to ask him about it, you know, to find out if he'd
been out doing something debasing in some alleyway, but it
seemed unkind.

"You sure you're okay?" I asked instead.

His voice was quiet and sad. "When your life is a series of
fuck-ups, eternity can be a very, very long time."

"Ain't that the truth? Well, maybe that's what you and
I have in common, Daniel Parrish."

He laughed. "Had a bad day, love?"

"The worst."

"Me, too." I could feel his body relax a little. His hand
came up to play with the short spikes of my hair. "The pixie
cut suits you," he said. "It makes you look tougher. Wiser."

Jaded is what he meant, I thought. I looked more like a
woman who's had fate kick her in the teeth a couple of
times.

"Yeah," I said, enjoying the feeling of his fingers mas-
saging my scalp, the knots in my neck. "It's easier to take
care of."

"Hmmm. Smells good, too."

Irish moss. It was in the stuff I used to give it a little
lift. I returned the favor and breathed in his scent: leather,
sweat, and sex. Parrish was comfortably what-you-see-is-
what-you-get.

I guess that's why I let him kiss me. His lips were chilly
against my forehead, but they were smooth, firm, and familiar. I never forgot Parrish was a vampire. Strangely, I found
comfort in that. His cruelty would never surprise me. He
was what he was.

When his lips touched mine, I pulled him in for a hard,
bruising kiss. I wrapped my hands around his neck and

levered myself around so that I straddled his waist. He looked surprised, but I could tell from the pressure between my legs that he was pleased with the new development.

I probably shouldn't start something like this, but I was still angry at Sebastian, and Parrish was oh so kissable. I pulled back and let my fingers roam through his hair.

And he had such gorgeous hair. The color always reminded me of burnt sienna, a deep, rich red-brown. There was just enough of a curl to give it fullness. I twirled a lock in my fingers, feeling the silky smoothness.

"Do vampires have to wash their hair, or does this come naturally?"

He blinked up at me for a moment and then laughed. "Your moods are mercurial."

"What?"

"You're easily distracted," he said.

"Am not," I said with a faux pout, kissing him again.

"Yes, you are," he insisted between kisses. "It's part of your charm. I often have to work exceedingly hard to keep your attention."

"So you like the challenge?"

"I do."

To show me just how much he liked it, his hands found their way to the front of my shirt.

His palms cupped my breasts, while his thumbs expertly teased the erect tips of my nipples. Not that he'd needed to do much to excite me at this point; warmth had arched along the fibers of my nerves the moment our bodies touched. When he pinched my nipples and gave them a slight twist, it was unexpectedly pleasurable.

I forgot to breathe.

"I command your attention now, don't I?" Parrish smiled, and his fingers continued to pull and stretch.

"Oh, yes," I said. My body rocked against his as he kneaded my flesh. The hollow between my legs ground into the hardness of his erection. My fingernails dug into the skin of his broad shoulders.

"Good," he said, giving me a tweak painful enough that I cried out. "Because I have something I need to tell you."

"What?" I asked breathlessly. Releasing my white-knuckle grip on his shoulder, I tugged my sweatshirt off over my head. The cool air on my naked flesh made me shiver.

"I'm jealous of Sebastian," Parrish murmured into my skin. His hands moved lower to grip my buttocks, while his mouth covered my aching nipples. He sucked hard enough for me to almost wish his fingers were still there.

Almost.

"Sebastian who?" I said between moans. At this point I wanted him so bad it was starting to hurt.

I felt his laugh vibrate against my rib cage.

He pitched forward, and we tumbled onto the floor. Or rather, I fell, and he pounced. His lips locked on mine; his cock, still restrained by his jeans, pressing me to the floor. His kiss was deep and probing, and I responded unthinkingly, passionately. I pushed hard against him, sliding along the shape of him until I dragged out a fierce, low growl. Propping himself up on his hands, he lifted himself from me long enough for me to work the buckle of his belt and unzip his jeans. With his help, I squiggled out of my pants.

Parrish chuckled darkly at my anxiousness.

"Oh, shut up."

It took me a moment to register that Parrish had no underwear on. I got his pants down as far as his knees, and then considered them his problem. I had other things on my mind. My hand stroked the smooth hardness of him, drawing out a shuddering moan from him.

I was so ready that he slid deep inside in one smooth stroke. Even so, my breath caught on his shoulder. My own heat insulated me from some of the shock of the coolness of his flesh. Luckily, Parrish didn't give me much time to contemplate the wrongness of feeling the strength of his erection versus the clamminess of his body. When he started moving urgently, my body responded in kind. Kisses smothered my lips, my hair . . . my throat.

When his mouth covered the space behind my ear, I tensed, expecting to feel the sting of fangs. Though he didn't bite, I twitched as he continued down the line of my neck. Once he reached my shoulder, his lips came back up to nuzzle beside my ear again. "Do you want me to bite you?" he asked, punctuating the question with a hard thrust.

Maybe some quivering part of my inner thigh did, but after watching Sebastian rip into Feather tonight, the only answer could be, "No."

Plus, there was something about how Parrish phrased the question that felt wrong, like it was some part of a rehearsed script.

I managed to say it again, stronger this time: "No."

His fangs had already descended, and I could feel the tiniest prick against my neck. Just when I was ready to fight, he stopped. Pulling back to look me in the eye, he sounded stunned at being denied. "You said no?"

"Yes." Then I realized how confusing that might be, so I reiterated my point: "I said, no."

Parrish nuzzled my neck with his nose. "No, really?"

"Really. No."

"You're already bleeding." The disappointment showed in more than his voice. He'd stopped moving.

I started noticing the icy temperature of his body where it pressed inside me. "Excuse me if I don't trust you to be satisfied with just a taste."

Parrish laughed and then kissed my lips hard. He wrapped his arms around my waist tightly, protectively, the way I secretly loved to be held. Into my ear, he grunted, somewhat painfully, "Garnet, you always leave me wanting more."

I wanted to continue having sex, but it was clear Parrish's interest had cooled, shall we say. With some effort, we disentangled. The space between my legs ached with unspent passion. Parrish looked deeply pained, but he resolutely lay beside me on the floor, letting our bodies touch. One of his hands roamed the curve of my shoulders. Calloused fingertips trailed along the taut skin over my rib cage, slowly moving toward the mound of my belly. I shivered again, only this time with more heat.

His lips hovered over the tiny puncture wound he'd left on my neck. "Your beauty is unparalleled, my love," he whispered in my ear.

It was such a sweet, poetic thing to say. My brain was still fuzzy from the sex, so without thinking I said, "You're such a big romantic, Parrish. How can you stand to do it for money?"

Parrish looked stricken. I covered my mouth as though to shut the barn door after the horses had gotten out. His jaw twitched as he recovered his composure. He stood up, his eyes locked on mine as though daring me to take in his powerful, magnificent, naked body for a moment. Then he stalked into the kitchen. I heard him rooting around in the refrigerator. "I'm starving," he announced.

"Uh, help yourself to anything you find," I said, pulling myself back up onto the couch, feeling stupid and mean. I hate the way my mouth and brain refused to work together. I hadn't meant to bring it up, especially now that I knew it was true.

I heard bottles clinking.

"I'm sorry," I said, loud enough to be heard in the kitchen. "Really sorry, Parrish. It's just . . . it's not like you, is it? Normally, if you were hard up for cash, you'd knock over a bank or something."

I heard a small chuckle. "You can only do that so many times," he said. "A smart thief is judicious."

Locating my sweatshirt on the arm of the couch, I pulled it over my head. I waited for Parrish to say more. Around my knees I wrapped the brown-and-white afghan I picked up at an estate sale for fifty cents.

Parrish sauntered back into the living room. He'd helped himself to a super-green smoothie from my fridge, and then joined me on the couch. He threw an arm around my shoulder, like there was no tension between us. Despite myself, I snuggled into it. Parrish's body temperature might be unsatisfactory, but he still had a comforting solidness about him.

"I'm surprised you didn't sell Sebastian's grimoire," I said.

"I suppose you are," he said. Peeling off the top, he took a long swallow. He made a face. "Ugh. This tastes like wet sod."

"That's because it is. I think the main ingredient is wheatgrass."

"It's unhealthy," he said, setting it carefully on the floor.

"You drank it. Aren't you going to get sick?"

"Until the fangs retract, I can eat or drink anything I'd like without major consequences, remember?"

Interesting. I hadn't realized they were still out.

"You could have sold the grimoire to the Order." I continued, with a glance at the arrow stub in the wall. "They seem pretty determined."

Parrish removed his arm from around my shoulder to pick up his leather pants where they lay half under the couch. He stepped into them without standing. "I didn't contact the Vatican, Garnet. How could I? I know what they are to you."

"But, if you needed money . . . ?"

"You think I'd sell you out for the Pope's gold? You must not think very highly of me."

He stood up to tuck himself in, zip up his fly, and buckle his belt. I knew what I was supposed to say, but our respective positions put me in the wrong frame of mind. I couldn't help but imagine him doing something like this in some dark corner of a sleazy street. "You'd rather sell your body?"

Parrish put his hand on his narrow hips, looking extraordinarily available and sexy all at the same time. "It's nothing I haven't done before."

That surprised me.

When I didn't say anything, he continued. "The exchange of money for sex is the oldest profession. People have done it since the dawn of time."

"People, sure. But *you*?"

His expression, which had started to grow hard, softened a little. He turned away, his eyes scanning the room as though searching for his shirt. I knew exactly where it was. His tank top was under my leg. I pulled it out and offered it to him like a white truce flag.

"I wouldn't think Madison would be a big enough town for . . . all that," I said. "I mean, you're careful about doing too much thieving to alert the police. Aren't you worried about getting caught?"

He took the shirt from me with a shrug. "You know the phrase 'Don't do the crime, if you can't do the time?' Armed robbery is a felony. What I do . . . even if they have a law against it, wouldn't be more than a misdemeanor."

So, it wasn't *precisely* his body he was selling. Even though I still wasn't happy with the situation, things had become infinitely more tolerable. If someone wanted to pay Parrish to bite them, well, that was their problem.

"But . . . why?"

"The job satisfaction is enormous," Parrish said with a smile that didn't reach his eyes.

"No, seriously," I said. "It just doesn't seem like you, Parrish."

He placed a hand over his heart. "I'm flattered. However, perhaps you would be surprised to discover how difficult it

is for a man such as myself to find honest work. I have no
letter of introduction, no résumé that does not include the
words 'highwayman' or 'bank robber,' and an inability to
search for employment during the daylight hours."

I thought about that for a moment. I'd worked third
shift at a twenty-four-hour grocery once, back in college,
but I'd had my interview during regular nine-to-five hours. I
also got the call to come interview during the day. I could
imagine Parrish going through all the trouble to apply for a
job, say as a security guard, only to never get the job because
the call would come while he slept.

Even if he got the job through some miraculous timing,
most places with multiple shifts rotated staff through the
various hours so no one would be burdened with always having to work late night. Similarly, it always seemed there
were mandatory staff gatherings that would happen during
the day. How frustrating to always be off the time zone of
the main culture. "You're probably an illegal alien, too. I'll
bet you don't have a social security card or a passport."

"You'd be right." His tone softened when I didn't give
him grief about his current profession. "I shipped overseas
in a cargo hold. The manifest claimed me as a corpse, which
was in fact true. I snuck in alongside war dead." He gave a
little shrug at the memory. "It was the only way to travel
back then."

"Wow. I hadn't really given it much thought. I'll bet
there are a lot of things you can't do."

"I've heard the Internet makes some things a lot easier
now. I wouldn't know. I've rarely had a place to call my own,
much less the disposable income to purchase a major appli-
ance like a computer."

"Yeah," I said. I could relate to that. The only computer
I used was the one we had at work. I hated how inaccessible
not having one at home made me. To be so cut off from so
much culture and opportunity must frustrate the hell out of

someone like Parrish, who was already an outsider. "No wonder all the vampires want Sebastian's formula."

His eyes narrowed, and his voice was clipped with unfiltered anger. "Yes."

"Are you being careful?" I asked.

Parrish shut his eyes. His jaw clenched. "I don't have to be."

"Yes, you do. I worry about you."

"Do you? Still?"

"Of course." I didn't hesitate. I had never entirely gotten over Parrish, and tonight was a testimony to that. But Sebastian complicated things. Even if I was angry with Sebastian after the whole Feather incident, he was still out there. I'd still have to see him again, one way or another. "But—"

Parrish's finger touched my lips. "I'm desperately in love with you, Garnet. Surely you must realize that by now."

I hadn't.

Parrish apparently didn't notice my stunned expression, or maybe he chose to ignore it. "I could have gone anywhere to escape my debt. A larger, more metropolitan center would have better served my need to disappear. I came here because you were here. Quite simply, I wanted to be with you."

Oh, what crappy timing.

It also ruined a theory I'd had percolating in the back of my head. Since I didn't want to deal with Parrish's unrequited love at the moment, I blurted, "So, if *you* didn't tell the Vatican to look for Sebastian here, who did?"

To his credit, Parrish rolled with the abrupt subject change pretty well under the circumstances. "What the bloody Christ are you talking about? Can't we talk about us?"

Wow. Daniel Parrish wanted to talk relationship. I'd really hurt him. He pulled away and crossed his arms in front of his bare chest.

"I'm sorry, okay?" I said. "You have to admit that our previous relationship was, well, fraught."

I couldn't think of a better word that took into account all the ghoul girlfriends and nights spent alone wondering whose blood—or other things—he was sucking. Being jealous, then feeling stupid for even imagining I could tame a wild thing like Parrish, followed by realizing I probably wouldn't particularly like him domesticated, anyway.

"Garnet," Parrish said my name as if it were a command for me to pay attention. "We just had sex. Wasn't that 'fraught'?"

He had me there. How could I explain all the mixed-up emotions that had inspired my libido? "Um, yes?"

He pulled his shirt over his head in a fluid motion. Then he rubbed his bare arms as though wishing he had more clothes to put on. He shook out his hair, which shimmered in the low light like red gold. He stared at me for a moment, not saying a word. His lips compressed into a thin, angry line. "Forget it."

Forget he said he loved me? I pulled the afghan tighter around my bare legs. "How can I? Parrish, it's not that I don't—" Oops, dangerous ground. There was no denying that my feelings for Parrish were strong. Did I love him? I was certain I had once. I probably still did.

Before I could finish untangling my thoughts, he put up a hand to stop me. "I get it, Garnet."

"You do?"

"Sure," he said. "Don't worry about it."

I frowned at him. I'd missed something. "What are you talking about, Parrish?"

Parrish shrugged. "I'm not the kind of guy who inspires happily ever after. You don't even trust me to bite you. You never did."

Ah. I wondered how long it would take before this old argument surfaced. Well, given the nature of our coitus interruptus, I'm surprised it hadn't sooner. "It's not about trust. If I wanted to give blood, I'd donate to the Red Cross."

His eyes flicked over the bruise on my shoulder. "Yet Sebastian convinces you somehow."

"He took liberties with us," I snapped. "Get over it."

The mixture of horror and surprise on Parrish's face made me mentally replay what I'd just said. I supposed the "us" made me sound a little insane, but I couldn't quite fathom why he still gave me the you're-scaring-me glare.

"What?" I asked.

Parrish continued to gape. Freak the mundane was one thing; I never expected to get the what-the-hell-*are*-you rapid blinking from a vampire. Then I remembered. Parrish had never met Lilith.

"Oh," I started. "When I said 'us,' uh, I meant 'me.'"

His thin lips jerked up in a kind of smirking smile, which was much better than the look of abject fear. "I see. So then the speaking with two voices at once was just some kind of Freudian slip?"

Two voices? Had She spoken through me? "Creepy."

"I'd say."

Here was the part where I should have started volunteering the whole story of how I'd walked in on the Vatican's cleanup crew that night and drew Lilith down from Heaven, or up from Hell, depending on your perspective. Instead, I stared at him blankly, not knowing even where to begin.

Parrish hadn't balked when I'd told him I needed help with some heavy lifting that turned out to be several bodies. He'd even suggested I aerate the bodies with a pitchfork to help the decomposition gasses escape. He could have told me to get lost, especially considering that I'd broken up with him two days before, but he'd been a calm in the storm—a homicide expert to lean on.

Clearly, he must have suspected I'd had some kind of magical help, but he'd let me keep my secrets. He never asked any questions, not even when he saw the vestments . . . or the damage I'd done.

Later, I found out through a tiny mention in the metro section of Minneapolis's Star Tribune that the coven's house had been destroyed by fire. I always suspected that Parrish had something to do with it. I hadn't been able bury my friends in secret. I'd wanted their families to have bodies to claim. I'd insisted we leave them exactly where they lay that night. Parrish made a strong argument about forensic evidence and how Wiccans did not need the sensational press blathering on about what would look like some kind of occult murder scene, but I'd started sobbing so hysterically that he backed down.

Now Parrish sat down on the couch and waited patiently for me to say more, his pale blue eyes scanning my face. A tiny smudge of blood clung to his lower lip. I used my thumb to wipe it off. "That night," I said. "Didn't you ever wonder how I'd done it? Killed all those agents, I mean."

He rubbed the back of his neck with his hand. "Someone tore their throats out."

"You thought I did that?"

"You *did* do it, Garnet."

"My body did," I corrected. "Lilith did the killing. I . . . channeled Lilith."

Parrish nodded, like he wasn't completely surprised by this revelation. He tucked a stray curl of auburn hair behind his ear. I recognized it as his contemplative gesture, especially when he started rolling the tip of the strand between his thumb and finger. "I see," he said. "And She's taken up residence, has She? As a payment for services rendered?"

I hadn't thought about it like that, but I supposed it was true. I'd assumed Lilith had become grafted to me by accident, since I'd built no protective circle, hadn't grounded, called wards, or any of the usual safeguards required for that kind of powerful spell work.

"And now the priests are back," Parrish said with a nod

at the arrow on the wall. "Do they know about your Goddess-in-residence?"

"I think so. At least, they do now. They had a sensitive with them."

"To fight Sebastian," he surmised. "But they found you, instead."

"Yeah, and I still don't get how they knew to look for Sebastian here. I mean, the first agent I ran into might have followed Izzy and me back here, but how would they know he was coming over tonight or that the grimoire might be here?"

No one else besides Parrish knew about the missing grimoire, and he swore he didn't narc. Sebastian would hardly give up his own secrets. Who did that leave? Mátyás.

When Parrish didn't respond, I asked, "Have you heard of a dhampyr?"

"Dhampyr." Parrish rolled the word around in his mouth, as though trying it out for the first time. "Damfear," he said again, slowly, exaggerating the pronunciation. "A dhampyr is the sexual offspring between a human and a vampire. Often said to have magical abilities and an extended life span. Sometimes turns Queen's evidence on his vampiric parent and becomes a hunter," he said. "A complete myth. No such creature exists."

"I met one."

Parrish raised an eyebrow. "You're full of surprises. First you find the formula that will free us all from the night, and now you've met the son of a vampire. Incredible. Next you'll tell me you've met a werewolf."

"No werewolves."

"Good," Parrish sounded genuinely relieved. "So, how is this dhampyr involved with your current situation?"

"I think he's an informant to the Vatican."

Parrish laughed. "The Vatican doesn't hunt vampires."

"They do if they're also Witches."

"Ah, excellent point," Parrish said, then he yawned. "I think I need to go to sleep soon. The sun is coming up."

I glanced at the window reflexively, having forgotten that it was covered in blankets. Even so, I doubted I would see any trace of the sunrise to come. Parrish always seemed to know hours in advance of the actual event. "Do you feel the rotation of the earth or something? How do you know?"

"I checked your clock. And, earlier, the almanac."

So much for the spooky Spidey-sense theory.

"You shouldn't stay here," I said. "I have a sneaking suspicion Sebastian sent the Order on a wild-goose chase. When they come back, they're going to be pissed off and looking for some vampire blood to spill."

Parrish's shoulders drooped slightly. He glanced at the clock again. "It's far too early in the morning to hustle up another place to crash. I'm afraid I'm just going to have to take my chances here."

I winced at how casually he said it. "No. I can't take the risk, Parrish. If you'd be willing to give me a ride somewhere to retrieve my bag, I could give you some cash for a hotel room. I really think you'd be safer elsewhere. I hate the idea of how vulnerable you are during the day. The Order could slaughter you."

He looked like he was going to protest, but then he stopped himself. "So you *do* care."

"Of course."

"Well, then, dear lady, lead on."

Sebastian's shiny black Mafia car sat under the streetlight. Parrish had parked his dusty, battered Harley right behind it. While Parrish fiddled with the saddlebags, I peered in through the windows of the car at the interior.

It seemed ominous that it was still here. I hadn't been

terribly surprised to see it when Izzy dropped me off, but I figured Sebastian would have been back for it by now, what with dawn mere hours away. But then I remembered morning wasn't necessarily a problem for Sebastian. He could doze on a park bench like a transient if he wanted to, I supposed.

I was turning away when my eyes caught the glint of metal. Keys. Wedged in the crevice of the bench seat were Sebastian's car keys. What the hell?

"We must make haste," Parrish said, coming up beside me to put an encouraging hand on my shoulder.

"Yeah," I said, trying not to let the keys bother me. "Let's go."

It was that eerily quiet time, which could be classified as either late, late night or early, early morning. The bars had been closed for several hours, and newspaper deliverers were only just waking up to head to work. Parrish's motorcycle roared down the empty streets, shattering the peaceful slumber of birds not quite ready to herald the coming dawn. The bitter cold moisture of morning dew clung to my face, and I could see hints of a frosty glitter on stretches of grass.

My arms wrapped tightly around Parrish's waist as the wind tore through my hair. We buzzed past closed restaurants, empty parking lots, and lonely, deserted-looking service stations. At this time of day, the highway stretched before us as we rode in the strobe of streetlamps.

Parrish really poured on the speed when we turned off onto the county road, seeming to delight in my panicked clutches at his stomach as he wove around hairpin curves and up and down rolling hills. Moonlight bathed the passing cornfields in silver and gray.

Thanks to Sebastian's wards, Parrish drove right past the farmstead. I yelled over the roar of the engine for him to turn around, and he did, even though he nearly drove past it a second time. After he cut the power and toed the kickstand into place, he asked, "This is the place?"

I saw it now with magical eyes. The image of the abandoned house floated like a ghost over the brightly painted clapboard exterior. "Yes, he's using wards to deceive you."

"Wards?" Parrish stayed on the bike as though he was tempted to leave in a hurry. "He's a Warlock?"

Remembering Sebastian's preference, I corrected, "Alchemist. Remember, that's why the Vatican is after him."

"Ah." There was something of a sneer in Parrish's tone, as if he thought Sebastian too hoity-toity for his own britches.

I started to head toward the door and then remembered the last time I walked in somewhat uninvited. More than wards guarded the house. If I wanted to get to my damn backpack, I was going to have to get past Benjamin, the poltergeist.

"Oh, crap," I muttered.

"What?" Maybe it was the nearness of dawn, but Parrish sounded jumpy.

"There's an attack ghost attached to the house."

"You can't possibly be serious."

And Benjamin might like me less now that I've slept with his master and violated his sanctum to boot. Or maybe Sebastian had instructed Benjamin to keep his distance. "Only one way to find out," I said, and marched resolutely toward the door.

As I walked, I unfurled my magical senses, reaching to unlock them with each step that brought me closer to the decrepit/well-maintained porch. Tangled weeds shimmered and became orderly rows of rosebushes and pansies, then, with a blink, appeared to be cocklebur and milkweed once again.

My body tensed into full-alert mode as I mounted the creaky steps. I closed my eyes and let my magical senses guide me to the door, which, in my mind, pulsed with a dark violet hex of warning. I reached through it carefully and put my hand on the doorknob.

Only to find it locked.

Seventh House

❦

KEYWORDS:

Wrath, Contracts, Bitchiness

"What's wrong?" Parrish's voice startled me. He'd come up behind me to peer nervously at the door. Magic apparently made him twitchy, because I could almost feel him holding back the urge to look over his shoulder. "I saw a flash of purple sparks, and now you're standing next to a brand-new door."

My magical senses showed that the hex had broken where my hand touched the knob. I shrugged. "I'm surprised. The wards are easy to break," I said. "But we're screwed; the door's locked."

He laughed. "That's something I can handle. Do you want him to know there was a forced entry or not?"

"Not."

Parrish turned on his heel and headed back to the bike. At first I wondered if he was going to take a running leap at the door, but he rooted around in his saddlebags for a moment instead. I watched him pull out something that looked like a power drill, though I couldn't see it very clearly in the darkness. He was fitting something on the tip as he came back up the stairs. He saluted me with the jagged bit, before placing it in the lock. "Daniel Parrish, thief cum locksmith, at your service."

The power drill—like thing clattered in the lock for a second. Parrish fiddled and clattered some more. Removing the tool, he put his hand on the knob, and the door swung open smoothly. "After you, m'lady."

I gave him a playful poke on the shoulder. "You just want to make *me* deal with the ghost."

He raked his fingers through his wind-tangled curls and blanched a bit. "Damn straight."

"I had no idea you had such a magical phobia."

"Magic is outside of my realm of understanding," he said simply. "I can't see it. I have no control over it. Yet it is part of my very fiber. It's . . . well, freaky."

"You dated me."

He gave me a sarcastic smirk. "You were part of my immersion therapy."

"Nice."

I'd not yet crossed the threshold. Deciding I couldn't delay any longer, I took a deep breath and stepped inside.

Parrish, my brave protector, backed up to the edge of the porch stairs.

Touching a hand to my womb, I coaxed Lilith from Her slumber. A twinge, heavy, deep inside told me she'd begun to stir into wakefulness. Behind me, I heard Parrish take in a sharp breath. I glanced around wildly but saw no sign of Benjamin. My backpack sat under the coat rack, right next to my foot, however, so I looped the strap around my shoulder and took a backward step out the door. I shut it with a firm click.

Putting a hand, palm up, an inch from the door, I retraced the lines of the hex mark. I poured my own energy into it, and the color shifted into a slightly bluer shade. Then I rubbed my stomach gently as I slowly closed down my magical talents. One by one, I released the elements I'd drawn to me, and inwardly, I felt Lilith groan in disappointment as she settled restlessly back into sleep.

Kneeling on the porch, I quickly opened the secret compartment of my bag. I counted out five one hundred dollar bills and handed them to Parrish. "This ought to pay for a nice hotel for a few nights."

He looked at the money, and I thought for a moment he might protest. With a shake of his head, he tucked it into his pocket. "I owe you."

"It's a gift. Just get yourself somewhere safe before the sun comes up."

He checked his watch. "Then we'd better go."

Parrish raced back to my place like a banshee out of hell. I thought I saw the speedometer top off at a hundred and twenty plus, so I squeezed my eyes shut to the driving wind and tried not to think about what would happen if I simply let go of him. The fear of being thrown off was very present on my mind, since the air tore at my pack, trying to rip it from my shoulders and me from the bike.

I kept thinking that our little breaking and entering escapade had been entirely too easy. Where had Benjamin been? It seemed entirely possible that the ghost had the same allergy to sunlight that Parrish suffered, but we still had an hour before dawn. Last time I'd had a sort of key: Sebastian's business card. Then the door had been open, and Sebastian had been at home. Even so, Benjamin had tried to kill me. What stopped him this time?

Sebastian had said something about the full moon making the ghost more agitated, and, while that had just barely passed, I still would have thought Benjamin would have made an appearance, especially considering that Parrish could qualify as a real threat, being another vampire, a stranger, and all that.

Benjamin's absence made me worry about Sebastian for some reason. With Benjamin's guard down, I found myself wondering if Sebastian was okay.

Then I wondered if I should care. I mean, when last I saw Sebastian he was tearing into Feather like she was some kind of rare steak.

I chewed my lip. I would just feel better, I told myself, if I knew where he was.

Parrish gave me a hurried kiss after he dropped me off in front of my apartment. The sky had just begun to lighten to indigo. Trees took on the hint of dimension, becoming blacker silhouettes against blue. Birds chattered in earnest. I couldn't remember the last time I'd been up this early, or awake this late. I'd forgotten how noisy sparrows were just before the sun came up.

I hefted my bag further onto my shoulder. I could still hear the faint roar of Parrish's motorcycle in the distance, and I wondered if I should've gone with him. The Vatican was bound to make its appearance again soon. I reminded myself of my resolve to stay and fight. I'd ward the bejesus out of this place, and then I'd let Lilith eat them for breakfast.

After dropping my bag just inside the door, I fed Barney some kibbles. As she twined around my legs, I started the coffeepot perking. I'd need some magical supplies for a good, solid warding. My apartment was generally protected against ethereal bad vibes, which clearly hadn't done anything to slow down the Vatican—although since no one had died, you could say the spell *had* worked exactly as intended.

Coffee steam filled the kitchen as Barney crunched her dry food. The first reddish light of dawn shone through the tower windows. Transition. A powerful time for any spell. From my bedroom altar, I grabbed my athame, a velvet pouch containing sea salt, and a glass herb jar of High John the Conqueror root.

So equipped, I headed back downstairs and outside. The air still held a touch of coolness, but the sun had already begun to warm the day.

I stood in the center of the narrow porch, directly in front of the door. Facing outward, toward the street, I cradled the athame in front of my chest. I let out a breath, intending to start deepening my consciousness, and found myself staring at Sebastian's car.

I closed my eyes, trying to visualize the elements, but my brain focused on one thing: he was going to get a ticket if he parked there much longer. My neighborhood was permit-parking only. Worse, it seemed like a major beacon to the Vatican that Sebastian was still here—even though he wasn't.

While I *was* trying to prepare for their inevitable return, I didn't want to open the door only to get nailed by their bowman because they were expecting a vampire. Okay, I probably wouldn't be quite so welcoming to them this time around, but the point was still valid. I didn't want the agents to be coming on any stronger than need be. My element of surprise was Lilith. Thanks to Sensitive they were expecting me to have some kind of serious magical firepower, but I didn't think they knew exactly whom they were dealing with. Even so, she wouldn't do me any good if I were already dead.

My concentration completely ruined, I decided to move Sebastian's car. The keys were still in it; after all, I'd seen them on the front seat earlier. I'd stow it a couple of blocks down, where the parking was less restricted.

I noticed that there was a figure now slumped in the front seat. Though his head pressed into the steering wheel and black hair shrouded his face, I recognized Sebastian.

I knocked on the window. His head twitched as though he wanted to lift it but couldn't. I pulled at the latch. I'd been expecting it to be locked, so I wasn't ready when the door swung open easily and Sebastian nearly tumbled out. I grabbed his shoulder just in time. Baring his fangs, he . . . well, what can I say? He hissed at me, like a cat.

Sebastian looked sick. He still wore the black trench coat he'd donned for our date, but he'd lost the tie. His white oxford was missing a couple of buttons. It was bloodstained and torn. One of the shirttails had come untucked. His usually neat hair was unbound, and it fell in lanky strands in front of his wild, animalistic eyes.

"Help me," he croaked, clutching my jacket with both hands. "Please, Garnet."

"What's wrong?" Could it still be the loss of blood? From what I could see, his stomach had healed.

"The sun," he said, squinting at the bright rays poking through the clouds.

The sun? I gaped at him stupidly. His plea sounded like he'd cribbed it from a B movie. Anyway, daylight wasn't supposed to be a problem for Sebastian.

"Please," he begged again. He looked truly frantic. I could see the damage the sun had already done. Black patches dotted his face. The skin under his eyes and under his cheeks had sunken.

Even so, considering his behavior earlier with Feather, I should have probably slammed the car door and abandoned him to his fate. I guess I'm a soft touch when it comes to vampires in need. I gave his shoulders a gentle shove in the direction of the passenger side. "Fine," I said, trying to sound grumpy. "Move over."

From my previous experience hauling corpses, I knew I couldn't possibly drag Sebastian into the house by myself. I'd call for help, but there was no time, and besides, I'd probably used up all my favors with my friends. Anyway, Parrish had given me an idea. I ran to the house, grabbed my to-go bag, and locked up.

Sebastian had managed to get the key in the ignition before passing out. It still took me several tries to remember how to operate the old car. Sebastian huddled close to the floorboard, as far away as possible from the bands of sunlight that fell across the seat. I shrugged out of my jacket and tossed it over him. Then I popped the clutch, and stuttered and stalled down the street until my body remembered the rhythm of driving a manual.

Luckily, we didn't have far to go. By car, State Street was less than five minutes from my house. So it wasn't long at all until I pulled into the underground parking lot of a hotel a block and a half from the State Capitol building.

I killed the engine once we reached the very bottom row. The car lurched forward when the brake released and hit the wall with a crunch. Sebastian stirred. From under my jacket, he murmured, "You suck at driving a stick."

"Yeah, well, you're alive."

The parking garage smelled dank. Low, concrete ceilings held rows of exposed bulbs and barely concealed wires. White painted stenciled numbers proclaimed that our car occupied the two hundred and twenty-seventh space.

Sebastian pulled himself up onto the seat. He cranked the window down, though I could tell it cost him a lot of effort. Leaning back against the seat, he shut his eyes. "I'm sorry about your friend. Is she dead?"

"No, although she would have been if I hadn't magically intervened. Or Lilith, I mean."

Though his eyes never opened, his brows knit together. "Since when is Lilith a healer?"

"Since I tried to call on another Goddess for help," I said with a shrug. I fiddled with Sebastian's key chain. He had a number of charms hanging from the ring, including a bottle opener. How boy.

"The jealous type, then," he said with a closed-mouth smile.

"I guess so." I shrugged.

"I *am* sorry," he said, still not looking at me. "I should have had more control."

"Yes."

He cracked an eye to look at me. "You've never felt it, have you? When you're wounded like that, it's so strong. It's . . . insanely intoxicating."

I was with him until that last line. "Your excuse is that you were drunk?"

Sebastian laughed a little. "No. Yes. I guess I can't explain it."

"You'd better try, or I'll start this car up and drive you right to the sunniest spot on the beach."

He took in a hiss of breath. "You'd kill me?"

"You wouldn't be the first," I reminded him, though I'm sure he could tell I was bluffing.

Sebastian lifted his head from the rest and turned to look at me. "Then you understand how powerful the desire to allow yourself . . . to be *uninhibited* can be."

I did. A cold twist in the pit of my stomach made me realize how much I did. Lilith sighed contentedly in her slumber. I might have called on Her in desperation, but I didn't rush to kick Her out, now did I? Part of me liked having Her there, and having access to all that destructive power—the ultimate power of life and death.

I didn't like to think about that at all. While I mulled over the implication of his statement, Sebastian had laid his head back down. Glancing over at his aquiline profile, I noticed a particularly angry looking black splotch on his cheek. "So, what happened to you? I thought the sun wasn't your enemy."

"The formula protects me from the sun. The formula's powers are fading."

"The mandrake." So, by not having it in the store, I really had been issuing Sebastian his death warrant. Then

I remembered something else from our first conversation. "Please tell me you don't need to perform your ritual on a full moon."

He sighed so sadly that I knew the answer before he said it. "I do. At least, I think I do."

I looked at his gaunt, pocked skin. "You're not going to last another twenty-eight days."

Sebastian straightened his shoulders. "I might surprise you."

Considering how badly he looked right now, I'd be stunned if he lived to see another day. To be fair, the bullet hole seemed to have healed. "The formula isn't working, but blood still fixes you up, I see," I said, glancing at his stomach.

"Yes," he said. Turning away, he stared out the window at nothing. "Though I seem to need a lot more than I used to."

Yeah, Feather discovered that firsthand, didn't she? Yet I couldn't stay mad at him. It wasn't his fault. His formula had failed him—he was dying.

"So, right now the problem is the sun, I said. So, if you can stay in the dark, you'll be okay for a while."

Sebastian ran his hand along the interior door handle. "As long as I get enough blood, I believe that's true. It's hard to tell, since I was so recently wounded both by the Vatican and by the sun, but I feel as strong as before."

"Just hungrier."

He didn't look at me when he said, "A lot hungrier."

A headache sprouted between my eyes. I rubbed my forehead. "But you only have to last until the next full moon," I said hopefully. "Then you can mix up your formula, and you'll be back to normal, right?"

He shook his head.

Then I recalled what he'd said when we were discussing his corpse-wife Téreza. "But, you've never been able to duplicate it. There's something occult missing in your notes."

"That's why I wasn't terribly angry when I discovered you took my grimoire. I would have preferred you asked, but I have other copies; besides I thought, *Well, if Garnet's looking the formula over, maybe she can tell me what I'm missing.*"

Parrish still had the grimoire. Plus, I'd just given him five hundred bucks—enough to live on until he contacted his London buyer. Oh, and I'd conveniently let him know that the Vatican had interest, too. He was probably snug in some five-star hotel right now, dreaming of all the money he'd make when he started the bidding war over Sebastian's flawed formula.

Or Parrish could just keep the grimoire from me out of spite, since I all but spurned his love for me.

Smart, Garnet. Truly Brilliant.

"Why didn't you just tell the Vatican the formula was fucked up when they had you against the wall?"

"Do you think they'd have believed me? They hardly wanted to believe the truth when I gave them my safe-deposit box key. Anyway, I don't think it would have mattered much. The Vatican has enough arcane knowledge that they could probably fix the problem, if they wanted to."

Suddenly, it hit me. "Great Goddess," I said with a shiver. "They could turn the Order of Eustace into super-vampire soldiers."

"Well," Sebastian said, clearly trying to contain the horror of that thought, "that would certainly make their Witch hunting more effective."

That observation could qualify for understatement of the year. "Yeah," I said.

After a moment more of contemplation, he added, "You do *have* my grimoire, don't you?"

"Uh." He was going to be so mad. "Actually, I . . . uh, loaned it to a friend of mine."

"You *what?*"

Yep, he was mad. Sebastian sat up straighter and turned

toward me so that I was inches from his bloodshot eyes. The mottling of his skin spotted darker with anger. His hands clenched as though he were holding back the urge to shake me or strangle me or both.

I pressed myself against the door of the car in order to put a little distance between us. "Okay, 'loaned' probably isn't the right word. He's holding it for me until things are safer. It's lucky he had it, too. Otherwise, the Vatican would have confiscated it already."

Sebastian seemed unconvinced. "How can you be sure it's safe with him? What if he's some kind of undercover agent?"

"For the Vatican? Hardly. Parrish is a vampire."

Oh shit. The words just flew out of my mouth before I could stop them.

"You gave my grimoire to a vampire?" Sebastian had gone from angry to livid. I swore I could see the veins on his neck about to pop. At least his fangs hadn't descended yet.

Though they probably would. I didn't have a good answer. Parrish had been clear about how valuable the grimoire was to the vampire community. Sebastian must realize it, as well. Worse, I couldn't guarantee that Parrish would return the book, even though he had done so once.

When I didn't say anything, Sebastian's jaw twitched. "You can trust him, can't you?"

Well, no. He was a professional thief. Then again, Parrish had come through when I needed him the most. "He helped me cover up a murder."

Sebastian grunted. "What an excellent character reference. And you thought it was a good idea to give him my grimoire?"

"He's a nice guy, really. I mean, once you get to know him." Oh, shut up, Garnet. You're not even convincing yourself.

"Jesus," Sebastian said.

"I'm sure we can get it back from him," I said. "He brought it home last night when I didn't think he would."

"Home?" Sebastian said. "You're living with a vampire?"

"He's an ex!" Who I slept with—or nearly so—but I didn't want to tell Sebastian that part right now.

"Ex? You gave my grimoire to a murdering ex-lover of yours? What, are you insane or just stupid?"

His fangs were down and in my face. I fumbled for the door latch, thinking that putting a steel door between us seemed like a good idea right now. Sebastian grabbed my shoulder firmly but not so hard it hurt. He seemed to realize that his anger had me spooked, because he took a moment to consciously school his expression into something resembling calm.

"Please, please tell me you can get it back, Garnet."

Could I? Parrish had said last night that he loved me. "I'm sure I can."

He removed his hand from my shoulder and sat back a bit. "I'll have to trust you. I don't see I have much choice. I need that damned book back. It's my working copy. It has all my most recent notes."

I let out a breath I didn't realize I was holding and released my death grip on the door handle.

"You dated a vampire before me?" Sebastian's head tilted backward onto the seat. "Should I be jealous?"

I shrugged. "Parrish was from a different lifetime."

"But he's living with you now."

"It's temporary."

Sebastian shut his eyes. "Isn't that what they all say?"

My cheeks colored a bit. He was right, of course. It was *such* a line. Besides, Parrish had made his intentions clear: he *was* totally trying to worm his way back not only into my bed but also into my heart. "It's not going to be like that," I said. "I have you. Besides, Parrish comes with a set of problems that isn't going to go away just because he's in Madison instead of Minneapolis."

"Oh? And what problems are those?"

The same ones I'll have with you, eventually, I thought but didn't say. After all, if I didn't let him bite me on a regular basis, Sebastian was going to have to feed on other people, too. Hell, he'd already had Feather, and that had made me jealous enough.

"I'd rather not talk about him, if you don't mind," I said.

Sebastian arched his eyebrow without opening his eyes. "Hmmm."

"Hmmm, what?"

"Sounds like unfinished business," he said.

"And never will be—unless I stop dating vampires," I said.

He cracked open an eye. "Oh, so it's a vampire problem, is it?"

"It's a biting problem, Sebastian. I don't like being used as a food source by my lovers, so sue me."

"Ah," was all he said, then Sebastian fell silent. After a moment, I thought he must have gone to sleep. I'd have taken it personally, except that we were well into the daylight hours. The sun was taking its toll on Sebastian's ability to stay with me.

I wondered what I should do. He was safe here. Unless there was a freakish Midwestern earthquake that split open the earth right above this particular hotel, sunlight was not going to find its way through several stories of concrete and steel.

It still seemed risky to just leave him snoozing in the car. A security guard could decide Sebastian was homeless, sick, or at the very least dodging the hotel room rental fees, and call the cops.

The hotel was just upstairs, but we'd have to somehow navigate a sun-filled lobby. And any room would invariably have a window, so there wasn't much point in even bothering—unless I wanted to tuck Sebastian under the bed, which could lead to all sorts of interesting scenarios if the cleaning crew discovered him.

Crap.

Selfishly, I didn't want to miss another day at work. Since I'd decided to stay and fight the Vatican, I wanted to keep my job. I was in danger of being fired if I kept up with the unscheduled absences. I should know; I was the manager.

I poked Sebastian on the shoulder. He stirred slightly. "How do you feel about sleeping in the trunk?"

I explained the various problems with his current napping position, and he finally grudgingly agreed. "I'm going to be a prisoner in there unless you find a way to prop it open. There isn't an internal release."

"No wonder the Mafia loved these cars," I said. In my previous car you could release the seats and crawl into the interior of the car. I knew because on those Minnesota winter days when the temperature hit an arctic minus-twenty and the doors had frozen shut, I'd used that alternate entry in order to start the car.

"It might be too small for me," he said. He opened the door and pulled himself slowly, painfully around to the back. I looked for a trunk release for a few seconds before I realized there wasn't one. Stupid, inconvenient old car.

He did fit, only barely. Though I agreed to come back once night had fallen, we used one of his bungee cords to jury-rig a kind of internal release. Really, the cord attached to the handle of the trunk, wound inside to where Sebastian latched the other end to the spare tire. That kept the trunk closed but also allowed it to remain open a crack.

Praying no one would find the arrangement odd enough to investigate, I left Sebastian with the intention of heading to work. The clock in the hotel lobby told me I had more than enough time to grab a quick breakfast in their overpriced restaurant. It was still o'-insanely-early, not even seven, so I drank several cups of bitter industrial coffee and fortified myself with a cheese omelet and several pieces of soggy, butter-soaked toast.

I started to feel vaguely human again, almost normal. The sun felt warm on my skin, and I whistled the chorus of a half-remembered Toby Keith song as I walked the few blocks to work.

I should have realized that was a bad sign.

The real estate agent was waiting for me when I reached the entrance to the magic shop. I recognized the ubiquitous cut of her fashionable, navy blue business suit a block away and nearly turned to run. But what was she going to do? Murder me on the streets of Madison? That seemed awfully public for a supposedly secret religious order.

Then again, hardly anyone was around. This might be the best time to leave a body out in public for the police to discover later.

Well, two could play that game.

I rubbed my belly to waken the beast within. Lilith twitched across my abdomen anxiously. I felt her strength settle into my bones. My pulse slowed to a measured, calculating, Zen-warrior pace.

It felt good.

Sebastian was right. I did know about the siren call of power.

What was I thinking?

This was *so* not okay.

Eighth House

❧

KEYWORDS:

Death, Sex, and Rock and Roll

I tried to settle Lilith back down, but she wasn't having any of it. With Lilith's calculating eye, my brain registered some new information about the agent. Taller than me by several inches, she carried herself loosely, like an athlete. Her soccer-mom fashion couldn't quite hide the bulge of muscles or the hint of a shoulder holster. I don't know how I'd missed the signs before, especially since those sensible shoes just screamed "nun."

Lilith hated her. So much, in fact, that I found the muscles in my arm twitching as She calculated the effort it would take to grab her and press my thumbnail into the hollow of her throat.

The image was so vivid that I had to turn away. To keep Lilith from killing her, I focused my attention on getting the right key in the door. The keys jangled as my hand shook.

"I'm not interested in any real estate," I said, trying to sound casual.

"You're not feeling the urge to relocate?"

I got the key into the lock and twisted it instead of her neck. The key broke apart with a metallic rending sound as the lock clicked open. The agent had the sense to look nervous when I turned to say, "Listen, Sister Mary Real Estate, I'm not running this time. State your business or get out of my way. I have a shop to open here."

Lilith rumbled through my intestines, gurgling Her desire for a fight.

"I can save Sebastian," she said.

The tension in my shoulders deflated slightly. She'd said the one thing I hadn't expected. Still. "Why should I believe you? What do you get out of it?"

We stood under the awning of the shop. My fingers gripped the mutilated head of the key, which I pointed, somewhat murderously, at the agent's heart. She seemed to notice it, too, and took another step back.

Her mouth twitched, as though she were trying on several responses and not liking any of them. I waited, and as I did, I realized that the agent didn't have an answer, because anything she said would be a lie. She was trying to play me and wasn't doing a very good job of it.

Something in my expression must have given away my thought process. She twisted her lips into an *Oh, screw it* line and pulled a gun from her jacket.

"You will lead me to him," she said, pointing the barrel at my chest.

I'd never seen a real gun so close. It wasn't anything like the toy revolvers the boys in my neighborhood used to pop caps. There was no Lone Ranger pearl handle, no gleam of silver. Matte-black and sleek-looking, it looked vaguely military, although I couldn't say why I thought so.

"Move," she reminded me.

Lilith tingled with anticipation of a fight. *No way*, I thought. Goddess or not, I didn't trust Lilith to dodge a bullet. Besides, neighboring businesses had begun to go through the morning stretches of opening. Bobby from the pizza joint across the street was setting plastic patio furniture on the sidewalk. Too many witnesses here.

I opened my mouth, and Lilith said, "Follow me. He's hiding in the storeroom."

For a trained assassin, she swallowed the bait easily. Carrying a gun can make a person overconfident. The way she purposefully strode through the store, it seemed obvious to me she felt she'd bagged her quarry already. I wondered what rewards the Order bestowed upon her for her kills. Women didn't exactly get to advance in the ranks of the Catholic Church beyond nun. I supposed she could become a mother superior or something like that. Maybe she was simply greedy for monetary gain or fame or some other earthly pleasure given as dispensation for a job well done.

We snaked through the aisles of Witchcraft paraphernalia. Her nose crinkled slightly at the sight of a collection of tarot cards.

"The formula is magical, you know." Despite the danger of the gun, I couldn't help but poke. "You're going to have to go against everything you believe."

"Not everything," she said, brushing her finger on the hierophant on an open tarot deck. The card showed a male figure sitting on a throne wearing vestments, a miter, and leaning on something not unlike the Christian cross. Though my previous association with the image was always of a high priest, when she touched it so lovingly, my first thought was *Pope*.

Christian magic. Catholics had a long history of it. Could most people even imagine hunting a vampire without such tools in hand? Holy water, cross, a wooden stake of oak, maple, aspen, ash, or whatever you believed to be the same wood as that of the Cross. You wouldn't dream of going near the undead without it.

Holy Mother, this agent could be a Catholic Witch.

Suddenly, I could far too easily imagine her higher-ups sending the good sister undercover. As a woman, she'd be much more easily accepted into a coven. Much of her Catholic magic could be explained away by the similarities between the Goddess and the Virgin, some of which were nearly indistinguishable. Hell, her dying and rising God wasn't a particularly new idea for Pagans, either. In fact, we had it first.

She could fit into the magical community pretty easily without even having to compromise her faith too terribly much.

Just imagining that kind of personal betrayal caused Lilith to send a stab of pain across my gut. I stumbled with the effort to keep Lilith from slaughtering the agent right here and now.

Her hand touched my shoulder gently, "Are you all right?"

Something in my eyes made her gasp and make the sign of the cross. I could only imagine what it was like to look the Queen of Evil in the eye. Honestly, I was surprised she had the chance to react. Lilith could have chosen this opportunity to push me away, like She'd done at Sebastian's place. Though, perhaps the planetary conjunction that gave Lilith such unusually powerful control over me had slipped its orb of influence. Or maybe my warding against Lilith had worked better than I hoped.

Of course, if all that were true, I'd intentionally called up Lilith to the surface to do this woman harm.

That disturbed me.

As did the genuine look of concern that the agent's eyes had held when she saw me stumble. I never expected them to be nice. Not even a little bit.

I pulled myself upright, "What's your name?"

"Rosa."

A soft, pretty name for a killer. Why had I asked that? I didn't want to know her name, especially since Lilith was planning on storing her corpse in a box next to the dry ice refrigeration unit until I could find a better way to dispose of it.

Rosa. It made me think of my father's strange obsession with finicky, delicate tea roses the colors of lemons, salmon, and snow. Which led me to wonder about her parents—who they were and why they named her what they did.

Focus on that gun, Garnet. Reminder: this woman is a trained assassin. Who gives a rip if she's got family somewhere? The people she killed had families, too, just like all my friends in the coven.

"Roses and Garnets," she said, reaching out to straighten one of the Kwan Yin figurines in the display on the bookshelf. "Funny how they're both associated with the Virgin, isn't it?

Or the Goddess, depending on your perspective.

"Don't go there," I told her.

She batted her eyes innocently.

I clutched at my stomach, which ached with Lilith's desire to be unleashed. "You don't want to make that connection," I said. "Because I already get it. I know what you are. You recite their Latin spells, preside over their arcane rituals . . . you're a Witch, just like me."

The cross at her throat glinted in the sunlight menacingly. "Not like you."

"No, not like me," I agreed. When pain tore at my womb like a knife, Rosa held out a hand to me.

"We can help you. Exorcise your demon."

Did she know about Lilith? No, I thought, there was no way. All of those involved in that night were dead. Except me.

"Right," I said, trying to sound sarcastic through clenched teeth. "And then what? Kill me?"

She smiled almost beatifically. "All you have to do is renounce your evil ways. Repent, and the Kingdom of Heaven is yours."

It actually sounded reasonable. But, these were the same people who showed up at my apartment last night with a longbow and pinned my boyfriend to the wall, who, had he not been supernatural, would be even more dead now. "Listen, if you want Sebastian, we should probably get moving."

"Yes," Rosa said with, I told myself, a hint of bloodthirstiness.

Because she was evil.

And evil must be destroyed. Right? Was it justice?

Yes, Lilith whispered, that was it. Lilith's warmth spread slowly upwards—no pain now, only hot, angry power. I stood up straight and took in a deep breath, feeling Her heat fill me.

The storeroom was only a couple of steps away. In a matter of seconds, Rosa would realize I'd lied to her about Sebastian's whereabouts, and I'd have to make my move. Lilith's power hummed along my nerves, making my whole body feel taut, ready.

I stopped with my hand on the door. It would be so easy. I could just shut my eyes and let Lilith take care of everything. I wouldn't even be there, not really. All I'd have to do was deal with the after. And I'd had lots of practice cleaning up blood lately.

I allowed my hand to turn the knob, reminding myself that Rosa wasn't just some stranger I planned to ax-murder. She, or people like her, had brutally murdered my friends. Rosa was far from innocent.

Closing my eyes, I pushed open the door.

But I couldn't walk through.

Rosa collided with my backside when I stopped midstride. "Run," I told her.

"What? Why?"

"Because if you don't, She'll kill you."

For a moment, she looked like she might laugh in my face, but then I caught a waver in her bravado, a hint of fear flashing behind her practiced, steely gaze. She proved sensible. Her low-heeled shoes clattered as she turned and fled. The bells on the door jangled as my veins coursed with fire.

I went away . . .

. . . and Lilith destroyed $745 worth of inventory. And broke a window. And most of my fingernails. I found six new bruises on my arms, three on my legs, and the knuckles of my right hand were so painfully swollen I wondered if I'd broken something vital. My back ached, and I'd be spending the rest of the day figuring out how to replace all the stuff and how I would manage without a paycheck for two weeks when I paid the store back for all the damage.

But no one was dead.

And that, I decided in the end, was a good thing, the best thing.

It was not an easy decision to reach, however. I spent a lot of the time feeling uneasy while I swept up broken pottery and bagged shredded bits of several copies of the Welsh folklore cookbook. I'd let a Vatican killer go. On purpose. All because I'd asked her name. Shouldn't I have let Lilith rid the world of one of the bad guys?

Even as I asked myself these questions, I knew I'd done the right thing. It was the more complicated thing, because now Rosa would very likely come back sooner, this time with reinforcements, but I didn't want to have killed her just because it was convenient. Then I really would be the monster they thought they were hunting.

It was one thing to let Lilith defend me from danger but completely another to intentionally lure a victim into a dark corner for the sole purpose of murder, even if that person had a gun pointed at my head. Lilith, I'm sure, would argue that it wasn't so much murder as long-range defensive planning. Kill her now, so you wouldn't be at her mercy later.

Even so, I couldn't say I regretted sparing Rosa's life. It got me thinking about my own culpability in the deaths of the agents I'd summoned Lilith to slaughter in Minneapolis. What else could I have done? It felt right to take a life for a life at the time, but had it been? For the first time since it happened, I wasn't a hundred percent sure.

Propping open the back door, I hauled the garbage, one or two bags at a time, to the Dumpster. I'd just finished the last trip when I ran into William. He was dressed in black and had dyed his hair to match. Under his glasses, I could see badly applied eyeliner.

Holy Mother, he was going Goth.

"Oh my God, Garnet, what happened? Was there a break-in?"

I glanced over my shoulder at the broken window. It would be a good explanation and one that could net the store a tidy insurance settlement, if only I didn't have the corresponding cuts on the backs of my hands.

Yet, what to tell William? I'd told him about Lilith last night, so the truth was an option. But I was embarrassed to admit that I'd done all this destruction myself.

"It's taken care of," I said, which was mostly the truth. I'd eventually have to come clean with Eugene, the absentee owner, but luckily he was currently in Finland attending a spiritual retreat on trancing your way to better profits.

"Man, I can't believe it. On top of everything else," he said, following me back inside. "The stars must be really misaligned, huh? Is this what happens when a bunch of outer planets all go backwards?"

I held the door to the main room open for him. "Partly. But for me it has to do more with Lilith. The asteroid. And the Goddess," I was so tired I was starting to babble. I stopped myself. "The point is, it's not contagious. It's my problem."

"Hey, *su problemo, mi problemo, amigo.*"

"Okay." I smiled. "Help me find a board for the window."

The first part of the day passed slowly. William spent much of our downtime trying to get me to relate the story of dealing with the police over the break-in, but rather than make up lies, I told him I just wasn't up to talking about what happened. When he wasn't asking about that, he wanted more information about vampires.

"So," he said, while polishing the silver jewelry with a cloth, "where do you find real vampires?"

I had the case open and was spraying window cleaner on the underside of the glass top. I ripped off a paper towel and started wiping. "I found my first at an all-night café near Banning State Park."

"In Minnesota?"

"Yeah," I said, spritzing the top. "I was visiting my folks, and, well, there's nothing to do in Finlayson, so I'd driven down to the casino in Hinckley to hang out with some old high school friends who were working there. Anyway, I stopped in the truck stop on the way home. For some reason the place was crowded. I ended up sitting at the counter next to him."

"How did you know he was a vampire?"

"Honestly I didn't at first. We just started chatting and hitting it off, and when I found out he was from Minneapolis, too, I gave him my phone number." In hindsight, that should have been a clue. I was ultra paranoid about giving out my number, but Parrish had worked his glamour on me . . . or maybe just his charm, since if he'd just wanted to lure me off for some tawdry sex and a nip on the neck, he probably could have convinced me to take him out to the back of my car.

"So he was totally passing as average?"

I nodded, though I knew Parrish would bristle at the idea of being referred to as average anything.

"So anyone could be a vampire."

I wasn't sure where William was going with this. "I guess. Why?"

He'd finished his work and waited for me to complete dusting the interior of the case. "I want to find one," he said, leaning back against the register.

"Why don't you ask Feather?"

"I did," he said. "We had a huge fight about it."

"She didn't want to share her needle, eh?" I hadn't meant to say it, but the words slipped out.

Before I could apologize, William shrugged and said dejectedly, "Yeah."

William changed the subject shortly thereafter, and we didn't talk about vampires for the rest of the morning.

I'd just let William go for his lunch break when Má-tyás Von Traum walked into the store.

He stopped the moment he noticed me behind the counter, and he slowly replaced the scrying mirror he'd been examining. Mátyás still courted the Euro-trash look with a burnt-orange silk shirt and black trousers. The bright color should have been gaudy on him, but something about the fabric brought out the vaguely golden cast to his skin and the deep blackness of his hair. Give the boy a bit of curl, tie a scarf over his head, add some gold hoop earrings, and he'd have looked stereotypically gypsy.

"If it isn't Daddy's Witch-for-hire. How nice to see you again," he said, making it perfectly clear he felt it was anything but.

"What are you doing in my store?"

Mátyás gestured at the arrangement of curios meaning-fully. "Browsing, I believe."

"Maybe I can help you find something," I said, trying to play the part of courteous store manager between gritted teeth. "Did you have something specific in mind?"

"Actually, I'm looking for a vampire, about this tall," he said, holding his palm out flat about three inches over his head, "looks a bit like me, only far less attractive, and he dresses like an auto mechanic."

"That's a very popular item," I said. "Had a customer in earlier looking for the same thing."

"Really?"

He managed to pull off "surprised" convincingly. The man should have been an actor, because I suspected Mátyás knew all about the Vatican's interest in Sebastian. Someone had to have told the agents to look for Sebastian at my place. Sebastian must have told Mátyás his plans at some point.

"Yep," I said, feigning interest in arranging the pens near the register. "Actually, there was so much interest in that particular item last night that it was nearly pulled off the shelf permanently."

"That would have been tragic," Mátyás said. "I take it I could still get my hands on it for the right price?"

Lilith twitched restlessly across my stomach. I took a deep breath to contain my swelling anger. "Depends. If you're purchasing for resale, it seems to me you stand to make a tidy profit. Maybe I want to be cut into the deal."

He laughed. "You want the Pope to perform an exorcism on your mother, too?"

I couldn't even begin to form a response to that. I was taken aback on so many levels, but mostly by Mátyás's colossal stupidity. "Do you really think that the Order is go-ing to make good on a promise like that?"

A tiny crease appeared between his eyebrows.

Even though he hadn't said anything, I continued as if he had. "Okay, you're right. Maybe they will. I mean, why would they lure a dhampyr to Rome on a false promise, especially one that'd be transporting his magically preserved Witch mother?"

Mátyás stiffened slightly. "My family is Catholic."

"I'm sure that will spare you. I mean, clearly, they're taking Sebastian's Catholicism into consideration, right?"

He had no response.

"Doesn't matter," I said. "I'm not going to roll over on Sebastian."

"No?" He returned his attention to the display of jeweled palm-sized mirrors. "I'd hoped you were at least a little serious when we started negotiating price. Are you interested in money? Because I stand to inherit a lot of it."

I wondered if there were estate laws dealing with people who were already dead, but I imagined if the government had any say in the matter, as long as you were making money and paying taxes, they'd consider you some sort of version of alive. No, get serious, Garnet. If the government knew about vampires they'd make sure inheritance laws favored the living and that they somehow got double-taxed for being dead.

"If not money, something else?" Mátyás continued when I didn't respond. He turned to look at me. "How about a chance to be off the books? Clear your name with the Order? Surely a life unmolested holds some kind of appeal."

I shook my head, though I had to admit that the idea of not being constantly harassed or chased from town to town for the rest of my life did interest me. "I don't think you have that kind of power—"

I stopped myself. A picture was forming in my head. "But Rosa does, doesn't she? She's your handler. She's the mastermind behind this whole thing. Leader Guy isn't in charge at all, he's just the muscle."

Mátyás looked a little shocked that I knew Rosa by name, but he quickly composed himself. "She's got the ear of people in power. She could smooth things out for you."

"It's not worth Sebastian's life."

Mátyás put his hands in his pockets and sauntered over to stand opposite the register. There was a raised platform behind the counter, so I stood a few inches taller than him. He pulled his bangs away from his eyes and gave me what I imagined passed for a sincere look for him. "Let's get serious, Garnet. You don't even know my father. How long have you two been going out? A month? A week? Days?"

Somewhere around sixty-two hours and counting didn't seem like a good response, so I said nothing and concentrated on not giving away the answer with a blush. "I'm telling you, Mátyás, I'm not interested in giving Sebastian up."

"I could make your problems go away, Garnet. Painlessly."

"So, you're leaving? Great." I turned away and pretended to sort receipts. I got kind of into it for a few seconds, especially when I didn't hear anything more from Mátyás. Maybe it was being in the zone, but a crazy thought struck me. I put down the pile of receipts and turned to find Mátyás leaning against the jewelry case. "You didn't join the Order, did you? Please tell me you didn't."

"I'm not sure why you care, but I didn't. Not yet, anyway. They offered when they found out I was Catholic. Their sensitives get a lot of dispensations."

I leaned in close enough to smell his aftershave or hair product. Whichever it was, he smelled faintly of roses and frankincense. "Don't do it. Seriously, don't fool yourself into thinking you're safe with them. You're always going to be a dhampyr in their minds, Mátyás."

"I, my dear lady, am God's judgment on vampires. Born of a vampire, impervious to vampiric magic. Designed perfectly to hunt and kill that which gave me life. Poetic, isn't it?"

I could see the Church liking the sound of that. "Still,"

I said, sounding less convinced even to my own ears. "Why would they perform the exorcism? Your mother was"—or should I say—"is, a Witch."

"They're thrilled with the idea. The exorcism will drive the demon from her soul. She'll be free to move on. They get two birds, don't you see? My mother will be finally and completely dead."

Of course. He had this whole thing worked out. Even so, I thought he was a fool to trust them. I shook my head. "Maybe so, but you're a magical. The Order is your enemy. Always."

We held each other's gaze for a moment, and I thought by the crease between his eyebrows I might be getting through to him. Then he opened his mouth: "A very impassioned speech, Garnet. Bravo."

"I'd like to say that you and the Order deserve each other, but, you know what? I hate seeing anyone played so thoroughly by them, even a jerk like you."

William chose that moment to return from lunch. The bells on the door jangled. If Mátyás had planned a witty retort it was lost in William's enthusiastic greeting. "Hey! Guess what I just found out? I can hire a vampire for sex!"

Ninth House

❧

KEYWORDS:

Faith, Justice, Misjudgment

William stood in the doorway of the shop looking ex-tremely pleased with himself. I tried to imagine what Má-tyás must see: a scrawny, pale Goth boy with hair so newly dyed that it was, quite literally, shiny.

Then, noticing Mátyás standing beside the counter, William flashed me an oops I didn't-notice-we-had-company face. But the damage had already been done.

"I'm surprised you have to pay," Mátyás said, then turned his cold amber eyes on me. "Or is Daddy charging a fee these days?"

"William isn't talking about Sebastian; he's talking about—" I stopped myself just in time. Did I really want to give Mátyás the ammunition that I had another vampire lover who was probably the hustler in question? No, I didn't think so. I feigned confusion and turned to William. "What *are* you talking about?"

"Oh," he said, clearly surprised that I decided to continue

the conversation. "Well, I was talking to these guys on campus—like, Goth guys—I'd seen them around before but never talked to them. I always thought they were poseurs, you know? So, we were talking about how to find real vampires, and, anyway, one of them shows off his bite marks. Says he got them last night here on State Street in an alley for fifty bucks."

Ugh. I felt embarrassed for Parrish. "Just biting, though, right? Nothing else."

Mátyás shot me a glance, which I pointedly ignored.

"That's extra, I guess," William said with a shrug, though his eyes darted back and forth between Mátyás and me. "Who's your friend?"

"Extra?" I blanched. "You mean, you can buy . . . ?" I couldn't finish it. It was hard enough to think my ex was giving out a bite for cash.

"Oh!" William said, with a nervous glance at Mátyás, who grinned at him mischievously. "Not that I'd want the extra. I mean, I just heard."

"I've heard the bite is plenty sexual," Mátyás said.

William came up to join me behind the counter. He stood just slightly behind me at the register, and all but leaned over my shoulder to stare at Mátyás. The spicy/greasy smell of the Mexican food he'd had for lunch permeated his clothes. "Yeah, that's what the other guy said, too, but he might have been just trying to, you know, freak us out." He reached over me and held his hand across the glass countertop to Mátyás. "I'm William, by the way."

They shook. It was all very manly. "Mátyás Von Traum. Sebastian's son."

"Sebastian? Like, Garnet's Sebastian?" When Mátyás nodded, William added, "Hey, how's he doing? He left in a bad way last night."

"Actually, I'm not sure. He never came home. You don't know where he is, do you?"

William shook his head.

"Nice try," I told Mátyás. "Anyway, Mátyás was just leaving."

"I was," Mátyás said, but instead of turning to go, he leaned an elbow on the countertop. "But I'd love to stay and hear more about this vampire for hire. How old? What's the pedigree?"

William brightened. He put down the prayer beads he'd been distractedly rearranging and crowded near me again. "Hey, I just learned about the significance of all that, but, thing is, he's new to town. No one knows for sure."

"He can't be that old, if he's willing to sell so cheap," Mátyás said with an air of knowledgeable disdain.

"Why not?" William asked over my shoulder.

"Because the older the biter, the bigger the kick," I supplied.

Mátyás nodded. "Yes, any vampire over, say, a hundred, would be worth way more than fifty bucks per. Besides," Mátyás said with a shake of his head, "prostituting yourself seems very New World, don't you think? I'll bet he's just some American who was turned in the late twentieth century."

"Nah, Todd, the donor who I was talking to, he said the guy definitely had a British accent of some sort."

Mátyás shot me a glance, as if to confirm that we weren't talking about Sebastian. When I shook my head, he continued, "He could be faking it. I doubt Todd and this vampire really did all that much talking."

William shifted his feet. I could almost feel the blush radiating from his cheeks.

One of Mátyás's evil grins spread slowly across his face. "Why, William," he said. "I do believe you're a virgin donor."

"Not a donor at all," William said grumpily, turning away. "I'm going to reshelve the astrology section."

Crossing my arms in front of my chest, I gave Mátyás my I-hope-you're-satisfied glare. Mátyás, for his part, looked somewhat disappointed at William's hasty retreat. He watched William make his way to the back of the store, then turned his attention to me. "So, you know this new vampire?"

"I might," I said. "You certainly know how to talk groupie, don't you?"

He shrugged. "You know what they say: find the ghoul, find the vampire."

I had *not* heard that. Frankly, I hadn't known that there were quite so many pat little sayings about vampires. "Where'd you hear that? Vampire-hunting school?"

"Only stupid people with death wishes *hunt* vampires. I merely locate them."

"So, you're a vampire detector?"

Mátyás smiled—a sincere, you-actually-amused-me grin—placed a hand on his chest, and said, "It's my special gift."

That, and being surprisingly charming for a guy I mostly couldn't stand, I thought.

"Let me know if you change your mind about my offer, Garnet," Mátyás said. "I could make the Order forget about you."

"And all I'd have to do is sell Sebastian out? Gee, what a deal," I said.

Mátyás pursed his lips and turned toward the door. "You're going to discover how misplaced your loyalty is, Garnet. I only hope for your sake it's sooner rather than later."

I didn't have a good response to that since "Oh, yeah?" seemed kind of weak and overused. Instead, I watched him leave with my mouth hanging open, which was equally cliché and idiotic.

Goddess, I hated that guy. I rubbed at my sore knuckles,

thinking how much more satisfying it would have been to have bruised them on his jaw instead of on boxes of books.

William wandered toward the front of the store, feather duster in hand. "Thought I'd do the window display," he said. "Oh, and Matt or whatever his name was? He's a jerk."

I laughed. "Yeah, I figured that out."

With a serious nod, William began using the tips of the feathers to tease cobwebs from the corners of the window shelf. I returned to the receipts in earnest.

After I finished, I called a window repair place and made an appointment for them to fix the storeroom window I/Lilith broke. I returned a few calls from various sales reps and placed an order or two. Having unearthed the number of Eugene's hotel in Finland, I stared at it for a long time before deciding that was a job for another day.

William, meanwhile, had dusted, polished, reorganized, reshelved, scrubbed, swept, and mopped everything in sight. "I'm a nervous cleaner," he said, when I caught him standing on a step stool, hand-vacuuming the velvet runners that decorated the top of the Witchcraft book section. "Last night was freaky. I'm still processing."

Thinking while engaging in busywork, an interesting trait. "Is your Mars in Virgo? Maybe Mercury in the sixth house?"

William stepped off the stool with a smile. "That's the Garnet I know and love," he said. "I've missed you."

I nodded, though it occurred to me that the old Garnet he knew was, in a lot of ways, just a persona adopted since coming to Madison. "So," I asked. "You okay?"

"Yeah. My worldview shifts all the time, remember?" His smile was a little thin, however.

I put a hand on his shoulder and gave it a quick squeeze. "Are you really going to hire a vampire tonight?"

He shrugged. "Maybe. I mean, why not? I'd like to see what all the fuss is about."

When I saw Parrish next, I'd have to tell him to be gentle with William.

"Don't look at me like that," William said. "I can take care of myself."

I didn't want to argue, so I changed the subject. My knuckles had been aching, so I asked, "Do you think I'm a violent person?"

The question had been on my mind since my conversation with Rosa this morning. I enjoyed the feeling of Lilith's power moving through me, and I'd been thinking that maybe there'd been a reason She picked me that night I called Her down.

"In what way?"

"Generally speaking. Do I seem prone to anger?"

William rubbed his chin with the tip of the DustBuster. "You've never been an unreasonable or irritable boss, but I've always gotten the sense that it was better not to piss you off. You seem like the sort who could do serious damage, you know?"

I nodded. The real issue was: was that Lilith or me he sensed?

William wasn't finished, however. Without prompting, he added, "Cold, though. Not hot. You seem like the sort to be calculating and methodical when seeking revenge."

Now that struck me as interesting. By Her nature, Lilith was an instrument for crimes of passion, not long-drawn-out grudges.

"Thanks, I guess. That answers my question. Buy us a couple of mochas from next door?" I asked, pulling some cash from my pocket.

"Sure," he said, taking the money. "But I really want to finish this last shelf first."

I went back to my own busywork and thought about William's assessment of my character. Possibly some part of William could see behind the perky Goth disguise to the woman who'd wrapped six bodies in landscaping tarp and dumped them into a cemetery's lake. Lilith hadn't done any of *that*. I'd done it. Well, with Parrish's help. He'd done some heavy lifting and donated some supplies. But other than a few tears of frustration, I'd handled it all pretty calmly. I made the key decisions. At the basic level, the whole thing had been down to me.

I rubbed my knuckles absently. The swelling had receded, and an ugly, blue-black bruise had started to form along the ridge of bone. My hand ached every time I moved a finger. No more punching boxes for me. Not that hitting people was any softer. I knew that from experience, too.

Maybe I *should* repent.

My battered body would probably appreciate a life without the blackouts and the bruises afterwards. It would be all right not to have to bury any more bodies, honestly.

Fine for me, maybe, but I couldn't give up Sebastian, despite Mátyás's warning that my loyalty was misplaced. The Order wouldn't have any mercy for Sebastian. They couldn't leave without a parting shot, quite literally, last night, so I had a hard time imagining they'd allow Sebastian to renounce his evil ways and return him to the fold without any more serious consequences.

I hoped he was okay, stuffed into the trunk like he was. Checking the clock on the wall, I sighed. It was only three in the afternoon. Mother of All, the day crawled when you were anxious for nightfall.

William stuck a mocha next to my elbow. The chocolatey steam tickled my nose, and wrapping my hands around the cup, I brought it to my face to breathe it in deeply. I could almost feel the caffeine scent activating some dead brain cells.

"You look tired," William said. "It's pretty quiet around here. I could mind the store, if you want to go home and catch a few z's."

Just the suggestion of a nap made my eyelids feel heavy.
"I'd like that, but it's hardly fair. You were up just as late as
I was."

"True," he said, adjusting his glasses with the tip of his
finger. "I'm just being gentlemanly."

"That's what I thought," I said, but I yawned despite
myself.

"Aw, go home," he said. "I won't tell the boss. Promise."

I didn't go home, however, because I half expected the
Vatican agents to be lying in ambush for me there. Instead,
I made my way up State Street to the hotel parking ramp.

It was one of those amazing, perfect spring days. The sun
sparkled on every surface—reflected on shop windows,
warming the concrete sidewalks, catching on the edges of
buildings. The sky was robin's-egg blue, without a cloud in
sight. Other than the occasional diesel fume from a passing
bus, the air smelled crisp and clean. I thought long and hard
about taking a detour to the nearby bookstore, Room of
One's Own, buying a paperback or two, and finding a warm
spot to sit with my mocha, spending the afternoon soaking
in the sun and reading.

Instead, I wandered through the hotel, playing at losing
a trail, à la James Bond, and finally made my way into the
low-ceilinged, musty, dark, underground lot, and crawled
into the backseat of Sebastian's car. The smell of exhaust
clung to the back of my throat, and the fluorescent lights
snapped and hissed just outside the window. I set my cup
down carefully on the floorboards and closed my eyes. I
meant to just rest for a moment. Take a short nap.

I was not made for a twenty-four-hour economy, I
thought as I drifted to sleep.

* * *

Sebastian woke me up with a gentle shake. Drool stained the upholstery under my cheek, and I had that hot, achy, I-slept-too-long-in-a-cramped-position feeling tingling just under my skin.

"Mumph," I said. Sitting up slowly, I reached for the cold cup of mocha. I took a cautious sip and found it tolerable. One thing I enjoyed about sweet coffee drinks was that they didn't taste all that bad hours later.

Sebastian sat in the space my head had previously occupied. He ducked behind the seat and gestured for me to do the same. "Someone's coming," he whispered.

"You woke me up for this? Wouldn't we have been safer sleeping?"

"Shhhh."

I heard footsteps then. Clomping jackboots of Vatican agents, I thought, though I didn't at first know why I made that connection. Then it hit me. There were no other noises. No happy how-was-your-day-dear cell phone conversations, no fumbling for keys, or the beeping of a nearby car coming to life. In fact, there were no nearby cars at all. Whoever was coming this way was coming for us.

The scuffling of boot heels stopped. I glanced over at Sebastian, who stared past me at the window over my head.

"I want you to stay in the car," he said in a low voice.

A sweet, chivalrous gesture that was completely misplaced. I put my hand over his. "Don't risk hurting yourself again," I said, giving his fingers a squeeze. "When I step out there, I want you to play dead. Go down and stay down, got it?"

"No, Garnet," he said, and I expected some sexist comment about a manful desire to protect me, but instead he finished with, "I need the blood."

"Oh," I said, letting go of his hand. "Okay. You first."

Sebastian threw open the car door and crouched low. He leapt, pantherlike, onto the roof. Or, at least, I assumed that was where he went, since I couldn't see him through the window when I lifted my head to peer out. Instead, I saw Mátyás standing in the center of the aisle he'd been walking down, arms crossed in front of his chest, glaring at the car roof disapprovingly. He was alone. I peered into the shadows, but I saw no hint of backup in the form of uzi-toting monks.

"Very dramatic, Papa," I heard Mátyás's voice drawl sarcastically. "Ooh, will you be turning into a bat next?"

I was stepping out of the car when Sebastian pounced.

It was a flying leap, skimming over my head. I ducked, but I must have messed up Sebastian's trajectory, because he collided less than gracefully into Mátyás, sending both of them sprawling. Belatedly, I felt the sting of his toes on the top of my head.

Sebastian didn't lose the advantage, however. Mátyás hit the concrete pad with a thunk so loud that I winced in sympathy. Sebastian knelt on top of him. He wrenched Mátyás's head to the side, exposing his throat. I'd been coming up beside them but stopped, immobilized by shock, as Sebastian lowered himself toward Mátyás's pulsing jugular.

He stopped before taking a bite, however. "Tell me why I shouldn't kill you." Sebastian's voice seemed surprisingly loud in the empty parking lot.

"I came to offer peace," Mátyás rasped.

Sebastian chuckled low in his throat, his lips brushing skin. "Eternal peace? I can offer that as well, child."

I didn't realize I'd been inching backward until my shoulders pressed against the slightly slimy wall.

"I'm sincere, father. Ask her," Mátyás said, looking at me, his eyes wild with fear. "I negotiated with her earlier."

Sebastian turned to glare at me. "Negotiated?"

Yeah, that was my thought, but the look in Sebastian's eyes made me consider my words carefully. "Mátyás came into the shop around noon. He wanted me to tell him where you were."

"And here you are," Mátyás said. "Garnet led me right to you."

Sebastian must have tightened his grip, because Mátyás groaned. "You're making a piss-poor case for your life, boy."

"My life?" Mátyás's voice chose that moment to break.

Sebastian stared at him. I couldn't see what passed between them, but Mátyás's eyes frantically scanned his father's impassive face. Mátyás wiggled as though he wanted to reach out to Sebastian.

"You're hurt," Mátyás said. "What's happened, Papa?"

Sebastian broke his dark stare and let go of Mátyás's exposed throat. "It's the formula," he said. "It's weakening."

Mátyás's hands grasped at his father's. "All the more reason to go to them. The Church can help you."

Sebastian seemed to be considering it. His shoulders relaxed, and he sat back a little.

"They can help us all," Mátyás continued. "You. Me. And I'm bringing them Mother. Once the exorcism is performed—"

The glare Sebastian shot Mátyás stopped further discussion. "You're an extremely foolish boy."

"Why?" Even from across the parking lot, I could hear the desperation in Mátyás's voice. "Because I want us to be a family?"

"Your mother is dead."

"Yes, and together we could finally bury her," Mátyás said.

In a strange way, I understood. Mátyás hadn't lied when he said he'd come in peace. He wanted to make things right between himself and Sebastian. He hoped that if the Order could free his mother's trapped soul, then they could put the hurt her undeath caused behind them. It was kind of noble in its own way.

But the Order had nearly killed Sebastian last night. They weren't interested in making happy families. They wanted the grimoire.

"I'd like that," Sebastian said quietly, the dark fire gone from his eyes. "But we don't know that it would work."

"It will. It must."

Sebastian shook his head slightly. "It doesn't matter, Mátyás. We can't give them what they want."

"Why not? Your formula isn't working."

Sebastian laughed. "Only after a thousand years."

"But it didn't work on Mother."

"I never gave the formula to your mother. I tried to turn her with a bite," Sebastian said, pulling himself off Mátyás to sit beside him. If the situation hadn't been so serious, I would have laughed to see them lounging there so casually in the middle of the traffic lane of the parking garage.

Something must have clicked for Mátyás, because he sat up straight. "It could work? They could turn themselves into vampires?"

So we'd been right. That was what the Order intended to do with Sebastian's formula.

Mátyás had sold the Vatican a bill of goods—or, at least, he'd meant to. He'd been banking on the fact that the formula wouldn't work. He was less of a jerk than I thought.

"I don't know, but the possibility is there—a strong possibility," Sebastian said. "I don't know. My experience with Teréza made me gun-shy. I thought a blood transfusion would be enough to save her, and it wasn't. It was a horrible mistake. Once she was dead, it was too late. The formula must be drunk by a living person."

So, Parrish and his vampire friends were out of luck. There was no Holy Grail—no cure for their particular brand of vampirism.

"At least, I assume," Sebastian admitted with a defeated sigh. "I . . . your mother's death shook me profoundly, Mátyás. I had never loved anyone enough to want to live with them forever besides your mother—and then to have things go so horribly awry. It was devastating. And then there was you. . . . I knew that my blood had tainted you, as well. I thought the formula must surely be a curse, a poison. Thus, I found myself unwilling to experiment with any other lives. Not with my blood, nor with formula. I have never attempted to duplicate it."

Mátyás's gaze seemed to linger on the dark splotches on Sebastian's face. "And now you have to."

Sebastian didn't say anything. The answer was obvious, as was his need for blood.

Mátyás turned his head to expose his neck again. "Drink," he said.

Sebastian hesitated, clearly moved by his son's sacrifice. He took Mátyás into his arms in an embrace, and then plunged his fangs deep into his throat. I heard Mátyás gasp in pain and surprise.

I turned away. I didn't like being bitten, and I had no desire to watch someone else being drained, either. I made my way back to Sebastian's car. The car did not come with a radio, I discovered in my search for distraction. I kind of wanted to see what was happening, but just when I thought I'd take a look, Sebastian opened the door and slid into the driver's seat.

He smelled like blood. In the enclosed space, the earthy, metallic odor was unmistakable.

Of course, it smeared his chin and chest.

Sebastian started the car.

"The parking attendant is going to call the cops unless you have some napkins hidden in this car somewhere," I remarked as dryly as I could, given how much my hands shook as I cranked the window down a crack.

When Sebastian steered around Mátyás's prone form, I couldn't help but ask, "Sebastian, uh, everything work out with you and Mátyás?"

"Under your seat," he said.

"What?"

"Handi Wipes." After groping around for a moment, my hands seized on a canister of alcohol wipes. I offered them to Sebastian, who pulled out a fistful. "He's not dead," he said.

Well, I'd hoped the hell not. After all, Mátyás had offered freely. Of course, so had Feather, and she'd nearly died. Sebastian scrubbed at his face, smearing it pink.

"Ugh. You're making it worse. Pull over a second and let me do it," I told him.

Sebastian wedged the car into a space one floor up between a minivan and a pickup truck covered in political stickers. As soon as he shifted into park, I began daubing at his face like a mother hen.

"I'm having some trouble with control lately." He shut his eyes and leaned his head heavily back onto the seat.

"I noticed," I said, finishing my ministrations by buttoning up his coat to hide the stained shirt.

"I can't seem to get enough. The Hunger . . . it's never been so strong before." Sebastian shifted into reverse and pulled the car back out. As we started circling our way upward, Sebastian fished a wallet out of his back pocket and handed it to me.

"It'll be okay," I said lamely. I didn't have a better answer.

"Part of me wanted to kill him, Garnet. My only son."

I couldn't precisely say that I knew how he was feeling, but I'd been wrestling with a similar question all day. I'd decided that what separated the good guys from the bad guys came down to intent. How could I continue to feel morally superior to the Order if I started acting like them? I'd killed, but so far, the deaths on my hands could mostly be considered self-defense. I recognized that in truth, there was an element of something much nastier, like Lilith's— and my—desire for vengeance, but when I'd walked through that door, they were the ones holding the weapons. For now, that's what was important.

If I could stay on that side of the line, I could live with myself.

"I know," I said finally. We were approaching the ticket booth, so I handed Sebastian a twenty. "But you didn't, and that's what counts."

"Yeah," Sebastian said, as he handed the ticket and the money to the bored-looking attendant wearing a Somali-style head scarf. She handed Sebastian his change and mumbled a thank-you without really ever looking at him. I wondered if we could have driven out with his face completely smeared in blood, after all.

"The worst part? I'm still hungry," he said, as we pulled out past the early evening crowds headed to the bars on State Street. "I need that formula, Garnet. You do have it somewhere, right?"

"Yeah . . . about that." I chewed my lip. Finding Parrish might be a problem. Then I had an idea. "Do you remember William from last night?"

Sebastian gave me a concerned glance through narrowed eyes. "I nearly killed his girlfriend, right?"

"Yeah, that's the one." I smiled. "We're going to help him pick up a hustler."

I sent Sebastian two doors down to the clothing boutique for a new shirt while I collected William. The Closed sign hung in the window, and all the lights were out. Though I couldn't see William, I assumed he was in the back counting out the till. I reached for my key to unlock the door, then remembered I'd broken it. I tried the door anyway. I was surprised when it opened, but more so to find William's key ring hanging on the other side. Sloppy and very unlike him. I left it as I found it, intending to drag his butt out here to show him the evidence of his absentmindedness.

As I approached the storeroom, I heard voices. At first, I thought maybe William had tuned the store stereo system to NPR to keep himself company while he worked, but then I recognized a few words, chiefly, my name.

Someone's muscular arm propped the door open slightly. Black T-shirt and the dull glint of the muzzle of a large automatic weapon slung over said shoulder was all I needed to tell me the Vatican agents had cornered William. I pressed myself against the bookcase when the agent turned to glance toward the interior of the shop. I willed myself to melt into the shadows as he scanned the room.

"We have lots of grimoires," I heard William protest. "You want a book of shadows? We have a million blank ones. Or I could order you the book by Curott by that name."

"Don't play stupid with us, Warlock."

Mother of All, they thought William was a player. Which, as funny as that might strike me on one level, meant he was in real trouble. I had to help him, but how?

I thought about the display of wands at the front of the store. There was a silver-plated one with a big honking amethyst crystal at the top that could probably do some serious damage if I swung it hard enough. Problem? I'd only get one shot. These guys had guns.

I always had Lilith, but I'd never asked Her to distinguish between friend and foe before. Somehow I imagined She'd just as likely slaughter William as save him, especially if he bolted, which any sane person would. No, Lilith was a last resort only.

Taking a deep breath, I closed my eyes and felt for the part of me I usually kept under lock and key. Purple light streamed out, filling me, surrounding me. I visualized myself surrounded by a bubble of luminescent purple mist.

"What I need," I told the universe, "is a distraction. Something big enough that all the agents will go and leave William unharmed."

I held my hands out—my right hand, palm up; my left, palm down—and began to spin in a clockwise direction. Golden light swirled in a spiral from my fingertips, creating a kind of magical tornado. I could feel the power building. When it reached its peak, I released it through the top of the bubble and sent it in the direction of the storeroom.

A cell phone trilled.

I could hear a brisk exchange, then: "We have to move out. Now. The source has been attacked. We'll deal with you later."

With a thanks to the universe, I rested my palms on the floor and grounded any excess energy charge I might be holding. While I crouched behind the shelves, the agents hurried past me. I felt rather than saw Sensitive pause, but he followed his compatriots out the door without a word. Once the door closed, I stood up and drew the purple mist back into myself.

When I opened my eyes, William was standing in the doorway of the storeroom gripping a crowbar in his hands as though it were a baseball bat. "Garnet? Is that you?"

"Yes," I said. "Are you okay? They didn't hurt you, did they?"

William lowered the crowbar with a relieved sigh. "Those guys. They were looking for you."

"I know."

"Are they the ones who broke in this morning?"

"No," I said.

"Are you sure? Because they have guns." He stopped his litany long enough to take a breath. Then he added, "They thought I was a Warlock."

I couldn't help but crack a thin smile. "Pretty cool, huh? I guess the new haircut is working for you."

"Yeah," he said, returning the smile with a bubble of hysterical laughter. He shook his head. "Man, I tell you, when outer planets go retrograde, the world gets really fucked up."

"I blame Lilith, myself," I said.

"That's one seriously badass asteroid, then."

I nodded, though I wasn't sure he could see me in the darkness of the store. "Yeah. It is."

"I should probably put the money in the safe," William said. "They didn't take it. I offered, but they didn't go for it. Sorry about that. I mean, the money. I just wanted them to go away. I fucking hate guns. Can I offer a suggestion? The police. I could call the police. I've got a pretty good description: guys carrying guns."

"First things first. Why don't you go over to Holy Grounds? I can take care of things here."

William seemed deeply relieved. "Cool." Then, he said, "Oh, and that special delivery you ordered finally came. I left it by the register."

When I made it to the coffee shop, I discovered Sebastian and William sitting together on the couches in the back. They looked chummy. I was surprised, considering the last time William saw Sebastian he was tearing his girlfriend's throat out. William had probably gone into full denial mode.

Sebastian had found a red silk shirt, which in combination with the black trench coat and jeans made a striking ensemble. He'd also taken the time to comb his hair and tie it back with a black ribbon.

William, meanwhile, looked frazzled. The dye job, which in the daytime had made his hair appear all shiny and new, now looked monotone, like a bad wig, in the artificial light. Sitting next to Sebastian, William seemed skinny and frail. Breakable. I worried that he wouldn't be up for our Parrish-hunting adventure, but all he had to do was point us in the right direction.

"I understand they're quite cold," Sebastian was saying as I approached.

"Yeah, but worth it," William replied. "All the time you were there you never even got your feet wet?"

I plopped myself into a nearby ratty, floral-print, over-stuffed chair. Even though one of the springs was missing, it felt good to take a load off and sink into the upholstery. I was planning on telling Sebastian that the special delivery had turned out to be his mandrake and that I had it with me in the pocket of my jeans, but their conversation distracted me. "What are you guys talking about?"

"Mountain climbing," William said. "Well, specifically, mountain lakes."

I nodded. Business at the Holy Grounds was winding down. Besides William, Sebastian, and me, only a few other customers remained. A barista I didn't know busily wiped down tables and prepared the place for close. I wondered where Izzy was. Had she taken a day off after all the excitement last night? I hoped she was okay. At least the new barista didn't seem bothered by us stragglers.

"You mountain climb?" I asked William. It was unchari-table, but I couldn't quite picture William rapelling down the side of a mountain. I guess I always imagined that sort of thing took more muscles than William seemed to have.

"My dad was into it," William said with a shrug. "He's originally from Washington State. When we went back to visit grandma, we'd hit the mountains for a few days."

"Huh," I said. The boys compared notes about the best trails and equipment and stuff I couldn't begin to under-stand. But we had more important things to consider. "Did your Goth friend say where he found the vampire hustler?" I asked William.

"That's kind of a major change of subject," William noted. He adjusted his glasses with his finger.

Sebastian had been taking a sip of coffee, and he nearly

choked. "*Vampire* hustler? You're not talking about your ex-boyfriend vampire, I hope. The one who has my grimoire?"

"Yeah," I said, chewing on my fingernail in anticipation of Sebastian going ballistic again. Instead, he seemed to be concentrating on taking slow, even breaths. I thought I heard him counting to ten.

"The skanky vamp biting for bucks on the dark end of State Street is your ex-boyfriend?" William asked. The look on William's face implied he hoped I washed after interacting with Parrish.

"Parrish isn't skanky. It must be someone else," I said. Here was something I hadn't counted on. What if there were two vampire hustlers in Madison?

Sebastian shook his head. "Unfinished business," he muttered.

William glanced back and forth between Sebastian and me. "You guys aren't thinking about having some kind of three-way, are you?"

"Eek!" I said, just as Sebastian said, "Good God, no."

"Oh, well, it's just I heard that there's another vamp who'd be up for something like that if the price was right."

My expression must have given away the fact that I suspected *that* vampire was Parrish because Sebastian said, "Nice. So the kinky one has my grimoire? Things just get better and better, don't they?"

"He told me he didn't do that, just bite," I said, and instantly regretted it.

Both of the boys gave me the and-you-believed-that? look.

I frowned. I didn't like hearing Sebastian besmirch Parrish's character, especially since I knew how embarrassed Parrish was by the whole affair. I desperately wanted to defend Parrish's honor, but every excuse I thought up sounded lame. Anyway, Sebastian would just give me grief about still being hung up on Parrish. Instead, I said, "Look, Parrish will give the book back if I ask him. I'm sure of it."

"Are you guys talking about the grimoire that the Vatican wanted?" William asked.

"What do you know about the Order?" Sebastian demanded of William.

"Our Roman friends just paid a visit to the store," I explained. "Apparently, they thought I might have hidden it there."

"Instead you gave it to your ex-lover, who is apparently selling his bite on the street," Sebastian muttered into his coffee. "Where it's much safer."

"Actually, it is," I pointed out. "Anyway, I thought you told the truth about the copy in your safe-deposit box. They should be off the scent."

"I imagine the Order is merely being thorough. They've got the microfilm, now they want the original. Besides, as I said, my most recent notes are on the paper version."

"You made backups?" William asked, then with a sage nod, added, "Sweet."

Sebastian smiled at William. "Yes, a number of them. The original is in a rare book collection in Budapest."

"Smart." William nodded.

"Not necessarily," I pointed out a bit cruelly, but I was still feeling the sting from Sebastian's constant dissing of Parrish. "After all, something must have put the Vatican on to you in the first place."

"You mean other than my son?"

"Yeah," I said. "As neat and tidy as it would be to blame all of this on Mátyás, I doubt the Vatican would invest this kind of manpower to hunt you down simply on the word of a dhampyr."

"Why not?" Sebastian asked.

"What's a dhampyr?" William added.

"Because," I said, hoping to answer both questions at once, "Mátyás is a magical. He's got vampire blood running in his veins. The Order might be operating in conjunction with him, but they're totally playing him, Sebastian. Once they get what they want, he's dead."

"The Vatican wouldn't waste a perfectly capable vampire hunter," Sebastian said with a shrug. "Especially considering he's the only one of his kind."

"Why would they want a vampire hunter, Sebastian? They hunt Witches. And now they're going to use your formula to make an army of holy vampires. I'd think the last thing they want in their employ is someone capable of destroying them. Mátyás is screwed."

Sebastian took a sip of his drink and then made a face. I wasn't sure if his disgusted expression reflected his feelings toward the beverage or my comment. "Shit."

"Yeah," I agreed.

We were all silent for a moment, lost in our respective thoughts. I looked longingly at the coffee bar, wishing that the barista hadn't already closed for the night. I'd kill for a strong cup of coffee. I had a feeling tonight was going to be a long one.

"Are you . . . you seem like you might be very old," William said. Though it was phrased like an insult, William made it sound like a huge compliment.

"Very, very old," Sebastian said with a nod, looking deeply into William's eyes. He'd thrown an arm over the back of the couch at some point, and his fingertips brushed the fabric of William's shirt. For his part, William seemed to lean into Sebastian's touch, like a lover.

"So, is it true what they say? The older the vampire, the stronger the kiss?"

"Oh, yes, definitely," Sebastian said with a smile. And suddenly, when their eyes met, there was that intimacy again. Sebastian's hand now rested quite obviously on William's shoulder. His fingers splayed so one of them could stroke the line of William's neck.

"Wow," William breathed.

"Yes." Like a cat, Sebastian had crept closer to William, even though I swore I'd never taken my eyes off them. Their knees touched. He was totally coming on to my friend. Right in front of me. I knew Sebastian was hungry, but couldn't he wait until they were alone to try to score one on my buddy?

"Hello? Break it up, boys," I said. "We still need to get Sebastian's grimoire."

William blinked as if shaking off a spell. "Oh, right. Uh, follow me. I know the bar the Goth guy was talking about. It's not far at all."

Since State Street is a pedestrian mall and only buses are allowed to drive it, we decided to walk. People—tourists and students mostly, by the look of them—crowded the sidewalk. We actually had to shoulder our way through bodies clustered near entrances to various establishments.

Strangely, a glance one block in either direction showed only empty sidewalks. Apparently people came to Madison to see State Street and nothing else.

I scanned the passing faces for Parrish. I'd given the boys a verbal description of Parrish's vitals, but they both looked baffled at the concept of a Leo's mane, so I didn't have much hope that they'd be able to identify him.

When I had a chance, I grabbed Sebastian's elbow to pull him close. "Back in the coffee shop, what were you playing at?"

Sebastian's pupils had expanded in the darkness. Only a sliver of brown remained. He looked high. "What do you mean?"

I jerked my chin in the direction of William, whose shock of black hair dodged around a gaggle of UW jocks and through a pride of bar floozies. He was only a pace or so in front of us. I kept my voice low as I said, "With William.

All the touching." Sebastian gave me a blank look, so I added, "All the lingering gazes. I thought I was going to have to throw cold water on both of you."

"Jealous?"

"As a matter of fact, yeah."

"Don't be," he said. "I'm so hungry anything looks good."

That was kind of a dis of William, so I gave Sebastian a disapproving frown. "You had Mátyás less than an hour ago."

"Yes, but I didn't take nearly as much as I wanted, and most of that went toward healing the sun damage from this morning." His gaze followed the floozies as they passed, lingering on exposed and ample assets. "That wasn't nearly enough."

Now he not only looked like a junkie, he talked like one, too. Just in the past couple of hours, Sebastian had started to look gaunt, a little too skinny to be sexy, particularly around his cheeks, like his skin was stretched tight over bone. In fact, the word *cadaverous* sprang to mind. I wondered how long it would be before his thirst became unquenchable and he died.

We came abreast of William when we gathered at a corner, waiting for the traffic light to change. A silver Ford Taurus came within a foot of us, and I recognized the driver at the same instant she recognized me. It was Rosa.

Brake lights flashed. I grabbed Sebastian's hand, and then nearly dropped it. His skin had already become icy cold.

"Run," I shouted to William, who still stood on the corner, while trying to drag an uncooperative vampire into oncoming traffic. "Vatican."

A couple of stoner college types we'd been standing next to gave me a wide-eyed stare at the last part of my warning, but everyone started screaming when Rosa stepped out of her vehicle and aimed a .45 in our general direction.

And William coldcocked her.

There was a crunch of bone, which could have been his knuckles, but the effect was the same: Rosa went from shocked to unconscious. William looked at his fist like he'd never seen it before.

Sebastian and I ran back over and pushed our way through the growing crowd of curious onlookers. Rosa's nose had caved in. Blood covered her face and a large portion of her power suit.

"I think I broke my knuckles," William said quietly, as if to himself.

Sebastian reached down to relieve Rosa of her gun. I noticed him pause at the sight of all that fresh blood. His hand hovered over her wet cheek, and I thought for a moment he might dip his finger for a taste. He stopped himself and pocketed the gun instead. Rosa moaned.

I looked through the crowd for someone with a cell phone. I spotted a geek boy with a utility belt containing both a cell and a BlackBerry and Goddess knew what all else. "You," I said, "Call 911."

Then I clasped hands with William and Sebastian and dragged them away from Rosa's body.

We ducked into the first bar that we came to. I ensconced the boys at a dark corner table and flagged down a harried-looking waiter. The waiter gave us a long, disapproving look. I could only imagine what he thought of us: two Goths and a pale guy. We must have seemed like a matching set, all in black. "I'm starving," Sebastian muttered.

"Honey, I doubt we have what you're looking for," the waiter said.

"Oh?" I asked, after exchanging glances with William. "What do you think we're looking for?"

"Two doors down," he said, with a sardonically arched

eyebrow. When we didn't get whatever hint he tossed us, he put a fist on his narrow hip. "Look around, darlings, this is a sports bar. You'll like the atmosphere at the Cavern much better."

The Cavern? That sounded cheesy. Sadly, I could totally see Parrish hanging out at a place like that.

Sebastian, however, looked like he was ready to pick a fight with our judgmental waiter.

"Thanks for the tip," I said.

"Rude little prick," Sebastian was muttering, as we pushed ourselves back out into the ebb and flow of State Street. "I should have eaten him."

"I think I broke my knuckles," William said.

I was a little disappointed to be on the move again, since I was worried that William had slipped into some kind of post-violence shock.

"It'll be okay," I said to both of them. My own bruised hands ached in sympathy for William. To Sebastian I said, "Can you give William one of your cards? It's been such a crazy night, I'm worried we're going to get separated."

"Sure," Sebastian said, handing one over.

The Cavern proved easy to spot. The exterior of the windowless, one-story building was painted black. The throb of industrial metal pulsed through closed doors. Pale, skinny boys with lots of tattoos and leather pants hung around the entrance, trying to look menacing. Their withering glances might have worked on me if I hadn't been holding hands with a thousand-year-old bloodsucker and amazing beta-male punching guy.

I ignored the not-so-scary boys and pushed open the door. Before my voice was lost in the relentless pound of the music, I said, "We'll collect the grimoire from Parrish, and then we can all go home and go to bed."

"Sounds good," I heard William say.

At the door, a grim-faced, bald bouncer collected a five-dollar-apiece cover charge and then waved us into the dark, smoke-filled interior.

The Cavern was misnamed. The place bore more resemblance to an amphitheater.

On the level we entered there was a coat check and the long, dark wood bar you might find in any tavern in Wisconsin. Neon beer advertisements reflected off a rear mirror and rows of bottles of hard liquor. That was where the similarity to a typical club ended.

A sunken stage occupied the center of the room. On progressively lower tiers, tables and chairs had been arranged. At the very bottom, just above stage level, stadium-style seating began.

The place was packed. I couldn't see a single seat unoccupied. Apparently, we were relegated to the standing-room-only section. People crowded around a metal railing, watching the show. I poked my head around a friendly looking shoulder to see what all the fuss was about.

I'd thought finding Parrish in the crowd would be difficult. I should have known he'd find a way to be center stage. Really, he was such a Leo.

I heard a sharp intake of breath as Sebastian came up beside me. "Dear God."

"That's for real," William added. "Isn't it?"

It was.

In the middle of a red-tinted spotlight, Parrish stood. His teeth sank deeply into the exposed throat of a bound, gagged, and very fetishized victim. That is to say, there was lots of leather, buckles, harnesses, piercings, and other S&M/B&D gear.

Two steel poles had been sunk into the stage floor. The woman was stretched tautly between them, secured by chains and handcuffs that rattled every time she flinched.

She wasn't exactly naked, but she might as well have been. The corset she wore pushed her already ample breasts into a jiggling mound of flesh. There was a cutaway that would have exposed areolae, but, apparently in deference to decency laws, a nipple shield with corresponding painful-looking clamps covered the naughty bits.

At least at the top.

The thong exposed an amazing lack of hair between her legs. I'm sure I was supposed to be titillated by the sight, but all I could think was: *Wow, she must have paid a fortune for electrolysis.* I was also sure the people in the seats behind her must have had a great view of her mostly naked buttocks.

Then there were the thigh-high boots. Even though the heels on them looked like they could have been registered as torture devices, I was actually jealous—they looked cool.

Yet, in my opinion, Parrish was even sexier. He had on his form-hugging leather pants, but he was bare chested. Always an excellent fashion choice for him. The stage lights cast deep shadows that only highlighted the angles and muscles of his body.

As we watched, Parrish moved around his victim's body, slowly puncturing exposed flesh with sharp canines. Tiny droplets of blood ran from each carefully placed wound. The woman shivered and pushed against the restraints at every bite.

Even so, I'd say she was enjoying it. So was the crowd.

I have to admit I must have gotten into it myself, because I never noticed Sebastian leaving my side. Like the rest of the room, I watched in surprise as Sebastian leapt over the stadium seats to land behind Parrish. Grabbing a fistful of hair, Sebastian forcibly pulled Parrish from his victim.

Then he slapped him.

I don't know what I'd been expecting, probably something more on the lines of a William-style roundhouse. Instead,

Sebastian tapped Parrish with a courtly, gentlemanly, I-challenge-you-to-a-duel, girly-man smack on the cheek.

The two men exchanged words. I strained to hear them over the booming bass and the angry shouts of the spectators. The woman strapped in a compromising position on the stage struggled furiously against her bonds, but she was completely forgotten when Parrish returned Sebastian's slap with a punch in the gut.

"What the hell are they doing?" William asked.

Beating the crap out of each other as far as I could tell. Because, just then, Sebastian came back with an uppercut that popped Parrish's head backward with a snap.

"We have to break them up," I said.

"Yeah, but how?"

It was times like these that I wished magic were more sensational. If I could call down a fireball or whip up some kind of cosmic light show, I could distract the crowd long enough to get down there and haul them both out. I closed my eyes and tried to think. Taking in a few slow, deep breaths, I centered myself. I thought maybe, if I cleared my mind, something would occur to me.

In the pocket of my jeans, I felt the Mercury dime heating up.

A gun poked me in the small of my back. "Your time is up, little Witch." It was Rosa.

Tenth House

❧

KEYWORDS:

Bad Luck, Orthodoxy, Ambition

The muzzle of the gun poked me like a sharp stone in the rib cage. Rosa placed a firm hand on my shoulder, and her lips brushed my earlobes as she said, "Nice and easy. We're going to slip outside."

I shuffled in the direction she suggested, propelled by her iron grip. William, who had been engrossed in the action onstage, looked at me askance. His face twisted into a frown when he recognized Rosa.

"Don't even think about it," Rosa mouthed over the noise of the bar.

William took a hesitating step forward. I shook my head. He'd gotten far too involved in all of this mess anyway. I wouldn't be able to live with myself if I lost another friend to Vatican assassins. William backed away, but out of the corner of my eye I saw him reach for his cell phone as he headed for the rear exit.

With everyone's attention on the fight between Sebastian

and Parrish, Rosa easily maneuvered us through the crowd toward the exit. My mind raced as I tried to think of what I could do. I couldn't risk kicking her or trying to twist out of her grasp; the gun was far too close. Lilith wasn't an option with all these people around, unless I wanted to kill them all. I kept hoping to catch someone's attention, but with the way Rosa held me, the threat wasn't obvious. To anyone looking, we probably seemed like lovers. It wouldn't have mattered. Rosa could have been carrying an antiaircraft missile while wearing a flying nun outfit for all that anyone cared. Everyone was focused on the vampire smackdown. Even the bouncer had abandoned his post.

Which was my first break. The front door area was jammed with people intent on a closer look. Rosa and I were fighting against the tide, which meant our progress slowed dramatically—at least until Rosa got the clever idea of moving us along the wall.

Which was my big break. Beyond the coat check, illuminated faintly in the darkness, was a fire alarm. The letters Pull Handle in Case of Emergency were printed in glow-in-the-dark yellow paint on the hand-sized switch. I decided my imminent demise definitely qualified. With Rosa concentrating on getting us to the door, I grabbed the bar and pulled with all my might.

When the Klaxon blared, I felt the pressure against my back lighten slightly. It was enough.

I twisted to one side but moved in tighter. My intention was to crowd in past the business end of the gun. Since I saw mostly elbow and the startled expression in Rosa's eyes, I figure I'd done it. I stomped on the bridge of her foot as hard as I could, hoping to shatter bone. Her scream of pain was lost in all the chaos. Just then, the bodies we'd been fighting against surged back toward the exit. I crouched and pressed myself flat against the wall. I watched as the fleeing crowd swallowed Rosa whole.

I wedged myself into a pocket between the desk surrounding the coat check and the wall. Even though I curled myself into as small a ball as possible, I still managed to receive my share of kicks and shoves. Someone had turned off the music and was using the loud speakers to advise everyone to make an orderly exit. The voice also reminded us to stay calm and to remember that the closest exit might be behind us. I pulled myself up and looked around as best I could. There did seem to be an alternate exit on the opposite side of the bar. The question was, could I get there?

I didn't want to have gone to all the trouble to lose Rosa, only to end up on the same sidewalk after the evacuation. More importantly, Parrish had probably stashed his motorcycle—and thus the grimoire—in the alley. It would also be the most likely place for a rendezvous with either Parrish, Sebastian, or both.

After weighing my various options, I decided the safest and most direct route was to crawl over the top of the bar. I felt a little foolish clambering up onto it from a stool, but no one was watching me. I slipped and stumbled over various hastily abandoned drinks. Yet, somehow, I made it to the other side of the room without being molested. When I slid off the bar, I easily followed the flow of people streaming out the back.

Most people clustered just outside the doorway under the awning. A halogen security lamp brightly illuminated a narrow, cobblestone alleyway clogged with Goths and cigarette smoke. Everyone seemed to be on a cell phone or chattering anxiously with one another. Some had managed to smuggle out their drinks and were making a party of it all.

The alley ran perpendicular to State Street. I could see the neon lights of the shops and bars down one end. The majority of the crowd congregated in that direction. Still, I didn't feel safe from the Vatican agent yet. She could be lurking anywhere.

I headed in the opposite direction. A small parking lot occupied the space between the club and another establishment. Twenty or so vehicles vied for room along with a number of Dumpsters, recycling bins, and a stack of wooden pallets. About half of them were motorcycles, and most of the motorcycles were Harleys. I made my way over to them, hoping I'd recognize Parrish's saddlebags despite the darkness and all the people milling around.

The first bike I approached clearly belonged to someone named Butch, as the vanity plate spelled out. Butch, a heavily muscular woman wearing a leather vest and sporting tattoos that might have either been dragonflies or faeries, didn't appreciate my scrutiny of her saddlebags. I apologized profusely and scurried off toward the next likely candidate.

And ran right into Sebastian.

At first, I almost walked past him, since his back was to me as he rooted through the bags. Then I recognized the trench coat. And the fangs.

"Garnet," he said. He sounded relieved to see me. An ugly slash decorated one of his cheeks, but otherwise he looked undamaged. "The grimoire is here," he said, showing me the tip of the leather-bound book before returning it to its hiding place. He swung his legs over the bike and started it up. "Let's go."

I almost said no. I didn't want to leave without knowing Parrish was all right, but Sebastian interrupted my thoughts.

"We don't have much time," Sebastian said. "The Hunger is consuming me. I need to perform the spell as soon as possible."

"But it's flawed."

"Maybe. Maybe not." He shook his head. "We have to try. I don't know that I can survive much longer."

Just then I spotted Rosa—who was difficult to miss with

her bandaged nose and two black eyes—making her way down the alley toward us. That decided things for me. I clambered onto the back. I held on tightly as Sebastian reversed the bike out of its parking space and roared down the alley away from State Street and out into the night.

While we idled at a stoplight, I got up the nerve to ask, "Where's Parrish? I mean, you have his keys."

Okay. So, I didn't say I was quite up to asking the tough question, the one that went more like, "So, did you kill him, or what?"

I couldn't imagine him handing over the keys to his beloved bike while he still had any say in the matter. At the same time, however, I didn't see Parrish so easily defeated that Sebastian would only have a scratch on the cheek to show for it. Still, Sebastian was almost five times older than Parrish.

When Sebastian didn't answer, I tried a different approach. "Why did you bitch-slap him, anyway? What was that about?"

Against my cheek, I felt his chest rise and fall in a deep sigh. "I don't like performance art."

The light changed, and the speed of the wind rushing past swallowed any chance of further conversation.

What did that mean? Was Sebastian offended because Parrish violated some kind of vampiric code of secrecy by doing his business onstage in front of everyone? That seemed somewhat unlikely, since Sebastian hardly ran in the same circles as most vampires. It wasn't like he was the local chair of the Secret-Keeper's Vampire Club.

He'd said "performance art," so something about the public nature of Parrish's show must have rankled him. But what? Could it be some kind of chivalry thing? Maybe he didn't approve of the situation the victim found herself in?

He must have known she was willing, though. That she was into it seemed pretty obvious to me.

When we sailed through the next set of lights, I found myself disappointed.

I hoped Parrish was all right.

I squeezed my arms tighter around Sebastian's slender waist.

When we next stopped, Sebastian surprised me by speaking first. "Listen, I was jealous," he said. "It was far too easy to imagine him doing those despicable things to you."

Oh, right. The whole ex- versus current-lover thing. I should have thought of that right away.

Parrish was so dead.

"You killed him, didn't you?"

"If I told you I made him regret ever touching you, would that make me sound sexy or scary?"

"Both?" Especially since that made it sound as though I had a chance of seeing Parrish walking around again someday.

I felt Sebastian's shoulders relax somewhat.

With bar-close still a couple of hours away, the night pulsed with activity. Cars flashed by, carrying with them the throb of bass turned up to window-rattling levels. Though cooler, the air still held a touch of the day's warmth.

Cottonwood seeds floated in the headlights like snow. We approached the lakes. They smelled faintly fishy, but couples strolled around the shore boardwalks. Overhead, bats flashed dark wings as they snatched insects from the sky.

"Where are we going?" I asked at the next stop.

"Do you know anyone at Circle Sanctuary?" Sebastian asked.

Circle Sanctuary was a covenstead in a small town outside of Madison. They owned acres of land, all of which they had dedicated to the Craft. "No," I said, although strictly speaking that was a lie. I was passingly familiar with their newsletter editor, since the store bought an advertisement every month. "Why?"

"Because I was hoping for an alternate place to perform the ritual," he said. "I imagine my house is crawling with Vatican agents by now."

"So why go back?"

"The elixir, the main ingredient of the spell, is there."

I gave Sebastian's waist a squeeze. "You'll die without it, Sebastian. We have to go back."

"I'd hoped to be a bit stronger before having to fight them," Sebastian said as the light changed.

"I'm strong enough for both of us," I replied, but the roar of the engine drowned out my words.

I was thinking of Lilith, of course, not me. I didn't feel particularly strong. I ached. Lilith's earlier tantrum had left my muscles battered and bruised.

The road widened. Buildings got farther apart, and green spaces grew wider and wilder. The smells shifted from exhaust to clover. City lights dimmed, and the stars above seemed brighter.

I squeezed Sebastian's waist, willing him to read my mind. We could just keep going, I thought, not deal with any of this and just run away.

Except that come morning, Sebastian would be a crispy critter.

What else could we do? I'd come to realize that I was culpable in the deaths of the agents in Minneapolis. Lilith might have done the dirty work, but I was the one who asked her to do it. I couldn't ignore that truth anymore, and I refused to be responsible for any more deaths. If we went in to Sebastian's with the intention of killing, we were the murderers, not the Order. I couldn't live with myself; it would be better to be dead.

It would, actually. It would be much better to be dead. If

the Vatican thought we were dead, it would be case closed. The file that carried my name would be stamped *Fini* or whatever the Latin was for "Done." No one would ever come looking for me again.

The same would be true for Sebastian, although he had a head start in the being-dead department.

Being dead was sounding better and better.

Except for the whole ceasing to exist part, that was.

But the thought had some merit. How could we convince the Vatican agents we were dead? Staging our deaths seemed risky, especially since the Order was actively attempting to help us achieve that goal. I could just see us playing dead in the middle of the living room, and the Vatican deciding to be thorough and putting a bullet in my head while cutting off Sebastian's.

What if we could implant the image of a successful raid in their minds? That seemed much more possible. Sebastian, being a vampire, had access to the whole "glamour" thing, although I had no idea if it could work on that kind of scale. Maybe if I could boost his magic with my own, somehow?

The feeling of the motorcycle slowing derailed my train of thought. Sebastian pulled the bike into a tangle of weeds that served as the shoulder. "We need a game plan," he said, cutting the engine.

"I was just thinking about that," I said. "What if we convince the Vatican we're dead?" When he raised his eyebrows, I told him everything I'd been thinking.

He didn't laugh out loud. In fact, he seemed to be considering it. "The biggest problem I can see with your idea is that there's no guarantee that the Order won't just come in with guns blazing."

I got off the bike to stretch my legs. The long grass brushed against my calves. "Yeah," I said. I bent to pluck a seedpod from its leafy sheath. "Plus they have a sensitive who could warn them that magic was happening."

"Probably as assurance against precisely this sort of thing," Sebastian said.

I chewed on the grass stem, thinking. "How can we get around him?"

"Well, we could kill him," Sebastian said matter-of-factly. I couldn't read his expression in the moonlight.

I just shook my head.

"Or, we could just kill them all."

"Yeah," I said dejectedly, "That's what I was afraid of."

Sebastian said nothing. I stared up at the stars. Venus shone brightly in the sky. I recognized a few constellations: Cassiopeia, or as my astronomy professor in college taught us, "the Big W," and, of course, Ursa Major, the Big Dipper.

Well, then. "I can't do it, Sebastian," I said.

"You have to. My life depends on it. Yours, too. They're not going to let you go." Sebastian took a deep breath and tried to put on a little smile. "Besides, I need your help with the ritual. I'm counting on you to fix it."

"I don't know, Sebastian," I said. "Your magic is really old. I'm just a garden-variety Eclectic."

He laughed as he started up the engine. "Who happens to have called down a Goddess."

"About that," I said. I pressed the flat of my palm into the curve of my belly as though to cover Lilith's ears. "I don't want to use Her for this."

"Then I guess I'm really, finally dead," Sebastian said quietly. My mouth worked as I tried to formulate a response. Just then his cell phone rang. He cut the engine. "Who the hell could that be?"

Turns out it was William calling to let us know he and Parrish were safe and headed back to my apartment to check it out for me. He also had some bad news.

"William saw Mátyás and the female Vatican agent heading in our direction," Sebastian said as he snapped the receiver shut on the phone. "They're coming after us. With weapons. We've got to go now."

I nodded resolutely; I guess we did.

"Are you sure?" he asked, as the engine sprang to life with a roar. "Because if you're going to be watching my back with that Goddess of yours, I don't want you to have a change of heart."

"I'm with you," I said. "But I've never been entirely sure Lilith is on your side, Sebastian."

He'd been about to pull onto the road when he paused to look back at me. "What do you mean?"

"She stole your grimoire in the first place, remember?"

He frowned at that. "I thought maybe that was her equivalent of leaving a sweater behind, you know? A way of making sure we had a second date."

"We'd already planned a second date," I said. "She wanted to cause you grief."

"Why?"

"Because you took Her blood."

"Oh." Sebastian's voice sounded small. "And that's bad?"

"I got the impression it was," I said.

"You can make Her help us with the ritual, right?"

No way. "Sure."

"Good," he said, taking us farther into the darkness. "Good."

About a half mile from his farm, Sebastian stowed Parrish's bike in a ditch. He disappeared into the night with a promise to reconnoiter and return shortly with a full report. Meanwhile, I sat, feeling useless, in a slightly damp patch of hawkweed and shepherd's purse.

I lay back to enjoy the stars. It was so dark that I could see the filmy haze of the Milky Way stretch in a broad band across the sky. A flash of an asteroid burning up in the atmosphere caught my eye, and, at the same moment, Lilith woke.

The sensation was becoming all too familiar. I felt a tiny nudge, like accidentally bumping shoulders with someone at the Minnesota State Fair. Then, completely without my consent, I got up, and my legs started walking my body toward Sebastian's place.

Eleventh House

❦

KEYWORDS:

Agitation, Desire, Rebelliousness

Lilith made quick work of the distance. I had no idea my short legs could move so quickly—probably they couldn't; I'd be paying for that overextension in the morning if I was still alive.

The farmhouse looked dark. Even so, Lilith moved in a military-style half crouch around the building to the rear entrance. I have to admit, from the outside, I looked pretty cool in commando mode, especially when I KO'd the agent who was hiding behind a lilac bush. Lilith gave him a nasty karate chop to the back of the head. She rolled him over roughly and curled my fingers into a claw around his throat. If I'd had control of my eyes, I'd have squeezed them shut. I did not want to see her rip this poor guy's throat out.

Luckily, Sebastian interrupted her. He looked a little taken aback to see my hand wrapped around the passed-out agent's throat, but he calmly said, "I was about to come get you. I think that's everyone. I took care of the other two."

Lilith nodded. My sense was that she knew better than to speak to Sebastian if she wanted to keep her presence a secret. Not only did she talk like a Goddess, she had a different voice than I did.

As we walked up the back stairs into the house, I understood what Sebastian meant when he'd said he'd taken care of the Vatican agents. Leader Guy and Sensitive's lifeless eyes stared up at me from where their bodies were stacked neatly against the foundation, vampiric puncture wounds darkly spotting their throats. *Oh, Sebastian*, I tried to say, but couldn't, since Lilith had complete control of me. Even so, I knew it was kill or be killed.

"If only I had the mandrake."

Lilith produced the root from my pocket.

Sebastian smiled. "Garnet, you're a gem."

If I'd had control of my throat, I'd have groaned at his pun. As it was, Lilith smiled stiffly at him.

"Well," Sebastian said, placing the grimoire on the small, rectangular coffee table in the living room, "We should get started."

Lilith helped Sebastian lay out his ritual. They made space in the living room by moving furniture closer to the walls and rolling up the Persian rug. He brought down various articles from his sanctum, including a black viscous fluid in a test tube. As he produced items, she arranged them. I watched with fascination and no small amount of dread. She was weaving something magical to be certain, but it was not good.

At one point I saw Benjamin waver into existence, but with a stern glance from Lilith, he disappeared again.

After the last piece was in position and the candles were lit, Sebastian nodded in approval. "You've been studying my grimoire, I see," he said.

Lilith took my clothes off.

I must say I was just as shocked as Sebastian appeared to be. After the initial surprise wore off, his eyes roamed over my naked body hungrily. From the perspective of being outside my body, I had two thoughts: I needed to get out more—my skin was incredibly white; and it was time to get serious about joining a health club.

"Oh," Sebastian finally managed to say, as he started to shrug out of his own clothes, "Skyclad. Right. Good idea."

Sebastian naked was a fine thing to behold. Lilith might not appreciate it, but I did. Candlelight glowed along the edges of his skin, making muscle stand out as though in relief. I especially enjoyed that line of hipbone that pointed to the shadows between his legs.

Lilith trailed my fingers along Sebastian's taut stomach as she walked past him to the coffee table, which they'd placed in the middle of the room as a makeshift altar. From it, she took a knife. I supposed that the weapon was technically Sebastian's athame, but it looked much deadlier than anything I'd ever used in ceremony.

Lilith slashed my palm with it. She must have cut deeply, because blood flowed freely. I heard Sebastian breathe in the scent of it.

Starting in the north, She began casting the circle. Sebastian watched with wide eyes as Lilith slowly paced around the room clockwise. Drops of blood formed the physical boundary, but where each drop hit, a spiritual wall began to take shape. A shimmer, like a heat mirage on summer asphalt, separated the inner space from the rest of the living room. A bubble formed around us.

When she reached the spot she started at, Lilith made a second tour around the perimeter. This time, she stopped in each of the cardinal directions. Swirling her hands slowly in the air, Lilith conjured a guardian at the first cross-quarter, east. Even from my Lilith-eye perspective, I could barely see the figure. I could make out the misty shape of bare breasts and long, flowing hair that seemed to be constantly blown by an unreal, unseen wind. In the south, Lilith formed a similar guardian. Only this time, the woman seemed made of smoke, with glowing embers for eyes. In the west, the womanly shape glittered like sunlight on water. The northern guard stood firm and dark as obsidian. They all had the same face, a horribly beautiful face I recognized from my dreams: Lilith's face.

As she finished her final round, the walls of the circle became more opaque. The bubble had taken on a pearlescent sheen that shifted and swirled like gas on water.

This was the strongest circle I'd ever cast, and it torqued me that I didn't have anything to do with it, not really—although that was *my* blood all over the hardwood floor.

Sebastian stepped up. He picked up a stick that branched into a V-shape at the tip. He followed the path Lilith had made around the room, adding his energy to the circle. A dark mist trailed behind his deliberate steps like a living shadow. I literally felt the ground shift when he finished. It was like a mini-earthquake. "We are between the worlds," he said, his eyes glittering in the candlelight.

No shit.

And this was just the boring part of the ritual.

Sebastian returned to the altar and the grimoire. He knelt on the floor to get a better look at the words on the page. Lilith came around to stand in front of him, so that he appeared to be supplicating her. While his attention was on the book, she squeezed my cut hand so that a drop of blood landed in the test tube containing Sebastian's formula. A second tightening of my palm, and a splash of blood fell onto the crown of his head. He must have felt something, because he looked up at us then.

What was Lilith doing?

Sebastian began an incantation in some language or

another. Lilith did not provide subtitles. Occasionally, however, I heard her whisper a word, and two seconds later Sebastian would repeat it. I had no idea if she was adding strength to what he'd already written or changing it completely.

I had a bad feeling that she was doing the latter.

But to what end? For someone so cranky about Sebastian having taken her blood, she certainly had no problem spilling it now. Of course, that was part of what worried me. Blood was binding. She was putting a hex on him, and he didn't even see it coming.

Of course, she was binding me to it as well.

Sebastian got to the end of what was written in the journal.

Lifting the vial of the dark liquid, he drank it in one gulp.

Then he looked up at us with a sheepish smile. "This is the part where I've written, 'and here a miracle occurred.' I have no idea what I did to charge the formula."

"I have an idea," Lilith answered with a seductive smile. She held out a hand. "The Great Rite," she said, her voice resonating strangely.

Sebastian didn't notice; he was too busy getting an erection. Typical boy Witch—one mention of the Great Rite, and it's an instant hard-on. The Great Rite is sex within the context of a ritual. Well, to be fair, when done right, it's more than just some kind of spiritual public display. It's *the* primal force. It's power of God and Goddess joined.

Considering what happened when Sebastian added his energy to the circle, the vampire/Goddess pairing had the potential to be earth-shattering. Unfortunately, I was going to be a disembodied spectator.

"Uh, this is very different from my original spell," Sebastian said, though he didn't pull away when Lilith cupped his face in both hands. "Are you certain it will work?"

"Absolutely," Lilith said with a bedroom smile. I couldn't tell if she was leading him on or not. Without a doubt, they needed something powerful. The moon was out of phase, and Sebastian couldn't hope to duplicate every aspect of his first working. The Great Rite, particularly one involving Lilith Herself, would make up for a lot of missing pieces.

Sebastian seemed to be falling under Lilith's spell. All of the subtle things she changed might have the effect of making Sebastian more susceptible to suggestion.

Lilith held out a hand, and Sebastian took it. He had started to rise from his knees when Lilith exposed his palm and cut it with the knife she still held. He cried out in surprise and pain. She pressed their palms together so that their wounds touched, like you would with a blood brother or sister.

I felt something. Even in my disconnected state, I sensed the flow of power. Though I couldn't see it, somehow I knew Lilith was drawing blood into herself from him. This was not some kind of congenial mixing of power, a shared bond. She was taking from him.

He had no idea. In fact, he looked like he thought he was already getting the best sex ever.

She leaned over the altar and whispered in his ear, "You'll make a beautiful sacrifice, child."

"Thank you," he said sounding completely dopey and dazed.

With a gentle lift of her hand, Sebastian rose to his feet. She led him a short distance from the altar and kissed him. It was a long, deep kiss. And I found myself in the very strange position of being extremely jealous of my own body. However, I was not so blinded by my anger that I failed to notice that Lilith had not dropped the knife. In fact, it seemed to hover dangerously close to Sebastian's heart.

I had to do something.

I felt a wave of panic as Lilith's knife moved closer. I'd have hyperventilated if I'd had any lungs. Worse, being unable to take steady breaths, I didn't know how to calm myself. I kept thinking if only I could breathe, I could do my concentration exercises. If I could focus, I could unlock my magic.

Suddenly, the scene in front of me faded, and I found myself standing in front of the vault where I kept my magic. I ran my hands over the hard steel door, feeling the rough, cold metal beneath my fingers. It had never seemed so real.

Of course.

The place Lilith "shoved" me was the same place magic lived. The astral plane. The space between. The place where rituals happened.

There was no need to panic. This was my place of power. I owned this space.

I unlocked the door easily. Then, with a thought, I shifted back to where Lilith held a knife to Sebastian.

The ritual space Lilith had woven was a dark tangle, like a spiderweb. Lines of black energy crisscrossed the interior of the bubble. The space felt stuffy and close. It was hard to move through.

Lilith's kiss held Sebastian mesmerized. She used the flat of the blade to caress Sebastian's hip and thigh. In my astral state, I could see the flow of power. Sebastian's energy, his life, was being drained.

His life energy poured into Lilith. Her long, wild, salt-and-pepper curls flowed in a ghostly halo to the floor, surrounding my body like a shroud. A tiny silver thread connected my body to my consciousness. Compared to the thick, crackling stream that transferred between Sebastian and Lilith, my lifeline looked skimpy. I tugged on the line and moved in closer.

Only to become caught in the sticky cords.

Lilith broke the kiss to look at me, but she smiled when I struggled uselessly against the bonds. She returned her attention to Sebastian, dismissing me.

You're killing him! I tried to shout, as I struggled against the astral bonds.

Lilith ignored me and continued caressing Sebastian. Then she slowly lifted the knife from his body and pointed it in the direction of the eastern guardian. A pure bolt of jet-black energy shot out of the tip of the athame like some kind of anti-laser. The guardian stumbled and started to bring up her shield when the blast hit her square in the heart chakra. Then, as if realizing she was not under attack, she slowly dropped her defensive posture and stood up straighter.

I watched in horror as she began to solidify. On more than just the astral plane, I felt a gust of wind ripple through the circle. The pages of the grimoire flipped wildly. Outside the circle, I could see curtains billowing.

Sebastian's knees buckled. Lilith put a hand under his arm to steady him.

In the east now stood a flesh-and-blood woman. She looked at her hands, inspecting them, as though the sensation of wiggling fingers and thumb were new to her. I watched her take a shuddering breath.

Yet, somehow, I knew the guardian couldn't survive outside the circle. She was only one aspect of Lilith, and until she was merged with her four remaining sisters—the fourth being Lilith, the Goddess herself—she would be incomplete.

I pushed against the bonds again. An astral hand broke free, only to be captured again by the sticky webbing. If Lilith finished the spell, She could break free of me and become human. She would be the dark Goddess incarnate. And, I suspected, that would be bad, really bad, for any mortal foolish enough to get in her way.

Lilith pointed the knife in the next direction, south. The power, this time, was narrower, as though waning. Sebastian's eyes fluttered shut. His face had become gaunt and strained. I could smell the woodsmoke of the southern guardian, but only the unearthly glow of her eyes had become brighter and more frighteningly real. Lilith broke her kiss and glanced in frustration at the half-formed southern guard.

"The flow of blood will bind this spell," Lilith intoned as she turned the knife on Sebastian.

I couldn't let her do it.

Drawing every ounce of my magic to me, I visualized myself as a bright flame. Heat poured over me, through me. The cords that held me dissolved into ash at my touch. Just as knife touched flesh, I threw my astral self around Lilith.

She/I screamed.

I was back in my physical body. Flames consumed me, scorching every inch of skin. Searing pain caused me to drop the knife. I doubled over, my arms around my waist. I clutched frantically at my womb. All I wanted was for the burning sensation to stop.

No, I thought, not me. Lilith. Lilith was trying to use my own body's sensations to stop my attack on Her.

I had to push on. Let the heat penetrate deeply, completely. Accept the pain, not fight it. Easier said than done, however. I'd never hurt so much in my entire life. I felt like I was being ripped apart. Despite the agony, I held on to the vision of Lilith trapped inside my body, surrounded by a bubble of impenetrable fire.

That's when the guardian struck. She grabbed me by the shoulders and pulled me upright. I took a page out of William's book and balled my hands into a fist and gave her a good punch in the stomach. She looked surprised. Then mad.

I was in big trouble.

Twelfth House

KEYWORDS:

Atonement, Imprisonment, Escape

That's when the cavalry kicked the door down.

The sound of shattering wood broke my concentration. On the astral plane, the image of Lilith shimmered momentarily. The guardian paused in mid-motion, like a robot awaiting a command.

I never thought I'd be so grateful to see Mátyás. Or Rosa and a very bruised priest/bowman, for that matter. They made a fairly tattered-looking army. Besides Rosa's blackened eyes, the bowman had a light slash across his forehead, and Mátyás's throat was wrapped in gauze.

Some rescue, I thought. But then I remembered they were here to kill us.

As if following some unspoken command, the archer nocked an arrow and took aim. The nasty-looking tip pointed right at me. The archer let the tension go. The guardian lifted her hand. I saw a ripple on the surface of the bubble. The arrow disappeared.

"Did we get them?" It was Mátyás.

I saw Rosa's hands pressed against the wall of the circle. "No," she was saying. "It's solid."

"If it's my father's magic, I can break it," Mátyás said confidently, though his voice was scratched and rough. He punched at the barrier, only to have his fist forcibly repelled. He nearly fell back onto his ass.

Which I might have found a bit amusing, except I was too busy fighting for my life. The guardian chose that moment to launch herself at me. She rammed the full force of her shield against my body, knocking me to the floor. Inside, I heard an evil chuckle. The muscles of my throat seemed to constrict on their own. I gasped for breath.

The guardian, meanwhile, moved to stand over Sebastian where he'd fallen.

Your death, Lilith hissed in my internal ear. *Is a sacrifice I will savor.*

I clawed at my own throat desperately, trying to pry loose hands that weren't there. The harder I pushed, it seemed, the stronger she became. I gasped for air as her grip tightened. I glanced over at Sebastian, hoping for a knight-in-shining-armor Hollywood hero moment from him. But he didn't stir. He looked as dead as I was about to become.

The guardian reached to pick up the knife I/Lilith had dropped when I took back control of my body. With Lilith's voice, the guardian said, "His death will give me the power to manifest; yours will be my release."

No! I wouldn't let that happen. I tore and kicked at her like a madwoman.

The next thing I knew, an arrow came sailing within an inch of my head. "How could you possibly miss?" Mátyás shouted. "They're three feet in front of you."

"It's like shooting through water. I'll have to adjust my aim."

"This is our last arrow dipped in holy water," Rosa said, handing it reverently to the archer. "We must pray that the sanctity of our righteousness will conquer their wicked magic."

Aim for the Guardian, I tried to say, but it came out more like "Ah."

A dark curtain formed at the edges of my vision. My magical eyes could see the circle imprisoning Lilith beginning to fade.

This was it. I was going to die.

As it happened, just then, the arrow hit me right in the calf. It missed bone but tore through muscle with a shock. In the pain, my anger and desperation slipped away. I forgot, for a split second, about Lilith's invisible death grip on my throat. I stopped fighting her. Her grip loosened, or rather, the ethereal fingers that had been digging into my throat were no longer quite as solid as they had been.

When I stopped pushing, she lost power. The guardian, alerted to the shift in power, pierced me with a menacing glare, but the jig was up. Lilith had been feeding on my anger and fear.

So I stopped giving it to her.

I took a deep breath and, despite the pain in my leg, I willed myself to be calm. It was like taking the air away from a fire. The guardian slumped limply, like a marionette released from its strings. The spooky glowing red eyes in the south, which had watched the whole battle, winked and then extinguished.

I took in another slow, calming breath, and the east guardian began to flicker. Her physical form dissipated into mist and returned to its place on the circle. I released the tension in my shoulders. I trusted myself to have the power, the strength I needed. Just me. Not any Goddess, other than the one I was.

A moment of twinkle, and then, with a pop, the guardian was gone. I could feel Lilith resuming her place deep inside me. Contained, for now.

This was the time to cast the spell of illusion on the Vatican agents.

I looked over at Sebastian, who, to my surprise, was looking back at me. I thought he was a goner after all the power Lilith had taken from him. I reached my hand out. If we were going to die, we should at least be together.

When he took my hand in his, something happened.

I felt stronger. Strong enough to control Lilith to use Her power as my own. Her power had become mine. I could feel it rippling through my aura. I put my hand on my stomach and pushed with our combined power. White-hot fire poured from my fingers, encircling her in a flaming prison. Her frustrated screams shook my belly, but the spell held.

The strength of the circle worked to my advantage. Lilith and Sebastian had made the interior almost invisible to those on the outside. They could barely see us. Thus, it was a matter of projecting the image of the arrow hitting home, stabbing me through the heart. Thanks to Lilith, Sebastian already looked dead, but I added the image of the previous arrow sticking out of his chest. To complete the illusion, I visualized the circle collapsing in on itself with a bang.

"Are they dead?" I heard Rosa ask.

"They look dead," the bowman said.

"Something's not right," Mátyás said as he approached the edge of the circle. "There's still something here. Some kind of power."

"It's residue," Rosa said.

"Grab the book and let's go," the bowman said.

I'd have to let Mátyás inside. As he approached, I allowed a spiral to form in the circle. It popped open like a lens when his foot crossed the threshold. I snapped it shut behind him, confident the others couldn't see due to the opacity of the magic Lilith and Sebastian had woven into the circle's creation. Once inside, I couldn't maintain the illusion. Mátyás scanned the scene. His father lay crumpled to one side of the altar. I sat on the floor beside him, holding his hand, with an arrow sticking out of my leg. We were both naked.

The bloodied knife lay within reach. As I moved toward it, Mátyás's boot slapped down on the blade.

"This is an interesting situation," he said with a slow, ugly smile.

"Take the book," I told him.

"I could kill you both."

"You could," I observed, trying to sound casual. Meanwhile, Lilith raged inside me. Her talons jabbed against the wall of fire I had surrounded her with, slashing along my intestines. All I'd have to do was let go. She'd rise and swallow Mátyás whole. And probably kill me in the process.

Mátyás knelt down and looked at his father's wan, gaunt face. Sebastian had passed out again from the effort of joining our power for the spell. Mátyás surprised me by smoothing a stray lock of hair back into place. It was a kind, almost loving gesture. "Or I could let him die in his own way," he said softly, almost to himself. Then he shook his head, as though trying to banish an unpleasant thought. "Not that he deserves my sympathy. I offered my throat, and he nearly killed me. All I wanted was for us to be a family."

"He wants that, too; I'm sure of it," I said. "He was sick, Mátyás, from the sun. He couldn't stop himself. He felt terrible about it, he told me so."

Mátyás's mouth screwed into a painful, thin line. I could tell he wanted to believe me, but a century of hate stood in the way. "Yet he left me lying in a pool of my own blood in the middle of the garage floor for the Vatican to find. Somehow that doesn't seem like the act of a loving father. I mean, for chrissake"—his voice broke with barely contained emotions—"he could have at least propped me up against a wall. How about a blanket in case I went into shock, eh?"

I winced. "We didn't have time, Mátyás. We thought the Vatican agents were hot on your heels. They would have killed us."

Mátyás raised his hand, forestalling any more argument from me. "It doesn't matter. My father already gave me his answer. He doesn't want peace between us, except for the eternal kind. And he can have it. Fortunately, without the spell, he won't last. It will be very painful and humiliating for him to know he was too impotent to save his own damn life.

"And you," he said turning to me, his eyes wild and glassy like an injured animal's. "He'll kill you to try to save himself. It's all very poetic. I hate to ruin the beauty of it by stabbing you in the heart."

Well, me, too.

He stood and picked up the grimoire from the coffee table. His finger reached out to snuff one of the candles on the altar. He contemplated the arrangement with a smirk, as though considering messing it up. Like a child, he knocked a few things to the floor, crushing the vial that had held the formula beneath his heel. "Even if I've miscalculated and you two manage to survive somehow, I'll still get what I want once I hand this over. Mother will get her Papal exorcism."

Standing in front of the circle's wall, he glanced at me. I obliged by opening the portal between the worlds. He stepped through. "It's over," he told the Vatican agents. "They're as good as dead. I have the spell. Let's go."

If the agents noticed Mátyás's semantic lapse, they didn't say anything. I held onto the image of us lying dead until they walked out the door. Mátyás paused, glancing back. His gaze lingered for a moment on the prone body of his father, and the door closed behind him with a click.

I squeezed Sebastian's hand but got no response. Giving me his reserves had finally exhausted him. He lay completely still, not breathing. His skin was as clammy and cold as death. Of course, he didn't have to breathe, and ever since the spell wore off, he'd lost his body heat, but it was still disconcerting. "Are you dead? I mean, more?"

"Ugh," he murmured.

That sounded positive.

I felt even more encouraged when he lifted his head, but the look in his eyes was wild. He bared his fangs. "You let him take the book," he said. "Mátyás is right. I'm as good as dead."

"Don't be an idiot," I said. I sat up so that I could get a good look at my leg. I wanted to pull the arrow out, but I didn't want to rupture anything important in the process. At least this shaft was significantly slimmer than the one the bowman had used when he'd impaled Sebastian to the wall earlier. I might be able to break off the ends.

When I glanced around to see if I could find anything to use as a bandage, I noticed Sebastian still gazing at me forlornly.

"You finished the incantation, Sebastian," I said. "You drank. All we have to do is raise the energy to charge the ritual."

He lay his head down, as though defeated. "How are we going to do that?"

"I think Lilith was right. We need to perform the Great Rite."

"Seriously?" The floor muffled his laugh. "Garnet, I don't think I can."

I gave him an affectionate smile. "We'll just have to take it slowly."

Sebastian tipped his head up to look me in the eye. "I'm going to have to feed, Garnet."

"I know," I said. "You can take from me."

"But . . . you hate that. And you're already wounded."

We both stared at the arrow in my leg.

"Any ideas?" I asked him.

Sebastian sat up. I noticed his elbows shaking under the strain, but he set his jaw fiercely.

"Let's make a tourniquet to start with," he said, reaching for my hastily discarded shirt. He used his fangs to start a tear at the hem and tore it into strips. He handed the pieces to me, and I knotted them together until we had a fair-sized bandage. We saved out a smaller section for the tourniquet.

Sebastian expertly constricted the tourniquet so that the skin prickled as though it was falling asleep. Just as I was wondering if he'd learned these skills on the battlefield, he said, "Wartime experience."

His eyes lingered on the small amount of blood clotting on either side of the arrow. I had to say that the wound was surprisingly clean, considering how much it hurt.

"Ready?" he asked, grasping the arrow.

I nodded.

He snapped the arrow. I screamed. The walls around Lilith expanded. I quickly reined them in with a steady, calm breath.

Sebastian used the rest of our makeshift bandage to field dress my leg. Once that was finished, he released the tourniquet. Despite my pride, I whimpered.

He winced in sympathy and said, "Are you sure you're up for sex?"

"I'm good," I gasped. Besides, I was certain I could siphon some of the sex magic energy to heal my leg and cement my control over Lilith.

"We're going to have to share," I told Sebastian. "I'll need some of your magic if I'm going to keep Lilith contained."

"And yourself from passing out."

"There is that," I agreed with a smile.

"And you think sex will do that?"

"Not just sex. Magic sex. And, yes, I do." I'd moved close enough to kiss him, so I did. I let my lips linger softly on his. Our breath mingled, and a tingle that was more than pleasure ran down the length of my body. Sebastian noticed it, too. Our gazes locked, and we both knew this would work.

My fingers traced the line of his jaw as his hands ran through the short mop of my hair. I spread my hands across the expanse of his chest while Sebastian massaged my shoulders.

We moved in harmony; each action had a perfect reaction. I kissed each of his battle scars. He counted the freckles on my back. His tongue pressed into me, and mine enveloped him.

Despite his concerns, he rose admirably to the occasion.

"You're beautiful, Garnet," he said when we paused to take a breath.

"Funny, I was about to say the same thing about you."

Lilith pushed against her restraints. I maneuvered Sebastian so that he could easily enter me. Even as I gasped with pleasure, Lilith recoiled at his nearness. We began to move together in slow, even strokes. As the urgency rose, so did the power. Sebastian was more than just my lover at this moment. He became the conduit for the God, whose strength matched that of the Goddess.

Me.

Lilith and I were equals now. Or would have been, had not Lilith's strength been sapped by weaving the spell of binding and her attempt to manifest. I had the upper hand.

I clutched at Sebastian's shoulders, driving him deeper. I could feel his skin heating with our passion. He had begun to heal. I kissed along the line of his collarbone. His lips pressed against my throat, but he held them there as if waiting for permission.

I began to weave the spell by imagining Lilith trapped

like a djinni in a bottle. She could not escape into the world, and I would have control over her power if I chose. When I felt I had the image secure in my mind, I put my hand on the back of Sebastian's neck, cradling him closer. I arched my body to meet each of Sebastian's thrusts.

He understood my meaning.

The bite surprised me, even so. There was only the tiniest flash of a pinprick, and then, only ecstasy. Power roiled and flashed in the air around us. I felt my heart pound through the spot where his teeth sank into my flesh, matching the rhythm of our bodies.

We came in a clap of thunder. Magic surrounded us, binding us.

Spent, we lay tangled together, unable to move. It was sunrise, and we were still inside the circle. I wondered if its magic could protect him if the formula failed. I stretched my wounded leg experimentally. It twinged, but it definitely felt much better than it should. I could feel Lilith's power sleeping inside me, so I knew at least some of the spell had worked.

Sebastian stood up. The Great Rite had returned his physical strength, as well. Using the wand, he traversed the circle in the reverse direction, counterclockwise. I took Lilith's knife and limped the perimeter, releasing the power she'd raised. The curtain lifted. The living room came slowly back into focus, and, with it, the first rays of sun peeking over the horizon.

I squeezed Sebastian's hand when I'd finished.

"The circle is open," he said.

"But unbroken," I continued.

"Merry meet," we said in unison, "Merry part, and merry meet again."

Beside me, Sebastian tensed as light continued to fill the

sky. The sunrise was a combination of pink and green. It spread slowly across the cornfields, touching the rows with gold. Sebastian took in a hiss of breath, and I held tightly to his hand. I had faith. Our sex and our ritual had healed something in me I hadn't even realized was broken. Saying the words of closing again with someone I trusted so profoundly reminded me why I'd fought so hard for the coven in the first place.

Sunlight touched our toes. We both waited to see if Sebastian would burst into flames. The light crept up his body, and he flinched at every inch.

He was safe.

We were safe.

And we only had two bodies to bury.

I could live with that.